The
Orchid House

The Orchid House

Published by The Conrad Press in the United2 Kingdom 2021

Tel: +44(0)1227 472 874
www.theconradpress.com
info@theconradpress.com

ISBN 978-1-911546-86-3

Typesetting and Cover Design by: Charlotte Mouncey, www.bookstyle.co.uk

The Conrad Press logo was designed by Maria Priestley.

Printed and bound in Great Britain by Clays Ltd, Elcograf S.p.A.

The
Orchid House

Jane Sheridan

For Jonkes who made this journey possible

1

It was a mid-March morning, and winter still held the east coast of Kent in its grip. Determined winds streamed across the English Channel, clutching rain-laden clouds. The people of Kent shivered, and waited for spring to arrive.

Ginny caught sight of her reflection in the bedroom mirror; she didn't like what she saw - not one bit.

Tall and graceful, with a dancer's figure, Ginny wore her clothes well. Today she had unintentionally dressed to match her mood - grey. Grabbing a red scarf from the top drawer of her dressing table, and swapping her comfortable black boots for stylish tan brogues - she looked again. Her black hair, curls tamed for the moment, lay at her shoulders. With a flick of her wrist, Ginny knotted her hair in place with her favourite tortoiseshell clip. Looking in the mirror again Ginny was satisfied that now at least, she looked a bit more cheerful.

Doubts about their weekend away in Devon had plagued her since she'd woken up. The idea of a romantic weekend with her husband, had morphed in her mind into what could possibly be the weekend from hell with David in his present grumpy and uncooperative mood. But there was no turning back now, she decided.

Ginny decided to walk the couple of miles to her mother Ellen's house, to drop off Bertie, a spaniel-poodle crossbreed, for the weekend. The path to her mother's cottage lying on the outskirts of Sandwich on the Kent coast, would take her through the town and out into the fields skirting the River Stour. Bertie twirled uncontrollably in excitement as soon as he saw Ginny picking up his lead,

'For goodness' sake Bertie, calm down - in fact be a good boy and sit,' she said in mock anger, a command Ginny knew would be totally ignored. She smiled to herself remembering David's words declaring him the most disobedient dog he'd ever had the misfortune to own.

By the time Ginny was ready to set off she was cheered to see the sun peeping through the heavy grey clouds. She threaded her way through the narrow streets of Sandwich town centre and along King Street. Walking briskly to fend off the morning chill, and then on to Strand Street, through the Barbican and finally out onto the quay.

The sight of the river never failed to lift her spirits, and today, as usual, a boat sat moored, beckoning prospective seal watchers. Ginny shivered at the thought of the cold winds out to sea, and began to wish she had put another warm layer on. Following the river along the towpath until she reached open fields, she let Bertie, who'd been straining to be free, off his lead. The banks of the river, now mudflats after years of silting, were home to wading birds, their scrawny footprints temporarily etched in the soft alluvium. Reeds lined the river, their roots easily embedding in the soft silty mud, their summer's feathery flowers now a delicate tracery atop slowly rotting stems.

Bertie, thrilled at being free at last, cavorted around Ginny's legs with abandoned joy, creating mayhem with every dog they met. Ducks circled in the dingy water, feet busy paddling against the tide getting nowhere. The annual mating ritual had begun; a startlingly violent affair. Ginny watched a female duck being set upon by six determined amorous drakes. Bertie thought the frantic flurry of wings hugely exciting, and tried to join in with a mating call all of his own.

The footpath meandered by the side of the river following its gentle curves through farmland and eventually out to sea. An elderly couple stopped to admire Bertie and to chat about the vagaries of the British weather. There was something about the silly, hairy exuberance of the dog that made everyone smile. She turned to watch as they walked away, hand in hand, and wondered if she and David would be like that in twenty years time? She hoped so; if only they could get over this… but what exactly was *this*?

The sight of her mother's flint cottage tucked away, down a little-used lane, cheered her, as it always did. She knew tea homemade cake and conversation would be waiting for her.

'Are you OK, darling? You're a bit quiet,' Ellen probed with all the instincts of a terrier. Ginny settled in the wicker chair, in the tiny kitchen, surrounded by plants on every surface. Her mother, she knew, didn't miss much, but Ginny wasn't ready yet to voice her… her worries.

'Is David all right?' Ellen said, bang on target.

She summoned up a bright smile, making sure she didn't catch her mother's eye. 'Yes he's fine. Busy at work. You know what he's like, Mum, always busy.'

'Yes I do,' Ellen replied, cryptically.

Ginny didn't miss the flash of annoyance on her mother's face. The last thing Ginny wanted was a discussion about David's shortcomings. Quickly changing the subject she asked her mother about the latest plant in her collection; a striking pansy of the deepest, darkest purple. The subject of David was soon forgotten.

After an hour of chat, tea and cake Ginny decided she'd better get home and finish off her packing. David she hoped would be home just after lunch, as he promised. Ellen's effortless hospitality had made her reluctant to leave the cosy warmth of her mother's cottage and face what could turn out to be a disastrous weekend ahead.

Opening and closing drawers and cupboards, hoping to find some inspiration for what to take with her, Ginny decided on something warm, and remembering her mother's earlier advice - something waterproof for the Devon rain. Throwing jeans and woolly pullovers into her bag, followed by a handful of underwear, and finally a silk nightdress; the red one, she knew David liked. Would he notice? *Of course he would - wouldn't he?*

David had already packed. Ginny had heard him that morning, stumbling around the bedroom in the semi-darkness of the commuter's world.

'See you at lunchtime, David?' Ginny had said, sleepily, 'you won't be late, will you?' She heard what sounded like a grunt of agreement from him. 'It'll take about five hours to get there, and we're expected for dinner.' Ginny added, 'and the later we leave the worse the traffic will be.' Another grunt followed.

Ginny lay thinking in the not-quite-dawn gloom, of the weekend ahead. She was hoping this trip to Devon would remind David of their happier times together; of holidays with their three boys, before they all went off to boarding school. She smiled as the memories came flooding back of their tramps over the moors - the boys fighting and laughing in equal measure, leaving her and David free to hold hands, and wonder at the landscape. The boys were too old now to come with them – too independent, more interested in sport and their friends. She knew boarding school was supposed to teach them – independence, but… *No I'm not going to think about my boys - not now.*

Unnerved by his recent quietness, and the growing realisation that he didn't seem to want to talk to her much anymore, Ginny was more than surprised when David agreed to go to Devon for a weekend. She had expected to have to use some persuasive arguments. She decided it was best not to mention she was hoping it would be a romantic weekend. The recent silence of their home had started to give her a hollow feeling in the pit of her stomach. Her plans to kick-start their marriage again in Devon suddenly felt doomed to failure.

Glancing at her watch, Ginny saw David should be home any minute - if he kept to his promise, that is, she thought. Zipping up her leather holdall, and applying a slick of ruby-red lipstick, Ginny went downstairs, leaving her bag by the front door.

Too restless to sit, she decided to wait for David in the Orchid House, a glass conservatory leading off the kitchen. Checking her watch after making a final walk around her precious orchids to see that they had enough water and warmth for the weekend, she saw with impatience that it was two-thirty and David was already late.

'David,' Ginny asked, the reception on his mobile really poor. 'Where are you?' She could barely hear him over the noise of the train on its tracks, drowning out his words. She just about heard *half an hour* and *Rochester*.

Hearing at last David's car turn onto the gravel drive she went to open the front door for him.

'It's getting on for three, David,' she fumed trying without any success to hide her irritation. 'You promised you'd be home by one at the latest. We're probably going to miss dinner. What's kept you? You promised,' her voice trailed off, as the words thudded between them.

'Ginny, it'll be fine,' he said, turning to cross the hall to the stairs.

'You promised me, though,' she tried to stifle her anger that accompanied the accusation. *Why didn't he seem to care anymore?*

'Stop being so… impatient,' David said, 'I couldn't get away.' He stood at the bottom of the stairs, running his hand through his hair.

In that one gesture seen so often, Ginny could gauge his impatience with her. It was high. Deciding it wouldn't help anything to have an argument, 'I'll put my things in the car and wait for you there.'

'I need to change. I can't go like this,' he called after her, gesturing to his formal suit and tie. 'I won't be long.'

They left in quivering silence. Making a huge effort to calm down, Ginny loosened her tight hold on the steering wheel taking a deep steadying breath.

'If the traffic's not too bad we should still get there in time,' she said generously, glancing at the dashboard clock.

'Mmm.'

Ginny flicked an irritated glance at David but something softened inside her when she saw how comfortable he looked. Stretched out on the cream leather seat of the BMW 5 series, with his eyes closed and envied him the ability to ignore the atmosphere circling round him; probably having to deal with tricky customers at work, she decided.

She saw he'd changed into chinos, and one of his beloved cashmere sweaters, with a polo shirt under, both a soft-blue, matching his eyes. His short curly, prematurely grey hair made him look distinguished rather than older than his almost-forty years. His skin, smooth was still slightly tanned from skiing. She sighed. He could still make her heart race, even when he was being annoying. She wanted her loving David back not this quiet truculent one. Where had he gone? Not too far away she hoped.

'I'm sure we'll get there on time,' he said, 'stop worrying. A muscle in his cheek was twitching. Why did he have to sound so impatient? Ginny wondered. Wasn't he looking forward to the weekend, not even a little bit?

'I can't wait for my horse ride with Veronica tomorrow,' Ginny said, trying to lighten the atmosphere. 'She's such a generous person lending me one of her horses, don't you think? You wouldn't find many hotel owners willing to do that would you?'

'Mmm,' David said, without opening his eyes.

Cheered at the prospect of a canter over the moors, and despite David's bad mood, she put her foot on the accelerator and moved into the outside lane. She couldn't wait to get there now.

2

Mile by mile, some slow, others fast, the bright red BMW cruised comfortably towards Devon. As the hours passed, and with David asleep beside her, Ginny, driving by instinct, used the time to plan. Deciding that she and David needed time together with no distractions. What better way to reconcile their differences, even if she didn't know what they were - exactly than a walk over the moors together?

As the miles sped by, and out of the worst of the traffic now, Ginny thought back to the places she and David had stayed at in Devon. Buckfastleigh, Lydford, Okehampton – such special places conjuring memories of her family at their best. David relaxed and happy. The three boys using up their boisterous energy climbing tors, and running wild over the moors. Even now she could hear the boys' shouts of excitement, as they acted out their complicated games, leaving her and David to enjoy each other's company, and the scenery. The moors were a unique place for them, and if they couldn't talk there... *No*, Ginny decided she wasn't going to think any further ahead.

She leant back in her seat and stretched as best she could to ease the tension in her body, and thought about Tavy House and the welcome she knew they would receive. Veronica, and her husband Charles, the owners of Tavy House and all the land for miles around, had created a wonderful place to stay. Relaxed comfort amidst faded Victorian grandeur.

As Ginny drove past Exeter, dusk was just beginning to fall making her eyes feel tired peering through the fading light, She wished David would wake up and take over the driving. *Why don't I just wake him up and ask him? Why don't I? Pride? Annoyance? Pig headedness more like.*

Ginny breathed a relieved sigh when at last she reached Mary Tavy and knew the house was only a short distance away. The last few miles had seemed endless; her shoulders ached with tension, and her head throbbed with tiredness. She called David's name, and watched as he reluctantly made himself wake up. Tired and dispirited by David's quietness, Ginny brought the car to a halt in front of the house, and saw with pleasure Veronica, waiting for her in the doorway.

'Difficult journey?' Veronica asked with sympathy, making Ginny wonder what Veronica had seen on her face. 'That was brilliant timing, you've got time to freshen up before dinner.

'We left later than I'd hoped,' Ginny explained. Trying very hard to stop herself flicking a look of annoyance at David,' and the traffic… well you know what it's like on a Friday evening?'

'You're here now,' Veronica said, 'and all you have to do is relax for the rest of the weekend.'

'That sounds amazingly blissful,' Ginny said, turning to look at him, 'doesn't it, David?' He nodded, and gave Veronica a quick smile.

They followed Veronica across the black and white tiled hall, and up the wide, curving staircase. She was happy to listen to Veronica's chatter about the weather, the other guests, the latest crop of lambs, and the health of her horses. It was balm to her frazzled mind; she felt her spirits lifting at the familiarity of it all. *It was a good decision to come here, after all.*

'I'll see you both in the dining room in about half-an-hour?' Veronica asked. 'What time do you want to go for a ride tomorrow, Ginny? Would ten o'clock be all right? It'll give me time to clear away breakfast.'

'Yes, that's great,' Ginny answered, feeling excitement at the thought of riding over the moors. 'I'm hoping for a quick walk to the river before breakfast. That's if I wake up early enough. I doubt you'll want to come with me will you, David?'

'Not early, no, I'm hoping for a lie-in.' David said, with a smile at Veronica. 'You like going on your own anyway.'

Do I? Since when? Ginny wondered, and then realised he was quite right she did like to slip away for a short walk before breakfast. But she wanted this weekend to be different.

'I'd like you to come. That's if you want to,' Ginny said. But she watched with disappointment as he shook his head.

'No thanks, Ginny. What time tomorrow am I clay shooting with Charles?' David asked.

Ginny saw his pleasure at the prospect, so something made him look happy at least, she thought bitterly.

'I'm pretty useless,' David said, 'I wonder if Charles has remembered? I think I nearly hit one of his cows the last time.'

'I'm sure he would have remembered *that*,' Veronica answered with a raised eyebrow. 'About ten, I think. I'll ask him and let you know later.'

Brent Tor bedroom, named for its view of the tor, was Ginny's favourite. She waited with a sense of anticipation as Veronica opened the heavy oak door, and switched on the lights. The room looked just as inviting, as Ginny had remembered it. She looked over at David and gave him a bright happy smile. The smile he gave in return nearly reached his eyes. She so hoped he would enjoy the weekend. She staked all her hopes on it.

'I can't wait to see the view in the morning,' she said, with more cheerfulness than she felt, trying to dispel the chill settling around her heart. She headed over to the full height sash windows; with remembered pleasure she touched the great swags of satin and brocade that framed the windows. Rich ruby-red, and butter-cream patterns swirled over the heavy brocade curtains. The same material had been used to upholster two armchairs both sides of a table of such lustrous walnut, that it could have been used as a mirror, Ginny thought. She warmed herself on the beauty of it all, and on the memories of past, happier times - it made her want to cry for the crushed feeling in the pit of her stomach.

She shook her head free of her thoughts. Tomorrow would be different. Ginny hoped it would be a fine blue day, free from Devon rain, so she could see Brent Tor puncturing the skyline at the horizon. She sighed with anticipation, and looked at David hoping he shared her optimism.

'Are we all right, David?' she asked, when he came out of the bathroom. She could see he was startled with her direct question. *Did he need time to make his mind up?*

'Ermm, yes, why not?' he said, not looking her in the eye.

Why not indeed? She thought.

'It's so lovely to be cooked for,' she said with pleasure, 'I'm really looking forward to it. Veronica's a really great cook. She trained with one of the best London chefs; I can't remember his name for the moment. I'd love to do that.'

You're already a great cook, Ginny. But he didn't say it. He said nothing. His blue eyes found hers for a second, and to Ginny it seemed that they held a question.

'What, David?' Ginny asked. But he shook his head and returned to his unpacking.

She thought back to all the entertaining she'd done for him over the years, helping him win clients - helping him become successful, and finding to her surprise she enjoyed the role of hostess. She was a good cook and Port Lodge, once they had done all the renovations and built the glass conservatory, was a wonderful home and garden to entertain in. The conservatory became known as the Orchid House as it was now bursting with orchid plants of every hue and variety, alive with colour, and their perfume heavenly. She loved watching her guests' pleasure at the sight, whilst enjoying their aperitifs, before moving into the dining room.

'You didn't have to cook if you didn't want to,' David said eventually, deliberately misinterpreting her meaning. 'We could have eaten out.'

'I know, but I wanted to. I wanted to help you, to help your career,' she said, determined not to let him upset her. 'That's why I did it. I enjoyed it. You must know that. Surely.' At least she saw he had the grace to blush, and she heard him mumble something as he walked over to stand in front of the big gilt mirror over the fireplace, running his hands through his hair, brushing an imaginary speck of fluff from his pullover. She turned away hiding her disappointment.

'Do I look all right?' she asked, some time later when she'd finished getting ready. Before the words were out she regretted asking, afraid she wouldn't get the answer she wanted.

It was a deceptively simple dress, she had chosen for dinner. Cherry-red and outrageously expensive - it never failed to lift her spirits. They had bought it together in Paris. David, flush

18

with his annual bonus, and with love for her, whisked her away on the Eurostar for a surprise weekend.

A pair of flat strappy sandals, and chunky silver necklace completed the outfit.

'You look very nice,' he answered, with a half smile.

It was something at least, she thought.

'Do you remember buying this dress? It was so romantic,' she said dreamily.

'I remember,' he answered.

'David… ' she reached out a hand. But he had already gone out of the door.

3

Making her way down the grand stairs to the dining room, Ginny felt a sense of isolation engulf her, even though David was walking right next to her. Could she get used to living on her own if she had to? *Why am I thinking like this? Tomorrow things will be sorted between us.* A great dinner tonight, a good night's sleep and the magical air of the moors, and it will all be all right - her instincts were telling her so. *Nothing's going to get in my way.*

The air, in the hall, was suffocatingly heavy with the scent of lilies. The smell reminded Ginny of death, and she hurried through into the dining room.

The grand walnut table, supported on legs both ornate and strong, was set for six. It could seat ten. The patina of the wood, polished lovingly for years, reflected the flickering candlelight. In the evening light the room felt intimate, a place where secrets could be told. They were watched over by portraits of past incumbents: aristocrats from a different era, gazing at them from their lofty poses, severe and imposing. The sideboard, laden with fruit, still had space for an ornate silver candelabra - alight with flickering candles. A chandelier hanging over the centre of the table, cast a myriad of tiny pinpoints of light over the diners. Perfect, Ginny thought, absolutely perfect. A moment of sheer pleasure stole through her aching heart.

Ginny and David, sat down at the empty spaces in the middle of the table between a young couple seated at the end, and another couple, older, possibly retired, she guessed. Relieved to see everyone's cheery smiles in greeting - she might be glad of their company if David carried on being so distant.

'David, have you seen the menu?' Ginny asked, 'home reared lamb - your favourite.'

Before he could answer, Veronica swept into the room carrying bottles of wine in silver buckets, ice rattling as she walked. She exuded energy and a zest for life. Ginny envied her. She looked marvellous as usual, her *boho* style of skirt and top, embellished with zips and colour, really suited her. Her renaissance-esque hair of auburn curls completed the picture.

Veronica smiled to welcome them all, followed by a short introduction of everybody. From past experience Ginny knew that after a couple of glasses of wine there was a good chance they would all be happily chatting together. Pushing from her mind the possibility that David might not join in, she suddenly realised she was starving. Lunch at her mother's now seemed a long time ago.

Veronica served everyone asparagus tart, on exquisitely patterned plates, pouring each of them a glass of a delicate sparkling wine in vintage glass flutes.

'Sharpham Sparkling Pink, a local wine,' Veronica announced. 'Enjoy your meal.' And with that she left them.

Ginny held her glass towards David for a toast, 'the future,' she said. *Now why did I say that?* Feeling momentarily foolish she was relieved to see some genuine warmth in his smile, when he touched her glass. Her stomach flipped with pleasure. *Maybe just maybe.*

'This is delicious, are you enjoying yours, David?' Ginny asked. 'I hope I'll be all right riding a strange horse tomorrow,' she added as she took another sip of the pink wine. 'I've got so used to my own horse, and all his foibles. I'm not sure I'll be able to ride another one. I don't fancy bolting on a horse over the moors.'

'You'll be fine,' David answered, concentrating on his dinner.

'Because?' Ginny asked.

But before David could reply, the young woman, Veronica had introduced as Philippa, interrupted, 'I'm sorry but I couldn't help overhearing you saying you were going for a ride tomorrow. It sounds amazing, I'm so envious.'

She seemed a sweet young woman, Ginny thought, late twenties perhaps, her light brown hair tucked childlike behind her ears. She wore a silk top with a pink flamingo on the front tucked into jeans. She looked effortlessly pretty, Ginny thought, with no make-up or jewellery.

'Yes, I'm really lucky,' Ginny replied. 'I'm going with Veronica, on one of her horses. Do you ride?'

'I did but not anymore,' she replied, 'I went off to university, and then got married, and now I work, there just doesn't seem enough hours in the day to ride.'

Nearly her own story, except for going to work, Ginny thought wistfully, and wondered how it would feel to be Philippa's age again. The whole world in front of you – if you don't become pregnant, that is.

She was jolted out of her thoughts by Philippa asking what work she did.

'Erm… I don't work,' Ginny said. 'I do charity work, and run our home. We have three children,' she added quickly to cover up an unexpected feeling of embarrassment. She looked at David for support as she spoke, and watched with disappointment as he looked at Philippa instead.

'What about yourself? What do you do?' Ginny asked quickly, hoping to deflect attention away from her.

'I'm a scientist,' she replied. 'I work in a laboratory mostly. I wear a white coat, and look down a magnifying glass most of the time - that sort of thing. It can get awfully tedious sometimes. But then... something really great happens and makes it all worthwhile.'

Worthwhile? Is my life worthwhile?

Ginny could see that David was listening to Philippa with a look of interest.

'What about you, Ian, are you a scientist too?' Ginny asked, turning to the swarthy serious looking man.

'Yes, we work together, that's how we met.'

Ginny saw the proud, uxorious smile he gave his wife, and the grin he received in return. Ginny felt a sudden burning jealousy - she wanted David to smile at her like that. She wanted him to be proud of her too. She wanted so much from him it hurt.

'Do you find enough to do at home?' Philippa asked, politely.

Ginny could see how hard the woman was trying not to judge her, and was grateful.

'Although I'm not paid,' Ginny explained, 'I think of what I do as work. Running the home and family; the three boys keep me busy. I've done a lot of entertaining for David's clients, helping him with his career. *I'm not convincing anyone. I'm not even convincing myself.*

'Will you go back to work when the children are older?' Philippa asked.

'Yes,' she answered, and was pleased to see David raise his eyebrows in surprise. It was about time he took some notice of her. 'I've been thinking about it recently. It's difficult trying to decide what to do. But I'm thinking of going back to university and finishing my degree.'

Ginny realised that her answer was as much a surprise to herself, as it was to David, judging by his raised eyebrow.

'What's your research about, Philippa?' David interjected, giving Ginny an opportunity to think about her declaration of going back to university. *When? How?* Hundreds of questions suddenly tramped their way across her mind. None had answers… yet. All of a sudden she started to feel her future begin to take shape; it was a good feeling. She broke away from her thoughts to find David looking at her thoughtfully. *Good.* She smiled at him with more confidence than she had felt for a while. It was about time he didn't have everything his own way, she thought, with a certain smug satisfaction.

'How long have you been thinking about going back to university?' David asked, quietly. 'You haven't mentioned it before.'

Ever since you've disappeared from my life. Ever since you insisted my boys went away to boarding school. Ever since now.

'I've been thinking about what I'm going to do for a while now,' she lied.

Why haven't I thought about it sooner? Why had she chosen to bring up her children rather than work? Had she decided it would be easier to stay at home? Ginny wondered about all these questions, there didn't seem to be any obvious answers as yet. And then she recalled the café in Crickhowell. She and David had gone to the Brecon Beacons, for a few days' honeymoon. Feeling very pleased with themselves that the wedding, small and civil, had passed without a glitch - all despite the displeasure of both sets of parents about her pregnancy. She and David didn't care, ok it hadn't been planned but they would manage. They were in love.

It was a July day and the sun was celebrating with them. They had sat outside, at a table with a view of Table Top Mountain in the distance, she remembered. Her sundress, bright blue cotton with white swirls, showed her pregnancy for the first time. They had been so excited. They had held hands and chatted about their future; Ginny remembered the laughter and love.

She replayed their conversation that day about David thinking it would be a good idea if she stayed at home after the baby was born. His new job, he said, meant he would earn enough for both of them. 'Why not stay at home and bring up the children?' he asked.

She remembered her astonishment; she wasn't ready for this adult conversation. She didn't see herself at home. She didn't see herself anywhere, except in David's tiny flat, expecting his baby. Her thoughts went no further than that. *How could I have been so naive?*

She had stayed at home, and the conversation wasn't raised again. She didn't need her own money. David had been right about that, and her boys had needed her, he had been right about that too.

'The food is delicious isn't it?' the woman sitting on her other side asked. Ginny had to drag herself back from the café table at Crickhowell, to the dining room at Tavy House.

'I'm sorry I was miles away. Veronica's a great cook isn't

she?' she smiled at her neighbour in agreement. Taking a more careful look she could see that the woman's face was full of character. Her eyes held a liveliness that Ginny had missed at first. Ginny was happy to talk about the easy subject of food.

The couple, Betty and Jack, turned out to be enthusiastic listeners, and seemed genuinely interested in her. Before long she found herself telling them about her unfinished degree, and her plan to go back to university. *Well it was on her mind, wasn't it?*

'It's difficult going back to a career after children isn't it?' Betty said.' I've seen it so many times, women trying to work and bring up a family - they all look exhausted. And it's so unfair I always thought, that as well as everything else, they all seem to suffer from guilt. I don't envy you trying to figure it all out. But I don't blame you for wanting to work too, and earn your own money.'

My own money? Why have I never thought I needed that? Ginny wondered. She realised immediately it was because David earned so much it would have seemed greedy to want more. She was only just beginning to realise that it wasn't about how much money, but more about the independence it gave you. All of a sudden, she realised that she wanted that independence.

A delicious aroma interrupted their conversation; Veronica arrived with the main course of home-reared lamb, celeriac mash and a melange of seasonal vegetables. The room became silent again in appreciation, giving Ginny time to absorb this tsunami of ideas that were flowing over her. She felt breathless with excitement. The meal, Ginny finally noticed, was served on a medley of beautiful china plates of different hues and patterns.

Much later, tired, and slightly drunk but with her head full of possibilities, she found herself climbing the grand staircase up to the bedroom unexpectedly alone. She had been taken aback when David told her he would follow in a bit. *When?* She smiled, wishing everyone a goodnight; she wasn't going to let anyone see her disappointment, least of all David.

She had tried to communicate silently with David. *Come to bed with me.* He ignored her entreaty.

4

A little later, David climbed into bed next to her, and with-out a word turned his back towards her, and fell asleep. Ginny tossed and turned, trying hard not to feel rejected.

Owls hooting across the valley, and David's quiet breathing were the only sounds she could hear. Sleeping, he looked so relaxed. She thought of the unspoken words between them, accumulating like water behind a dam on the point of bursting. In the oily blackness of the bedroom, sleep elusive, Ginny tried to pinpoint when she first noticed the fading of David's desire for her. Of course they didn't – couldn't talk about it – it wasn't their way anymore – it was too… personal. Didn't he know she would blame herself? Didn't he know she would question her attractiveness? Didn't he care?

Her hand itched to touch the bare skin at the nape of his neck where his hair curled slightly. Ginny couldn't remem-ber the last time they had touched. Really touched. Days had turned so quickly into weeks, weeks into months. She edged nearer to him, and breathed in his scent; the smell of lavender mingled with the smell of his skin, so familiar it made her want to weep for what she seemed to be losing.

Ginny whispered, 'David, are you awake?'

She heard a murmur. Had he really been asleep after all?

'What is it?' he asked, quietly.

'Well, I thought,' she whispered, '… as we're on holiday…

you might like to… I know we're tired but… ' Her voice trailed into silence, embarrassed.

She heard another murmur. She couldn't see him in the darkness, but she could hear that he'd shifted his position, and she could tell he'd turned towards her. She felt surprised, after the way things had been between them recently, and a sense of delight shot through her.

Ginny reached out a tentative hand, and touched his shoulder, which was bare. His skin felt smooth, warm and infinitely sexy. She trailed her fingers down his back until she felt the beginnings of the gentle slope at the small of his back. He lay quite still. Her hand carried on exploring gently, her eyes closed, her mind absorbed, the feel of his skin, his scent transporting her to a world of pleasure. She felt a shift in his body, a slight movement towards her. Her fingers started to travel back and stopped at his waist. Dreamily the tips of her fingers moved sideways and lower.

She felt David reach out, his arms encircling her, his breath close. She shivered with anticipation as his skin touched hers. She opened her eyes, now blurred with pleasure. Their bodies knew each other so well, there was no need for thought, no decisions, just recognition, familiarity, comfort, delight.

Some time later, lying by his side, feeling relaxed, happy and close to him, the aridness of the last few months seemed to have faded away. She felt they had made a real connection; the barrier between them had momentarily toppled.

Ginny felt David shift his weight as he turned away from her. She wanted him to talk to her, to hold her, but soon his deep slow breathing told her that this time he really was asleep.

A tear, hot and sad, slid slowly down her cheek into her pillow. *Had anything really changed?*

Wanting the day to be over, she fell asleep at last, dreaming of searching for David on the moors.

5

Bella Boswell woke early on Saturday morning to hear the bells of St Clement's church, Sandwich chime six o'clock, and thought of her plans for the day. Feeling selfish, she wished Ginny was going to be with her, instead of in Devon. Careful not to wake her husband, Steve; she slipped out of bed shivering in the chill of early morning and headed for the kitchen. While the kettle boiled, she watched out of her kitchen window the pink and orange dawn breaking, revealing an early morning mist hovering in the distance.

She dragged a chair over to the welsh dresser to retrieve her diary, hidden away from Steve on the top shelf. Her diary had become more than a record of her days but her confidant - the only safe place for her thoughts. It was her friend – it felt like her only friend. Or so she had thought until recently… It was all there chronicled in her spidery writing on the pages of her diary.

January 15 *Met a lovely woman walking her dog on Sandwich recreation ground. I wish I looked so… vibrant. Heard a woodpecker. Steve slapped me, annoyed his dinner was cold. I think work is getting him down.*

January 16 *Christmas definitely over, Steve back at work and in a bad mood. Kitchen wasn't clean enough today so he pushed me into the edge of the table – a big bruise on my hip. Life's difficult -Ben and Issy the only light. Not allowed to use the car*

I've been told I have to walk everywhere. It took me all morning to do the shopping. Arms are really sore.

January 31 *Saw the same woman on the rec again - talked about dogs - I was too shy to say much. She told me her name was Ginny – short for Virginia – I like it - she said she didn't. Steve came home from work in bad mood again. He spent all evening shouting at me. I tried to keep out of his way.*

February 5th Saw Ginny on the rec. She wanted to know about the bruise on my cheek –told her I walked into a door. Did she believe me? I don't want her to guess about Steve.

She read back over all she had written in February. It told the story of walking with Ginny on the rec and Steve's abuse. She didn't want to dwell on the latter part. It was far too depressing. Instead she picked up her pen to write about the unbelievable events of the last couple of days.

March 12th Ginny asked me to help with election canvassing. ME! I felt so excited to be asked. They're all (canvassing team, leader Peter) meeting in Ash on Tuesday and would I like to come? YES PLEASE I said before remembering Steve would never let me go. What was I thinking? Steve will go mad. But to be asked…
    Issy lost another tooth, she doesn't like her 'gappy' smile, but I do, she looks so cute.

March 13th *Tuesday I've asked Steve if I can go! I planned everything yesterday evening his favourite meal, his favourite beer, a smile on my face. He guessed in a minute. He saw through it all. 'I know you're up to something?' he'd said, 'what is it? What do you want?'*

I felt my body twitch with fear, my smile that I had been so determined to keep, already gone. and I could feel my teeth clenched with tension. I just couldn't bear to disappoint Ginny, so somehow I forced myself to ask.

'WHAT' he roared. I thought the roof would come off the house he shouted so loudly. But later I couldn't believe it (and still can't) without any explanation he said I could go. But I had to be EXTREMLY willing in bed that night.

March 17th Ginny went to Devon yesterday for the weekend, she won't be here today when I go canvassing in Wingham. I've got to do it on my own! When she phoned me yesterday she asked if Steve and I would go for supper in a couple of weeks time. What's happened to my life??? If only it weren't for Steve...

Looking back over her diary, Bella saw how quickly Ginny had become a friend. An unforeseen gift; Steve could only see her faults: she was too thin, her hair was too straight, her face too pale. Nothing was right about her. She was so thankful that Ginny seemed to be able see beyond the mousiness of her. Could she somehow see the colourful woman hidden behind the careworn, dull facade?

Bella, suddenly hearing Steve's footsteps thundering down the stairs, quickly rushed into the kitchen with her diary. *He must never ever find it or she would die.*

She plastered a smile on her face. At lunchtime she'd be cycling to The Anchor pub in Wingham, to meet the other canvassers. The thought filled her with dread and excitement in equal measures. *If only Ginny weren't away in Devon.*

6

That same Saturday morning, while Bella was writing in her diary, Ginny woke to a feeling of excitement. Her mother had been right; everything, well nearly everything, did seem better in the morning.

David was curled towards her still deeply asleep; his hands tucked under his cheek like a child, like Tim their youngest. In that moment she felt the thread, despite everything, connecting David and her, and their three beautiful sons. It was still intact - just about.

Realising she had only just over an hour before breakfast, she quickly dressed in warm clothes, and her old walking boots, leaving David a jaunty note: '*Gone fishing – back for breakfast!*' She slipped out of the bedroom, tiptoeing down the grand staircase, and out into fresh air and freedom.

The house was still wrapped in sleep, the day not yet quite begun. She stood looking over the valley, for a moment, her memory filling the gaps in the landscape hidden by the early morning mist. The grass beneath her feet was still damp with dew; Ginny could feel the cold seeping through her shoes.

Walking briskly, she felt a sense of relief as she headed out onto the moors. In front of her lay a scene, straight from a Constable painting. A rolling landscape with huddles of mature oaks in endless fields, drawing the eye inexorably towards the river. The Burn, snaked its way in silver glittering loops until it was out of sight beyond the horizon. A rural idyll; one of rolling hills, cows and sheep, all made miniature by distance.

The path leading to the river skirted between fields and moor, in places it was no more than a sheep trail. Ginny followed the path eventually emerging onto the edge of the moors. She quickened her pace. She didn't have long before breakfast

She turned for a moment to look back at Tavy House. She could see it sitting confidently on the top of the hill. It's grey stonewalls giving the impression of strength - strength that would be needed to withstand the determined force of the easterly winds. Its plainness couldn't disguise its fine proportions.

Ginny heard the river before she saw it. Burn River, bloated with winter water, was in full flood; it galloped and hissed its way between the pillars of rock dropped in its waters by no man's hand. It was this rush and hiss she could hear, nothing gentle, full of power and vigour. Rounding the next bend she saw the river in all its fury. This was nature, she thought, in its destructive beauty, it made her want to reach out for comfort, for a sense of *other* to witness this roil with her.

She followed the riverbank looking for a route down to the water's edge. She needed to stop somewhere to reflect, to meditate - to get everything straight again in her head. She found a flat-topped stone safe from the eddies, and sat facing the weak March sun. Letting her thoughts roam, the sun warm on her face, they came to rest on the most pressing one. The one she had been avoiding for months: David and her. *My marriage is failing.* Last night's love making, she realised, had meant nothing at all. They were no further on.

She picked up some small stones and threw them into the calm water, making it ripple. She threw the stones harder and harder until her emotions, held back for so long, no longer fettered escaped from their prison. She shouted in pain and frustration as the stones churned the water. Her tears, which she had held back for months - flowed.

Filling her lungs deep with the cold fresh air permeated with the smell of iron ore, she forced herself to regain her calm. She slipped off her shoes, dipping her toes in the icy water; she relished the physical jolt – it was bitterly cold. Her tears dried, she realised she felt better after their release. Better able to cope with what was before her – whatever that was. She still didn't know. She knew she at least had taken the first step. She was no longer in denial about her marriage. What was happening to them went so deep - it had touched the very heart of their relationship. Did David feel the same? *I have to save our marriage somehow.*

She wondered if she was kidding herself that her plan to go for a walk this afternoon, would make anything difference between them. Ginny could imagine it now, hand in hand, the two of them alone on the moors, heading to the top of Brent Tor. Her and David, as it always used to be, talking through their problems. Their problems, she had hoped would seem smaller in that vast landscape. She could see them laughing happily together at how each had misunderstood the other. It would be all right. She was determined. It had to work. If it didn't work… She realised she had no other plan. No plan B. She couldn't bear to think of them going home without some sort of resolution. She didn't know how long they could go on as they were. It had to work. Their marriage depended on it. *On a walk?* She was beginning to realise that this whole weekend had been based on her optimism only

- she was being ridiculous it was never going to work. Dread engulfed her.

Ginny sensed too much time had drifted she needed to get back, or she'd be late for breakfast. Putting her shoes back on, feet now numb with cold, she started the walk back to Tavy House her heart weary with each step. She watched the sky match her mood. The brilliant blue of earlier, so full of energy, was now draining of colour through blue to pale grey.

She saw the ruddy-red chimneys of Tavy House reveal themselves in the distance as she neared the house. She turned for one last sight of Brent Tor. It rose with its church atop, grey on grey, only the barest of shadows differentiating man's hand from God's.

7

David instantly regretted his harsh words to Ginny as she left for the stables after breakfast. And she had seemed so excited too. He thought how pretty she had looked, with a bloom on her cheeks from her early morning walk. Her eyes though, held something different, something sad, he thought. He shouldn't have been so miserable, spoiling her morning, the way he had.

She was right, it wasn't her fault his plans for clay pigeon shooting with Charles, had been scuppered. "Charles was needed" was the message given by Veronica at the breakfast table. "He was very sorry, but Charles had to go and meet the vet". David of course understood, or so he told Veronica. Ginny had looked at him with hesitation on her face – he could tell she was on the point of cancelling her ride to keep him company. It was the fact that in the end she didn't change her plans that had made him so churlish.

'Well, I hope *you* enjoy yourself,' he said, 'I'm sure I'll find something to do,' and then watched her face fall with dismay. He had left her standing there her mouth open with astonishment. Shame engulfed him. He nearly turned to apologise, but instead he carried on walking back to the house.

He opened the door to their bedroom to be greeted by a shaft of butter-yellow sunlight. Enticed over to the window to admire the source of the brightness, he stood gazing at the hills streaked with sunshine. So different, he thought, to the grey and suffocating air circling over London. He was glad to be here, he realised all of a sudden, even though his plans for the morning had fallen through. Ginny had been right; they needed to spend some time together. He remembered with a stab of guilt how pretty and interesting he had thought Philippa last night, and was shamed by the comparison he had made with Ginny. She had, he knew, done everything for him, and he hadn't defended her.

How long had it been since she was everything to him? How long had it been since Ginny stopped being the ebb and flow of his life? He felt her hurt with every look she gave him, with every nuance of the beautiful planes of her face, her skin pale against the darkness of her hair a Celtic beauty – his Celtic beauty. But now, that beauty seemed faded irredeemably in his eyes, the lustre edged with tarnish, or had his eye dimmed? A cataract? His vision blurred? He wished it were so; it would be easier to forgive himself for those bruised eyes of hers.

For all his married life, he knew she had partnered him, in all his endeavours. She had built a home around him, and their three sons. He had accepted it all, he had relished it, lapped it up. And he, in his turn, had worked hard to make her proud of him. He had succeeded - they had succeeded.

But now when he looked in the mirror, instead of seeing a young ambitious man he saw a man about to become forty, still looking the way he always did - fit, strong, intelligent with clear sky-blue eyes. He didn't see a husband, he didn't see a father, instead he saw a man yearning for freedom. Where had the time gone from his student days at King's College, London?

Not only had he pursued his love of numbers at university,

David recalled how he had also pursued Ginny. That was nearly twenty years ago. They complemented each other; he sensed it immediately. He remembered how her beauty had stunned him, and he, a man of numbers, of logic, was blown away. Everything he thought he knew flew away on the air, when he saw her. Those clear eyes swept through his reserve and found the joy of him. She saw beyond the quiet methodical nature, and showed him his other side, his human side. Ginny's more mercurial nature needed his calming hand, he soothed. Her gift was the brightness of her very soul. He took - she gave. It was the way it had always been between them. It was the way it still was, David thought - shamed. He remembered the fast pace of it all. He'd found himself spinning; numbers so ordered, now tumbling all around him. Ginny moving into his flat creating a vortex he didn't think he could survive. But he did survive, and from then he was her acolyte.

From the beginning their passion was something he had never experienced before – by comparison, his other relationships felt like teenage fumblings. With Ginny it was comfort, and glorious moments, he never knew which to expect. Plans for a life together, a future became an unspoken horizon.

The gods laughed as they loved - Ginny fell pregnant.

8

The sun was sparkling, not a rain cloud in the sky as Ginny left Tavy House, and walked round the back of the house to the stables. But instead of feeling the thrill of the planned ride on horseback across the moors, she felt tears sting her eyes.

The smell of leather and polish greeted her at the door of the tack room. Saddles and bridles were hung in orderly rows with a plaque above of each horse's name; Sultan, Iggy, William, Daisy... Below them were a row of wellingtons and riding boots, some dusty, some polished. Veronica was already in the tack room busy checking the saddles and bridles ready for their ride.

'Veronica, this is such a treat for me,' Ginny said, trying not to show the hurt she felt at David's words. 'I'm so grateful.' She would deal with the sharp words when she and David were out walking; until then she was determined to enjoy this adventure on the moors.

'You're doing me a favour really,' Veronica replied, looking snug in a bright blue jacket and fur-lined hood. 'Oz needs the exercise, and I don't usually have time to ride two horses.'

Ginny watched with pleasure as the horses came rushing and whinnying over to the gate to great them. Ginny offered her hand out to Oz, a dark bay Irish cob. He was hanging his head over the gate in anticipation of a carrot, not so very different from her own horse.

'The horses are hairy and muddy, I'm afraid,' Veronica said, 'I've got a couple of brushes and a hoof pick, for a quick groom. But we need to get going if we want to get back in time for your walk later this afternoon.

'Tell me about, Oz,' Ginny asked, stroking his muzzle, 'he looks very sweet.

'Oz, is very kind, you won't have any trouble with him,' Veronica replied.

Sitting on their horses and ready to go, Veronica warned Ginny before they set off, 'if a mist comes down and we lose each other - it's never happened before - so don't worry. But if we do get separated,' Veronica said, 'head for the chimneys on Tavy House, they can be seen for miles around, even in a mist. The horses know their way home too, so if there's any problem just give them their head. Let them find their own way home.'

As they set off, Ginny turned her face to the sun, enjoying its mild warmth on her skin. The air was invigorating, and cosy in her down jacket, Ginny had a sudden feeling of well-being. David for the moment forgotten.

As they rode, Ginny enjoyed listening to Veronica's tales of the farm and stories about guests at the hotel. One guest Veronica recounted had stolen a painting from one of their bedrooms; another had scratched their initials in one of the best pieces of furniture in the house. Her own news seemed less exciting. She realised sadly she didn't have much news of her own, unless you considered a failing marriage newsworthy, she thought.

Ginny was suddenly aware of movement; she saw a bird plummet to the ground, and then, almost as quickly rise back up into the air.

'A kestrel,' Veronica explained, 'watch while it hovers - it'll get something this time.'

And as Veronica said the words, the hawk with ginger-brown feathers and cream speckled underside, swooped back down to earth, and just as quickly rose again with what looked, to Ginny, like a mouse dangling from its beak.

'Such savagery,' Ginny said. 'I know they have to live but… '

'It's what happens in the wild, Ginny,' Veronica said, 'it does seem cruel though.'

'You've gone quiet,' Veronica said, looking worried.

'Are you all right?'

'I was just thinking about that poor mouse,' she answered.

'But not just that… it made me think about how fragile life is. How we need to make the most of it, I suppose. I hope the mouse did. That sounds absolutely ridiculous, doesn't it.'

'Out here it gets you thinking,' Veronica answered, with a sweep of her arm. It's so huge here and we're so small. We can't control this space as we do our own. I think it makes us feel vulnerable.'

'You can just see the church, now that the mist has lifted,' Veronica said, pointing ahead. 'The legend goes that the devil was roaming the moors looking for victims; he'd already killed all the giants and witches. And then, the devil saw a ship coming up the Channel, so he created a terrible storm. The ship's Captain, seeing that all would be lost any minute, prayed to Saint Michael and promised if the ship, the Virtue, was saved, then he would build a church on the highest land he saw when he reached safety. And that… was how Brentor Church came to be built on the top of the tor.'

'Can you imagine having to climb all that way to church?'

Ginny asked, 'I'm not sure Saint Michael did anyone any favours there.'

Ginny laughed, seeing Veronica's eyebrow raised, 'I know, I've missed the whole point, but couldn't Saint Michael have said, "no it's OK, build me a church at the bottom it'll be much easier for everyone?" I wonder if life felt much simpler then.' And seeing Veronica's look of scepticism, tried to explain, 'today's world seems so full of debt, recession, getting a mortgage, a career, children as well as homemaking. And not enough time to do anything well.'

'Hmm, maybe.' Veronica said, 'I'm not sure how much fun it would be washing your clothes in the river, or living on berries.'

'Ginny laughed, 'no, maybe not. But imagine travelling everywhere by horse… wonderful.'

'Is that why you didn't have a career, Ginny?' Veronica asked quietly, 'so you would have more time? I know it's none of my business, but you don't seem your usual self at the moment, and David too… he seems preoccupied.'

'It's the moors,' Ginny lied, 'and that damned kestrel - it's got me thinking. That's all.' And once more she saw Veronica raise an eyebrow. She hadn't believed her for a second.

9

Uncomfortable with his own company, now that the shoot with Charles was cancelled, David decided to take the car into Tavistock. He picked up his jacket and felt in the pockets for the car keys. All of a sudden he realised Ginny had taken them to get her riding boots out of the car.

'Damnation,' he muttered under his breath, 'she must still have them. What a bloody... nuisance.'

He raced round to the stables, hoping she might still be there, or at least near enough for him to call out to her. But as he reached the path, he saw them just ahead but still too far in the distance for them to hear him shout.

'Damn, damn, damn,' he muttered to himself. A sheep in the field next to the path blinked at him. Now what?

Looking around there was no one but him and the huge landscape. He may as well go for a walk; there didn't seem much else for him to do. He decided to follow the same path as the horses until he thought of a better plan.

There was nothing to distract him except the buzz and dart of insects in the hedgerow. He strolled without aim for about half an hour, beginning to enjoy the lack of urgency of his steps. Noticing a river, in the distance, he decided to head that way and follow it, realising at the same time how ill equipped he was for walking on the moors. He should at the very least have brought a map with him and water, waterproofs, something to eat, chocolate, compass, everything in fact that was in his rucksack, all ready and prepared. Except it was now locked in the boot of the car and Ginny had the keys. *Damn. What could go wrong? It's not as if I'm doing anything strenuous. Is it?*

With more energy, he set off towards the river hoping he could figure out how to get there. He recognised this person - a challenge to face.

When the track came to an end, David branched off onto the moors; the narrow and heavily rutted sheep trail he was following seemed to be heading in the right direction. There was still no one else in sight, only sheep and heather. Alone with his thoughts he faced the worst of them. The knowledge that he was bringing their marriage to its knees, made his stomach churn with apprehension.

He thought of Ginny's amorousness the night before. He had been surprised that given the way things were between them, she had even wanted to make love. It shamed him to think of Ginny trying so hard to bring them closer. What was he doing? Absolutely nothing. And then he remembered Philippa asking Ginny about her career. He remembered now, once more with shame, how he had made it difficult for Ginny to pick up her career after the children had gone to school. They still need you at home, he remembered arguing persuasively. He had to confess it had suited him, and he thought at the time it had suited Ginny too. But now he was beginning to wonder. He was beginning to wonder about so much recently.

In the silence of the moors he raised his arms out to the sky and yelled his feelings of pent up shame and guilt.

And then quite suddenly he saw something on the skyline. Two dots in the distance, heading for the tor - could that be

Ginny and Veronica? Should he go and find out – try and catch up? And then realising it was a ridiculous idea. 'I'll stick to my plan and head for the river,' he said out loud to a group of sheep grazing contentedly. His voice disappearing on the breeze.

The physical demands on his body, as the climb got steeper, began to feel exhilarating. The pull of his lungs, the sweat on his face, the heat of his body trapped in his jacket as the path climbed higher and higher. He didn't even know if he was going the right way. He didn't care. This was the challenge he wanted to be facing - physical hard work, banishing all thoughts. He didn't want to think anymore.

He stood still for a moment, to catch his breath, and let the wind dry the sweat from his skin. He circled slowly, he could feel the power of the landscape taking hold; releasing tensions that he hadn't, until that moment, realised existed.

10

Ginny and Veronica had been riding for an hour or so. And now free of mist at last, the church at the top of Brentor was clearly visible. The terrain had grown wilder, the higher they rode; Ginny noticed how sparse and tough the grass was, still brown tipped from winter. The horses picked their way slowly round the jagged granite boulders that were strewn along the narrow path.

Tired and needing to stretch her legs and stiffening knees, Ginny hoped they were planning to stop soon.

Feeling grateful Veronica hadn't probed any further about why she was quieter than usual, she concentrated on her riding: straightening her back, relaxing her hands, and giving Oz all the help he needed to negotiate the steep path.

Who would believe I had problems anyway? She thought. She knew her life must seem idyllic - a successful and attractive husband, a big house and garden, expensive cars and holidays, three sons at private school? She shouldn't have anything to complain about – and that, she realised made it all the harder to confide in anyone. Bella perhaps? But Bella had so little, how on earth could she tell Bella she was unhappy? She wondered how Bella would get on canvassing without her this afternoon. She had occasionally seen steel in Bella's eyes, and knew instinctively that Bella was stronger than she appeared. She was beginning to worry that Bella's bruises were something to do with her husband. *But it couldn't be, could it?* There just seemed one too many doors that Bella had accidentally walked into.

Veronica turned round, 'you look pensive?'

'All this,' Ginny said, quickly putting aside her worries about Bella, drawing an arc with her arm. 'I was thinking of riding off into the sunset.'

'Are you trying to escape?' Veronica asked.

'The simple life - no cars, no mobile phones?' Ginny replied, ignoring Veronica's question. 'Getting anywhere would take a day.'

'Oh, yes, that would be lovely,' Veronica said, 'but... reality would set in pretty quickly, I'm quite sure. I think you'd miss your *caffe latte* more than you imagine.'

They both laughed, 'you're probably right,' Ginny acknowledged, 'but just think... '

'It sounds to me,' Veronica said, 'as though you want to escape from your own life. But maybe not on horseback – didn't I just see you rubbing your knees just now?'

Ginny laughed, 'I don't want to escape, well not exactly. I know I'm lucky with what I have - but just at the moment... none of it seems terribly important.'

'What do you mean?' Veronica asked, sounding curious.

'I don't work, not paid work anyway, so my time is almost all my own now that the children are away at school. Is it enough to be at home? That's what I'm thinking about. And I'm nearly forty. It's time for change.'

'And David? What does he think?' Veronica asked. Ginny could see Veronica wasn't going to let this go.

'Well... ' Ginny hesitated, 'I'm not sure I want to know

what he thinks. I'm not sure I need to know what he thinks' she amended, feeling almost embarrassed, as though it were a confession.'

Veronica was waiting for Ginny to come alongside her on the wider grass verge. 'Why don't you look for a job that would give you the same satisfaction as bringing up the children? Earning your own money is not just about having more money, it's about a sense of achievement.'

Ginny pretended to be taking a moment to admire the view, when really she was trying to digest what Veronica had just said. She had begun to wonder, in the last few months, if David's life had somehow become more important than her own.

Ginny returned her thoughts to the moors and Oz, who by now was blowing hard, as he struggled up the steep slope, his coat darkening with sweat.

'We'll stop at the top and let the horses get their breath back,' Veronica said.

'I enjoy what I do... mostly, even though I don't get paid,' Ginny said continuing their conversation. 'I love my garden - pottering about in the Orchid House, and my charity work, of course: at the moment I'm canvassing for the general elections. And I don't need any money. David earns enough for both of us. Wouldn't you call it greed for me to want more?'

Why do I sound so lame? Ginny thought.

Veronica broke the uncomfortable silence, 'I don't need to work either. I could be a team with Charles, helping on the farm. But the difference for me is that I want to work - I want that feeling of independence. It's not how much you earn, it's the fact that you've earned it, using your skills and talents. I want to have a sense of me, not just 'us'.'

'That's what I've been thinking about,' Ginny said, 'and I'm beginning to see that if things aren't right between David and I, then I don't want to be using his money.' She paused for a moment letting that idea sink in. 'It all seems so clear suddenly.'

Hallelujah...

Ginny could feel a smile broadening on her face – she had just got past the most enormous hurdle. *OK so it's taken me a while to get here. But I'm on my way...*

They rode on, the path winding up and around the tor, the going getting tougher for the horses, the pace slow and careful.

'Ginny, you clearly love your children,' Veronica said, suddenly, 'I've been thinking about it. You and David have used all your energy making their lives as contented as possible. That's a wonderful thing to have done for them. I think you are being too hard on yourself. My children would have loved a mother like you,' Veronica continued. 'I think you're under-selling yourself, if you consider these years you've given your children as being without value. But I think you're right – you need to make changes – but for *you* this time.'

Ginny nodded, too much to think about to speak just yet.

'See over there, that grassy area?' Veronica asked, pointing over to a patch of green in the distance, 'that's where we're stopping. The horses can graze there, and we can sit and eat our picnic.'

'I'm sure my knees will hold up that far,' Ginny said smiling, her stomach beginning to rumble at the thought of food. 'Breakfast seems a long time ago. It must be all the fresh air.'

After a few minutes more riding she said, 'I thought I would want motherhood and homemaking forever. But what happens when it doesn't want you? I never anticipated the boys being away at boarding school. Not for a second did I anticipate it would be just David and I at home this soon.'

Ginny could feel her throat constrict with pain, but as long as she kept her eyes on the tor and not Veronica, she felt able to continue. Her face to the sun, Ginny let loose words, that up until now had been drained of life by her determination to keep silent.

'When the children grow up,' Ginny said, 'and move away from home - go to boarding school - what do you do then? Look after your husband? But what happens if your husband suddenly doesn't want to be looked after anymore?'

Ginny sniffed, and felt Veronica's hand on her shoulder.

'How long has it been like... this?' Veronica asked, gently.

'Forever it seems - now I've begun to notice,' Ginny replied, her voice choking. 'If I'm really honest, it's not just David. Somehow it feels as though... we've both lost our way. That's why I thought the peace and quiet here might help us. I hoped we could talk, where there are no distractions – go for a walk just the two of us, you know?' Ginny sighed. 'But now... I don't know. But I do know I want our marriage to work but not the way it is now. It has to change. I want to be an equal.'

'Marriage needs an overhaul at times – its organic, isn't it?' Veronica said, her face tilted to the sun. 'I know you'll find a way.'

Ginny nodded, Veronica was right. She would find a way.

'That's the river Burn,' Veronica said, pointing to a thin silver ribbon glinting in the early afternoon sun.

It was time to tell someone of her plan, Ginny thought and who better than Veronica? 'I was toying with the idea of doing a landscape-gardening course,' she said. 'Going back to university

- I think it would be something I'd enjoy. I haven't told anybody yet about the landscaping part, not even myself... not really.'

'Well there you are then – things are already taking shape,' Veronica said, encouragingly. 'It sounds like a wonderful idea to me. You're always talking about your garden, it sounds as though you've done amazing things - you obviously really love it.'

'Do you know, for the first time,' Ginny said, almost to herself, 'I'm beginning to see that I can't just leave my life and happiness in David's hands, and then complain when I don't like what he's decided.' *Why did I ever think I should?*

Ginny paused and looked around from the sweep of blue sky to the threatening black hue forming in the distance. She could smell the metallic salts buried deep in the peat. All around her were the signs of winter. It was only the purple heather that hinted of spring.

'It's this place, you know – it allows you to think differently,' Ginny said.

They stopped for a moment, forming a tableau of horses and riders, silhouetted on the tor by shafts of sunlight. There was no one to see them. So completely alone, it sent a shiver through her. What if... and then she remembered she had a mobile and more prosaically a picnic to eat.

The two women carried on uphill at a leisurely pace, the hint of green they had seen earlier becoming, with each step, a reality; the horses tired now, content to amble if allowed. It wasn't too much longer before they arrived at the top of the tor. Dismounting at long last, they let the tired horses meander in the heather, and graze where they could. Ginny stretched out her aching back, as she sat down on the large, flat granite stone Veronica had found for them facing the sun. Out of the breeze, it almost felt warm.

'Thank you so much, again, Veronica, for suggesting this ride. It's what I needed to get a sense of perspective.'

She wondered fleetingly what David had decided to do that morning, as she settled down to their picnic. She felt ravenous.

11

The very few clouds in the topaz-blue sky that David could see, reminded him of puff balls in the desert, bowling along merrily, at the mercy of the breeze. In the distance, he could see a tractor, army-green with sun-yellow hubcaps, toiling up the hill, followed by a plumage of seagulls looking for worms in the newly tilled soil.

He wasn't certain, but he thought he could see a pair of buzzards in the distance, soaring through the air in what could only be described, as playful: David felt envious of their effortless freedom.

He realised with surprise, he had never experienced loneliness before. His life, usually so ordered, so busy, full of people, so full of Ginny, was now like a broken abacus: the beads ordered and useful one minute, and the next, scattered and dysfunctional. He smiled to himself at his choice of analogy: once an accountant always an accountant, he thought. At least he could count on his work, he realised.

Wondering if Ginny was enjoying herself on the new horse, he realised she was never far from his thoughts. She was a reference point in his life. A wayfinder - drawing him home. Did that mean he still loved her? *How I wish that were so.* He felt tears prick the back of his eyes. He sniffed, and hurried on.

Enjoying the swishing noise of his footsteps on the gravel track, David spotted the river just ahead. As he neared, he could see the river was more like a stream, shallow and slow. David scrambled through the bracken and rough grass to reach the edge where he could see the water was clear, running over small multi-coloured stones rubbed smooth and round by the currents. He breathed in the many-layered scent of the river; iron ore, peat bog, upland grass all merged – absolutely nothing like the Thames. No sewage. No detritus. So many things were absent. This river though, the Burn, was delicious - life affirming. Further along this lowland stretch, and many miles distant from its mother river the Tamar, David could see that the river had shed its winter waters, engorging the peat bogs.

Was this where Ginny had been before breakfast? He should have gone with her. He wished he had. She loved water – he knew she would have taken off her shoes and paddled despite how cold it was. He knew her so well. Why did this have to happen to him, this jarring, this jangling of nerves, this dissonance? He wanted everything to be as it was. No he didn't and that was the trouble. He wanted something else – but he didn't know what. What a terrible mess.

As he walked, the view shifted from moorland to upland, and finally to the tor. He wanted to imprint this on his mind for the time when he was sitting in his living room wanting to escape - this memory would sustain him, he knew. A flock of sheep suddenly appeared on the track in front of him, startling him. They jumped in a huddle one on top of the other until order was restored from momentary chaos. *Why do I want to escape?* Not from this though, he thought. He didn't want to escape from this.

It was time, he thought as he walked: he had nothing better

to do than think of Ginny. Where? When? How? Why did his marriage all of a sudden feel like a trap?

An image flashed into his mind, of his mother, sitting by the fire unravelling an old pullover. He recalled asking her why she was undoing all her hard work.

'To start again,' she had answered, simply. The look on her face, so clear to him all these years later – it shone with excitement at the prospect of a new beginning. *Is that what I want - a new beginning?*

All these years later he began to see what his mother was talking about. His mother's knitting reminded him of their marriage. Could all the strands of their marriage be knitted back again – knit one purl one. Ginny had knitted for the boys when they were little. The clacking of the needles restful to his mind, tired after a day's work. The soft cashmere of their early life had now turned into a finely woven hair shirt.

David clambered over some bigger boulders; his thin city shoes were by now letting in water, totally unsuitable for the rugged and boggy terrain. As he began to follow the river along its upland stretches towards it's source, there was silence except for the murmuring of the river, and birds calling to their hopeful mates.

His watch told him he had eaten almost two hours ago, and he was beginning to feel hungry and thirsty. *Damn, damn, if only I had my rucksack.* He was surprised at how challenging the walk was becoming and for the first time began to have misgivings about being on the moors with no emergency supplies. He was only supposed to be going for a stroll, after all, until Ginny got back, but now he was miles from anywhere. The river was now at least two metres below him and had deepened into a murky blackness.

He continued walking; heading towards higher ground, following the bows and loops of the river. Memories were all around him here – of him and Ginny, the boys - running and chasing, sandwiches and chocolate, laughter and tears. Family stuff. He wished he could bring back that same feeling instead of this black hollowness in his stomach.

He missed the boys; he couldn't tell Ginny that, she'd been so against them going away to school, he couldn't own to his doubts now. It would destroy her. Had it been the right thing to do? He could see with disappointment his oldest boy, William, nearly a man at eighteen-years-old, growing aloof. He barely came home now in the holidays, choosing instead to spend his time with his pals instead. It was only what he had done at that age, after all. But then he hadn't known how a parent would feel about the separation – it was only now. He knew Ginny found it hard, right from the beginning. Each son leaving, one, two, and followed by their third son, Timmy, became more of a wrench for her. And he had to pretend that he didn't care – that it was best for them. But he had cared. He did care. He just couldn't say it. He couldn't show it. He had to pretend to be that stereotype of a father – distant, disconnected. Inside he wasn't distant or disconnected - as his heart beat, so did he love them. But wasn't it part of their growing up – growing away – didn't she just have to get used to it? Didn't he? He had overruled her, and still felt guilt at his dogged intransigence.

He was so deep in thought that it took him a while to realise the river had disappeared, and began to panic that he maybe lost with no waterproof clothing and soaking wet shoes. The sky, so blue before, was now turning a troubling grey. Would they send out a search party? Would anybody care enough?

Ginny would – he knew. He could always count on her. That was the essence of Ginny.

And then with relief he heard the distinctive sound of water gurgling, rushing over stones and rocks, and knew he wasn't lost after all. The river would show him the way. Before dark he hoped, with a shiver.

He'd been aware of the call of birds all morning he recognised the stonechat and the crows, but there was something else now he thought he could hear. A thin sort of sound, he didn't recognise. Could it be an animal? A bird? He couldn't be sure what it was and then… there it was again. Faint but there nonetheless. This time though, he thought it sounded more human – it couldn't be a bird, could it? He shrugged, he didn't know much about birds anyway. Ginny would know what bird made that long high-pitched reedy sound that floated away as soon as his ears found it. And then again. There was something about the sound that was making the hair on the back of his neck stand up. And then again, but nearer this time. He must be walking towards it. David was beginning to have a really horrible feeling that the sound might be human. He could now hear urgency in the voice; a voice that was most distinctly human. He thought he could hear distress too. He started walking quickly, not sure which direction to take, trying to catch the sound again, before the breeze whipped it away.

'Help… please help… will someone help…' A high thin voice was calling, desperation all too evident. David knew he had to find whoever it was, and quickly.

12

While Ginny was eating her picnic in the lee of Brent Tor, Bella was cycling hot and flustered, along Wingham High Street, past bright-white thatched cottages, and award-winning civic planting. She could see Peter and the other canvassers, already waiting for her outside The Anchor pub.

'Sorry I'm late,' she mumbled, sweat pouring down her face. She hadn't wanted to explain to them that Steve had demanded, at the very last minute, that she iron him a shirt - it might raise too many unanswerable questions. Disgusted with her timidity at not mentioning that there were at least ten other ironed shirts hanging in his wardrobe. She had quickly ironed the shirt - but she couldn't tell these people any of that. 'One of my children suddenly had toothache,' she said, gulping in explanation, apologising to Issy, in her head.

'This is, Bella,' Peter said introducing her to the rest of the group, 'for those who haven't met her before.'

Bella could only smile weakly at them, as she tried to get her breath back, surreptitiously wiping the sweat off her face.

They set off straight away, deciding they would canvass together in the High Street

and then split up to canvass the lanes off the main street. Wingham was a small pretty village between Sandwich and Canterbury, boasting a Post Office, and a General Store, not forgetting the three pubs dotted along the High Street.

'Don't worry,' one of the group, whispered to Bella, picking up on her anxiety, 'we'll be in twos or threes.' Bella smiled at her with relief.

Despite the kind woman's earlier reassurance, it wasn't long before she found herself quite alone, standing outside, The Bungalow. Instead of fresh cut, spring green lawns, and nodding daffodils, like the rest of the houses in Water Lane, The Bungalow had flattened mud for a garden, and the only signs of spring were some valiant weeds poking through the bare earth.

Tentatively approaching the gate, Bella noticed it was only hanging on by one hinge. The front garden, full of abandoned cars and motorbikes, looked deserted. Bits of greasy engines and machinery were strewn everywhere. It looked more like a scrap yard. The neighbours must hate living next door to this mess, she thought, glad to it wasn't her.

Opening the rusty gate cautiously, Bella was startled to see a man in a dirty grey vest, suddenly appear from the side of the house, followed by a massive black dog. She was relieved to see they hadn't noticed her yet. Bella quietly pushed the gate closed, and wondered frantically what Ginny would do? Steve had done this to her, she thought angry with herself for being such a coward. He had reduced her confidence, layer-by-layer, vanquishing everyone from her life, except him. He had turned her into this feeble being. Well she would show him, she suddenly determined.

Ginny she knew, would have marched up to the front door, telling the dog to 'sit and be quiet'. She so wanted to be able to tell her how brave she'd been. *You should have seen the dog, Ginny; it was bigger than a house*. She could hear Ginny's laughter.

'Hello,' Bella called out. 'Oh no,' she muttered to herself, as the dog raised his head and looked directly at her. The next second he let out an ear piercing howl and leapt towards the gate, closely followed by its owner.

'What do you want?' The scruffy, unshaven man asked, appearing from around the corner of the house – the sound of the dog's barking deafening. He came to a standstill in front of her, and with his hands on his hips, waited for an answer. As Bella took a step back in fright, he advanced towards her. She could see his arms and neck were emblazoned with tattoos: spider's webs crawled up his neck, devils heads, and snakes wrapped around his arms, and some others on his chest that made a blush rise on her cheeks. Bella looked up at his face to see him leering at her, delighting in her discomfit.

Bella knew he wouldn't consider her a threat - a pale, under-nourished looking woman. If only Steve wouldn't glare at her at mealtimes, she might be able to eat more.

No. This bullish man wouldn't feel threatened at all by her, she thought. And the dog wouldn't either. Dinner was dinner, however bony.

'Shut up, Spike,' the aggression in the man's voice matched the snarl on the dogs face, loud and intimidating.

The four-legged version of scruffy and unshaven, instead of tattoos and piercings, sported a dangerous-looking spiked collar.

Spike stood snarling at the end of his chain, saliva drooling from his cavernous mouth, looking as though he were about to pounce. Its bared teeth were the colour of wet sand, dark and yellowed, and bigger than any she had seen this close up.

Bella wanted to squeal in fright, and run. But it was as though somehow she was glued to the ground.

It was the dog that made the next move. With an athletic leap, Spike's front paws were over the gate. And Bella suddenly found in her fright that her feet were working at last. She ran as fast as she could.

Bella only stopped for breath when she judged she was safe, and could no longer hear the man's laughter. Apart from her heart pounding like bellows, and birds calling, there was no other sound. There was no sign of Peter, or anybody else, in the lane and as she stood recovering she wondered what to do next. Should she go home? To Steve?

After a few moments, once her heart was beating normally again, she decided she would go on to the next house on her canvassing list. The Manor House - she hoped it wasn't as grand as it sounded; she didn't think she was ready to cope with any more difficulties. Spike had been enough for one day.

The end of Water Lane was edged with open farmland. Some of the fields she could see were starting to turn green, as the first crop made a bid for life. The lane on the farm side was bordered with a scrubby hedge, of hawthorn and wild roses inextricably entwined. In another week or so the hedge would be alive with hawthorn blossom and bumble bees dozy from their winter's rest.

'Are you on your own?' Peter said, from somewhere behind her, making her jump. She turned to find him looking extremely pleased with himself. 'All for Ann round here,' he said. 'It's no surprise though is it? It certainly looks like Tory country.'

Not sure what Peter was getting at, she nodded in agreement.

'Everything's going all right, I think,' Bella said, 'apart from

63

having to run away from a dog, and a man laughing at me. I somehow don't think he'll be voting for Ann'

'I saw that dog - absolutely terrifying,' Peter said, in agreement, 'I don't blame you for running. If it had been me I wouldn't have gone near the place. It looked a complete mess. You were brave to even try.'

'Brave?' Bella asked surprised, trying to judge whether he was serious.

'Of course, the whole place looked scary. You did well.' Peter answered, smiling encouragingly.

She was suddenly reminded of the old Bella; the Bella she had begun searching for, the one before she had been subsumed into Steve's dictatorial ways. *So she was still there.*

Growing up in the dim and dingy industrial Kent towns of Medway, Bella had imagined this exact rural life for herself, many years ago. Rabbits, enticed from their winter discomforts, scampering everywhere. Pheasants escaped from last season's shoot, either running kamikaze-like across the lane, or standing stock still waiting to be run over.

It reminded her of childhood visits to eccentric Auntie Millie. The memories so vivid had stayed with her into adulthood. Auntie Millie was her mother's youngest sister. She owned a smallholding on Romney Marsh, on the south coast of Kent. To Bella's eleven-year-old eyes, more used to grey and smoking buildings, the marshes were a fairy-tale of green, seemingly endless marshland, dotted with sheep and cows idly grazing.

The crow of a proud cockerel had woken her each morning, and the excitement of being given the job of collecting hens' eggs for breakfast was a feast of experiences beyond the imaginings of the urban Bella. She had never seen so many rabbits.

She remembered sitting on the crumbling stonewall at her aunt's house trying to count them.

'You'll never do it, girl,' her aunt had said, laughing kindly. And she couldn't - not even if she quartered the field, they were so fast and busy, hither and thither, and hither again.

She never forgot the exhilaration and freedom she had felt on those marshes.

Bella had dreamt since those visits that her life would be like her Auntie Millie's. She hoped she would grow up to be like her: wild hair, wrinkles from an outdoor-life, eyes glowing with energy. The hope was still there, even as a twenty five-year-old, preparing for marriage, that she and Steve would one day bring up their children on a small-holding: a few goats, sheep, chickens, exactly how she remembered it as a child.

She hadn't told Steve her dream before they got married, and when she did, a few months later, when they were relaxed, lying in bed, bodies entwined – he laughed. He laughed so hard, she remembered, he nearly fell off the bed.

'Oh Bella, a smallholding? Who is this Auntie Millie anyway? I've never heard you talk about her? Chickens? Geese? You? Me?' He had said with such ridicule in his voice, that she almost felt a breeze on her cheek – as if it were her dreams flying away. She watched him convulse with laughter, tears streaming down his face. 'Chickens, geese,' he kept on repeating. She lay silent, her face white, surprise at his nastiness robbing her of speech.

It had taken her a long time to forgive him, she should have recognised something in Steve that day. She had seen an ugliness that she couldn't quite forget, however hard she tried. But she let optimism live, he might change his mind, she could persuade him, love would do the rest. He was a scientist, she argued, maybe they didn't have the same dreams. Looking back, she wondered how she could ever have been so naive?

Bella's aching feet brought her back to the realities of Water Lane. It was worth a few blisters to have broken out of her narrow world, even for this short time. She would manage the discomfort. Steve had taught her all she needed to know about that - the pain of blisters was nothing compared to what she had experienced at his hand. She shuddered at the thought.

'Are you all right, Bella? You've gone pale? Was it the dog? Did he upset you? He can't get you now, you know,' Peter said to reassure her, at the same time pushing his glasses up the bridge of his nose; a habit she was beginning to recognise he used to hide his embarrassment. Bella was astonished at the kindness she could hear in his voice.

'My feet hurt a bit, that's all,' she said, 'the soles of my shoes are a bit thin. I'm fine apart from that.'

As they walked along the lane trying not to wince as her blisters rubbed, half listening to Peter chattering on about the candidate, she realised how timely the lifeline Ginny had thrown her had been. How close to drowning she had nearly come.

13

Straining to hear above the noise of the river, David turned full circle waiting for the call again – but no matter how intently he listened he heard nothing. As he neared the river his feeling of trepidation intensified. He knew, but at the same time didn't know how he knew, that something was wrong, and maybe even terribly wrong. The sound of rushing water drowned out everything else. He left the path and headed through rough grass to where he thought the river must be, stumbling as he went. His feet tripped on the uneven ground, littered with loose stones and protruding rocks; tussocks of long grass seemed to wrap themselves around his feet. He felt ungainly and foolish glad there was no one there to see him. He wasn't doing it well. He liked to do everything well.

He stood still for a moment checking if he could still hear the river. Was it possible he had imagined those hair-raising cries? Could it have been a fox howling? He knew they could sound human sometimes. He so wanted it to be an animal. He felt totally ill equipped to help anything in trouble. He hurried off again along a grassy slope, climbing down towards the river edge.

Instincts, he didn't realise he had, were urging him on. Climbing out of a dip in the ground, he finally found the river. It was now only a scramble down a steep stony bank beneath him. The river, shallow but fast, lay snaking its way between and around boulders shaped into honeycombs, by its timeless energy.

It wasn't so much the river that filled his eyes with wonder, but a sight that he couldn't immediately understand. His brain faltered, pausing with incomprehension. He couldn't immediately process what was in front of him. He wanted to shake his head, to rid himself of what he could see. He forced his lungs to catch an anxious breath. It was a sight he knew would haunt his sleeping hours for the rest of his life.

David realised the sound he had heard, just as his instincts had told him, were in fact cries for help. Standing on the top of the final scree that would take him to the water's edge a few metres below, he couldn't work out what it was he could see.

A girl with her back to him seemed to be standing waist deep in the water. *Why the hell was she doing that? It must be freezing in the cold winter water.* He didn't know why, but he didn't want to disturb her yet. He slithered down the bank; the water's hiss muffling his progress. He edged closer, cursing the rattle and spray of stones as his feet slipped and slid in the loose screed, until at last, he was standing at the edge of the water, breathless, grazes stinging his hands. Frightened, but with no reason he could immediately think of, David could now see she was a child. A pale honey-coloured ponytail was tied high on her head in a violet-blue bow – her pretty face, thin and neat, with a scattering of freckles across her nose. David felt his heart pause with shock. Her cries, muted by the river's energy, were being carried away on the breeze into nothingness. How on earth had he heard? No one could possibly hear that thin child's cry… and yet here he was. By some miracle he had heard her cries for help.

She turned at his call, and he saw her fear change to utter relief when she saw him. She was saved; he could read on her face. He ran stumbling over the stepping-stones until he was by her side. He saw that she was a slight girl - eleven-years-old perhaps. He only knew about boys; they probably matured differently. Her blonde hair was dark in places with river water. His heart contracted at the sight of her face; it was streaked with dirt where tears had run and had been swept away by her fingers. Her eyes, huge with fright locked onto his own, were full of silent pleading.

'What's happened?' he asked, feeling the inadequacy of the question. There were so many questions he needed to ask. 'Why are you alone? What are you doing here? Why can't you get out?' He desperately wanted to ask, but could see that his panic was upsetting her. Her relief was quickly being replaced by the fear he had first seen.

'It's all right. It's all right,' David soothed. 'I'm here to help.' (*if I can* - he didn't say). 'I'll get help. Don't worry. I'll find a way of getting you out.'

I shouldn't have said that. What happens if I can't?

It was only then, when at last he was beginning to think straight, that he noticed her mouth was edged with blue. He realised how dangerously cold she must be. His heart clenched at the sight of her distress.

He tried again, but this time he spoke slowly and calmly so as not to frighten her. 'How long have you been here? Why are you alone?'

'I'm stuck…' And with that she began to cry; silent tears glided down her cheeks landing in her hair at her shoulders - she didn't bother to brush them away. David could feel his heart beginning to break.

'My foot is stuck,' stuttering and stumbling her way through these few words - her face looked so stiff with cold. 'My dad's gone to get help.' With these words a fresh bout of weeping assailed her.

How frightened she must have felt alone here, waiting for her father to return. He couldn't bear the thought of it. 'How long have you been here?' He didn't want to know the answer. He could tell it must have been quite a while. What could he do? Feelings of inadequacy and panic rose - it took every vestige of his self-control to quash them and to keep his face bland and smiling.

'I don't know,' she replied, quietly crying.

He was no expert, but the girl didn't look well at all. Ginny always looked after the boys when they were ill, but even he could tell that standing in the water for any length of time would be dangerous.

'What's your name?' he asked gently, making his voice soft, so he didn't worry her. 'Mine's, David.' The bleak look in her eyes frightened him; he realised she was being taken beyond her strength. She looked exhausted.

'Grace,' she whispered.

At the loveliness and simplicity of her name, David felt tears sting his eyes. There was anything but grace in her plight, he thought. He realised he still didn't know why she couldn't just get out. *Just get out,* he wanted to shout - *just get out - walk away.*

David could feel his own fears escalating; ignorance creating wild scenarios – sharks, animal traps, metal spikes. What? What? What? He had to calm down. Stay cool. Think. Take a deep breath.

'Grace, I'm going to try and help you,' he paused, wondering what if anything he could do. Could he live up to his easy words? The last thing he wanted was to get her hopes up. 'You aren't alone now,' he continued, 'are you able to tell me about what happened?' David asked, dredging up, from he didn't know where, another David, a forgotten David, gentle, instinctive, caring, interested in another's essence, no thought of himself. Poor Ginny, he thought, suddenly understanding how she had known before him how much he had changed. A want so strong rose in his breast; he would do anything to help this young vulnerable girl. The revelation nearly blinded him.

'My foot…'Grace said quietly and then stopped - the effort all too much for her. Her words so difficult to understand, David had to hide his impatience.

'Yes go on,' David urged gently. 'Your foot… ?'

'… is caught,' she mumbled.

'Is caught?' He repeated stupidly.

Her words sent shivers through him in every direction – it was what he had feared – it was what he least wanted to hear.

'First of all I'm going to try and get you a bit warmer,' David said as cheerily as he could muster. 'Let me put my jacket around your shoulders.'

The awkward squatting position on the small stone next to her, was making his thigh muscles shout - stretched hamstrings making their presence felt. Although the stepping-stone next to her was flat, it was barely broad enough for both his feet, he felt unbalanced and awkward. With all the gentleness he could muster in his unnatural position, he tucked the jacket around her, careful not to touch her. Careful not to show her how cold he was already feeling without it. Close up, he could see a watermark where the river had crept up her jacket. Osmosis, a long forgotten chemistry lesson arose unbidden.

'Dad tried to get me out,' Grace said, almost to herself, 'but couldn't. His phone wouldn't work here, so he went to get help.'

Grace's teeth were chattering so much, David could barely make out what she was saying.

'I don't know where he is now,' she added, her throat catching with the words, tears plopping, large and glistening, onto his jacket.

He could see Grace was trying to be brave - biting her bottom lip to stop it trembling, beads of blood congealing on her lips. She wrapped her arms around herself to keep her body warm, but looking at the colour of her thin pinched face he saw that the cold was winning. He tried not to imagine how cold she must be. *What the hell should I do? What the hell can I do?*

'Can you remember how long ago was it since your father went for help?' David asked – more for something to say – the answer wouldn't make any difference. She shook her head. Time, he supposed, had stood still for her.

He knew it had to be a while ago, and wondered why he hadn't seen her father walking the paths, but supposed there were many routes he could have taken.

'Can I rub your hands, Grace?' he sounded parental, he thought, and it made him think of his own boys. 'It will warm you up.'

But, he couldn't remember when he had last felt this anxious about his sons. He had let Ginny do all the worrying. He earned the money didn't he? He felt reassured with that thought. But not as reassured as he would have liked. Was he a bad father?

He reckoned looking at Grace, she might have been in the water for anything up to an hour. But really David knew, it was only a wild guess. He looked to see if he had a signal on his phone. *Why didn't I think of that earlier?* There was no signal – her father had been right.

'Damn,' he said, under his breath. 'Damn.'

In a second, he went from wondering how long her father had been gone, to how long her father was going to be. He didn't like the look of Grace's colour, it was now more grey than pink, and he noticed she was shivering uncontrollably. *Hypothermia?* He would be shivering too, he thought, standing in that water. Anyone would. He rooted around in his trouser pocket hoping to find something – anything - that might be of help. There was nothing. Absolutely nothing.

He set his mind to try and remember what he knew about hypothermia. He'd attended a first aid course many years ago - if you get too cold for too long you died. That was about it. He couldn't remember the symptoms or how long was too long? He didn't know. *If only I had listened more.*

All the while, the river was eddying round the boulders and gurgling where the beds were shallow. Grace had been unfortunate, he thought, and that was an understatement, to have found the only deep pool in this section of the river. The pool was so deep and the water, impenetrably dark, it was making it impossible to see where or how she was trapped.

David recognised that no experience in his life so far, had prepared him for this predicament. He had thought himself resourceful, but his brain, however hard he tried, couldn't compute this problem. Couldn't dent it even.

David summed up in his head what was happening around

him, hoping it would jolt him into some sort of action. They were alone in the middle of nowhere; he had no way of contacting anybody; he knew nothing about young girls; or about hypothermia. Her father had already gone to try and find some help, so it didn't seem a good idea for him to do the same – he couldn't bear to leave her now anyway. He felt... bound to her in a very primitive sense. She needed him – the thought was startling. All that was left was to keep her company and try to release her foot. *Simple.*

At least he could talk to her, he suddenly decided; distract her until her father returned.

'I'm on holiday here for the weekend,' he told her, feeling silly talking almost to himself. Grace had her eyes closed, and he wondered if she was actually listening. 'I was supposed to be having a shooting lesson today but that was cancelled, and instead I went for a walk – and found you,' he added, trying to sound upbeat.

He thought he had seen a flicker of interest in her pale blue eyes.

'Did your dad try to move your foot?' he asked, wondering how that would be possible without getting into the water.

Please not that, he thought.

David stood up to stretch his legs; his knees were now aching from the awkward position.

Grace finally nodded. So her father had tried to get her out – but how? He wondered.

'Would you like me to rub your hands and try to get some warmth in them?' David asked, worrying about the correctness of touching a young girl. *Surely in an emergency it would be all right?* How complicated the world seemed to him at times, he thought. She nodded her permission. He took both her hands in his, and started to rub gently; they were cold, ice-cold and felt like lifeless dough. *At least I'm doing something at last.*

David looked around for inspiration. Ahead of them was the babbling water, benign, wandering through on it's way out to sea. It should have been heaven, but a fluke accident had turned it into a hell. He carried on chatting and found that Grace was eleven- years-old; she was on holiday with her mum and dad, staying in Tavistock. All this was said in a slow faltering voice, as though she was finding it difficult to breathe. *Where was her dad? Why had he taken so long?*

All the while David talked to her, keeping her calm, trying to distract her, his mind was racing trying to think of what to do. He could only come up with two options: either he had to try and dislodge her foot, or he had to find help. What finally decided him was that the waterline on her jacket had risen in the short time he had been with her, it was well above her waist now, and if he was feeling cold, then what must she be feeling? Alternately crouching beside her, and standing up to stretch - David's mind buzzed with permutations. *Useless permutations.* Her colour hadn't changed but can you get greyer than grey? David wondered.

'Grace, I am going to have a look to see how your foot is trapped.' David could see fear and hope fighting on her face. 'I know your dad has already tried, but I might see something different. OK?' What the hell could be different he didn't know – but he couldn't just sit and watch her slip away from him into a silence so frightening that he felt he couldn't bear it a moment longer. With no more ways of keeping her warm – he had given her his pullover and jacket, and held her in his arms so that she gained some warmth from him: it was now time to try something else. Action.

'You won't leave me will you?' Grace said suddenly, startling David. She was still able to talk - it was something at least.

'No,' David said, catching hold of her hand. 'I'll wait with you until your father gets back.'

Grace's look of relief made him hope he could keep his promise. Deciding to try the first option he had on his extremely short list of dislodge Grace's foot or go for help. And as he'd just promised not to leave her, it was now a list comprising one solitary item. DISLODGE GRACE'S FOOT. That's how he saw it in his mind - in capitals with flashing neon lights – it seemed absolutely impossible. Did Grace know that?

'I'm going to get in the water and see what's going on with your foot,' David said, and at the same time heard the ridiculousness of his words.

He went over to the far bank to where the thin and barely-warm sun was shining; his teeth chattered as he stripped off his trousers and t-shirt. It was a typical early spring day – chilly - what did he expect? He immediately shook with cold. He mustn't even think about it, or he wouldn't be able to take one step into that ice-cold water. Knowing he was not a particularly strong swimmer, and had no diving skills that he could remember, he began to worry if he was up to the challenge. He wasn't. He really definitely wasn't.

He gave Grace a confident smile to hide his flailing doubts. She didn't smile back, but he noticed that her eyes never left his face. Not once.

He felt the complicatedness of life grip him. *Why me? Don't I have enough problems to deal with at the moment?* He looked at her pinched ill face and thought himself a self-pitying bastard.

David stood at the water's edge irresolute, frightened. His skills to date were with numbers: things that added up whichever way you looked at them, it was always black or white. Ginny dealt with the in-between things, the greyness of life. That was the way he liked it. The life he had chosen - not a young girl with her foot or feet (he didn't know which yet), stuck, in the middle of nowhere, where there was no bloody phone signal, no one for miles, and cold beyond imagination. She was depending on him – he couldn't fail her, as he seemed to be failing everyone else at the moment. *Where was all this self-pity coming from?*

David edged his way into the water immediately realising he needed to put his shoes back on – the pebbles, benign-looking from a distance, were like sharp needles in the underside of his foot. So now, on a patchy blue-skied spring day out on a remote part of the moors, he didn't exactly know where, he stood in his boxer shorts, flapping loosely in the breeze, and his favourite hand-made Italian city brogues. *What must I look like?* It was almost comical. He was glad there was no one to see - having quickly decided that Grace didn't count. Her eyes were fixed on him like a laser beam - direct, unwavering.

Feeling ridiculous, his milky-white winter body exposed for the first time that year, it was only when the water encroached over the top of his shoe and touched his skin for the first time that he fully realised how desperate Grace's situation really was. The water was freezing. He wanted to turn and run as fast as he possibly could. *Coward – I'm a bloody coward.* He had to make the decision – run, or stay and help Grace. He looked at her; the beseeching expression in her red-rimmed eyes told him she had seen his moment of weakness. He blushed with shame.

'Please don't go – don't leave me,' her eyes begged, 'please try.'

David gritted his teeth trying to ignore the grip of ice-cold water steadily moving up his body as he waded further and further in. The water still looked jolly, bubbling merrily around them both. The birds still sang in the trees; they were happy it was spring, and they had escaped colder climes and were here for the summer. *Lucky, lucky them.* The new growth on the grass was rustling in the light, playful breeze. Every now and then an animal scurrying in the undergrowth was held in their vision. It was heaven. Except…

David tried not to think about the thread that Grace's life might be hanging on by. Life or death – did someone, God perhaps, choose which way the balance would swing? Luck, or bad luck? Bloody bad luck. Chance or choice? Today, now, life was serendipitous – here, in the middle of nowhere, in his city shoes and boxer shorts, in water more cold than any sensible person would want to be immersed in, he had to try and save another human being. Would he have chosen to be in this position? *Not bloody likely.* He liked his life to be predictable. He liked to make choices - to be in control. He liked, most of all, for it to add up. And again, as before, he saw the look in Grace's eyes willing him to have the courage to help her.

David waded in further; inch by inch the water rose up his legs, now above his knees, his thighs, and oh god – and then his hips, he could feel the blood leaving his lower extremities almost immediately. The water was above his chest now; he ran his hands over his face wetting it and his hair.

'I'm going to go under the water now,' he explained, teeth chattering uncontrollably. 'So if you feel something on your leg it will be my hand – don't be afraid. OK?'

He knew it would be a miracle if she could feel anything. Another miracle was needed for him to find her leg in this dark, murky water.

The water was now at his shoulders, and David had begun to have some idea of the excruciating pain that people experienced when they had a heart attack. A band of steel was getting tighter around his chest; he made an attempt to dive under the water, but immediately came up spluttering. He dived again, this time he filled his lungs with air, into the blackness of the water and began the search for Grace's foot. He lost all sense of bearing immediately. It was blackness everywhere, distorting his vision, disorienting him: fearful, frightening, and the cold allowed him no breath.

Something soft and gentle touched his legs; he shot out of the water in surprise. A fish? But he could see the weeds, now, waving gently in the currents. Beckoning, inviting. Sinister.

He went down again, this time expecting the blackness, and trying to remember without seeing which way was which. It couldn't be that difficult surely? He was out of his depth straight away, and he had to thrash his legs to stop himself descending into even grimmer darkness. He no longer knew which direction Grace was, so quickly had he become disoriented. *It was hopeless.*

He came up for air. Grace was transfixed, terror and hope competing; terror was winning. She didn't make any sound – none. David wanted her to roar and shout – he could deal with that better, he could soothe her fears, he could calm those – but for this silence of hers he had no strategies. He was so cold now, he could so easily have given up, but the look on Grace's face gave him the strength to go back down into that horrible murky world – cold as any hell.

Deep breath and dive; deep breath and dive; deep breath and dive... He was still standing on the stepping stones unable to will himself back into the water. He only just caught the sound - faint, weak - only just there.

'Please.'

He turned to look at her and nodded, he was a witness to her desperation. Eleven-years-old, and desperate. Life was so unfair.

'I'm going back in, Grace, OK?' she blinked, relief stark in her eyes.

David made another dive into the dense black water and instantly shot back up for air, the coldness of the water taking his breath away. He dived again and this time managed to hold his breath. He had never done anything like this before, and had trouble staying down long enough for his eyes to adjust to the darkness. But it was Grace's only chance; he had to try. It took a while and all his resolve but his eyes started to adjust. He could just about make out Grace's white legs in the gloom.

He came up for air again and immediately dived back in. The feeling that time was running out, drove him beyond his capabilities, beyond anything. But still he tried, determined not to fail her. And just when he felt he couldn't go on any longer, he found her feet and the boulders. *What had been so difficult?*

He floated back up to the surface to catch his breath. It seemed he had been in the water hours, but it was only a few minutes. The longest minutes he had ever lived. He now felt physically sick with cold, and he knew Grace must be feeling even worse. *Oh God.* She must by now be reaching the end of her endurance. He couldn't waste time reassuring her. He took a deep breath and dived again.

Air taken for granted, now became something he had to think about in all its complexity. Every breath was noticed, its shallowness railed against. He felt his chest trying to burst. He located her foot again, quickly this time, and searching with his hands he found the rocks that held her foot in their deathly grip. Was this some Greek tragedy being played out; was it Potameides, the mischief-making river nymphs, at play? Surely this could be no one's idea of pleasure? He rose out of the water again.

'Grace, I can see your foot it's slipped through a narrow gap between two boulders,' he explained, 'and your foot is now jammed there. I'm going to try and pull it out.' He didn't recognise his own voice. His jaw was stiff with cold, and his breath was coming in short rasping bursts.

She managed a nod of understanding, but he had his doubts if she really understood. Another deep breath, and he was gone, diving into the dark alien world of reeds and vegetation that only seemed to want to pull him down further into the river's depths. This time he found her foot in seconds and began trying to pull it out, gently at first, but when that didn't work he tried twisting and pulling – hard. He could see that her delicate skin was bleeding, grazed on the rough boulders. Curls of panic were forming in his stomach as he pushed and pulled at her foot in desperation; the water swirled round them leaving trails of her blood. He had failed.

He rose to the surface a defeated man. He couldn't look Grace in the eye – he had failed – and she would know what that meant. Or would she? What concept of death did an eleven-year-old have? Life was the only concept a young girl would have – the life in front of her, a life for living.

He had failed; from the despairing look in her eyes, Grace knew he had failed. She had grown wise in the space of an hour – the wisdom of experience. Too wise, too young. *Oh Grace* – his soul cried out for her. He noticed the birds were still singing in joyous chorus.

'Shut up,' he wanted to scream at them, 'can't you see what's going on? A girl may die here, and all you can do is sing.' He knew he couldn't vent his frustration in front of her, so instead he smiled encouragingly at her and squeezed her hand. She scarcely noticed. *Don't die Grace please.*

What could he do now? His brain was computing furiously. *What? How?* The river continued to eddy and burble over the stones, and all the while hidden from sight, a horror continued under the water. Her skin once pink with the bloom of youth, was now grey and clammy, her lips blue, and her eyes becoming more vacant with time.

Where was her father with help? David railed, his hands balled into fists of anguish he could never before have imagined.

A deep frustration shot through him; nothing seemed to be on their side. It seemed so ridiculously stupid that he couldn't move her small slender foot, and because of it Grace might die. Was he being melodramatic? *How am I going to live with myself now?*

He was so thoroughly chilled that David had difficulty getting out of the water: his legs felt like lifeless rubbery logs, and his hands having lost all sensation, felt as though they belonged to someone else. He finally managed to lift his legs out of the water back onto the bank.

David dressed under the scrutiny of Grace's red-rimmed eyes. He had never, in all his near forty years, experienced such desolation in a child's eyes before. Dressing proved impossibly slow, so numb were his fingers. He had to tell Grace, who by now was beyond terror, that all they could do was hope for help.

'Your Dad will be back soon,' he said, shame at his failure held his words back, 'and will bring help.' He wasn't sure what help was needed; who or what could move those two huge boulders?

He tried soothing her with a gentle voice and repeated that help was on its way, like a mantra. David didn't know if she took any comfort from him. He managed, by kneeling on the stepping-stones, to wrap his arms around her and the shuddering subsided slightly. His own legs and body stiff with cold felt clumsy and useless.

'Grace, stay awake,' David suddenly realised with panic that her eyes were shut, 'you must stay awake.' He wasn't sure why she should stay awake; maybe he had read it somewhere. Maybe his brain had found the imprint of the first-aid lesson at long last.

He could feel Grace slipping away from him. He started to pray, something he hadn't done in years. He prayed as though it were for his own child. This young girl had touched his heart - her predicament, her stoicism. *Would I be so brave in her position?*

'Where the hell are you?' He wanted to shout at the empty

space around them, beauty at every corner of the diorama. Perfect in every way - except this one small mote - a young girl, with honey-blonde hair, and huge terrified eyes.

The birds, continuing to sing oblivious of the tragedy unfolding, rose as one, disturbed by some predator. A flash of blue - a kingfisher arrowing it's way along the river. Just then he thought he heard something. *Please God, please God, please God, please God.* He hoped his silent invocation was heard. *Please God, please God, please God, pleeeease.* He carried on and on and on. There was no other noise even though he strained his hearing for that sound again – it never came. Such thin hopes dashed, brought on a feeling of despair so terrible that David felt a huge explosion of impotent anger.

In this moment, where the balance of life and death was hanging over Grace, he realised the importance of leading the best life you could – you never knew when it was going to be taken from you. He made a vow that whatever the outcome of this day's happenings, he would go back and try to put his life in order. It might be that Ginny and he needed to part; maybe they had come to the end of the road, but he must work that out for himself and act on whatever he found. Maybe she would like to part – he needed to ask the question – that much he must do as soon as possible. A resolution brought about in the presence of one of life's most spectacularly cruel events. Why Grace? Why this lovely brave girl? Nobody deserved this.

As Grace's breathing eased into a quieter slower rhythm so did the clamouring in his mind. He could feel tears sliding down his face; tears for both Grace and himself mingled together, inseparable.

14

A short while later, it was the birds' quietness that drew David's attention to a sound that didn't belong there. David unwound his arms from around Grace, trying not to cause her discomfort. She was quiet now and had been for a while - barely breathing, but still alive. Still alive – where had that thought come from? He was horrified even thinking she may not make it. *She had to make it.* He couldn't be thinking she might die? Could she die? David thought.

He couldn't wait for her father anymore: he couldn't be sure that her father had reached anybody that could help. Just as he realised the sound was a helicopter, and just as his hopes soared they were as quickly dashed, as he watched the helicopter fly past oblivious to their presence. That's it, David thought, I can't just stay here anymore – I have to do something. His mind screeched that he couldn't leave Grace. He wouldn't be able to bear the pitiful look in her eyes.

'Grace, Grace can you hear me?' David asked. She had gone downhill rapidly since he had been unable to release her foot.

'Grace, I have to go and find help,' he explained, 'we can't just wait here. We can't. I have to try and do something. I don't know what's happened to your father, but I must go and try. I know I said I'd stay but that isn't your best chance now. I have to go.' He sensed she had given up hope. She nodded eventually, imperceptibly.

He didn't tell her that he thought they might be running out of time. She nodded in understanding. He had to drag himself away from her. He had never in his life done anything as hard as leaving Grace, not even leaving his own children at the forbidding timber doors of their boarding school. He had done that; one, two and three times as each of his sons had each reached eleven. *Well my parents did that to me – right?* The expression of loss and grief on Ginny's face, each time they drove away up the tree-lined drive, haunted him still.

'Your father may come back with help before I do,' David said, trying to soften the blow. He didn't believe it – not for a single moment. 'It's a long way to the road, and he doesn't know the area, so he may not have got there yet. I have a mobile phone, and I'm going to try and get to higher ground, to see if I can get a signal. I promise, on my mother's life, I'll be back and soon.' *Why didn't I think of that before?*

Grace didn't need to know his mother had been dead for five years.

There was so little feeling in David's legs that at first he stumbled his way up the path. Heading uphill through the reedy grass and bracken, he couldn't feel them scratching at his legs. Every now and then he checked his mobile phone; he prayed that the next time he looked there would be those little blocks of colour – no, not yet, not even one. No signal. He rushed on, looking for higher ground; there must be some somewhere. The flatness seemed to be going on forever. He ran on, he had to get out of this valley, desperation clawing at his stomach. He had promised Grace five minutes and it was nearly that now.

He looked again, no blocks of colour on the mobile's screen, but instead, what he saw sent waves of panic coursing through his body. His battery was running low and nearly out. He cursed himself for not charging it the night before as he'd intended; he'd been too tired he remembered and had gone straight to bed – that chilly world that he and Ginny inhabited.

He stopped for a moment to catch his breath; his legs and arms were beginning to hurt as feeling came back now his blood was coursing through his body. He looked around him; surely there must be higher ground? All he could see was the scruffy wind blasted copse he had scurried through earlier. The trees… of course, the bloody trees, he screamed, *you stupid bloody idiot*. He looked around for an easy one to climb. He spotted a pine tree, bent by the wind, but still taller than anything else around, and ran towards it.

David wished he had gloves - *the ones in his rucksack*. The bark was sharp and crumbling, tearing at his hands. He began to climb, tentatively at first, his body trying to remember how to do it - he hadn't climbed a tree since he was a boy. He remembered shinning up the old apple trees in his parents' garden. They had an orchard that he and his friends had long summers of fun, climbing and falling. Playing games with complicated, ever changing rules that even they sometimes couldn't remember.

He also recalled summers of bellyache as the unripe apples took their effect - motherly forebodings coming true. David realised he was making a bad job of scaling the tree: it had too few branches for his liking. He had climbed only a few metres and was scratched and scraped already - his thin t-shirt no match for the knobbly protrusions of the tree trunk. At last he was beginning to gain height, rapidly now that there were more branches higher up – six metres now – would that be enough? He checked his phone. No. He carried on more slowly, as the density of the tree started to work against him. He was about halfway and checked his phone again, there it was, that wonderful blue square. *Thank god, thank, thank god, thank god,* he chanted at full volume in his treetop eyrie. He had no time to appreciate the view.

He phoned Charles, continuing his chant – would Charles have a signal in this satellite-arid world of Devon. *Please Charles, have a signal... please.*

'Charles here.' The calm tones of Charles had never been more welcome to David's ears.

'It's David,' he shouted, 'I have no battery, and very little signal so I have to be quick. There has been a terrible accident; can you find where I am from this signal? You must help...'

David gulped back his tears. 'There's a girl in the river. I must get back to her. I promised her I would only be five minutes. We have to save her.' His voice broke as he got to the end of his pleas.

'Slow down,' he could hear Charles telling him in a calm voice. 'David, start again but slowly, can you tell me what has happened and where you are?' That calm voice again. David's voice sounded like a screech in contrast. David tried to steady his voice and started to explain again.

'I have only a small amount of battery left,' David said, trying to keep the panic out of his voice. 'I walked out from Tavy House out towards Brent Tor I'm following a river and I'm by a small copse., There's no particular landmark, except for stepping stones across the river. Her foot's stuck under a boulder – she's freezing cold standing in the water. Please come.'

He was doing better now with the explanation. Charles's

calm murmuring in the background helped. 'Her father was with her,' David continued, 'but he left her to look for help. I reckon from what Grace has said she's been there for well over an hour – I have been with her for nearly hour – I can't free her foot, I've tried to, but it's so firmly wedged that I can't budge it. You have to get here quickly, she isn't well, it's so cold in the river,' and on a sob, 'I've tried everything, I can think of.' David's voice started breaking again.

'OK David, you're doing really well,' Charles said still calm, reminding David that he needed to stay calm too. 'I need to try and locate you. I should be able to do that from what you've described. I'll get the rescue team alerted. You need to get back to Grace. Try to keep her as warm as you can and don't let her sleep – talk to her, sing to her – anything to keep her awake. Can you do that?'

'I'll go back to her now,' David said, 'are you sure you know where I am? I promised her I wouldn't be long - she is so terrified. I think she's near the end of her strength, she's so cold, the water is freezing and she's up to her waist in it.'

'OK you go back to her,' Charles said, 'how did you get a signal?'

'I'm up a tree,' David answered. 'If it wasn't such a bloody tragedy it would be funny.'

There was nothing left to laugh about when his call to Charles was cut off - his phone was dead. He hoped he'd done enough to get the rescue team to them. Thank god he had Charles's number - and then he remembered Charles belonged to the Dartmoor rescue team. At last something was going their way. *Halleluiah,* he shouted, *Halleluiah*, and again and again as he climbed back down the tree, slipping and sliding - his hands red raw, stripped of skin – he didn't care. *Halleluiah*, he sang, as he raced back to Grace.

Halleluiah.

15

Ginny and Veronica were reluctantly packing away the remains of their lunch; the sky, although still blue, was now beginning to look washed out.

'I could have sat there all day,' Ginny said, as she put Oz's saddle back on.

Veronica smiled in agreement and declared, much to Ginny's relief, that the weather should just about hold out until they got back home. They started to make their way back slowly down the tor, skirting around granite boulders littering the ground. The horses knew what to do, relieving her of all responsibilities except to soak up the aching loveliness all around her. She didn't want to go back to reality. She wanted to remember every detail of patchwork quilt fields, bright green against their dark boundary hedges; grey ancient monolithic stones, impossibly difficult to construct edifices to God, purple-hued heather, and even the tough brown reedy grass seemed to have a rightful place in this landscape. She would try and store it all away for the dark days ahead. She didn't know when she would be back – with or without David?

'I'm not sure about your walk later on,' Veronica said, pointing skywards. 'See those black clouds over there? They're definitely coming our way.'

'I'm not sure I'll be able to walk after this, anyway,' Ginny said ruefully, rubbing her knees. 'It'll be a good excuse if it starts to rain.' *Where will my plans be then?*

A helicopter passed overhead drowning out their words.

'That's low,' Veronica said.

The horses startled, suddenly planted their feet squarely on the ground refusing to budge until they located the source of the noise. Ginny grabbed at her reins, nearly losing her balance.

'I wonder where it's going? You don't often see rescue helicopters out at this time of the year,' Veronica said, regaining her balance and reins, after the sudden halt.

'I hope nothing serious has happened,' Ginny said, and immediately thought of David, despite his harsh words that morning. Her first thoughts were still for his safety. Nothing had really changed, she thought.

'It looks as though it's heading for the river,' Veronica said, over her shoulder, 'it's less than a mile from here as the crow flies.'

'Do you have many emergencies on the moors?' Ginny asked, assuming that bad weather was the usual reason for accidents.

'Not that many,' Veronica answered, 'thank goodness, and when there is Charles is usually called out. He's a member of the Dartmoor Rescue Team.'

'Really?' Ginny said, impressed. 'I didn't know. He must be really brave to do that.'

'Charles knows the moors like the back of his hands,' Veronica explained. 'They need people like him. He's been in the team for about five years now; they need all sorts of different expertise. Charles used to be in the Marines before he inherited the farm, so he's had a lot of experience – they're lucky to have him.'

Ginny couldn't see David rescuing anybody, except perhaps from bankruptcy.

They sat for a moment watching the helicopter, both shielding their eyes as it flew sunwards, allowing their horses to settle.

'It's nowhere near us,' Veronica said, 'wrong direction. Someone may have got into trouble in the bog maybe, they sometimes do.'

'Look it's coming back this way,' Veronica said, 'they can't find them. Come on lets get going again, I'm beginning to have a bad feeling, not sure why – just a practice run maybe. Let's head for home. We've had a good ride: got to the top of the tor, had our picnic, so time to go home.

'I'm fine with that,' Ginny said, she had a bad feeling too, but couldn't be sure why. David? David surely couldn't have got himself into difficulty – or could he?

Both women eager to get home pushed on their horses. The day was cooling down already, and Ginny shivered despite her down jacket. The world silent around them, now the helicopter had flown away, except for the rustle of the cows in the bracken and the horses' footsteps – rhythmic, hypnotic.

Veronica interrupted her thoughts, 'Charles is called out about once a month, usually in winter though. The weather fools people; mists and rain can come in very quickly on the moors, disorienting people. Even for someone that knows them well, it's still easy to get lost.'

She knew David wouldn't go out unprepared, she remembered seeing his rucksack in the boot of the car that morning. Which now somehow seemed a lifetime ago. She was worrying about him for nothing – he would have been well prepared. He would know what to do.

Ginny relaxed, her mind more at ease, and her horse immediately relaxed too – he must have picked up on her anxiety, she thought.

'Do you ever take all this for granted?' she asked, having to speak loudly as Veronica was in front again, the track too narrow for them both. The path followed a drainage ditch, about a metre wide running down the hill to the lowlands as far as she could see. The banks on both sides were flat. Perfect riding, Ginny thought.

'Sometimes, I suppose I do,' Veronica answered. 'But it's usually because I am too busy, rather than grown contemptuous.'

Ginny sighed in envy; she dreamed of living in a little cottage on the edge of the moors, her horse in a paddock next to the house. Her fanciful thoughts were interrupted by the merry chirping of Veronica's mobile phone. The sound filled the silent moors.

'Hi Charles, what's going on?' Veronica asked.

Ginny watched Veronica's face paling, and the sight of it made Ginny catch her breath. *David?* Ginny's senses were on full alert, she just knew it was something to do with him. She could only guess what Charles was saying. All she could hear Veronica saying was 'yes…no…oh? No… how?' Ginny's imagination was filling in the gaps. Dead? Injured? Unconscious? *Oh David, please no.*

'We'll be there as soon as we can,' Veronica confirmed.

Where would they be? Ginny wondered. She didn't have to wait long before Veronica explained.

'It's David, Ginny, he's become caught up in an emergency,' Veronica said, her face stricken with worry.

'What emergency – where? What's happened? Is he hurt?

94

What accident?' Ginny gabbled, her thoughts ricocheting out of sequence into a maelstrom of fear. Her immediate instinct was to get off her horse, and run across the moors to help him. A blinding image blurred her vision for a second – David's rucksack was in the boot of the car with all his safety equipment. She had the car keys. He had gone out walking without anything. She gulped in terror. It was her fault he was in danger. She wanted to melt and disappear into the ground. She could feel her body falling apart. She couldn't breathe; her heart was beating so rapidly she felt it would explode.

'Ginny, Ginny, Ginny... David's fine,' Veronica said. 'It's a young girl trapped in the river. David's been trying to help her.' Then she heard Veronica's voice insistent, getting louder. Until finally she heard what she was trying to tell her.

Ginny gulped with relief at these words. Never had she heard such sweet words. And yet, her brain nudged her – a young girl?

'David isn't hurt,' Veronica repeated, 'he isn't hurt it's a young girl that's hurt. Are you all right, Ginny? You look terrible, are you going to faint? Whatever is it?'

'I've got the keys,' Ginny tried to explain and saw incomprehension on Veronica's face. 'To the car, in my pocket - David's rucksack was in the boot. He's got nothing with him. I thought for one awful second I'd caused his accident.'

'Ginny that's ridiculous,' Veronica said, her face tense. 'You haven't caused anything. And anyway there is plenty of spare stuff in the house. He only had to ask.'

'The rescue team haven't found David and the girl yet,' Veronica explained. 'David managed to call Charles on his mobile, but unfortunately it ran out of battery before they could locate him precisely.'

'He never keeps his phone charged,' Ginny said, shaking her head in exasperation. 'I tell him about it all the time.'

'The girl has been in the water for too long,' Veronica explained, quickly. 'The water's very cold at this time of year, it hasn't warmed up yet after winter, especially in the deep pools.'

Ginny could see worry etched on Veronica's face. She couldn't get a feel for what was going on - her thoughts still jumbled, her earlier fears for David, preventing her from thinking clearly. *Who was the girl?*

16

'Only six more weeks to go now,' Peter said cheerily, walking with Bella down Water Lane.

'I don't think I'll have any shoe leather left by then,' Bella replied. Peter smiled at her weak joke. She couldn't quite believe it.

'It's so quiet for a Saturday afternoon, where is everyone?' Peter asked, looking around him. 'Not even a car in sight.'

'Spike was certainly at home,' Bella reminded him, feeling surprisingly at ease in his company. He was just like a boy scout, Bella thought, who hadn't quite grown up. He was wearing khaki everything with lots of pockets: keys and his mobile hung from his belt. He must be about forty, she thought, and she remembered Ginny had told her he was unmarried. She detected loneliness under his boyish enthusiasm, and suddenly felt sad for him.

'We just need to finish these last few houses. One last push and you can go back to your family,' Peter said, encouragingly. *If only he knew.*

'I want to thank you,' Peter continued. 'I know you didn't want to come without Ginny.'

Bella turned startled eyes on him - embarrassed at being so transparent.

'You've done really well,' he said. 'Will you come again?'

She nodded, unable to believe at first that she hadn't been

found wanting. It was a start, she thought – it might be a beginning of something different.

'If I can,' Bella said, without explanation. 'I wonder how Ginny's getting on in Devon?' she asked him, changing the subject - she didn't want Peter asking awkward questions about Steve. 'I envy her those moors, and the sense of tranquillity you can find there. Have you been?' she asked shyly.

'Yes, marvellous walking country - it does rain though, doesn't it? Last one now. You do the Manor House on the left - it will be a treat for you,' Peter said, sounding mysterious. They stood outside a substantial black and white house next to a set of tall and exquisitely designed, wrought iron entrance gates.

'And that's only the gatehouse,' Peter said, pointing up the drive.

'I can't go up there,' Bella said panicking. 'It's going to be huge.'

'Yes, you can,' Peter said, simply, surprising her.

She agreed reluctantly.

It must be a very grand house, Bella thought, in awe. All she could see through the trees were chimneys, ramrod-tall - stark on the skyline.

Lime trees, tall and straight, flanked the drive. Ancient oaks and sycamores, scattered over the fields, made her think of kings and queens galloping on horseback hunting deer. The white paddock fencing, bordering the fields as she neared the house, made her search instinctively for horses. She didn't have to look far, before two horses grazing contentedly lifted their heads curiously and went back to their grazing.

The main house, at last, came into view. She paused to take in all its splendour. So this, she thought, was the Manor House she'd heard all about. Ruddy-red brickwork, bedecked with Virginia creeper greeted her. Crenelated square towers rose steeply from each corner. Knowing nothing about architecture, Bella could see, even so, how right it looked - its symmetry and proportions seemed so completely... perfect, she thought.

Standing awe-struck in front of the house, reminded her of the poem by William Davies she'd just been reading:

'*What is this life if without care there is no time to stand and stare?*'

What indeed? The poet, she thought, must have been looking at an idyll just like this. And, as if that wasn't enough, she marvelled, there was the house again, mirrored in the still waters of the lake. A lake, the size of which, Mr Darcy would not have felt ashamed rising from. Acres of daffodils just starting to bloom softened the double curved grey stone steps and led her eye towards the gardens as they rolled gently towards the fields beyond. *Perfect,* she thought, *absolutely perfection.*

'Hello, can I help you?' a man's voice, with a soft Irish brogue asked, from somewhere behind her. Bella jumped in fright.

'I'm sorry,' she stammered. 'I was... admiring the view. Are you Mr Knight?' she asked. Doubting he was, judging by his clothes, check shirt and jeans, finished off by muddy green wellingtons. Casual.

'No, wouldn't mind though,' he said with a twinkle in his eye. 'I'm the gardener - the head gardener.'

'Maybe I shouldn't be here? I'm sorry...' Bella trailed off as she watched with surprise, the most beautiful smile appear. She didn't think she had ever seen anyone's face light up so much, just by smiling. Not even Mr Darcy, who she had only just been imagining over there by the lake, had smiled so beautifully.

'That depends why you're here,' the man said expectantly, resting both hands on his spade.

'I'm campaigning for the general election in six weeks,' she answered, hoping the man would smile again. 'Well in that case,' he smiled again. 'You're in luck; they're both here today.'

'I'll go up to the house then. Thanks for your help,' Bella said, and found herself surprisingly reluctant to leave him.

Arriving after a few minutes at the grand arched oak door, she pulled the bell rope, and heard a loud clanging as the bell reverberated inside the house.

'Can I help you?' a blonde man, looking even less like the owner, in flip-flops opened the door, impatience plain to see on his face.

Overawed, and feeling the fool Steve always told her she was, she summoned up the courage to tell this busy man why she was there.

'I was hoping we could count on your vote for Anne Parham' she finally stuttered.

'Yes, you can,' Mr Knight said economically, preparing to close the door. 'I'm sorry but I'm in the middle of...'

'Who is it, darling?' a woman's voice called, interrupting him.

'Nobody, darling,' he shouted back, 'nobody.' That's about right, Bella thought – *nobody*. He did at least have the grace to blush when he realised how rude he had sounded.

'You will remember to vote, won't you?' Bella said mustering up some resolve. 'I would... we would be so grateful.'

She turned and started to walk back down the drive, and

discovered the head gardener was still where she had left him, planting saplings.

'Don't mind him,' the gardener said, guessing from her face it hadn't gone that well. 'He's busy that's all. Is he going to vote for the right one though?'

'I think so, he said he would anyway,' Bella said, shyly. 'Of course people tell you they're going to vote for your party, just to get rid of you.'

It seemed so easy somehow to talk to this man, she wasn't sure why, 'you only really find out on the day.'

The man nodded to show his understanding of the difficulties.

'What about yourself? Are you going to vote, do you live locally?' Bella knew she was babbling with nerves, and stopped talking, not wanting to bore him to death, like Steve told her she always did.

'Yes, I live in the gatehouse - you passed it at the bottom of the drive 'I'm probably not registered to vote; I've only lived here a few months. Is it too late?'

Lucky, lucky man to live somewhere so... gorgeous. She caught herself wondering if he was married. *Bella!*

'If you let me know your name,' Bella said, 'I might be able to do something about that - if you want me too, that is?'

Bella felt confusion steal into her face at her boldness. She worried it might have sounded like a chat up line?

'It's Will Green,' he explained with a smile, 'and before you say anything, I know it's a daft name for a gardener.'

'I wasn't,' Bella said flustered, unsure if he were joking with her, or not. 'I have to go now. The others will be waiting for me. 'But I'll look into it if you want me to,' she added shyly.

'Will you come back and let me know if I can vote?' he

asked, making Bella feel breathless with possibilities. *Don't be ridiculous, Bella.*

'You haven't told me your name?' he said, with a look that made her knees shake.

'My name?' She asked surprised, her mouth suddenly dry. He nodded. 'It's Bella.'

'Pretty,' he said, with another warm smile, making his eyes look bright in his tanned face.

She thought she could feel his eyes boring into her back as she walked away. *Don't be ridiculous, he wouldn't be interested in me, no one would.* At least that's what Steve told her so often that she now believed him. The mirror told the same story.

When she finally reached the gatehouse, the rest of the group were waiting for her; joining them, she heard the excitement of the day's campaigning, in their chatter.

'What have you been doing all this time?' Peter asked, 'we were worried.'

'I was talking to the gardener. He wasn't sure if he could vote,' she answered, their anxiety making her flustered. 'I said I'd find out for him.'

17

David found Grace exactly as he'd left her: mortuary-grey with cold. And still trapped. She didn't acknowledge his return. He knelt down beside her and took off his last layer, the t-shirt and wrapped it like a scarf around her neck. He tried to share the heat he'd generated from his running and tree climbing. His muscles squealed in protest at the awkward position. The watermark he noticed with horror, had reached her armpits – he couldn't bear to look.

But Grace was still there, he reminded himself, still breathing – just. *Thank God, thank God, thank God...* David didn't care which god had kept her alive while he was away, he was just grateful and promised himself that he would lay fruit, or whatever was appropriate, at the altar of the deity responsible.

Tears rolled unimpeded down David's face at the possibility of losing her. She might be dying, he thought with horror, and it was his own entire fault. *I failed her.* He could see Grace had deteriorated even in the short time he'd left her to get help. She'd stopped shivering – that had to be bad hadn't it? Once more he cursed himself for knowing nothing useful about hypothermia. *What else can I do anyway?* Charles had said she would definitely be suffering from hyperthermia, and to try and keep her warm.

He touched her cheek with the back of his hand; it felt clammy to his touch, and her skin mottled and icily cold. The bloom on her face completely gone; her eyes were closed and her mouth a thin line of grey. She was facing death, he thought. He hadn't seen death stalking so closely before, and he felt his stomach grip with terror.

The water still eddied around them, gurgling merrily on its way. How devastatingly cruel, he thought, that such beauty could be ripping the life out of this young girl.

'Grace, can you hear me?' David asked, 'I came back didn't I? Like I promised?' He could tell Grace was barely conscious; her head was resting on his shoulder, and her hands were in his for warmth. David felt the pulse in her wrist – so slow. Too damned slow. Come on, David, don't just let her die here in front of you. Come on dammit – do something.

'I got my mobile to work,' David said, remembering that Charles had told him to talk and sing, anything but let her slip into unconsciousness. 'Help is coming. We're a bit hidden here, but they'll be able to find us – don't you worry.'

David wished he felt as confident as he sounded. He told her he'd had to climb a tree to get a signal; he thought he saw a flicker of her eyelids at the mention of him climbing trees, but maybe he imagined it. He wanted so desperately to have seen that flicker. In that moment, he wanted her to live more than anything else he could think of. Grace had pushed every other single thought out of his head.

'My friend, Charles, is in the Dartmoor Rescue Team, and he's on his way. If anybody can find us he can. It's a bit of an awkward spot – middle of nowhere and hidden by trees. Did I tell you he was in the Marines? They specialise in finding people - so they'll find us as soon as they can.'

He didn't tell her that once she was found it would be very

difficult to get help to this isolated, and boggy spot. He found it hard to believe that he had only known Grace for less than a morning; it felt like a lifetime of responsibility for her.

Again he remembered Charles' words about talking to her and not letting her slide into unconsciousness. He tried desperately to think of a story to tell and could think of none. His mind had gone blank. He could tell her about work – it might not interest her but at least she would have something to listen to.

'Do you know what an accountant is, Grace?' David asked, not waiting for an answer. 'No? Well that's what I am. An accountant keeps an eye on the money side of a business – lots of adding up. Some people say it's boring and that accountants are all dull people. Grey. Well I don't think so. Do you think I'm dull? No don't answer that – you don't know me well enough, and I am sure you are too polite anyway. Do you like numbers Grace?'

Was that a nod he saw?

'I love numbers,' David carried on, 'Do you know that nature is full of examples which follow number patterns? Take a sunflower for example; did you know that the seed head grows in the same sequence as a Fibonacci number? What is a Fibonacci number you might well ask? Well, it's a really simple idea - the first two numbers in the sequence, or list, are zero and one and then the next number is just the sum of the previous two numbers, and so on. So that would be zero; one; one; two; three, five; eight; thirteen… and so it goes on and on. I wish I had a pen and paper to show you. How simple is that?' They sat quietly together for a moment, Grace, doll-like, lifeless - David his arms around her – tight.

'Somebody thought about it in the thirteenth century, you

know,' David said, almost as though to himself. 'That's a very long time ago, isn't it?'

No response, to his words. He continued after a while. He could see she was slipping away deeper into her own world.

'There were incredibly clever people around then too,' David carried on, relentlessly. It felt peculiar to hear his voice in the silence of the moors. You see being an accountant isn't just about adding up dull lists, it's about bringing numbers to life and enjoying their patterns. Can you think of any shells that you've seen? Do you remember if they had any patterns on them? Well it's likely they were Fibonacci spirals. When you get home, perhaps you can look it up on the internet, and draw a spiral yourself, it's really easy.'

When she get's home. The idea was beginning to seem almost impossible now, David thought.

'First of all you draw two equally-sized squares,' David carried on, anyway, 'and then you draw on top of them a square with its sides twice as big as the first square, and then alongside that you draw another square with its side the sum of those two squares and so on, so each square is the sum of the sides of the squares it's touching. Now I know that sounds complicated, and I can tell you it's very difficult to explain. Much easier to draw. Let me see if I can draw it on this stone with water, as long as it doesn't dry too quickly. Are you going to watch me?'

All the while David chattered on, drawing the Fibonacci squares, he could see Grace was still with him by the merest flutter of her eyelid. He didn't care as long as she was still thinking and listening. He dipped his finger in the water and started drawing another set of squares to illustrate his rather cumbersome explanation.

'So, you see, Grace,' he explained, 'each square is the sum of the two adjacent squares - well sort of. Now here comes the clever bit. In each square you draw an arc of a circle. Can you see how slowly an ever-increasing spiral is forming? Fibonacci's spiral. Clever isn't it?'

Grace eyes were still closed. He realised he was really enjoying teaching her, albeit an unwilling student and in the most dire of circumstances. He would have to remember that for another day.

'Grace, are you listening?'

She wasn't talking now, and her eyes were closing; he kept talking about anything that came into his head not caring if it made any sense. He knew that he mustn't let her sleep, however improbable sleeping might seem partially immersed in freezing cold water. He suddenly remembered Charles suggesting he sing to her – why would he suggest that? He didn't know any songs, never listened to pop music, except at full volume emanating from his sons' bedrooms, and he didn't think Wagner's Das Rheingold would fit the bill.

He suddenly had a picture of Ginny singing lullabies to the boys when they were babies; he remembered thinking how beautiful she looked, her face, suffused with love, open and sunny. She was happy then; he hadn't seen her look so happy for a long time. Then he thought of his own mother singing to him, it had been the most comforting thing in the world – Charles was right, he should sing to Grace.

'Grace, don't go to sleep please – I'm going to sing to you. Please don't laugh, it's a long time since I've done this, and I'm not sure if I can remember all, or indeed any of the words.'

David tried not to think of the needle sharp pain in his knees from the coldness and the hardness of the stone. Could he do this? He wondered. *Sing?* He felt foolish at the idea. Save Grace – save Grace – save Grace, a voice in his head kept insisting. Sing.

'OK, OK,' he said to the heavens, 'on your own head be it.' He cleared his throat. As if that would make any difference:

'Oh Danny boy, the pipes, the pipes are calling,'

David sang, his voice tentative at first, through lack of use and embarrassment, but deciding to plough on anyway:

'From glen to glen, and down the mountain side.'

As David sang, tears began to course down his face, a sadness overwhelming him for the death of his mother, for Grace slowly slipping away, and for himself and Ginny. So much loss, he thought.

Grace's grip was loosening with every minute. Where the hell was Charles? David wondered. *Where the hell are you?* He looked up to the heavens as though to find an answer. There was none. Only silence.

The summer's gone and all the flowers are dying.
Tis you, 'tis you must go, and I must bide.'

18

Ginny couldn't believe what Veronica had just told her. The horses were walking at a fast pace urged on by their riders. Veronica led the way, Maud, Ginny noticed, the older of the two horses was tiring - her long black tail was swishing with impatience at the speed she was being asked to go.

Here they were with God's creation at its most wondrous, and then this cruelty – she just couldn't believe it. Where was God's mercy now? Ginny asked herself. How did that happen – why had life got so difficult all of a sudden? The straight line of the future had become chaotic, unpredictable, tangential – anything but straight. *And it was just about to get more chaotic.*

'Tell me again will you, Veronica,' Ginny asked, 'I can't seem to be able to grasp what's happened. I was too worried about David to listen properly about the girl. How can David be in the river with a young girl?'

All the questions leapt over themselves as she tried to speak, all of it coming out at once. 'What's happened to the girl? How did David find her?' Ginny asked knowing Veronica probably didn't know the answers.

'I only had the quickest of conversations with Charles,' Veronica replied. 'He doesn't know much either. David's phone gave out before he could give Charles all the details. But he told him enough for Charles to know there's a young girl in dire circumstances who needs help.'

Ginny's earlier panic returned tenfold – her gut went into a painful twist. Oz sensed the sudden tension in his rider and started jigging around on the spot in anxiety. Communication was all to a horse; the primitive flight instinct still core to their wellbeing.

'All right, Oz' Ginny said, patting him on the neck. 'It's all right – calm down now.'

Her own fear was beginning to subside as she concentrated on soothing Oz. He could smell her fear and didn't like it one little bit.

'So what are they going to do?' Ginny asked. 'Where are we going?'

It was all so unreal. One minute they were having a lovely hack on the moors, and the next, danger and mayhem.

'Charles has asked that we head towards the river,' Veronica finally said, 'he thinks it might be easier for us to find where they are. Apparently we're the right side of the river, and the rescue team might have trouble getting to them quickly. He thinks the horses will be able to cope better with the boggy ground. Charles isn't sure if the helicopter will be able to land. On horseback we may be able to find them first and help navigate them to the right spot. It's a sort of needle in a haystack situation.'

Ginny could think of nothing to say, her mind was still trying to absorb what Veronica was telling her. She couldn't get out of her mind the unutterable relief she had felt when she found out that David was all right.

'Thank goodness David's all right, but we need to try and help this poor girl. Are you OK with that?' Veronica asked. 'We need to get moving and see if we can find them. The going will be difficult, and we'll be cantering downhill some of the way. But there are some good flat tracks down the other side of the tor and that's the right direction, it takes you straight down to the river. Are you OK with that?'

'No, I'm only a weekend hacker – I don't do cantering downhill.' Was what she wanted to say but Ginny knew she didn't have any choice. Her stomach churned at the thought.

Oz had suddenly become livelier, pawing the ground and snorting; he must have sensed the unfolding drama. She smiled as best she could to let Veronica know she understood.

'Can you see the river? Over there in the distance?' Veronica pointed. 'That's where we're heading, concentrate on that. We're going downhill, so sit well back, keep your weight over his back legs, that way he is less likely to slip. Just follow me – I'm not going to go fast, just an easy rolling canter. Come on then. You can do this,'

Ginny knew her feeling of terror must be showing on her face. Lives were at risk - there was no time to hang about. She lengthened her reins slightly and leant back, just as Veronica had instructed her.

Fortunately the horses sensed the urgency, picking their way carefully, but still faster than Ginny would have liked - downhill.

Silence was all around, except for the horses' breath sounding like pistons and the drumming of their hooves. In spite of their speed, the horses descended cautiously, constantly in danger of slipping. Ginny tried to concentrate on getting to that ribbon of water, glinting white in the sun, without falling off, and without letting fear totally overwhelm her.

Cantering around the side of the tor, they scattered sheep and grit in their path. She could feel Oz's excitement, and wondered fleetingly if the helicopter might not be needed for her instead. His hooves seemed to be beating out, *David in danger, David in danger, David in danger, girl trapped in river, girl trapped in river.* It did nothing to steady her nerves.

For what seemed like hours the sliver of white against the winter-brown of the moors didn't appear to be getting any closer. Then finally after a heart-stoppingly fast canter where the horses through some ancient instinct, managed not to slip, they arrived in sight of the river. The terrain, to Ginny's relief, was turning into a flatter, grassy slope, and Veronica decided, without discussion, to go for it. *Gallop. Oh God.*

Ginny held on, her hands gripping like claws on the reins, his mane and anything she could get hold of. Her legs gripped Oz's sides like a vice. The horses sensed an opportunity for speed and galloped without any encouragement from their riders. They knew they had a job to do. Ginny's mouth was so dry she couldn't swallow. Dust and mud flew from Maud's hooves ahead. She could barely see.

If there wasn't a tragedy unfolding, the speed, the noise, the motion of the horses might have been exhilarating, but as it was Ginny felt more frightened than she ever thought possible. And then suddenly, despite the racket they were making, she heard Veronica's phone ring. They brought their horses to an abrupt halt - their sides heaving, their riders gasping for breath. All four glad of a couple of minutes' respite - Ginny just wanted it all to end, she didn't think she could go on much longer, her legs felt so weak she didn't know how long she could keep her balance. And they still hadn't reached the river.

'What's happening?' Ginny heard Veronica shout to Charles. 'The reception is terrible; you'll have to speak up. Do you know anything more? Is David all right? And the girl?'

Ginny heard the anxiety threaded through Veronica's voice and was left imagining the worst.

'They haven't located them yet,' Veronica said after finishing her call with Charles, 'and they want us to carry on. They must be in a part of the river that's difficult to see from the helicopter. Charles is putting a boat in the water. He still reckons we have a better chance of getting there first on horseback.' Veronica said all this calmly, but Ginny could see she was fighting anxiety too.

'I know how hard this is for you, Ginny,' Veronica said, 'but you are riding brilliantly. There's nothing ahead that's more difficult than we've already done. It's flatter now so we've done the hard part. We might be their only hope we can't give up now. We must find them.'

Veronica had found her out. The riding was beyond her capabilities, and she knew the ground was only going to get worse. Ahead were peat bogs. Ginny nodded, even though she was exhausted, and her muscles were trembling with the effort of trying to stay on her horse – she knew she had to do it for David, and the girl.

'We must find them or the girl may die,' Veronica said. 'It's as desperate as that, I'm afraid.'

'Yes of course, we must find them - I'll be all right, don't worry about me.' Ginny made her voice sound strong and capable, knowing Veronica wasn't fooled for a moment.

'OK,' Veronica said, 'let's get down to the river as safely as possible. Hang on.'

'OK.' Ginny managed to squeak. *You coward Ginny, you bloody bloody coward.*

They started cantering again; mercifully it was getting flatter but the track was single file and badly rutted. It was a sheep track edged with dense bracken and lumps of grass. *Oz, please don't stumble,* Ginny prayed. She concentrated on Veronica's back swept low over Maud, jockey like – a natural rider. Under different circumstances Veronica would probably have enjoyed this helter-skelter ride. Ginny could think of nothing worse.

Once they'd started their descent and for what seemed like an eternity, Ginny had no time to think of anything but hanging on in whatever way she could - gripping with her legs and trying to keep her balance as they careered round bends, as if lives depended on them - *they did.* Her breath was coming in gasps. She felt winded. Pulling up sharply, when sheep didn't get out of their way fast enough, nearly had Ginny flat on her face on the ground a few times, but she managed to cling on - just. Her only thought was a prayer. *Keep them safe, keep them safe,* saying it to the rhythm of the beat of the horses' hooves.

Fleet of foot, the horses seemed to know that lives depended on them.

After what seemed an aeon of time, they slithered down some stony scree and came at last to the river. The river, busy and swirling many feet below them, looked dangerous. Already afraid for David and the girl, she shuddered at the sight. *Could they survive for long in this?* Their view along the river was blocked by a sharp bend in one direction, and large sharp edged black boulders in the other.

'I'm going to call Charles again,' Veronica said, her voice carried away by the roar of the water, 'and see which way he thinks we should follow the river. Get your breath back, and give the horses a moment to rest.'

This part of the river was at least twenty feet below them, and it was angry. The bank was steep and inaccessible, the water rushing impatiently past big granite boulders in its way. The sight did nothing to allay Ginny's fears.

The horses, glad to have finished the challenging descent, were now contentedly eating grass; their sides still heaving from their exertions, sweat sheening on their coats. Ginny wiped the sweat from her face. Her head felt as though it was about to explode with heat, and her heart was still racing. Veronica looked no better, Ginny thought.

'OK, Charles, but how are we going to get down to the river?' Veronica asked. 'We're so high up here.'

Hearing Veronica's tense conversation with Charles, Ginny had a sinking feeling that their ride was anything but over.

Veronica finished her call, 'Charles thinks they're up-river from us. He knows this part of the river, and the bank starts to slacken off from here. We can trot when the going is rough and then canter when the track allows. We have to take care as the track is at the edge of a steep drop.'

At Veronica's words, *edge of a steep drop*, Ginny looked down the bank to the river below. *And just when I thought things couldn't get any worse...* There was now the possibility she may fall over the edge of the cliff. This couldn't be happening, she thought.

'Unfortunately the path looks as though it meanders away from the river in places,' Veronica said, looking into the distance, 'so we'll have to listen out for them but I doubt if we'd hear them over the roar of the river – the last thing we want to do is ride past them,' Veronica added.

Ginny wondered how Veronica could be so calm, and realised that this was Veronica's territory out here on the moors. She knew it well.

'Ready?'

Ginny felt too exhausted and too worried to speak, and could only nod her assent. They slowly followed the narrow river path, which was only just wide enough for one horse, another sheep track, badly rutted. The river was wide at this point, large boulders stood proud along the river bed abraded by the fast-flowing water, creating angry currents as the water divided, scoured the river bottom and regrouped at the other side. Still angry.

Ginny wasn't sure which was more scary, the downhill descent or the narrow path with a sheere drop on one side into a swirling river.

19

It was the horses that found them. They slowed almost to a standstill, with ears pirouetting, like sound locating devices. They snorted gently in their uncertainty.

'What do you think they can hear?' Veronica asked, stopping and turning back to her. 'Do you think it might be them? I hope so. Let's see if we can get nearer the river again.'

Ginny suddenly felt her exhaustion drain away at the thought they might be near. They had already been at least half-an-hour walking along the bank river at high level trying to find them. She hoped they weren't too late. Urging the horses to leave the track they headed directly downhill to the river about twenty metres away.

At the point they reached the water it was not very deep or wide.

'There's a track on the other side – it might be easier.' Veronica took the lead, kicking Maud out into the river. Oz, needing no encouragement, followed willingly.

The horses sniffed the air, nostrils flared, still unnerved by something, as they waded over to the far bank up to their hocks in icy water.

'The horses are trying to tell us something,' Veronica said. 'I'm sure we're near but I can't see or hear anything can you?'

'No, nothing yet,' Ginny answered, 'I hope we're following the river in the right direction. Charles was sure wasn't he?'

Before Veronica could answer her, 'what's that?' Ginny asked, her heart thumping. 'There it is again,' she shouted this time. 'It's got to be them. Veronica, come on, this way. Look the horses have heard it too.'

A thin high-pitched sound could be heard, drifting along the river and disappearing quickly on the breeze. The horses, turned to face the way they had come, and as if by instinct they both set off up river again.

'There they are,' Ginny shouted, excitement making her voice shrill over the sound of the river, 'look, there, in the river,' she pointed frantically, 'I can just see them. Look – in the middle of the river.'

The noise they had heard was becoming more distinct as they got nearer. It was someone shouting to them in desperation.

'Help – over here – HE…LP, HE….LP, HELLOOO.'

'David, David… we can see you – hang on,' Ginny jumped off Oz and abandoned him to graze on the riverbank. She ran down the track, her legs wobbly with fatigue but her thoughts were only of David.

'David, I'm here,' she shrieked back. 'Here, over here.'

She ran the last few metres waving her arms and arrived at the edge of the river. Veronica was at her side in seconds.

'David, what's happened, 'Ginny asked, her voice shrill with concern, 'what's going on?'

'I'm all right… it's Grace… ' David said, and she turned away from him to see a sight that froze her to the spot with horror.

Nothing was all right, nowhere near all right; Ginny could see that straight away. Despite his words, David looked desperately ill, but it was the girl that transfixed her with worry. She was young, terribly young.

The girl was limp in David's arms. Ginny could see it was taking all his strength to hold her up. Was the girl conscious her face so pale it was almost transparent, her lips and tip of her nose, blue? Her mouth, bloodless, was closed tight with suffering. Ginny looked away for a moment to regain her composure. She knew she had to stay calm to be of any help at all. Grace opened her eyes for the merest second, and Ginny breathed out with relief. Thank God, she was still alive. They weren't too late. But the faraway look in the girl's eyes told Ginny she had begun her journey to another world.

'David,' Ginny said, quietly not wanting to disturb the girl, 'Veronica's calling Charles again, the rescue team is close by. He's arranged for a helicopter to come, and it will be here in a minute, now that we've found you. Everyone's been looking for you. It's nearly over – you've done marvellously – she's so lucky that you were walking here.'

David didn't seem to be listening to her. He seemed remote, faraway. *Was that singing she had heard? David singing?*

'David, take my jacket and put it around Grace,' Ginny said. 'Come out of the water, and I'll take your place, you're too cold.' His face, she could see was hideously mottled, his blue eyes staring madly at her. What has happened? Ginny thought frantically. *Where were his clothes? Why was he bare to the waist in this weather?*

Ginny could now see what had happened. But not why – that would come later. Grace was standing in the water and David had wrapped her in all his clothes and had his arms around her – he was trying to keep her warm. He was trying to stop her from… dying. A lump caught in Ginny's throat but she knew now was not the time for her own emotions. David, as she had expected refused to let go of Grace - he clung to her. A fierce protective look in his eyes. One that Ginny had only ever seen at the birth of their three sons.

'It'll be better for Grace,' Ginny said, gently, 'to have someone warm holding her – you're no longer able to do that. It will help Grace.' *Where was Charles – where was anybody that knew what to do?* She could see Veronica frantically on the phone and waving to the helicopter.

David reluctantly, after more cajoling, let Ginny kneel down beside him and let her unpeel his arms from around Grace. Grace's eyes flickered, but she seemed to accept Ginny was there to help her too. Ginny took off her own warm down jacket and thermal layer. Peeling away David's wet jacket and pullover she quickly wrapped Grace in her own warm clothes. Putting her arms around Grace, she breathed warm air onto her face. She could just about feel a pulse in the girl's neck, and could feel her lungs moving slightly against her own chest. Ginny needed all her resolve to ignore the coldness of the water lapping around her knees. It was as nothing to what Grace must be suffering.

'Sing to her – she likes that,' David said, his voice a whisper, all energy spent.

So, she *had* heard him singing then – how extraordinary, Ginny thought. Ginny watched David trying to scramble off the stones, and realised he must be paralysed with cold.

Veronica had seen him struggling too and was running towards him, a grim look on her face.

'David, I'll help you,' Veronica said, bending down to grip his hands. 'Charles will be here soon,' Veronica explained. 'The helicopter's trying to find somewhere to land, the ground's really boggy around here, and a second helicopter is on its way.'

Ginny could already feel numbness creeping up her thighs from the cold stone and the freezing river water. *What must Grace be feeling?* Ginny couldn't bear to think about it. She didn't like the girl's colour - pasty-grey, and her pulse thready and irregular. But she was alive. There was still a chance.

She could hear Veronica trying to persuade David he needed to get warm. 'No, no, no,' Ginny heard him say, 'I need to get back to Grace. She'll be so frightened without me. I only got out just for a minute – I shouldn't have done it. She needs me.'

Ginny had never seen David so impassioned - he seemed confused, irrational. She heard him telling Veronica he didn't know how long he'd been with Grace, but it felt like hours. He kept muttering about trees and spirals. He seemed, completely unaware that he too might be in danger from hypothermia.

'David,' Veronica tried again, her voice now stern as if talking to a naughty child, 'you're colder than you should be, you need to get warm as quickly as you can. Here put my jacket round your shoulders and this pullover of mine. You need the warmth.'

It was almost as though David didn't understand, Ginny thought. Maybe it was hypothermia, she couldn't be sure. She could see David couldn't tear his eyes away from Grace, and in those bloodshot and weary eyes was the look of a defeated man.

What had he to be defeated about? Ginny wondered – surely he must realise he had saved Grace. No one else would have passed this way and tried to rescue her. Grace was incredibly lucky that David had chosen to walk along this remote part of the river. Without David, the girl would have had no chance at all. *Grace is going to be all right.* She tightened her arms around Grace, ignoring the aching cold sweeping through her own body.

Desperately wanting to go to David to comfort him, Ginny knew Grace's life was hanging in the balance, but that David would live. For that moment Grace needed her more.

'David, you've done all you can for Grace,' she heard Veronica say to David. 'You must think of yourself now. You've been absolutely marvellous. Grace is all right with Ginny until Charles gets here. Then they'll get Grace out of the water, and fly her to hospital.'

'How are they going to get her out?' David's voice broke. He wouldn't be fooled for a moment, Ginny thought. 'Where's her father? Have they found him? He must be lost,' David asked, his voice slurring slightly.

'I don't know, yet' Veronica said, 'they're looking for him.'

Ginny saw Veronica's relief as he let her put the jacket around him. Veronica sat down on the stone slab next to him and put her arm around his shoulders. They didn't talk; David seemed to have retreated in his mind somewhere - but even so, Ginny saw his eyes never left Grace for a second.

She checked the girl's pulse again, and it seemed fainter than ever. Today had started so well, and along the way it had somehow descended into hell. *Come on Charles where has that damn helicopter gone?*

'Are you OK, Ginny?' Veronica called from the riverbank.

Only metres away from safety only two more steps to get to the bank – what had gone so horribly wrong for Grace? Ginny wondered. Had her foot just slipped? So bloody, bloody unlucky – life was so… unfair.

'I'm OK thanks, you look after David,' Ginny called back, 'I'll let you know if I need some help.'

'Are you sure you don't want me to take your place?' Veronica asked.

In that moment, Ginny began to understand what David felt about leaving Grace. This wisp of a girl, pale beyond possibility, was hanging on to the very essence of her life. Brave beyond comprehension. She hadn't given up. Ginny could feel the beat of her heart in her thin eleven-year-old chest. Grace could have given up, but she hadn't – she wanted to live. How fragile life was Ginny thought.

She remembered David telling her to sing. She began quietly at first, embarrassed. But then with more resolution she began to remember songs she sang to her own children. While she sang, she held Grace tight trying to pass on her warmth, just as if she were her own child. Was this what David had been feeling, this primitive connection to his absent sons?

Ginny recalled her yearning for a daughter. *Where had that thought escaped from?* She hadn't ever allowed thoughts of a daughter to flower… not since the miscarriage. She held them back, hammered them down. But there it was - surfacing when it was least needed. Her mind was playing cruel games on her. Had it been the same for David – had he wanted a daughter too and, like her, kept quiet about it?

20

It was while life stood still for a moment, the silence of the landscape enveloping them all, each one of them trying to control their own fears and panic, each with only thought for the others, that a sound, beginning softly and then more certainly, was heard. The tableau frozen in shared horror, suddenly came back to life.

'They're here, David, Ginny, look,' Veronica frantically waved her arms, her voice shrill with relief, 'look David, the helicopter's managed to land. The rescue team are here. They'll soon have Grace out of the river and into hospital.'

Ginny watched Veronica waving frantically to four men walking towards them with heavy looking rucksacks on their backs, and carrying a stretcher. Neat coils of rope lay across their chests, and belts round their waists were festooned with all manner of equipment. Ginny felt utter relief at the welcome sight. She was beginning to think that Grace couldn't hold on for much longer.

'Grace, love, they're here,' Ginny whispered. 'They've come to rescue you. You'll be all right now.'

Ginny stroked her face, gently, singing to her again, willing with every cell in her body that she would live, and that they weren't too late after all. Willing Grace to stay in this world with her, she whispered about all the things Grace still had to do in her life.

'How will they get her out?' David asked as the rescue team arrived at his side. 'She's completely trapped? It's her foot, it's stuck between two rocks.'

Ginny's heart contracted with pain at the sound of David's voice so full of despair. 'I tried and couldn't get her out. I failed.' David said, so quietly Ginny had to strain to hear him.

'Don't you worry, mate,' the oldest of the four said to him. 'David isn't it? We'll get her out.'

A million thoughts buzzed through Ginny's head, as she watched Veronica rush over to Charles where they embraced quickly. The embrace between Veronica and Charles – it spoke of love. Ginny shed another tear - for herself this time.

'Charles, thank god you're here,' Veronica said.

'What are you going to do?' Ginny heard Veronica ask Charles quietly. Their conversation was now a private one, and Ginny could only just catch some of their words. *What is it they don't want me to hear?* Something about David? Her heart constricted in fear.

'We need to see what's going on underwater,' Charles explained to Veronica, 'a diver's getting ready. I need your help to get Ginny and David away from here, as quickly as possible. I don't want them to see. Nor you, love.'

'See what, Charles? What do you mean?' Veronica asked.

'There's another helicopter on its way for David,' Charles said, ignoring her question. 'The paramedic will take a look at David in a minute when he's stabilised the girl, and got Ginny back on dry land and warmed up. David doesn't look well,' Charles added, 'I'm worried about his colour, and his speech is slurred. We need to get him to hospital as quickly as possible too.'

'Is David going to be all right?' Ginny shouted over to Charles.

'He's going to be fine,' Charles answered, 'we're going to get him to hospital in just a minute.'

Within minutes of Charles' words the rescue team began their work. Ginny was helped to the riverbank, her legs rubbery with cold, and taken over to sit beside David. She understood David's reluctance to let go of Grace. She felt she had deserted the girl, and she'd only been with her for barely ten minutes.

The paramedic wrapped David in foil and put a pillar-box red woolly hat on his head. Ginny knew that, in spite of his situation, David would be feeling ridiculous.

'Come on, love,' the thickset paramedic said gently. 'Ginny, isn't it? Strip off,' and at her blush of embarrassment, 'no one is looking, put this change of clothes on, you need to get warm too.'

Ginny nodded, realising foolishly it was not the time to be prudish. Exchanging wet clothes for dry ones: including a hat like David's, wrapped in a foil blanket, and given a cup of very sweet tea – it seemed that in the shortest possible time, warmth started to creep back in.

'You did a grand job there, you two,' the burly man said. 'You did exactly the right thing trying to keep the girl as warm as possible. Well done. I wish everyone was as sensible.'

Ginny looked at David who was sitting silently next to her but it didn't seem David had heard.

'Don't worry about him,' the burly man nodded towards David, 'it's a bit of shock; it's the cold that does that to you. He won't feel like talking for a while – maybe when he warms up. He'll feel better in a few hours, I'm sure.'

'How are you holding up, Ginny?' Charles asked.

Ginny nodded, and tried to smile but really all she wanted to do was lie down and go to sleep.

'She was marvellous, Charles,' Veronica said. 'The riding was hard for me, so for Ginny it must have been terrifying at times - she's was really plucky. The horses were brilliant too, weren't they Ginny? I'm so grateful to them they ran with wings, and kept us safe – it couldn't have been easy for them either. You know what the ground's like. It could have all gone so horribly wrong.'

'Well thank goodness it didn't,' Charles said, 'you're both OK and that's what matters. It'll be a story to tell the grand-children one day.'

'How are Ginny and I, going to get back home? Veronica asked. 'What about the horses, Charles?'

'The only way back is for you and Ginny to ride home,' Charles replied. 'I know it's not what you want, or Ginny for that matter, but there's no other way. You can't leave them on the moors. Unless you can think of one?'

Ginny's heart sank, how could she even contemplate getting back on a horse right now?

'David's become very withdrawn, and doesn't seem to want talk to anybody. Will he be all right do you think?' Veronica asked, moving away just out of earshot of David.

'He needs to get to hospital – he's probably got hypother-mia like Grace, but not so badly,' Charles replied. 'We're just waiting for the second helicopter.'

'I'll get Ginny back home as soon as she's warmed up,' Veronica said. 'I'll go and tell her now.'

Ginny knew what Veronica was coming to tell her, and

stalled her, 'Tell me what? I'm not leaving David even if it does mean we have to ride back in the dark. I'm not leaving him.' Her fingers gripped David's blanket. Even if their marriage was collapsing, she wasn't leaving him like this.

'Don't leave it too long,' Charles entreated, 'I don't want to have to worry about the two of you, lost on the moors in the dark.' Charles gave them both a hug, and left to take command of what was happening at the river.

'David, are you OK?' Ginny said, laying her hand on his, 'you did a marvellous thing, you know. Without you, Grace wouldn't be alive.'

David didn't answer, she knew he'd heard her; instead he remained huddled in his blanket staring at Grace. 'David, are your feet hurting?' Ginny asked, 'Mine are.'

'You did everything you could, darling, no one could have done any more,' Ginny said, putting her arm around him. She could feel his body shaking.

Ginny watched as Charles headed back towards them.

'David, are you all right?' Charles asked, crouching down in front of him. 'Are you able to tell me now what you know? David you're in shock with the beginnings of hypothermia, we're going to take you to hospital soon. But it would help Grace if you could tell me a bit about what happened. We're waiting for the second helicopter; it'll be here very shortly.'

Charles squeezed David's shoulder as he spoke, but Ginny didn't see any signs he'd heard.

'I was with Grace... I'm not sure how long,' David began suddenly in a shaky voice. His face was taut with anxiety, 'it all seems so... confused. I don't know where her father went? Has he been seen?'

'No, but we'll find him soon,' Charles reassured him. Another squeeze of his shoulder followed. 'We've sent a search party out for him. Did Grace tell you what happened? How it happened?'

'I think she just slipped crossing the river – and her foot caught between the rocks. So bloody unlucky,' David said, his voice breaking.' I don't know anything else. She hasn't really been able to talk much. I'm sorry - I'm not much help,'

'It's OK, David,' Ginny said, stroking his back.

'I don't know how long she'd been in the water before that,' David, added. 'I dived in to see what the problem was and found that her foot was stuck. I tried to free it, but couldn't: it's wedged between two large boulders, neither of which would budge. I feel so useless,' David stammered his way through his story, his teeth chattering. Ginny found it almost impossible to understand what he was saying, but it seemed to be enough for Charles.

'David,' Charles said, standing up again, his hand to his headphone listening. 'I've just heard the second helicopter's landed. They'll be here shortly with a stretcher for you.' Charles gave him a final reassuring pat on his shoulder.

'I'm not going anywhere without Grace,' David shouted. 'I need to know that she's safe.'

'You must, David,' Ginny implored. 'There's nothing more you can do for Grace now.

'David, I must go and attend to Grace,' Charles said. 'Please do as I ask, that's the best thing you can do for Grace now. I don't want to have to worry about you as well. OK? I promise to let you know how Grace is. Ginny and Veronica will be going back now too. They did a terrific job finding you, you know.'

Veronica came and sat down on the other side of David and put her arm around him. David didn't acknowledge her so trapped was he in his own world.

'Are you sure you are up to riding back, Ginny?' Veronica asked. 'I reckon it would take about an hour's ride from here. No cantering,' Veronica added, smiling. 'I promise.'

'Sure,' Ginny replied, her smile as brave looking as she could make it. Veronica looked pale and tired too, she thought, and definitely too tired for Ginny to start making a fuss. 'I'm up for that.' None of this was about her now; it was about Grace and David.

The thought suddenly struck her, that although she knew nothing about Grace - not her full name, not where she lived, not what she liked to eat, nor what colour she liked, or whether she had siblings – nothing – and yet somehow, Grace had stolen a piece of her heart. She knew Grace had come into their lives and changed them forever – who could forget the events of this day? It suddenly felt unfathomable, for David to have put himself in so much danger, for a stranger. Was this her David?

Ginny shivered, as she watched a black rubber clad diver flip over the side of an inflatable boat and disappear into the oily-black water of the pool. The boat and the equipment must have been brought in the helicopter, she thought, amazed at how organised they were. She couldn't tear her eyes away from the events unfolding before them. With fascination she watched as Charles, holding the boat steady, belayed the rope to the diver – keeping him safe. They all knew exactly what they were doing. It was a well oiled operation.

She watched the paramedic kneeling awkwardly beside Grace. *I know the awkwardness of that position, my knees still haven't recovered.* The paramedic wasted no time in setting up a drip, checking her temperature, blood pressure and her pulse. If anybody could save Grace, it was these men, Ginny thought, in awe of their skills and confidence.

Time seemed to hover motionless while they waited for the diver to resurface. Was everybody holding their breath or was it just her? Ginny wondered. And like a cork out of a bottle, the diver broke the surface of the water. Everyone's eyes were on him, but no one could hear the intense conversation between him and Charles.

'What do you think's happening now?' Ginny asked.

'Not sure,' Veronica replied, shaking her head, 'I'm going to find out though.'

Ginny watched Veronica walking swiftly over to Charles. It wasn't long before Veronica was on her way back her expression grim.

'We were just making plans for us to get back home,' Veronica said, as she sat back down next to Ginny. 'Charles thinks we need to go now as rain is forecast and the dense cloud covering means we will lose the light more quickly. It will be more difficult to make our way safely.

'I'm not leaving until David's gone. I'm sorry, to be such a nuisance,' Ginny said, turning her head away from Grace. 'You know something you're not telling me. Don't you?'

'Yes, but it isn't my information to say. Please trust me, Ginny.'

Ginny nodded reluctantly at Veronica, who she thought, looked unusually stressed.

'You're not being a nuisance,' Veronica said. 'Do you feel rested enough?'

'David hasn't said a word to me, not one. He just keeps staring at Grace.'

'Charles thinks David maybe in shock,' Veronica replied, 'he'll soon be on the helicopter and away to hospital. The second one is just landing now. You say goodbye to him while I catch the horses and sort their tack out. OK?'

'I want to go with David,' Ginny said, suddenly feeling horribly torn between Veronica, David and Grace. She wanted to stay, but realistically knew she couldn't. She sighed with a heavy heart.

'You'll have to leave David and Grace to Charles and his team. Don't worry about them for the moment,' Veronica replied, 'they're both being well looked after. The rescue team know what to do for the best.'

Ginny nodded. 'It's best we're out of the way, I suppose?' She saw the relief on Veronica's face.

'It'll only take about an hour or so to get back to the house, and then you can drive straightaway to the hospital,' Veronica said. 'You won't be too long behind him. David's just said he won't leave Grace; so you'll have to use all your powers of persuasion.'

Ginny walked over to David; her heart tightened in her chest at the sight of him. She hadn't ever seen him looking so grey and his face etched with pain.

'Darling, can you hear the helicopter? It's for you.' She explained gently, taking his hands in hers, she could feel how cold they were still, and began to rub them warm.

David turned his head towards her. 'I want to wait for Grace, I'm not going anywhere until Grace is out of the river.' He stumbled on his words.

'David you have to go,' Ginny implored. 'You aren't well,

and we have to do what's best for Grace now,' she continued, 'you've done everything you could for her, but now Charles wants you to go to hospital. If you stay you'll be… causing them extra work looking after you. They need to concentrate on Grace – not you.' She looked at him intently, knowing she had sounded brutal. But reading between the lines, she knew that Charles didn't want David to see what was going to happen next. He didn't want any of them seeing. She waited quietly, hoping her love for him carried enough weight still for him to do as she asked.

David turned his face away from her without a word and looked at Grace.

'Darling, please,' Ginny said, again, beseeching him, 'you must let them help you. You don't look well at all – please let them help you.'

David glanced back at Ginny, and for a second or so their eyes met and in that moment something passed between them. Something Ginny recognised from happier days. Their destiny shared. And then it was gone as though it had never been.

'Darling, I'm sure they'll get Grace out of the river,' Ginny was saying, as two paramedics came over to them.

'Come on, mate, time to go,' the paramedic said.

'I want to stay until Grace… has been freed,' David said, looking defiant.

'No, mate, you can't,' the paramedic said gently, but firmly. 'We need you in hospital. We don't want to keep the pilot waiting, now do we? There maybe other emergencies needing him.'

To Ginny's relief, David finally nodded, and with the aid of the paramedics she watched helplessly as David was lifted onto the stretcher. Ginny walked over to the helicopter with him holding his hand tightly. She didn't want to let him go.

'David, I'll get to the hospital as soon as I can,' Ginny said, 'you'll be OK, won't you? I wish I could come with you but there isn't room for me,' Ginny could feel her voice choking. 'I don't want to leave you,' she barely whispered.

The paramedics lifted David's stretcher into the helicopter. David didn't acknowledge her – he hadn't looked at her, didn't seem to care she wouldn't be going with him. She kissed his cheek, cold and clammy still. He wasn't well she reminded herself.

A few minutes later, Ginny heard the deafening engines of the helicopter, and watched as it rose and yawed into the sky, like a great ugly bird. Ginny was left with the sense that something important had just happened. But she had no idea what.

21

Bella stood with Peter and the other canvassers outside The Anchor pub enjoying the laughter and enthusiasm, now that the afternoon's canvassing was done. Bella looked around the group, ordinary people with ordinary lives, she thought. She envied them. Her life was far from ordinary.

'Did you meet anyone interesting, Bella?' They wanted to know.

Bella basked for a moment in the attention, 'only Spike, and Mr Darcy,' she answered. 'That's all.'

'Who's, Spike?' they all wanted to know, 'and Mr Darcy?' they clamoured with curiosity. She answered their questions shyly, but something stopped her from telling them about Will Green. She wasn't entirely sure why she wanted to keep him to herself – she would enjoy thinking about him later when she was on her own.

Only just realising the time, Bella said a hasty goodbye. Her fingers shook so much she could barely undo her bike lock, knowing Steve would be angry if she was late.

Arriving home out of breath, she parked her bike on the path at the side of her house, and saw Steve through the window. He was sitting in the living room with a beer in his hand watching out for her. She knew that look on his face – it was the anger she had feared. Her stomach started churning.

The house was unnervingly calm and quiet. *Where were*

the children? The living room looked cosy, inviting, when she opened the door. The fire glowed red, bright yellow sparks burst from the logs. Daffodils, picked from the garden the day before, were a splash of gorgeous yellow. *We could be so happy here.*

'Hi Steve,' she said, trying to vanquish fear from her voice. 'I'm back.'

At the sight of his glowering face, she could feel her steps beginning to falter. 'Where are the children? They're so quiet?'

'I've done what you have never managed to do as their mother,' Steve said smugly, 'They're now playing quietly in their bedroom. They were squabbling while I was trying to watch the footie, so I told them I didn't want to hear from them again, or there'd be trouble.'

Poor children, Bella thought, guiltily - *I should never have left them with him.* 'I'll just go up and see them.'

'Not so fast,' Steve said, getting up from his chair and barring Bella's way. 'What time do you call this, hey? When did I tell you to come home?' Steve asked, his words slurring as he advanced towards her. Bella felt a knot forming in her stomach as he came nearer. She watched as beer slopped on his shoes and the carpet with every step. She tried to edge around him but the largeness of him blocked her escape. She knew it wouldn't be long before his temper became a living creature: tentacles of horribleness would fill every corner of the room.

'It's only just after four, 'she whispered. 'I took a bit longer than expected. I'm sorry.' But she didn't really feel sorry, not deep down. It would almost be worth Steve's anger; she would put up with a lot for these last few hours.

'A bit longer?' He spat. The white gobbet of spittle landed on her shoe. She had learned to hide her disgust. The veins on his forehead stood out and throbbed, 'nearly an hour longer, you mean,' Steve growled, jabbing his thick finger in her shoulder.

'What you had to do was come home when I told you to. But oh no, that wasn't possible was it? Who is he?'

Who is he? Bella nearly laughed out loud at the thought of anyone finding her attractive. She backed away trying to escape him, but in her panic her foot caught the corner of the rug. Grabbing the back of the sofa, she managed to stop herself falling, but only just. She was now only a couple of steps from where he stood.

'Mummy?' Issy shouted from the top of the stairs. Bella could hear the wobble in her daughter's voice, and forgot her own fears in an instant.

'I must go to her,' Bella said, making for the door. 'She sounds a bit… '

'Mummy, I need you,' Issy shouted. 'Please come.'

'I'll be up to see you soon,' Bella called, trying to sound reassuring, not wanting her to witness Steve's anger. 'I'll be up soon, Lovey.'

'You didn't mind leaving, Issy or Ben, this afternoon, did you?' Steve accused, his nose inches from Bella's face, a hand went up and Bella found herself instinctively flinching. 'That's OK though, isn't it?' Steve said grabbing her hair.

'That's it,' Steve added, 'you're not going again. You've had your fun. You didn't tell me you were canvassing for a woman, did you?' Steve sneered, 'did you think I wouldn't find out?'

'She's a lawyer,' Bella answered back, knowing it would only make him more angry, but she just couldn't help herself.

'So?' Steve asked. 'What does any woman know about the

real world?' Steve asked, scornfully, 'women are all like you – bloody useless.'

Bella stood, silent. There would be no stopping his tirade now.

'What people want,' he continued, spittle flying from his wet red lips, words slurred, 'is someone who's strong and straight down the line - someone like me, not some whingeing woman.'

Bella's head was throbbing where he had pulled her hair, but even so the idea of Steve trying to persuade people to vote for him, was so unthinkable she could barely keep her face straight.

'You're not going again, do you hear me?' Steve repeated, 'I don't suppose you'll be missed anyway, what use can you be, you can't even say 'boo' to a goose? You are a goose, a stupid… stupid bloody goose.' Steve's voice was nearing a crescendo. Any minute now, Bella thought, the fight would go out of him, but not before… and there it was - his foot swung backwards, picking up momentum. And then… the pain, shooting down her leg as Steve's foot made contact with her shin. She knew it was nearly over and tried to breathe slowly to stop herself from shrieking.

'Get out of my sight,' he said lurching back to his chair, his face red with effort. 'See to the children,' Steve instructed her. 'I'll be up later, you can have an early night too,' he said, leering at her. His intentions abundantly clear. Bella's heart hammered at the thought of his fat hands crawling all over her – and much, much worse.

Just as the afternoon light was beginning to stutter into dusk, an owl hooted over the valley. Ginny saw with unutterable relief the chimneys of Tavy House slowly coming into view. Their ride was nearly over. She wanted to weep with exhaustion.

'Thank God,' she heard Veronica say under her breath. So she was tired too.

'We've only just made it,' Veronica said, 'it'll be dark in a few minutes.

'Mmm,' Ginny mumbled, as she got off Oz, her legs didn't seem to belong to her they felt so stiff.

With a last pat and a heartfelt 'thank you' to Oz, Ginny left the stables and followed Veronica back to the house.

'You go and have a quick shower,' Veronica suggested, 'I'll let mum know we're back; she'll have been really worried about us, and I'll rustle up something you can eat quickly before you go to the hospital.' She put her hand on her arm stopping her for a moment. 'You were wonderful today, Ginny,' Veronica said, 'so brave. Charles thought so too.'

'I've so much to be grateful to you for,' she answered, 'I keep wondering how today could have turned out as it has - you know?' How could they ever have guessed what would happen when they set out this morning? Ginny wondered wearily.

Ginny drove into the car park of Tavistock Hospital as the clock on the radio chimed eight. Her quick shower, and a dinner rustled up by Veronica's mother had done almost nothing to lessen her unutterable weariness. The hospital, a large rich-red Victorian building, was saved from a grimness, redolent of the workplace, by attractive yellow brick detailing over the large, arched sash windows. She climbed the steps, worn away by decades of footsteps, at the portico entrance and walked into a large and gloomy lobby.

She waited while the young woman at the reception desk finished helping another visitor. 'I'm looking for my husband. I'm not sure what ward he's on,' Ginny explained when it was her turn.

The woman smiled, showing even white teeth. 'Let me look. David Jackson, you say? Hmm,' she muttered, consulting her computer screen.

'Found him. He's on Lister Ward, which is straight down that corridor,' she said pointing, 'turn right at the end, go up the stairs and you'll find it on your left.'

'Thank you,' Ginny said, wondering how on earth she was going to remember all that. 'Would you be able to tell me about a young girl my husband helped to rescue this afternoon, from the river? Her name is Grace, I don't know her surname, I'm afraid.'

'I can't tell you about other patients,' the woman said, apologetically. 'I'm afraid we're not allowed to - it's a matter of confidentiality.'

She turned away not surprised, but still disappointed at the woman's answer.

At the entrance to Lister Ward Ginny could see the nurses were busy, so she walked through the ward without disturbing them. Finally spotting David lying on his side facing the window, she hurried down the ward.

'David,' she said. He turned slowly at the sound of her voice, and Ginny could see how desolate he looked. Her heart faltered.

'How are you, David?' she asked, sitting down next to him and reaching for his hand.

'What have they said to you? How are you feeling?' Ginny asked, but she could see from the blue shadows under his eyes, that he was far from well.

'Is there any news about Grace?' David asked, the tiredness in his eyes vanishing for a second.

Ginny shook her head and watched disappointment cloud his face. He turned away from her to look out of the window. She followed his gaze and could just about make out a courtyard garden, where a statue of Venus appeared to rise from neglected shrubbery.

'The woman at reception said she wasn't allowed to tell me anything about Grace, because of confidentiality,' she explained. 'I'm sure Charles will let us know soon.'

'Why are you so late? David asked. Visiting time started hours ago.'

Ginny looked at him in disbelief. 'Don't you remember Veronica and I still had to get back to Tavy House from the river on horseback? It took us nearly two hours; the horses were absolutely exhausted. If it wasn't for them we wouldn't have found you so quickly.' The effort to keep her voice steady was nearly too much. 'Is there anything I can get you? Is there anything you want?'

'I need to know what's happening to Grace,' he replied, irritably. 'That's what I want. Somebody must know, surely? I feel as though I've been here for ages?' David added, shifting himself up on his pillows, sounding like a petulant child. 'I want to go home.'

The chilling thought suddenly struck her - their marriage was all but over. *All he wants to know is what's happened to Grace.* There was no concern at all for her, Ginny, his wife. She'd suspected it at the riverbank that he no longer felt anything for her at all. But now she knew – he didn't feel anything for her.

She tried desperately to persuade herself that he was being like this because of his terrible ordeal. But she knew if he'd truly loved her, he'd have reached out to her, with his hand or with his heart. He would have shown some concern for her, some sense that they'd been in this catastrophe together. Some indication that he knew she had helped to rescue him and Grace. But no. She blinked her tears back.

Ginny took a deep breath, and took his hand in hers again. He's been through a lot, she reminded herself. He's not himself. Or is he? Ginny thought. Is this the real David – the one not hiding his feeling?

'All I know, is that Grace has been rescued, and is now in hospital,' Ginny explained as calmly as she could. She could feel her patience and sympathy beginning to fade. 'Veronica phoned Charles before I left to visit you, but he didn't know anything more.'

'How did they rescue her?' David asked all of a sudden.

'I don't know, David, I'm sorry,' Ginny didn't know why she kept on apologizing to him – none of this was her fault. He turned away from her again to look out of the window. She wondered as she sat there if she should just go back to Tavy House. She was aware that her life seemed beyond anything she had control over anymore.

David turned back to face her, he must have realised how rude he was being, she thought.

'The doctors said I'm all right,' David replied, 'they warmed me up and put me on a drip. They told me that I can go home tomorrow morning.' It was all so matter of fact, Ginny thought, as though hyperthermia was an everyday occurrence.

'Are you sure? Tomorrow morning seems very soon?' she asked, surprised.

'That's what they said,' he explained, with a shrug. Suddenly he glanced over at the box of chocolates, 'thanks by the way. Do you want a chocolate?'

Ginny shook her head. Chocolates were definitely not what she wanted at the moment. A hug maybe, a kiss, an acknowledgement of the part she'd played that day – but not chocolates.

Ginny could see a nurse approaching David's bed, and quickly got up gathering her things together.

'I'd better go, before I'm thrown out. I'll come back in the morning.'

David nodded his agreement. She could see his thoughts were already elsewhere, anywhere but with her.

'Time to go, Mrs. Jackson, you look as tired as your husband,' the cheerful looking nurse said, as he came to a halt at the end of the bed.

'I hear you've both had a day of it,' Shaun said with a look of compassion on his face. 'By the way, I've managed to find out something that might interest you. I know you were both asking. I've heard the young girl is going to be fine.'

As he spoke, Shaun picked up David's medical records from the end of his bed, 'I can't tell you anymore than that though. I'm sorry. But looking at both your faces, I can see that even that's welcome news.'

They watched him walk back to the nurses' station, his steps quiet.

'David, that's wonderful news isn't it?' Ginny said, turning to David with relief, 'she's doing OK. Thank God.'

She watched David trying to assimilate the news, and slowly he looked up and a faint smile crossed his face.

'Go home, Ginny, the nurse is right, you look tired.'

24

Ginny woke the next morning to a bedroom bathed in sunshine. She realised she'd forgotten to close the curtains when she finally got to bed the evening before.

A quick nightcap with Veronica and Charles, when she'd arrived back the hospital, had stretched to midnight and a bottle of fine wine from Charles' cellar. Sensing how late it was – she jumped out of bed only to find that her head was throbbing horrible. Hangover, or just plain tiredness? She wondered. She phoned David's mobile as she clattered around the bedroom. No answer. Was he all right? She dressed quickly; she must get to the hospital.

Her muscles rebelled with stiffness; a reminder of the awfulness of the day before. David ill in hospital. Grace – well she didn't know about her yet, breakneck speed on horseback. It was a day to forget in so many ways.

The breakfast room was empty except for Veronica clearing the table.

'Hi, am I too late? I've overslept,' Ginny said, thinking how tired Veronica looked too. *What a mess.*

Veronica's smile however was the same as always - bright and cheerful.

'Hi, Ginny, did you sleep all right?'

'Well apart from dreaming of water and young girls it wasn't

145

too bad,' Ginny said, not willing to admit to the terrors she had woken with in the night.

'I don't suppose Charles knows anything more?' Ginny asked.

Veronica shook her head, 'nothing we didn't know already. I still can't believe they're sending David home today?'

'Stay here another night. Your bedroom is available,' Veronica suggested again.' You're too tired to drive all that way today, surely? You look terrible – I suppose we shouldn't have stayed up so late. I don't know about you but my head is aching.'

'Mine too,' Ginny said, automatically putting her hand up to soothe her head. 'David's mind's made up,' Ginny said. 'He wants to go home, and that's it. There's no changing his mind,' she sighed, 'I've packed already. But I will try again - I don't want to drive all the way home today. But if I have to… '

'Come into the kitchen for a minute,' Veronica said, walking that way with a tray of dirty dishes in her hands. Ginny followed, glad to have put off saying goodbye for the moment.

Veronica went straight over to the coffee pot that sat on the kitchen counter.

'You can, at least, have some toast and coffee before you go,' Veronica said, handing her a large steaming mug, with pictures of prancing horses. 'I'll pack you a lunch to take with you.'

Ginny smiled, nodding her thanks, and felt the immediate comfort of the warmth of the mug. Perching herself on the back of a sofa, strewn with discarded sports equipment, Ginny surveyed the mess, and ate her toast. Newspapers, books, dogs, all fighting for space - so different from her own home, neat and tidy, and unlived in. A strong stab of envy swept through her leaving her feeling speechless. This was exactly what she wanted for herself. This was exactly what she didn't have.

Her thoughts were interrupted as she watched in bemusement as Veronica suddenly hit the palm of her hand against her forehead.

'How could I be so stupid,' she said to Ginny 'I do know something. Charles had a phone call early this morning, from Grace's father,' Veronica explained. 'The police found him wandering lost and distraught, he said.'

'Poor, poor man,' Ginny said almost to herself, shaking her head at the thought of what the man must have gone through.

'He'd fallen into a ditch full of water on the moors,' Veronica explained, 'dropped his phone, and the water must have got into it, so he had no way of communicating with anyone.'

'What terrible bad luck,' Ginny said, clutching her mug. 'The whole thing from start to finish has been about bad luck - hasn't it?'

'But also good luck – if David hadn't... ' Veronica reminded her.

'I suppose so,' Ginny replied without conviction. 'David's so desperate to know what's happened to Grace – it's affected him really badly. I've never seen him like this before – it's just not like him to be so emotional.'

'I'll tell Charles, David needs to know what's happening to Grace,' Veronica said. 'Charles definitely said, if it wasn't for David, he thinks Grace wouldn't still be alive... ' Veronica left the sentence hanging.

They stayed silent for a moment, not wanting to fill it with the questions and fears that teemed in their heads.

'Veronica, I must go,' she said, sadly. 'How can I ever thank you?' Ginny began, but found she couldn't say anything else, the words sticking in her throat, and tears threatening to overcome her.

'No need for thanks – but you know that,' Veronica said, 'I just wish it could have all been so different for you – for everybody.' Ginny nodded, she wished it could have been different too. 'Don't worry, Ginny,' Veronica said, 'it will come right in the end, one way or another. I know it. You're strong – I saw how strong you were yesterday. You overcame so many fears out on those moors. I know you can do it at home too.'

'One way or another,' Ginny repeated.

It had all been too much, and so terribly far from what she'd hoped for the weekend that Ginny wanted to runaway and hide. But she couldn't – she knew deep inside that this whole episode had to run its natural course whatever that might be. She had no control over events anymore. Hers and David's life was like a runaway train - on a collision course.

Veronica came over and put her arms around her.

25

It was eleven o'clock by the time Ginny finally arrived at the hospital, after saying an emotional goodbye to Veronica. The roads were quiet; Sunday morning traffic Ginny realized gratefully. The earlier promise of blue skies and sunshine had been a hollow one; greyness and Devonshire drizzle dashing even the most determined of people's hopes.

Ginny found David much as she had left him the evening before: lying with his back to the room, staring out of the window.

'He don't talk much do he?' the elderly man in the bed next to David said, as she walked past. 'Is he all right?'

'He's a bit tired, that's all,' she replied, smiling awkwardly.

'David, I'm here. How are you feeling today?' Ginny asked, bending over to kiss his cheek.

'Did you sleep at all?' she asked, when he turned towards her.

'No. I didn't sleep well, that man snored all night,' he said, pointing an accusing finger at the man in the bed opposite.

'Shh,' Ginny said, 'not so loud, he'll hear you. He looks very sick, he probably couldn't help it.'

'I know he couldn't help it,' David replied, more quietly to Ginny's relief. 'He still kept me awake all night, though.'

Ignoring his tetchy mood, she asked, 'don't you think it would be better if we stayed an extra night here? We could go back to Tavy House, or something - Veronica said our room was still free. It's not as if you'll be going to work tomorrow, and Mum wouldn't mind keeping Bertie for another day. What do you think?'

Ginny waited patiently for him to answer. He still looked frail, she thought. The thin cotton hospital nightgown was making him look so vulnerable.

'I need to get out of here,' David said at last. 'Out of Devon.'

He couldn't have been clearer, even though he didn't let his eyes meet hers. She would like to tell him that every muscle in her body ached, and that her head was throbbing from all the worry about him, and all the heartache about Grace. But she said none of it - only nodded her agreement.

26

Much later, after a day of interminable waiting for David to be discharged, they descended the stone steps and left Tavistock Hospital without looking back. Neither felt they wanted to return. Ever.

The drive home was tense – fraught with long silences, punctuated with stilted conversations. Two people in need of their own space to heal and recover were confined in the small space of their car - emotions thrumming.

'Sleep, David,' Ginny suggested, as soon as they'd found their way back onto the motorway, 'it's what you need, the nurse told you that as well.'

'Mmm,' David answered, his eyes closed.

'You'll need to take a bit of time off work,' she said. 'I'm sure they'll understand – you've worked hard for Silverman's all these years.'

'I'm going in to work tomorrow.' David said, into the strained silence, almost to himself. 'I've already decided.' *And nothing you say or do will change my mind,* Ginny heard in his tone.

'You're going into work tomorrow?' Ginny repeated, unable to believe what he'd just said. 'But that's crazy, David. You've only just come out of hospital. They said that you had to rest – hypothermia is dangerous – you need to give yourself time to recover.'

She gripped the steering wheel tightly, trying to contain her anger, 'I suppose you'll go whatever I say?' she asked, resignation palpable in her voice.

'I need to go,' he explained, more kindly, 'I can't sit around at home, waiting and thinking – can I?'

'I don't know, David. Waiting for what?' Ginny asked, bitterly. 'What more is there to know? Grace has been rescued, and is doing well and her father has been found and reunited with her. I don't see there's anything more to know. Or at least,' she hesitated trying to find the right words, the gentle words, 'that we've got a right to know.'

When Ginny next looked over at him, she saw with relief that he was fast asleep, and for the first time that day, she could feel herself begin to slowly unwind. The miles sped by uneventfully.

A couple of hours later they were on the M25 and halfway home. Evening was rolling in early under a slab of thick cloud. Ginny had used the peace and quiet to think about the idea she'd had for studying again.

Slowing down to join the end of the first tailback of the journey, Ginny saw that David was awake. To fill the uncomfortable silence between them she decided to tell him about her future plans. 'I've made a decision to go back to university. But this time to do Landscape Gardening.'

Ginny had no idea how he would react, but suspected it wouldn't be positive. She could almost hear the cogs of his mind working and held her breath waiting for his response. She decided in those quiet hours while David slept that no matter what he thought, she was still going back to university. And she thought David was stubborn - there was an irony there, she realised.

She could see she had taken him by surprise, 'when did you decide this?' he asked, quietly – she could see the gleam of his eyes as he turned to look at her. She kept her eyes on the road ahead.

'Only recently,' she said, trying to sound nonchalant

'Why, now?' he asked, eventually. 'Isn't it a bit late in the day?'

'Late in the day?' Ginny said, thrown by this unexpected direction. 'I'm not forty yet. What's that got to do with anything, anyway?'

'OK, OK,' David said. Placating. 'Why, now then?'

'The children don't need me as much now they are all at boarding school,' Ginny answered. She didn't mention that he didn't seem to need her either.

'It feels like the right time to do something different,' Ginny said. 'Something for me, this time.'

'What do you mean – this time,' he asked, interrupting her, irritated.

'I missed out on a career.' she said, more sharply than she'd intended. 'I didn't have a chance to finish my degree - if you remember?'

'And you think this is the right time to mention it?' he asked.

Stung by his anger, Ginny felt instant shame roll over her. He was right - she was thinking about herself – not Grace - not David – not the children. It wasn't a good time, Ginny realised. She should have waited until all this had blown over - her timing had been the worst, she admitted to herself - but would any time have been better? And would her newly found resolve have lasted?

Without another word on the subject, she saw David had closed his eyes and dropped off to sleep once more. Relieved to

153

have only her thoughts for company again, she settled down to think some more about her future. Instead of shame, Ginny all of a sudden felt a most wonderful sense of peace. She could feel an excitement bubbling at the prospect of what lay ahead for her. Excitement tinged with nervousness – it was, after all, a big step out of her cosy safe world that she had made for herself.

Arriving in Sandwich sometime after nine that evening, she drove through the gloomy streets, deserted except for a few dog-walkers braving torrential wind and rain. Pools of yellow light glistened on the wet surface of the cobbled streets.

Port Lodge was dripping with rain: rain slid off the roofs, the gutters were groaning with water, the down pipes were delivering a foaming gush into the gulleys - everything looked as though it couldn't soak up another millimetre of rain. Ginny switched off the car engine, closing her eyes for a moment. The constant swish of the wiper blades, the poor visibility in the rain, and the incompetent drivers she'd shared the road with for over six hours, had combined to give her a thumping headache – the silence was bliss.

'I've been thinking,' David said, as he carried the last bag in from the car scurrying to dodge the rain. 'It's probably best if I sleep in the spare bedroom tonight.'

'But why?' Ginny asked, following him into the kitchen.

She couldn't think of the last time they had slept apart – except for David's hospital stay.

'I'm so restless,' he began to explain, embarrassment reddening his face. 'I don't think I'll be able to sleep – I'll only disturb you.'

Ginny watched him busy himself with making tea for them - clattering mugs, filling the kettle, getting the milk from the fridge, and finally stirring sugar into his mug, all with a determined concentration to hide his discomfort.

So it's come to this, she thought, 'if that's what you want,' she said, shrugging and turning away from him - too upset to say anything more. She left the tea he had made her – a small act of rebellion.

She would be glad when the day was over and stayed downstairs until she heard the spare bedroom door close. It was only then she made her way wearily up the stairs to face an empty bedroom, and all that it foretold.

27

Bella heard the front door slam and breathed freely again. It was just after eleven and Steve had left the house for his usual Sunday morning round of golf.

She had listened to the church bells chime every quarter hour since four o'clock. The night hours had brought with it a terrifying decision. Bella could feel every part of her body ache - bruised after Steve's rough handling the evening before. It hadn't stopped at the kick. Steve's anger had spilled over once more in the bedroom. Sleep had been impossible. Pain, that no painkiller could dent, swept through her body in waves, leaving her breathless and afraid. The only sound she could hear were Steve's alcohol-fuelled snores filling the bedroom with angst. He would sleep for hours.

Bella slipped out of bed around six, as soon as fingers of daylight found their way under the bedroom curtains. Biting her lip, to stop moans of pain escaping, she crept silently out of the bedroom.

A creaking floorboard made Bella's heart stop for a second, but the house stayed silent and the rhythm of Steve's snores unchanged. She stood for a moment at the open door of Izzy's bedroom to look at her beautiful, sleep-flushed girl. Ben had slipped in next to her - one arm was flung lazily over his sister's shoulders. She determined there and then that her children's life would be nothing like her own.

Looking in the bathroom mirror for the first time in many months, Bella surveyed the damage. It no longer shocked her. She had seen a similar sight in that mirror too many times before: purple bruising over her right eye, and her cheek bone, a swollen lip. Nothing new there, she thought. What were new were the two faint blue-edged thumbprints on her neck – a shudder ran through her at the sight. It was more frightening than anything that had gone before. Steve's rough thumbs had only been there for a second. Her shriek, high and shrill had pierced his consciousness. Releasing her from his grip. Steve had backed away his face ashen. That was new too.

Quickly putting on her dressing gown that hung on the back of the bathroom door, she buttoned it up to the top – hiding most of the damage from her children's eyes. The rest of the bruising invisible to the eye was to her spirit. It was flayed raw - an angry-red open wound.

When Bella looked in the mirror a few minutes later, concealing make-up in hand, she thought she saw something different in her face – what was it? Studying her reflection more closely, she could see the same thin, dun-brown hair, the same washed-out face, more pallid than ever today. But wait, there it was again – elusive - like the aqua-blue flash of a kingfisher, a dart of light, of colour, of movement – gone even before she had time to focus. But this time she saw it - it was her eyes, she realised. A glint of life had come back into her washed-out blue eyes. Her spirit had not fled after all. It had just lain hidden, dormant.

Waiting for the painkillers to take effect, Bella wandered into the living room. The only sound in the house was the soft padding of her slippers on the stairs. Bella loved this time of the day – alone – peaceful – healing.

Curling up in the armchair next to the fire, she looked out of the window and dreamed of a different sort of day. A family day on the beach, a family picnic in the park, a day of… happiness. She listened instead to the real day beginning - the birds were singing to her – listen they sang – it's a new day – make it yours.

Then Bella remembered the decision she'd made in the night. It had all gone too far - far too far, she thought. Fearing for her life, for the first time the evening before, Bella knew she had to act, before it was too late. She had to confide in someone. A huge step faced her. She trusted no one anymore. And then she thought of Ginny. Doubts circled around her. Would their friendship – her only friendship - survive her dreadful secret? Bella wondered. But realising she had no other option left, Bella decided she would just have to take the risk.

Wrapping herself tightly in her dressing gown, as though it was all that kept her from falling apart, she thought of ten years ago to the day. Today was hers and Steve's wedding anniversary; a time for celebration, a time for cards and presents, but ten years of marriage to Steve had brought her bruises and unhappiness instead.

Last night she suddenly understood for the first time that her hope Steve would change, was nothing but a blind and useless dream. But she also now knew that his anger went through to his very soul. It wasn't shallow - it was a deep and rich vein. His anger was a living and breathing entity - a living demon. A beast that breathed, that fed on the oxygen of her presence – a beast that controlled him – controlled her. His anger defined him. It was in his every cell. His DNA. Bella saw it so clearly now. It was shocking.

Bella sat thinking unthinkable thoughts – she prodded and probed them – allowing them into the open. She let her thoughts breathe and take life, however frightening they were. She felt terrified at what she saw in front of her. She now knew Steve couldn't change - not wouldn't - but couldn't. There was a difference. A big, huge difference. And last night she had finally admitted it to herself.

Her fearful thoughts made her feel restless; she walked painfully into the kitchen and once more pulled her diary from of its hiding place.

She settled down in the armchair again and read the last entry - Valentine's Day.

February 14th 2am

Steve asleep. A letter arrived this morning that upset him. His face went a shade of red and then white. I thought he was going to have a stroke. I didn't dare ask him what it was about. It put him in an even worse mood than usual, shouting at the children and me and breaking my favourite vase deliberately, before he went to work.

He came home in the same mood and during dinner twisted my arm - he said dinner wasn't cooked properly. The sight of the children scurrying upstairs, dinner half-eaten, broke my heart. Arm not broken this time. Finding it difficult to write properly. Managed to keep out of his way upstairs with the children until he went to sleep in his chair –drunk. He might be apologetic in the morning – I doubt it. Some times he is and sometimes he isn't. No flowers or card for Valentines. He threw the one I gave him on the fire.

She noticed she hadn't written about what had happened later; what had happened when he eventually came up to bed. She couldn't write the words - the memory of his rough demands was enough.

She began to write about what had just happened.

March 21ˢᵗ 5am

> *Steve out of control. Really frightened now. I thought he was going to kill me last night. His hands were so tight around my neck. Can't go on like this. Must do something. But what???? Talk to someone. Talk to Ginny???? Would she listen??*

Bella read over what she had just written and decided it said all that needed to be said. Suddenly remembering that Ginny would be home from Devon that evening, she felt a surge of relief. Life always seemed more manageable, she thought, knowing Ginny was nearby.

Allowing her mind to settle wherever it roamed she thought about how it was their wedding day ten years ago today. Her thoughts teemed with memories of wedding dresses, flowers, love, happiness, honeymoon. She remembered thinking how happy she was.

Looking back, Bella realised Steve had managed to hide his anger from her before they were married. *Clever of him.* She could have seen the signs, if she had only thought to look. Even in the first days of their courtship, he was unsure about affection, of closeness. Naively, she thought he was shy. She had always been certain of his attraction to her - that was never in doubt.

This day, Bella checked her watch, seven hours and ten years ago, she would be walking up the aisle. She floated back in time and remembered how she had never seen Steve look so handsome or distinguished. His hair, dark and curly - cut short for their wedding. His physique, slim, powerful, his walk elegant, strong. She remembered her goose bumps of desire.

Why had this handsome man chosen her? She remembered thinking, with a shiver of excitement as she had walked towards him on her father's arm? She couldn't breathe, she was so excited; each step took her nearer to him – each step nearer to her dream life.

Even on her wedding day, her simple ivory wedding dress could not disguise her fragility - her gentle mousiness - her lack of presence. All she brought to the altar was her love. Would it be enough? She had wondered even then.

And then back to the reality of today. Back to the dying embers of her married life, to her bruises. She realised that all the love she had poured into her marriage, hadn't dented his anger towards her, or the world. Ten years ago, she could make his piercing blue eyes shine with passion.

Today, his cold arctic-blue eyes inflicted pain and chilled her to the bone.

28

Monday morning as St Clement's Church bells were chiming ten o'clock, Ginny hit the cast iron knocker on Bella's midnight-blue front door. Ginny looked across to the church and saw with disappointment the cloud filled sky held no promise of fine weather.

Just as she wondered if it was a good idea just calling uninvited, the door started to open. Through the gap Ginny saw Bella's eyes widen with surprise.

'Bella, it's only me,' Ginny said, taking a step nearer the door. 'I'm sorry to come unannounced but…' her voice trailed off seeing the consternation on Bella's face. She took a step back, ready to leave – but wait a minute, was that fear she could see on Bella's face?

'Ginny, I'm sorry but… ' Bella said, backing away from the door.

'Could I come in… please?' Ginny asked, 'just for a bit.'

Ginny had conceived her plan to call on Bella, when the hollowness of the empty space in her bed kept her awake most of the previous night. David had done as he'd said he would and gone to work that morning, despite her protestations. He couldn't miss the Monday morning partners meeting apparently. Frustrated by him, and worried for him in equal measure, she was, in the end, glad to see him go.

Feeling incredibly embarrassed at her intrusion, she stood

with one foot half in Bella's door, clearly unwanted. *It's my own stupid fault, I should have phoned first.* Her instincts though, were telling her not to go. Some sixth sense was at work. Her foot remained in place.

'Are you on your own, Bella?' Ginny asked, worried that maybe Steve was still at home. After what seemed an age, Bella nodded.

'Could we perhaps have a cup of tea together - and then I'll go?' Ginny said, her voice as gentle as she could make it, 'please?' To Ginny's relief, Bella nodded, and opened the door slowly – reluctantly.

She lost no time in stepping through the doorway, before Bella changed her mind. She followed her through the dark, narrow, half-timbered hallway, so it was only when they reached the kitchen that Ginny finally understood Bella's reluctance.

They faced each other in the bright sunny kitchen looking over a pretty courtyard. It wasn't the courtyard though that caught Ginny's attention; she tried, but failed to hide her shock at the sight of Bella's face. She could see bruising all down one side of her face, and was that a bruise on her neck? Could it be a thumbprint?

Ginny understood everything now. The mounting uncertainty had fallen away to reveal what she had begun to suspect. Bella's face was suffused with embarrassment and felt a sharp stab of remorse. She had come here to escape her own problems, maybe even to confide in Bella, but she instantly realised Bella was in desperate need of her help. Her own needs would have to wait.

'Bella, shall I go? I'm so sorry. I didn't mean to… intrude.'

They stood looking at each other, neither knowing what to say, or what to do next.

Bella turned and walked wordlessly over to the other side of the kitchen, picking up the kettle as she went, and filling it at the sink.

'What's happened, Bella?' Ginny asked, breaking the silence. Staying completely still, letting Bella decide what the next step should be.

'It wasn't a door this time – was it?' Ginny asked, after a few moments to break the unbearable tension filling the room.

Bella turned towards her, and Ginny saw tears rolling down Bella's face.

Rushing over to her, arms wide, Ginny knocked over a chair in the narrow, unfamiliar kitchen.

'Bella – come here – I didn't mean to make you cry,' Ginny said, with a catch in her throat. 'I'm just so worried about you.' She was so thin, Ginny thought, as she hugged her. Her fingers could feel the sharpness of her bones.

'You're right, of course - it wasn't a door,' Bella said. 'It never was.' A tremulous smile flitting across her face.

'Tea first I think - talk after - perhaps,' Ginny said, looking around her properly for the first time since she'd entered Bella's house.

Leaded windows overlooked what Ginny could now see was a tiny garden, created by someone with great flair for colour and texture: miniature box topiary, feathery grasses, nestled happily with sun yellow daffodils. A riot of tulips, all shades of orange through to red, and whites to yellows, planted in ceramic pots jostled for attention in every inch of space, all against a warm-red ancient brick wall.

Turning back into the kitchen, she looked at Bella for a second, with fresh eyes, and then took a moment to take in the pretty kitchen. She was surprised at how charming it all looked. Seventeenth century oak timbers ran across the ceiling and walls, marrying contentedly with the buttermilk paintwork. Matching blue chair cushions, and curtains gave the kitchen character. Colourful amateur pictures of landscapes, vases of flowers, bowls of fruit, jostled with Ben and Izzy's artwork. A scrubbed wooden table with a jam jar of yellow Forsythia, took centre stage.

Ginny took it all in at a glance, and saw in it a Bella who she had always guessed existed.

'Bella,' she breathed in wonder, 'it's quite, quite beautiful.'

She watched Bella move awkwardly around the kitchen, wincing with pain, trying not to let Ginny see. Ginny saw. But she also saw the pleasure of her compliment soften Bella's face - the pain forgotten for a moment.

And then she looked at Bella again; and saw the same thin, mousy woman, wearing unattractive brown-green layers – at such variance with what she saw around her. How could that be? Ginny felt pleased with herself that she hadn't judged Bella by her appearance.

'It's... what I can do,' Bella said, pouring the tea. 'I have such ideas... '

'Me too,' Ginny said, smiling.

'We can sort this out you know,' Ginny said, hearing an echo of Veronica's words from the day before, 'somehow – whatever it is.' Sadness descended at the thought of the empty place beside her in the bed last night, and her hopes for the weekend in tatters.

Bella handed her a piece of pear and rose water cake on a yellow striped plate.

'Mmm, delicious. Is there no end to your talents?' Ginny asked, in appreciation.

'The cottage is so small, smaller than you're used to– are you sure your comfortable? I can get another cushion if you want.' Bella said, rising painfully from her chair.

'Sit down, Bella,' Ginny said, and then more gently. 'There's no need, really. Everything's fine, beautiful in fact. So no more, "sorrys". OK? Not between us anyway.' 'You're not on your own,' Ginny added. 'I can help you.' But as she said the words, Ginny realised she didn't have the least idea what help she could give, or even what help was needed. But more than anything, she realised, she wanted to do something for this defeated and broken woman.

Ginny was relieved to see the corners of Bella's mouth lift into a half smile.

'Tell me, Bella' Ginny suggested, pausing, '... it may help, you know.'

The kitchen fell into silence. 'You don't have to,' Ginny added, 'we can just have this cup of tea together, and then I'll go. And we don't need to speak of it ever again. Or... '

Ginny thought how bleak that sounded.

A moment hung – an important moment for both of them. Ginny watched conflict and pain ripple across Bella's face. Ginny held her breath – waiting – dreading Bella refusing to tell her – but also dreading what she may about to be told.

'I'm sorry...' Bella began. Ginny pushed her hand across the space that divided them, and touched Bella's hand gently with the tips of her fingers. Bella startled, looked down with

166

consternation at Ginny's hand, and then slowly, thoughtfully, looked back up at Ginny's face.

'Is it Steve…?' Ginny asked again. The tips of her fingers were still touching Bella's, a gentle contact, reassuring. Bella nodded, silently, and Ginny let out the breath she hadn't realised she'd been holding. Tears fell down both their faces – both knew that a line had just been crossed.

'And a few weeks ago… ?' Ginny asked, determined not to waste the moment. Bella nodded again.

Wondering if she had the skills for this, Ginny could feel panic begin to well up. Could she make it worse? Ginny wondered. Then she asked herself what could be worse?

'Have you spoken about… it, to anyone, Bella?' Ginny asked. 'What about your family?' It made Ginny realise that however bad things stood between her and David, this was worse – far, far worse. Indescribably worse.

'My father's dead,' Bella continued, 'and my brothers are a complete waste of space.'

Bella's life history in such a short sentence, Ginny thought. How isolated she must feel, and with sudden understanding it became clear to her, how Steve felt he could get away with what he did. Bella had been made to think she was on her own. She shuddered at the thought.

'Like most families then – incomplete and dysfunctional at times,' Ginny said. For a second, a gleam of understanding passed between them.

'My mother has dementia and is in a home. I can't visit her as much as I would like.' Ginny could see how much this pained her, it would pain her too.

'I tried telling my mother,' Bella said, 'I knew she couldn't

understand though. She doesn't understand anything anymore.'
Bella's shoulders drooped as she spoke. 'But she did give me a
look, when I told her. It was as if… just for a second, she was
there with me, again. I miss her so much. She never knew about
Steve. I hid it from her - from everybody.'

The look of sadness on Bella's face wrenched Ginny's heart.

'They advised me not to marry him, you know?' Bella said,
'all of my family. Chaotic though they all were, they still saw
something I didn't.'

'They're your family,' Ginny said, pausing to think, 'I
suppose, whether you were close or not, they know you like
nobody else does. They sensed it maybe,' Ginny added helplessly, totally uncertain if she was right.

'He wasn't always like… this, you know?' Bella said, trying
to explain, wanting Ginny to understand.

'How long…?' Ginny asked, trying to hide her incomprehension of why any husband would want to hurt his wife.

'Just after Izzy was born,' Bella answered, biting her lip,
ashamed that she'd put up with it for so long. 'Steve does love
me – in his own way.'

'Eight years?' Ginny said, unable to hide her incredulity.
She put both her hands over Bella's, her breath stuck in her
throat. What Bella had gone through, Ginny could only
wonder at.

'We've been married ten years – it's our anniversary today,'
Bella said with a laugh that held no pleasure. 'Steve won't
remember though.'

It was while Ginny was trying to take in what Bella had just
told her, she noticed a square of paper laying on the table. It was
an ordinary piece of paper, but what had caught Ginny's eye

was the writing. It had been scored so deeply into the paper it had torn holes in places. The children probably, Ginny thought.

She looked up to find Bella staring at her intently with a face so pale it looked bloodless.

'What, Bella? What is it?' Ginny said, beginning to panic that maybe Steve had come home. The room suddenly seeming to have become darker - claustrophobic.

'What is it?' Ginny repeated in a whisper this time, not liking the desperate look on Bella's face. 'Bella, tell me. Please. You're worrying me.' Bella looked down at the piece of paper, and Ginny saw her recoil.

'It's my "to do" list,' Bella said, mortification now reddening her previously deathly pale cheeks. 'I'm given one every day.'

Ginny was intrigued that something so innocuous could cause such a reaction from Bella.

Ginny couldn't tell if it were Bella's writing, or not. But what was so worrying about a '*to do*' list? Ginny wondered. *Everyone wrote them —didn't they?*

Bella sat down, and start to pull at a loose thread on her cardigan.

The piece of paper lay between them on the table - Ginny's fingers were now touching the edge of it. She could see that at the top of the page the words 'TO DO' had been scored in red capital letters. But for some reason – she didn't want to pick it up. Instead, she tidied the crumbs on her plate, pushing them around the edge hiding the pretty rose pattern. Ginny's eyes kept coming back to the words, 'TO DO' - the letters had been gone over and over many times.

'Steve writes it for me. He was very angry with me this morning.' Bella said, her words sticking in her throat, shame suffusing her face. 'Hiding his guilt, I think.'

Ginny took a deep breath, 'can I look?'

Bella nodded, her face flushed with humiliation.

Ginny took the list, it was written on a square of cheap white paper, thin and semi-transparent. It had been torn from a pad, some gum still hung from the top margin. Steve, Ginny noticed had ignored the narrow, feint, blue lines. He had used a red biro, and because of the thinness of the paper, the ink had bled slightly leaving the writing fuzzy and difficult to read.

Her breathing slowed as she read:

1. *With a toothbrush clean all the toilets with bleach.*

2. *Take everything out of the oven. Clean the inside with oven cleaner.*

3. *Scrub the kitchen floor.*

4. …

The list was endless - detailed and demeaning; Ginny couldn't bear to read anymore. The man must be sick, she reckoned. No sane person would treat his or her wife or partner like this, surely? *Poor, poor Bella.* She was beginning to have an understanding of what it was like to be a victim of domestic abuse. She knew now why people didn't leave their abusive partners – fear – control – domination. She looked up to find Bella watching her intently.

'He writes it every morning at the breakfast table,' Bella said, biting her lip as she spoke to stop it trembling.

'Every morning?' Ginny couldn't stop herself exclaiming. 'Oh, Bella, that's… terrible.'

Bella nodded in agreement, her face long with unhappiness.

She continued, 'he writes it while he's eating his cornflakes that I have to put in his favourite bowl, with just the right amount of milk and sugar. His cup of tea mustn't be too strong, or too weak, and I mustn't make a noise stirring in the sugar, and then there's his toast... '

'Bella,' Ginny said, 'I'm so... sorry. What can I do to help?'

'When he's finished his tea,' Bella continued, as though Ginny hadn't spoken, 'he opens the drawer, you can see it at the end of the table, and takes out his pad of paper, and his red pen. The drawer squeaks horribly,' Bella added. 'I hear that squeak in my sleep.'

Ginny couldn't resist looking at the drawer with a horrible fascination - she was beginning to feel physically sick, she didn't think she could hear anymore. *Ginny get a grip.*

'He chews his pen for a bit,' Bella continued, 'while he thinks about what to write on the list for that day.'

Pausing, Bella looked out of the window, Ginny waited, her breath held.

'Each item always has a number – the ones that are important have an asterisk. He takes such care drawing those asterisks. Steve prides himself on that,' Bella murmured, her eyes far away.'

Ginny couldn't bear it a second longer. She was beginning to feel ill with repulsion for this sick, horrible man that Bella was married to. How could he? Ginny raged inwardly.

Ginny put her arms round Bella. 'Bella,' Ginny said, wanting to calm the situation, 'that's enough now, you're making yourself too upset. I'm getting worried about you.'

Bella's eyes widened, as though surprised to find Ginny in her kitchen. 'We don't need to do this all at once,' Ginny said, 'it's too much for you.'

Bella needed someone more skilled than her to help, Ginny thought, suddenly panicking at the responsibility of it all.

'Bella, what do you say we go for a walk? Ginny suggested, pleased with the idea. 'Let's get out of the house and take the dogs for a walk, and clear our heads.' Quickly consulting her watch, 'it's only just after eleven. There's plenty of time before you have to collect the children from school.' Ginny didn't mention the list of chores.

'I've had an idea – well, a couple really,' Ginny said, putting on her coat, 'it's why I came around this morning - to tell you. And I want to know how the campaigning went at the weekend.'

'You'll need some wellies on,' Ginny said, smiling to herself, hearing her mother in her words. 'It's going to be muddy over the fields,'

Bella looked over at Ginny, and gave her a tremulous smile.

29

They arrived in Ash, a tiny village on the borders of Sandwich, just as the clock of the eleventh century flint built St Nicholas Church pealed the half-hour. Ginny squeezed her car into the tiny village car park. The two dogs, Bertie and Rosie, tumbled out in unalloyed excitement.

Ginny, led Bella and the two dogs through the church kissing-gate and into the cemetery. The stone path next to the banks of memorial stones, celebrating the many lives and deaths of the locals, led straight out into flattish grasslands typical of south-east Kent. Ahead, lay overgrown hedges and wind blasted trees. In the far distance, the dot of a few cottages could be seen. The landscape was empty – no one to disturb them.

'Right then,' Ginny said, using a voice that was redolent of her days as head girl. 'Lets walk over to the pond; it isn't far and there's somewhere to sit out of this wind.'

When they had settled themselves, Ginny asked tentatively if Bella would start from the beginning.

'It's difficult to… ' Bella hesitated, hunched against the cold, hands pushed deep into her coat pockets.

'I know. And don't, if you don't want to,' Ginny suggested, her attention momentarily diverted. 'Bertie come here, at once. Stay near me, and don't even look at those sheep or you'll be shot - either by me or by the farmer,' she warned darkly.

'You haven't met Steve,' Bella eventually mumbled.

'No, I haven't,' Ginny agreed, not immediately understanding why that might be important, 'does that matter?' Nor did she want to. *Horrible man.*

'It's just that you'll only be hearing one side of the story. My side,' Bella explained.'

'Yes, but it's your side I want to hear,' Ginny said, 'and can I assume Steve doesn't have a black eye too?' And realising she may have gone too far, she laid her hand on Bella's arm for a moment. 'Sorry, Bella, that sounded harsh.'

'You tell me in your own way, and I promise not to be judgemental,' Ginny suggested, wondering how on earth she was going to be able to keep her word.

'You have to understand,' Bella said, 'he had a difficult childhood.'

'I'll remember that.' Ginny promised.

Bastard.

30

With the chill breeze caressing her cheek as it went scurrying on its way, Bella felt a surge of energy that had been missing from her life for too many years. Although she and Ginny had left the medieval church behind them Bella could still hear the deep sonorous bells tolling the quarter hours. The air reverberated with the joyous toll and sent a quiver through her body. What happened next, Bella knew with an inexplicable deep-rooted conviction, would change her life forever. The possibility that she might not have to live the life she had been forced to live, these last ten years with Steve, was making her feel dizzy with hope.

As they sat, Bella tried to decide where to begin – how could she find the words to explain to Ginny all she had been through? She hadn't missed for a second the decisive tone in Ginny's voice – she wasn't going to get away without telling Ginny the whole unpalatable truth. But at the same time she dreaded Ginny thinking it all sounded so pathetic - so miserable. How to explain, Bella wondered, to anyone when she didn't fully understand herself how it had all happened?

She could feel herself begin to crumble as she strove to find the right words to tell her story. None of the words that hurtled into her mind – abuse, physical violence, mental violence - spoke of how it had all made her feel. *Maybe that's where I should start - with my feelings.* It was only when she felt Ginny's hand on her arm, did she realise she was crying. Bella felt the comfort of Ginny's arm tucked in hers.

Ginny was right, Bella thought, it was the perfect spot to sit – the perfect spot for secrets – not another soul in sight or in hearing. They sat quietly by the edge of the pond watching ducks and moorhens busily paddling, oblivious to their onlookers. Reeds, waving gently in the faint breeze, edged the pond providing homes for many unseen creatures.

Bella could feel her face grow stiff with pain and cold. The feel of Ginny's arm through hers was, at the same time, embarrassing and comforting. She knew too that Ginny would be able to feel her trembling.

'Go on, Bella,' she heard Ginny say, so quietly it sounded like a whisper.

Was Ginny strong enough to hear what she had to say? The last thing she wanted was to frighten Ginny away - the thought of losing her friendship was more than Bella could bear right now.

But then Bella's sobs began to subside, and she found that although her voice had no strength she felt ready to say the words. She knew it was time. She decided she would just have to deal with the consequences whatever they were. She fixed her eyes on one of the ducks, watching it circle aimlessly. She daren't look at Ginny as she started her story.

'He hits me,' Bella whispered, and then, as her voice got stronger, she repeated the words louder and louder until the birds nesting in the reeds rose in a plume, forming mumurations against the cloud filled sky.

They weren't the only ones to be disturbed. Bella knew she now faced unknown waters - waters that might rush and roar, drowning her - leaving her defeated. She watched Ginny trying to catch hold of what she was telling her, and saw the look of incomprehension that was creasing her forehead and pinching her mouth into a thin line.

'Steve hits me,' Bella repeated, as though having found her words, she needed to hear them again and again. These words were new to her; she had never heard them before from her own lips. They were frightening - demanding.

'He hurts me... he hurts me... HE HURTS me... HE HURTS ME.' Bella could feel her voice rising in its awful refrain, edging closer, and closer to hysteria. And as her voice rose to a crescendo the rest of the birds fled the reeds.

It was only the pressure of Ginny's arms around her that kept Bella from falling. Falling into the abyss of the dark world that had suffocated her for so long. She could feel Ginny move closer, protective, supportive. Ginny was totally silent – saying nothing. Just there - where she was needed.

31

They sat there, the two women, by the pond, watching the scurrying clouds bring with them a deep grey gloom.

Each of them felt bewildered by what had just happened. Each of them with their own thoughts. Bella knew denial was now no longer possible. She couldn't bear to look at Ginny; her sense of shame was overwhelming.

'The first time,' Bella began again, calmer. The words took her back to a time she had long tried to forget, deep, deep buried. 'The first time Steve hit me, was when Izzy was a baby. A newborn baby,' Bella said for emphasis.

She looked straight ahead, she didn't want to see the look of horror on Ginny's face, but she knew it would be there. She could imagine it. 'I can't remember what I was like in those days – I remember being happy though – my life was full of hope and promise. Steve killed so much that day…'

Bella paused, her thoughts taking her back to those moments when Steve had walked into the nursery. Ginny was now her Ancient Mariner – she could no longer stop this tale.

'We were in the nursery… Steve and I had prepared it together for the baby. We'd had such fun. The pregnancy was a surprise – we'd only been married a year. We'd still been getting to know each other, when we suddenly had to start thinking of ourselves as parents.' It sounded to Bella that she was making excuses for what happened next.

'We painted the walls the palest of yellows. You know that colour of the autumn sun? Gentle, welcome – it was that yellow. The sun was always shining in the nursery. It seemed to be a sign. We put up muslin curtains, and if the window was open they would move in the breeze, like a gossamer web. We chose everything together. We bought mobiles and toys for the tiny nursery. We were both so excited and took joy in all our silliness. We spent time in the nursery together, sitting hand in hand, trying to imagine how it would be,'

Bella had to stop; looking down she found strands of her hair between her fingers where she had pulled it as she spoke. Lifting her head daring to meet Ginny's eyes, she saw compassion and horror in equal mix.

'Izzy was just two weeks old,' Bella continued, 'she was tiny, helpless, slightly premature, and we had to be extra careful with her. I was singing to her as I breast-fed her. I can still remember the song.'

Bella, in a clear pretty voice, quiet and gentle, started to sing:

'Hush, little baby, don't say a word.
Papa's gonna buy you a mockingbird
And if that mockingbird won't sing.
Papa's gonna buy you a diamond ring
And if that diamond ring turns brass,
Papa's gonna buy you a looking glass

'I was concentrating so hard on feeding Izzy and singing that I didn't see Steve come into the room, and that, do you see became part of the surprise? Part of the shock - I didn't know he was there until… '

Bella stopped again and gulped for air, her hand was gripping her mouth, her eyes tight shut, 'until… I was aware of a shadow across my cheek and a second later – the shadow had gone. It had been his hand. He hit me with such force that my mouth bled, instantly spattering Izzy's white shawl with drops of her own mother's blood.'

Bella heard Ginny's exclamation of horror, a long high note, 'no… oo.' But Bella was miles away now, her mind streaking back to the moment her life collapsed. *Blood red on the purest of white. Evil defiling innocence.* 'That moment has defined my life ever since,' Bella said.

Bella looked up, she could feel her heart racing, her cheeks hot, surprised to see the birds had slowly returned to the reeds and were chirruping their pleasure at being safely back home - for a moment, she couldn't remember where she was exactly. And then she saw Ginny, still sitting quietly beside her motionless, except for tears pouring down her face.

Looking back, Bella remembered the next five minutes in the nursery, memories came tumbling out freed at last from the dark recesses of her mind, but she could find no words to tell Ginny. Instinctively, Bella remembered, she had clutched Izzy to her, to protect her daughter from her own father. She opened her mouth in horror, to yell, to warn, to fight. The pain in her jaw, remembered, sharp, all the more brutal for its deliverer. No sound came – not then. The force of the punch had unbalanced her, and she remembered clinging onto the muslin curtain with one hand. Why wasn't it velvet, brocade, anything but this flimsy muslin material? Bella's other hand clinging onto the baby, she had to stop herself from falling, anything – anything - to stop the baby being hurt. Bella still dreamt about the sound of tearing muslin.

'Steve walked out of the room,' she told Ginny, 'with no explanation, no words, just the slamming of the door behind him. Can you imagine how that would feel? How that would sound? I hear that slam…' Bella watched Ginny shake her head, her face paler even than Bella's. 'It's OK Ginny, really, I got used to it – he never went near the nursery again – it became a place of safety.' Bella slumped in the chair, drained, all emotion gone and sang the rest of the song, quietly, to herself:

And if that looking glass gets broke,
Papa's gonna buy you a billy goat
And if that billy goat won't pull,
Papa's gonna buy you a cart and bull
And if that cart and bull turn over,
Papa's gonna buy you a dog named Rover
And if that dog named Rover won't bark
Papa's gonna buy you a horse and cart
And if that horse and cart fall down,
You'll still be the sweetest little baby in town.

32

Ginny was frozen, the bench by now felt hard and unyielding. For the last while, Bella's story had made her want to run away from the cruel world Bella inhabited.

'I should have left him. But I didn't,' Bella said, shrugging her shoulders. 'I did leave for a few days. I went back to my parents, which if I'm honest was only marginally better than being at home. Steve called every day after work, looking sheepish, begging me to come back.'

"Bella, I'm so sorry,' Steve said, 'I was jealous of your love for the baby. There didn't seem to be any room left for me anymore.'

'Those were the only honest words, I think I ever heard him speak,' Bella said, sadly. 'Eventually he wore me down - I couldn't resist the sorrowful look in his eyes, and of course, the promises that it wouldn't happen again. He looked like a frightened child. I just so wanted to believe him. I still loved him, you see?'

Ginny didn't see.

'I wanted to believe him,' Bella continued. 'You don't know how much I regret going back.'

'Bella... but why?' Ginny said, in a strangled voice.

'What else could I have done?' Bella asked, pleading with Ginny to understand her decision. 'I couldn't live at home, not with my brothers. They were as near as you can get to being villains.'

'There must have been some way?' Ginny said, unsure of her ground.

'Oh I know how simple it must sound,' Bella burst out, in her defence. 'But it's not. It's... complicated. I suppose at its simplest - I still loved him. So I forgave him,' Bella hung her head, and Ginny's heart went out to her. Maybe she would have done the same in her circumstances, thankfully she would never know.

'You wouldn't recognise the *old* Bella,' she told Ginny, 'that's how I think of myself, by the way. The *old* Bella wasn't a coward, she would have remonstrated with him – but there was Izzy to think of, and then later Ben and somehow I managed. It was almost like being struck down with a chronic illness that you had to live with, to get on with, to live your life in spite of it.'

'I have a voice in my head, you know, Ginny,' Bella said, 'that says all the things you are probably thinking, It sits on my shoulder remonstrating with me, accusing me of cowardice – it tells me how weak and mousy I've become – and I answer: *What can I do? I have no money, nowhere to go. He loves me really. One day he'll stop. He can't help it. He loves me really.*'

She didn't feel she could say anymore, and she could see Ginny was struggling with what she had just been told.

'Bella, I think you're the bravest woman I know,' Ginny said, 'you've been through some truly terrible times – and I'm sure you haven't told me the half of it. I'm glad actually, because I don't think I could listen to anymore without wanting to go and... oh - I don't know... confront Steve, or something. It couldn't have been easy telling me – and now I feel so inadequate. I arrogantly thought there would be something I could do. Make a difference somehow. But now… I feel so useless to you.'

'Don't say that, Ginny,' Bella implored, 'just by listening – you've helped. By letting me tell you. By sitting by my side. I know it couldn't have been easy for you to listen.'

Ginny felt a chill run down her spine, all this and the emotional chaos reigning in her own home – it was all too much. She mustn't let Bella guess though about her own problems. She forced a bright smile on her face.

In the distance, they could hear the bells tolling one o'clock.

'I must get back,' Bella murmured, 'I've stuff to do before I pick the children up.'

Ginny nodded, 'OK. But you do know, Bella, that what you've told me today about Steve, must be stopped – you can't go on like this. He might end up… '

'Don't say it,' Bella said, putting her hand up to her neck.

'It doesn't surprise me at all, what you've just told me,' Ginny said, hoping Bella might not feel so guilty. 'I'd begun to wonder about all those, 'accidents' with doors. Telling someone is the first step, the hardest step perhaps, and now you've done that maybe everything might feel a bit easier for you.'

As Ginny spoke, she pointed to a heron that had landed on the other side of the pond, 'it's lovely here isn't it? Just the right place to let go of all those horrible memories.'

'I'm sorry,' Bella began, looking downcast, 'if I'd known…'

'If you'd known – what then Bella?' Ginny asked. 'You'd have kept it locked away for another year or two?'

Bella nodded. 'You're right of course.'

Ginny got up, stretching, 'it's getting even colder, my back has stiffened up - all that driving yesterday, I suppose.' She didn't mention the four hours of riding over the moors. She'd leave that for another day.

'I'm so sorry, you must think me terribly selfish. I haven't asked you about Devon.' Bella said, getting to her feet too, and stamping the ground to bring some life back to her feet.

'Don't worry about that. I'll tell you all about Devon, another time - it's you I'm worried about, right now.'

'I think you need some advice,' Ginny said after a while, explaining quickly when she saw Bella's worried face. 'Professional advice I mean, legal advice, that sort of thing. I've begun to realise I don't know enough.'

'I'm not sure… 'Bella said, and shuddered. 'What if Steve found out?'

'He wouldn't, Bella, I promise you,' Ginny explained. Another promise I have to keep, Ginny thought, heavily. 'I've been thinking while you were talking, about this friend of mine, she's a solicitor. I'd trust her completely. She works in… this sort of area. She's changed her job recently and now works in Dover, at the women's refuge centre. She would know what you could do – what your options are – who to speak to – that sort of thing.'

For one awful moment Ginny felt the unwelcome weight of her responsibility towards Bella, and a sense of shame engulfed her. *I can do this – I must do this.*

'I'm going to phone Leila tonight anyway,' Ginny explained, forcing herself to sound confident. 'I wanted to ask about her new job anyway, and to hear about her new boyfriend.'

Ginny watched Bella turn pale, and realised it was too soon. Bella wasn't ready yet.

'I wouldn't say who you were,' Ginny reassured her, 'or where you lived, or anything like that. I'd just make a general enquiry, that's all.'

The clouds parted for a minute, and as they rounded the last corner, Ginny saw that the church spire was lit with a ray of sunshine. It seemed to be some sort of sign, but she had absolutely no idea of what.

'I need time to think about it,' Bella said. 'I feel… different now. I'm not sure if I can go through all that again with some-one I don't know.'

'I can't imagine how difficult it must have been for you. So don't worry about… anything' Ginny said, starting up the car and turning for home. 'I'm glad it was me you chose to tell.'

'Why did you call this morning, by the way?' Bella asked. 'Didn't you say you had something to tell me? What was it?'

'Don't worry, it's fine. I only wanted to tell you about my plan,' Ginny smiled, as she pulled out onto the road back to Sandwich – back to reality.

Ginny said little as she drove, her thoughts occupied her: thoughts of the terrible things Steve had done to Bella, and thoughts of how David was slowly slipping away from her.

The quay was quiet, when Ginny pulled in to the car park.

'I've decided I want to do some studying, 'Ginny said, and turned to look at Bella, 'I need to change my life too. But I'll tell you about it some other time. You've much more important things to think about at the moment. Come to mine for a cup of tea. Later in the week?'

'No. Tell me more, now, I'd really like to hear,' Bella demanded. 'It will take my mind off my own problems. 'But why do you want to change your life? It's perfect isn't it?'

Ginny raised an eyebrow. *Perfect?*

'OK, nearly perfect then,' Bella amended. 'You look so happy and… together.'

'Well… ' Ginny hesitated, she still felt foolish talking about it. 'I want a career.'

'What career? Why? When?' Bella asked, both women laughed at the staccato of questions. 'I thought you liked being at home?'

'I did. I do. Ginny announced, shyly. 'Come over Thursday? Are you busy? I'll tell you about it then.'

Ginny saw a sparkle in Bella's eyes, as she nodded her acceptance, realising for the first time how pretty her smile was.

'Have you been to see the gardens at The Salutation?' Ginny asked, and when Bella shook her head, 'I know the head gardener, Carl Jansen; he's my new neighbour. He started working there recently to restore the original Lutyens gardens.' *What a dream job.*

'I want you to come on a course with me - keep me company,' Ginny said. 'It's about the historic garden. Carl is giving the talk so we can both get in free.' Ginny continued, unperturbed by Bella's look of fright. 'It's in the day, just for a few hours, once a week. Please come with me? I don't want to go on my own.'

'But, how – could I?' Bella spluttered.

'It would be while the children are at school and Steve… '

'… would be at work – and would never know,' Bella finished the sentence for her.

'Ginny,' Bella said, her words tripping over themselves. 'I've changed my mind. I want you to talk to your friend.'

Ginny couldn't resist, even in the constricted space of the

car, flinging her arms around her. 'Bella, I'm so proud of you.'

33

Later that evening, Ginny was pottering about in the Orchid House, far away thinking of her future. David was already asleep - in the spare room. His perfunctory replies, when he got back from work, did nothing to make her think he was in a more receptive mood. He looked terrible, grey and haunted, and hadn't appreciated at all her mentioning it. No, she hadn't heard any more about Grace. And with that he'd gone straight to bed. A feeling of absolute rejection and loneliness swept through her.

Her mobile rang, giving her a welcome diversion from her annoyance.

'I'm so pleased you rang.' Ginny said, to her friend, Leila Mistry, a lawyer working with victims of domestic abuse.

'Are you all right, Ginny?' Leila asked, 'you sound… '

Ginny put down her gardening tools and settled into one of the old wicker armchairs.

'I'm fine,' Ginny replied laughing. 'I was just feeling a bit bored that's all.'

'You? Bored? Leila said, with disbelief.

'Tell me about your new job,' Ginny asked, hoping to distract her.

'Exhausting,' Leila replied, with a loud sigh. Work, work, work. I don't think I've surfaced since I started this new job, and it's only been a few weeks. I'm getting to be a really boring person. No riding, no going out, just more work.'

'It'll get better, will it?' Ginny asked. 'You're enjoying it though?'

'Love it,' Leila answered, quickly dispelling Ginny's fears, 'and yes it will get better in time when we have everything running smoothly.'

Ginny smiled at Leila's enthusiasm, pleased for her, and hoped that one day she might herself feel the same about her own job. Already - in her head - she was winning major awards for her landscaping projects.

'Tell me more,' Ginny asked.

'I work with Debbie, the manager of the refuge, who's a fantastic person - so calm and knowledgeable. She never gets ruffled – sadly she's seen it all before. But what's wonderful about her, is she hasn't grown at all cynical.'

Bella would need someone like Debbie, Ginny thought.

'I'm ashamed to say I've no idea… ' Ginny confessed, 'what goes on?'

'I work in a team: the police, social workers, and solicitors, that's where I come in, independent domestic violence advisors. All of us help support the women through the Criminal Justice System, and try to put them, and their family back on their feet.'

'And the refuge? Where does that fit in?' Ginny asked.

'The women,' Leila answered, 'who are trying to escape an abusive partner, can live at the refuge while the legalities, safe housing, criminal investigations, and financial help are sorted out for them and their children.'

'It sounds as though you're involved in something amazing,' Ginny said. 'I'm so proud of you - so proud of the difference you'll be making to these women's lives. Is it always women? I suppose it probably is.'

'Mostly, but not all,' Leila explained. 'It's not always about physical abuse, you know, it's also about humiliation, degradation – mental abuse. And women are strong enough to do that too.'

'But how does it all happen? How does anybody let their partner do all that to them?' And then Ginny remembered Bella, and realised exactly how it might happen.

'The victim thinks it's all their fault,' Leila explained, 'and are convinced that if only they were a better wife, husband, partner then the abuse would stop.'

Ginny immediately recognised Bella's situation.

'It doesn't usually stop though,' Leila continued, 'it's very difficult to persuade a victim of abuse, that it's not *their* behaviour that needs to change, but their partner's – and unfortunately more often than not – that doesn't happen.'

'What should someone do… if they're being abused?' Ginny struggled to find the right words. 'I mean what should they do… what's the very first thing they should do to get help?'

'We're not talking about you, Ginny, are we?' Leila asked, quietly.

'Me? No, it's not David and me. He's never raised a hand in anger to me. Ever. It's a friend of mine I'm talking about.'

Leila paused, 'it must have taken a lot of courage for your friend to tell you what's been going on in her life. Victims of domestic abuse are extremely good at hiding their real situation. So that must have been a huge step for her.'

'Yes, it was,' Ginny agreed. 'She's a really brave woman.'

'Ginny, tell your friend to phone Debbie,' Leila said. 'If I were a victim of abuse, I would want someone like Debbie on my side - no one's going to hurt her clients once they are under her protection. I'll text you her number later, Debbie's definitely the best person to start with. You've not spoken about this friend before.'

'No. I haven't known her that long,' Ginny explained. 'And there's only so many doors one person can walk into before you begin to wonder.'

'Debbie,' Leila said, 'is the embodiment of kindness and gentleness. She is like a tigress with her cubs. Tell your friend, it will be totally confidential.'

'She sounds just the person my friend needs,' Ginny said with relief.

'It's going to be the second hardest decision your friend might ever have to make,' Leila continued, 'the first was to tell you – so she's going to need a lot of help from you to make the second decision - which is to ring Debbie.'

'Don't worry about anything like that,' Ginny said, 'I'll help her with everything.' And thinking it was time to change the subject, 'don't forget you're coming over with your new boyfriend on Saturday. There's so much we need to catch up on. I want to hear all about him. Matt isn't it? And then there's your mother, is she still really cross with you?'

Leila chuckled, but Ginny could hear sadness as well.

'She's just about speaking to me,' Leila answered. 'She's still terribly disappointed, that I turned down yet another possible husband she'd arranged for me to meet.'

'You've not told her about Matt yet either, have you?' Ginny asked.

Ginny felt such sympathy for Leila, whose traditional Asian parents were insisting on an arranged marriage for her. And unfortunately, Matt was neither Asian, nor Hindu.

'There's nothing to tell them anyway; I've only known Matt for a few months. It's still too early to create a tsunami of emotion in the family. You can imagine how angry they would be. All these Asian boys I've turned down…'

'Would Matt become a Hindu?' Ginny asked cautiously. There was a pause at the other end of the phone and Ginny wondered if she was being too nosy.

'I would have to be very sure Matt's the one, to ask him anything like that,' Leila answered. 'And he would have to be strong enough to cope with the fallout from my family, and I might have to be willing to give up my family for him. So,' Leila paused again for a moment, 'I've decided it's not the right time to tell them. Or Matt for that matter, he might run a mile. And I wouldn't want that.'

"I'm really looking forward to meeting him.'

'Yes we'll both be there on Saturday, and he's looking forward to meeting you too,' Leila answered.

'I hope it works out for you,' Ginny said. 'I'll keep my fingers crossed.'

'By the way, how was Devon? You haven't mentioned it at all.'

How should I answer that? Ginny thought. Should I tell her the truth? She decided on the truth - Bella had – so she should too.

'Not that good, really,' Ginny replied.

'Oh no, why not?'

Ginny could hear Leila sounding more alert, her emotional antenna working.

'Come on, Ginny,' Leila said, into the silence, 'I can tell something's not right, and hasn't been for a while. So come on tell me - what's the matter?'

'You're too tired to listen to my woes,' Ginny said, laughing at how accurate Leila had been.

'I'm not tired anymore,' came the swift reply, energy bristling down the phone. 'You've just woken me up. Come on I want to hear this.'

'Well,' Ginny stumbled, caught off guard by Leila's insistence. 'Things between David and I, are…er…in the doldrums,' Ginny said, reluctantly. 'It's why I thought it would be a good idea for us to go to Devon. I'd hoped it might bring back – I don't know - a spark or something, to our marriage – help us make some sort of connection again.'

Ginny could hear the stillness on the other end of the phone – she knew Leila would be processing the information.

'OK…that seems like a good idea to me - getting away, concentrating on each other – that sort of thing?' Leila said, 'so did the spark come back? Did the idea work?'

'Not exactly. Instead… ' Ginny said, hesitating, 'oh, Leila, it's made things worse. Much, much worse – we're not even sleeping in the same bed anymore.'

'Ginny…' she heard Leila's concern, on the other end of the phone, 'I'm so sorry. But why? What on earth has happened?'

'It's so difficult to explain, even to myself,' Ginny admitted. 'I can't think how David and I got to where we are now.'

Ginny took a gulp of air, 'bringing up a family, creating a home, a shared life and I suppose I thought… that would just go on - forever.'

'Things can be fixed,' Leila said, quietly, professionally. 'You know that. You can get help – professional help. Was it something specific that happened or… '

'Not really, I just started to feel restless,' Ginny admitted, 'when Timmy went off to boarding school, and the house began to feel so empty. And it was then I noticed that David was just carrying on with his own life but it didn't seem to include me as much. And all of a sudden nothing seemed familiar anymore. I felt that everything had changed – my whole life had shifted.'

Ginny got up and switched on a couple of lights that were nestling amongst the orchids. The effect was instantly mesmerising – the orchids seemed to glow with colour. And through the glazed conservatory roof she could see pinpricks of stars sparkling above.

'Go on,' she heard Leila say.

'I'm too young surely for the - empty nest – thing?' Ginny said, 'I'm not even forty yet. Well nearly.'

'You had your children young though, don't forget,' Leila said, 'and they're all away at boarding school now. It's probably nothing to do with your age, I'm no expert, but all your children leaving home would be really hard for any mother. You know, I often wondered how you coped with that.'

'Did you?' Ginny said. 'I never realised.'

'I suppose I hadn't known you long when Tim went off to boarding school,' Leila said, ' what was it two, three years ago?'

'Three years – he's fourteen now,' Ginny swallowed hard to keep the familiar ache of sadness from engulfing her.

'But what's all this got to do with you and David?' Leila asked.

'David isn't happy either,' Ginny admitted. 'It was David that demanded they go to boarding school, not me. I didn't have much say in it.' Ginny could hear her bitterness swirling around the empty room. 'So he should be happy - but he isn't.'

'It sounds to me,' Leila said, slowly, thoughtfully, 'there's more going on than the boys all going off to boarding school.'

'David and I can't... ' Ginny corrected, 'seem to be able to talk to each other anymore.' Pausing, she summed it up, 'and when you can't talk… you can't put anything right. And that, Leila, is what happened in Devon. We didn't put anything right at all – in fact it was an unmitigated disaster.'

Ginny heard the silence down the phone, and knew Leila would be trying to figure out the right thing to say. She could do with a glass of wine. Uncurling her legs she headed for the bottle of red in the fridge and a glass from the cabinet and made her way through her orchids, back to the chair.

'Oh no…. this all sounds really horrid for you,' Leila said,

'And that's not all,' Ginny said, resignedly.

'There's more?' Leila said, her voice hesitant with worry.

'David had an accident while we were away,' Ginny said, reluctantly, and then stopped, unsure of how many problems she could offload onto Leila.

'Is he all right?' Ginny could hear Leila's voice sounded taut with sudden worry.

'He's all right… sort of,' Ginny said.

'Sort of?' Leila pounced on Ginny's words. 'What sort of accident?'

'Not an accident to himself – but to a young girl,' Ginny tried explaining.

Ginny heard a sudden sharp intake of breath at the other end of the phone.

'Ginny, whatever do you mean – a young girl?' Leila asked. 'Is he having an affair? Is that it?'

'No, nothing like that,' Ginny answered, wondering if in fact that was exactly what he was doing. *Was David having an affair at work? The wife was always the last to know.* 'David wasn't hurt, apart from mild hypothermia, that is.'

'Ginny, you're talking in riddles,' Leila said. '*Apart from hypothermia?*'

'David went out onto the moors for a walk while I was riding with Veronica – do you remember I told you about her?'

Ginny heard a loud crackle on her mobile, and for one frustrating moment thought she'd lost signal. D*amn.*

'Are you still there, Leila?'

'Yes, I'm here,' Leila answered, 'I've moved into the bedroom now to get a better reception. Go on, you were telling me… '

'While David was walking, he came across a young girl trapped in the river,' Ginny stopped, choked with the memory of seeing Grace, unsure now whether she could carry on.

'Sounds awful,' Leila said, the concern in her voice evident.

'It was, believe me,' Ginny said. 'The young girl, Grace, was alone and very cold, stuck in the water. David tried to rescue her, but he couldn't and then he tried to get help. Veronica and I had a hair-raising ride over Dartmoor to find them. And the marvellous, wonderful horses found them.'

'This is the shortened version, I assume?' Leila said, interrupting her.

'Yes, but it would take longer than you've got, to go into detail,' Ginny explained. 'Another time perhaps. And so now,' Ginny carried on, 'although Grace is still alive, we don't know what the rescue team had to do to get her out of the river. I'm not sure I want to know either - whether I can bear knowing. But not knowing is tearing David apart. Quite simply, he hasn't been the same since. It's affected him so much that he can't even bear to speak about the accident.' *Or to me.*

Ginny finished on a quiet sob – embarrassed at her show of emotion.

'Look, Ginny, I'm coming over? I think you could do with some company.'

It's too late,' Ginny said looking at her watch, nearly midnight. She must have been talking for longer than she thought. *Poor Leila.* 'You've got work in the morning. But thank you – I'll be all right, honestly. We'll talk some more soon. I promise.'

'Maybe David's going through a… mid-life crisis,' Leila suggested, 'and you just have to hang on in there until he's over it.'

'Well he was rather enamoured of a young woman staying at Tavy House when we were there,' Ginny said, beginning to wonder if maybe… no he couldn't be having an affair… could he? Ginny shivered, despite the heat in the conservatory.

'You must have kept all this to yourself for a while now then,' Leila said intuitively, 'I wish you'd told me about it sooner.'

'I wish I had now too,' Ginny said, sadly 'but you know at the time you think it's all going to blow over. Well… it hasn't'.

Leila stayed silent throughout. A good listener, Ginny realised, grateful for being allowed to get it out of her head, into words. Shared.

'David's obviously completely traumatised by what happened at the river, it must have been terrible for him,' Leila said. But that doesn't explain what's happened to you and him up to that point. Have you thought of counselling? It can be really helpful.'

'I'll think about it,' Ginny said, doubting David would agree to go. 'Anyway you must be exhausted, Leila. Thank you so much for listening.

'Don't worry about cancelling supper next Saturday?' Leila

said, 'it doesn't seem like a good time for you at the moment.'

'That's exactly why I need to carry on with the supper plans - something to think about. I don't want to sit around feeling sorry for myself. It'll give me something to do, and you know how I like planning a meal.'

'Yes, Ginny, I know,' said Leila, sighing good naturedly, 'OK, if you're really sure, I'm certainly looking forward to it. Who else is coming?'

'Unfortunately David has invited a colleague and his wife – I've not met them before and they'll be another couple - Bella and Steve, you haven't met them before. Bella is lovely, and I haven't met her husband, but Bella's told me a bit about him,' Ginny said, cryptically. They said their goodbyes, and she made her way to their empty bedroom.

34

It was an ordinary looking white rectangular envelope the postman delivered early on Wednesday morning to No. 3, Churchwarden Street, Sandwich. It could so easily have been junk mail, Bella thought, except for the bright green and gold Pharbos insignia. It now lay on the kitchen table waiting for Steve to come downstairs to open it.

Letters from Steve's work were rare: the last one, about six months ago, had been a formal reprimand, with the threat of sacking – a red warning. Blood red. Bella couldn't keep her eyes of it, the sight of it coupled with her talk at the pond with Ginny the day before, threatened to overwhelm her. Bella heard Steve's heavy footsteps coming down the stairs.

Bella remembered the first letter with a shiver – it turned out his anger also extended to his workplace. *Inappropriate language and behaviour.* The letter had said. What did that mean? How could he jeopardise his job like that?

And now, there was another letter – lying on the table. She kept her head down; she daren't meet Steve's eyes.

'What's the matter with you, this morning?' Steve said, arriving in the kitchen. It was then he spotted the letter on the table and snatching it up, and with a vicious, 'mind your own bloody business,' he slammed out of the house and into the courtyard.

Bella watched him surreptitiously through the window; he opened the letter, and after only a few seconds she saw him scrunch it up and throw it in the bin. All of a sudden she saw him lash out with his foot hitting the bin with resounding clang. It looked like news of the worst kind, Bella thought.

She didn't wait for Steve to come back in. Dragging the children with her, Bella scurried out of the house. She would retrieve the letter when she got back from school. She had to know what it said.

Bella loved the walk to school along The Butts, part of the old town boundary. It was a deep and straight drainage channel, now home to wildlife and an ever-growing population of ducks and moorhens. But in medieval times, The Butts had been used for archery practice in readiness for war; only birds flew its length now, straight as the arrows of earlier centuries.

Even preoccupied, as Bella was, her attention was caught by the graceful willows and alders, edging the banks of the stream. The tree's whippet thin branches, tips already spring-green, were moving gently in the breeze.

Chivvying the children along the path to school, Bella heard her phone bleep - it was a text message from Ginny.

Spoke to Leila last night – call Debbie - here's the number. Phone from mine if you want: Port Lodge, Sandown Road. I'm in all morning. I've got cake!

Having delivered the children safely to school, and only just in time, she stood at the school gates agonising about whether or not to go to Ginny's. She didn't want to become a nuisance – and there was that letter waiting for her in the bin. As she stood dithering, she saw another text arrive. She read with surprise what almost sounded like a plea from Ginny, *please come – I'd like some company.*

Never having been to Ginny's house before, she set off feeling anxious. Walking through the town and passing the supermarket, Bella wondered if she should get some flowers for Ginny. Deciding not to, Ginny probably already had a houseful, she carried on walking, passing the butcher and the chandlers, and arrived at the quay. Turning right down Knightrider Street, she loved that name, she headed out towards Sandwich Bay and the sea. She could already smell the salt of the sea breeze. The sun, struggling through the clouds finally found a gap, and for a few minutes Bella lifted her face and felt its warmth – wonderful, she thought.

Watching out for the field of sheep Ginny had described in her directions, Bella felt a prickle of fear down her back at the thought of making a phone call to the manager of the refuge. It was all going too fast. First, her confession to Ginny and now, phoning the women's refuge. Far too fast, she thought.

She breathed in deeply, letting her anxiety float away with the tumbling aerobatics of the lapwings, and the sight of the ruddy-red rosehips in the hedgerows, left over from winter.

Rounding a bend in the road, the tops of two barley sugar chimneys came into sight, just as Ginny described, with the distinctive red Kent-peg tiled roof. It couldn't be, Bella thought, and nearly turned and ran for home. Port Lodge, Ginny's home, was large, intimidatingly large.

Bella pushed open the intricate wrought-iron gate with some trepidation. The name *"Port Lodge"* was woven into the wrought iron vines and roses. Before her, she could see a tudor-esque black-timbered house, partially hidden by an avenue of tall meticulously clipped laurel hedges. Through gaps in the hedges, she could see bowling-green flat lawns. Through another, she saw flint walls forming a backdrop to deep flower borders being readied for their summer planting. It looked utterly wonderful, Bella thought transfixed.

As she gazed in appreciation, Ginny appeared from around the side of the house with an empty trug on her arm and some secateurs in her hands.

'Bella, I'm so pleased to see you,' Ginny said, smiling and welcoming her with a hug 'I was just about to pick some daffodils for you to take back - that's if you want them?' I love having a vase of them on the table - so cheery. Come along inside, and I'll make you a cup of tea.'

Bella, feeling too overawed to be able to think of anything to say, other than, 'yes please, 'thank you', 'that would be lovely', followed Ginny meekly, as she led her through a door that opened into a high-ceilinged and light-filled glass conservatory. It was like stepping into another world, reminding her of the conservatory at Kew Gardens. It was difficult to see where Ginny's glass-house finished and the garden began, so verdant and riotous were the plants.

'Ginny,' she breathed, in awe, 'this is just so wonderful.'

But Ginny had no intention of letting her look around, quickly leading her through into the kitchen. Bella looked at the miles of hand crafted beech wood cupboards – gleaming with polish; marble worktops - glistening with mica, and floor tiles – a cool, hard to keep clean, forget-me-not blue.

She put both hands to her cheeks at the embarrassment of what Ginny must have thought of her poky kitchen and tiny garden. She couldn't take it all in – it was so perfect.

'Bella, what is it?' Ginny asked, looking concerned, 'you look like the world is going to end any second. Are you all right?'

I can't do this, Bella thought, her mind blind with panic,

I can't stay here – it's all been some sort of mistake. Why has this woman taken an interest in me, when she has all this? 'I just didn't expect your house to be so…'

'… big,' Ginny suggested, 'I know – it is, isn't it? It's what David wanted - to entertain clients, to impress them. It usually worked.'

'I was thinking - beautiful – and big as well,' Bella agreed hastily, drumming up a vestige of a smile, 'what must you have thought of my little kitchen?'

'Bella don't be silly – your kitchen is gorgeous – it was so homely - I envied you that. This can seem a barn of a place sometimes, especially when I'm on my own. I'm not complaining though – I know I'm very lucky.'

Bella stood imagining the children running round the garden: playing on the swing she had noticed hanging from a big oak tree. Ginny was right, she was lucky. Very, very lucky.

'It's the garden that's really my home,' Ginny said, 'it's where I spend all my time - it's what I'm most proud of. Come on, I'll make some tea, and you can let me show off what I call, the Orchid House, it's just a conservatory really.'

The urge to escape from Ginny's house was receding. It was just a home after all, she thought – some home though.

'Which reminds me,' Ginny said, putting a tea-tray down on the wooden table in the conservatory: white mugs, teapot and milk jug, cake and biscuits were laid out, and looked very inviting, Bella thought. 'Do you like orchids?' Ginny asked.

'I can see you do,' Bella teased, sitting down and looking around her in wonder at what must be hundreds of different orchids. Colour abounded in every nook and cranny; from the palest creamy white to deep velvet magenta, 'and I can see why you call it the Orchid House, there's so many of them - they're amazing... I'm amazed,' she said, turning around to take it all in – they were everywhere, 'you must have a real talent- they're difficult to grow aren't they?'

'I've got the hang of it now – I've had plenty of disasters – I collect them from all over the place,' Ginny said, as she poured them both a cup of tea. 'David calls it 'my shed', it's where I disappear to.'

'I'd disappear here, too,' Bella agreed.

'You remember Carl, my neighbour,' Ginny asked, 'I was telling you about him the other day? Well, he wants to take some photographs for a gardening book he's writing,' Bella heard the pride in her voice.

Biting into a piece of cake, Bella thought how Ginny was right, it wasn't a patch on her own home-made one - and smiled to herself with pleasure.

'I did warn you that I'd bought the cake,' Ginny said, and Bella knew she'd been found out and smiled guiltily.

'Ginny...' Bella said, confused for a moment until she saw Ginny laughing.

'It's really good to see you laugh, Bella.' Ginny said, laughing, too. 'But now, to more serious matters - I spoke to Leila last night. She gave me this number for you to ring. Leila said Debbie was lovely, and she would... be very helpful.'

'I'm not sure if I can,' Bella said, looking at the name and number on the slip of pretty notepaper Ginny had handed to her. And then she thought of Steve's letter waiting for her in the bin and all that it presaged, 'but...'

'Yes you can,' Ginny interrupted.

Bella heard the determination in Ginny's voice.

'You're tougher than you think - I've seen it,' Ginny said getting up from her chair, as she spoke, 'but first, while you think about what you want to do, I'm going to show you my garden.'

Bella relieved to have put off the moment, followed Ginny through large folding glass doors and out into the garden.

They wandered happily around together for half an hour, through arches, past rose arbours, over lawns, along paths to the vegetable garden, and Bella saw the magic of what Ginny had achieved. Bella could scarcely believe that it had been a bramble patch when Ginny moved in ten years ago.

Returning to the Orchid House, Ginny asked, gently persuasive, 'are you ready, Bella?

Nodding slightly, but with a quaking heart, Bella took her mobile out of her jacket pocket. She couldn't bear to look Ginny in the face - she thought she might lose her nerve. Her fingers shook so much she had to punch the number in a few times before she got it right.

'Is that, Debbie?' she asked in a whisper? She watched Ginny quietly slip out of the Orchid House.

35

Bella went out into the courtyard as soon as she got back home from Ginny's.

Opening the bin, she saw the letter crumpled and torn lying on the top. Taking the letter back into the house, she flattened out the creases with trembling fingers. The words swam in front of her, but one word stood out from all the others - big, bold, and emphatic.

It was the bad news Bella had feared ever since he had got his first warning. She began reading the letter; the first few lines, were all that she needed to understand that her life was just about to get much, much worse. Suddenly aware that it was nearly school time, Bella quickly read the rest of the letter. Crumpling it again, as she hurried back out into the courtyard she carefully placed the letter in the bin exactly how she had found it. Steve, she hoped would never know she'd read it.

Time had taken wings in the peace of the Orchid House, and now she needed to dash to school. Life had stood still for so long, Bella thought, as she rushed along pavements busy with mums heading for school. But now her life seemed to have taken flight - towing her along, her feet barely touching the ground; she could scarcely believe it.

Her heart racing with worry at the thought of those words in Steve's letter, *misconduct – warnings - redundancy -* and then she remembered what Debbie had told her only that morning.

'You're not on your own now - not any more.' They echoed Ginny's words to her. She had immediately liked the sound of Debbie's voice, so calm, so reassuring..

Bella quickened her pace, a sense of urgency growing with each step. All thoughts of orchids had been replaced by thoughts of Steve's redundancy. Before her life got better it was first going to get much, much worse.

36

David was sitting at his desk, mulling over all that had happened that week: it was Friday and the end of a long day, at the end of a long week. He couldn't believe that it was only the previous Saturday that he had been in Devon trying to rescue Grace. She was on his mind, worrying if she was all right. He couldn't seem to be able kick start his life again – it was that not knowing. He sighed and idly turned over some papers on his desk.

David was trying, before he went home for the weekend, to put the finishing touches to a contract that he, and Joe, his associate, had been working on, but he somehow now felt he couldn't be bothered. *What's the matter with me?*

The client, he and Joe had been wooing for months and months had finally come through, and to their relief, earlier that day, finally agreed to sign a five-year service contract. It was a big value deal for them, and their company, Silverman Grant Accountants. He knew his directors would be delighted and wondered if there might even be some action about his directorship now. It had been intimated at higher levels recently - or so he had been told.

The adrenaline generated by today's achievement was making him restless - he wanted to celebrate; he didn't feel ready to go home, not yet anyway - a feeling, he noticed, that was becoming more frequent recently. The thought of Ginny waiting for him at home sent his heart sinking - he had to do something about it, he couldn't just let things go on like this. He was getting too used to sleeping on his own.

David swivelled round in his chair to look out of his fifteenth-storey window of Silverman Grant's offices, onto the River Thames below. He remembered nearly four years ago, the feeling of excitement, of finally having arrived when he was given this large office with a spectacular view,. Since then he had come to learn the life of the river: its seasons - sluggish brown in winter, lighter brown in summer, never blue, never inviting – but always fascinating. In summer, the smell of the river drifted through the building: organic, peaty - in winter, the smell, instead of peat, became decay. Some days, waves with dirty brown froth at their crest whipped up by the wind, sent the riverboats bobbing jauntily. It was never the same whenever he looked. He had grown to love it in all its moods.

Returning with a sigh to his paperwork, he was surprised to see Joe lounging in the doorway; his tall frame well dressed, as usual, in sharp designer shirts and suits. At twenty-eight-years-old he was an up and coming City accountant. David smiled he had been just the same at Joe's age.

'Hi, Joe. What a week, eh?' David said, turning back to his desk, and with a flourish signed the back page of the contract that had caused him and Joe such hard work.

'That last meeting…' He said, shaking his head at the memory, 'I thought it was all over at one point. He was a difficult client, wasn't he? But we swung it - we make a good team,' David added, scrutinising Joe. 'Well done. You played a big part in winning that client.'

'Cheers,' Joe said, accepting the compliment with ease.

David admired that about him – straight, and bright with it. He remembered Joe's interview and had liked him immediately, determining there and then to make him an offer he wouldn't be able to refuse. Joe hadn't refused, and as he got to know him he began to recognise something of himself as a young man - economic with words, but good with clients; they trusted Joe's calm manner, he was also someone that shifted the work without fuss.

'I'm off to the bar with the others,' Joe said, tilting his head towards a group of people David could see getting into the lift. 'I just popped in to say goodbye,' Joe added, putting his jacket and scarf on, 'unless of course team work includes going for a celebratory drink?' Not sure if he wanted a drink, David hesitated for a moment. He'd always headed home straight after work - it was a long commute two hours door-to-door, but the thought of having a drink with Joe, and maybe meeting some interesting people, suddenly felt very appealing.

'OK,' he agreed, surprising himself, 'why not? And after all, I owe you a drink after your hard work.'

'Great,' Joe said, straightening up from his slouch.

'I don't usually stay long, but it's good to unwind before the weekend, start it on a good note,' Joe explained, the surprise that his boss had agreed quickly gone from his face, replaced instantly with easy politeness. It was what Joe did well – to look as though life was unfolding exactly as he had planned it.

They walked out of the office together, collars up against the river chill; the bar, a short walk from their offices, was on Tooley Street.

'I'm going to see if I can get you a bonus on the back of this contract, Joe; you deserve it,' David could see he had caught

Joe's attention and was gratified to watch an expression of excitement flit across his face.

'Cool - thanks, David.'

'Where are we going, Joe?' David asked, wishing he hadn't mentioned the bonus until he'd spoken to the directors – he didn't want to get Joe's hopes up.

'Hays Galleria - have you been before?' Joe asked.

'Not sure,' David said, uncertain if he had or not. 'A while ago now, maybe.'

'It's the converted wharf on Hays Lane,' Joe reminded him, 'it used to be known as the Larder of England, because most of the dry goods for the capital came into its quays in the nineteenth century.

'Ah, yes, I remember reading about that,' David said, as they walked along companionably.

They turned off into Tooley Street and David whistled at the sight in front of him. Hays Galleria stood tall and imposing. An historic wharf building, of rich-red brickwork, couldn't hide its industrial origins. The space between the two wharves had been infilled with an intricate cast iron and glass-vaulted roof.

'I never knew this was here,' David said astonished. This was what he loved about London, no matter how well you knew it, there were still sights that took your breath away.

'It was burned down twice,' Joe told him, 'once in the Great Fire of Southwark, and then the Great Fire of Tooley Street.'

They pushed open the large glass doors and were greeted by a wall of sound. David finding the noise deafening, all of a sudden, felt a decade too old. Looking around him, he saw men and women, mostly he guessed in their late twenties and early thirties. They all looked confident, designer dressed; their voices at full tilt – the sound, David thought, of adrenaline from deals done or not done. He knew how they felt – restless, buoyed up with excitement – he knew exactly how they felt.

Joe and David forced their way through the throng, towards the bar - a sleek and highly polished affair - with a backdrop of bottles of wines and spirits and optics sparkling under brightly coloured down-lighters.

Everyone was standing; wooden tables and chairs remaining empty, the hallmark of Friday after-work drinks favoured by the City of London's wealth-creators.

A few minutes later, Joe arrived back at his side, a drink in both hands. David sipped his full-bodied red wine with appreciation, and as his eyes scanned the room he noticed a young woman trying to make her way through the jostling crowds. David watched her progress, his attention captured: she was tall, maybe just under six feet, almost as tall as himself and with the pale freckled skin of a true redhead. She looked arresting. He guessed she was the same age as Joe, late twenties perhaps. Her progress slowed, he noticed, by colleagues wanting to chat. He liked her easy smile, she looked quite charming, he thought.

'Sorry, what was that you said?' David asked, turning back to look at Joe, but before he could answer, the woman reached their side, and to David's surprise addressed Joe.

'Hi, Joe,' she said - open, friendly. David felt a quiver of excitement when he realised, that although she was talking to Joe, she was looking directly at him, her eyes wide and full of interest.

'Hi, Alicia, I've not seen you here before,' Joe said.

'First time, and maybe the last,' she replied laughing, 'it's a bit of a crush isn't it?'

David watched her turn her head from Joe to himself, as though the question was for him.

'This is, David Jackson, my boss,' he said.

'Hi, David,' Alicia replied, making eye contact with him, 'good to meet you. So you're David Jackson – I've heard of you.' Spoken, in what David recognised as an educated voice with a faint west-country cadence. He liked it. He liked the look of her even more. She was sleek: her wavy red hair rested on her shoulders. It looked expensively cut, if he was any judge - her generous mouth glistened with bright pink lipstick.

'And what have you heard?' he found himself asking, intrigued, 'what's Joe been telling you?' David saw out of the corner of his eye, Joe holding up his hands indicating innocence.

'Oh, it wasn't Joe,' she answered, 'just... people,' she said, smiling.

'Nothing bad I hope?' he said, suddenly realising, she was flirting with him. He'd got rusty. More like seized up, he thought ruefully.

'No, nothing bad at all,' she answered, her eyes flicking up to his and away again. He nearly missed it, he was sure she was saying something in that look but he didn't understand what. 'Great place isn't it, except for all the people?'

'Yes, amazing,' he said, as he admired the glass roof above, 'we're out celebrating a successful deal with Esse Construction,' David answered.

'I've heard about that,' she said, looking impressed, 'it must have been really hard work putting a deal that size together.'

'Yes it was,' David said, deciding not to be too modest, 'we

214

had some tough moments though - didn't we, Joe?' David turned to Joe but not before he noticed Alicia's smile of sheer appreciation.

'I wish I could work on a project like that,' Alicia replied, 'although,' pausing she added with a gleam of excitement in her eyes, 'I've been told there's an interesting project coming up soon in our department – I'm hoping it's got my name on it.'

David toyed with the idea of seconding her onto his own team, but quickly realised how it might look to his colleagues.

'How do you know, Joe?' he asked, watching her hop onto the empty stool beside him. He couldn't help noticing that her dress had risen slightly, revealing a little bit more of her smooth, shapely legs.

'I only started a couple of weeks ago at Silverman Grant,' Alicia explained.

'Even so, I thought I would have noticed,' David said, seeing a flush rise on her cheeks.

'And Joe was a friendly face at the coffee machine,' she finished, touching her cheek with her hand.

He'd been crass.

'I'm a trainee accountant here,' Alicia explained, as though anticipating David's next question.

'And you're still alive after the coffee?' David asked, 'I only tried it the once, and vowed never again.

He watched her smile at his weak humour. She seemed interested – or was she? David felt a rush of excitement at the possibility.

'Don't even think about trying the coffee again, it's definitely not changed for the better,' she said, smiling and swinging her empty glass in her hand, an unspoken request, implicit in the gesture.

She was definitely flirting with him, David realised – this truly delicious woman was actually flirting with him.

'A drink, Alicia?' David asked, reading her gesture correctly, 'and what about you, Joe?'

'Thanks,' Joe said, 'but I'll get them. I want to talk to Gerry at the other end of the bar, his head bobbed towards a man sitting at the bar, he's organising a charity run I'm interested in doing.'

As he watched Joe walk away leaving him and Alicia alone, David suddenly began to feel awkward, wondering how many people knew him here. Would they think he was chatting up this young woman? Was he being old fashioned? Was he a relic from a previous way of doing things? He had a choice, he realised – stay and chat - nothing wrong with that, he argued to himself; or go home to Ginny. He stayed. So what if someone saw him? What was essentially so wrong with having a drink after work? Conscience now under control, David turned to Alicia and asked about the project she was hoping to be involved in.

'It's a construction company in Exeter; they've just won a big hospital contract,' she answered. 'I don't know anything about construction – but I'm a fast learner,' she said, smiling with the confidence of a bright future ahead.

'I may be able to help you,' he said wondering if that was wise of him, 'this last contract of ours was in the construction sector.'

'Oh, really? That would be great,' Alicia said, her eyes gleaming at him.

'Do you know Devon well?' David asked, thinking about that faint lilt in her voice. And before she could answer, his thoughts were dragged back to Grace; rushing, swirling, freezing water began to engulf him - he had to swallow down hard on the lump that had suddenly formed in his throat. He hadn't thought about Grace once since he'd been talking with Alicia. A shaft of guilt hit him.

'Are you all right, David?' Alicia asked, 'you suddenly look... sad.'

Smart, sassy and now perceptive, David thought.

'I'm sorry,' he said with a smile, recovering fast, 'I was thinking about something that happened recently.

'It looks as though it's upset you - what happened?' she asked, a spark of interest growing in her eyes.

'Amongst other things,' he said, not feeling it was appropriate to talk to her about Grace, 'I was er... thinking about my last trip to Devon,' he said, starting to feel uncomfortable. There was no way he was going to tell her about Grace..

'And that was why you looked so sad?' Alicia asked.

David looked at her, seeing her concern, she didn't even know him, 'I'm sorry,' he finally managed to say, 'it was just... it's difficult to talk about, that's all. Maybe I could tell you when... ' He didn't know when, why had he said that? He was relieved when he saw she seemed to be more intrigued than offended.

'Yes of course,' she said, 'it sounds as if you know Devon well?'

'Yes, I've often been on holiday there,' he answered, batting away any thoughts of Grace. 'I was there last weekend.'

'I love it there,' Alicia said, 'where did you go?'

'Do you know Tavistock ?' David asked, the words felt like

stones too large in his mouth, threatening to choke him.

For reasons he didn't understand, he decided he wanted to explain his sadness to Alicia – he didn't want her to think badly of him. What did he have to lose after all?

Lowering his voice so only Alicia would be able to hear, 'there was an accident,' he began.

There it was, out in the open, and already he felt his burden shift a little. He had told no one, and wondered for a moment why he should want to tell this girl he had only just met.

'There was a young girl trapped in the middle of a river,' David said quietly, confidentially, 'and I tried to help get her out, but I couldn't.'

He stopped, he knew he was talking too fast but if he was going to tell her it was almost as though he needed to say it in one breath. 'And because I couldn't get her out I had to call the rescue team – the mountain rescue team, they flew in by helicopter,' he decided he wasn't going to tell her about Veronica and Ginny finding them.

'I felt…' he corrected, '… feel as though I let Grace down, that was the young girl, she was only eleven-years-old. I feel as though I let her down by not being able to rescue her. That's why I looked sad.'

David wondered if he'd made a mistake telling a stranger, albeit an attractive one - but it was too late now, there was no going back. He wouldn't blame Alicia for making her excuses, and moving on to find someone more exciting to chat to.

'Oh, David, that's terrible,' Alicia said, 'but how brave of you. So did the rescue team… get her out of the water?'

'Yes,' David replied, 'they rescued her and took her to hospital in Exeter.'

'Do you know how she is?' Alicia asked.

'I don't know, but I think she's going to be OK - she's alive anyway. If you'd seen her, you would know that was a miracle in itself,' David said. 'But the hospital won't tell me anything more.'

'Even though you helped save her life?' Alicia said.

David shook his head.

'No wonder you looked sad,' and as she spoke, Alicia put her right hand with its manicured, cerise-pink nails briefly on his shoulder. David gulped.

'I really hope she's going to be all right,' Alicia said, picking up her drink.

Over the top of her glass, David saw her smile at him with a warmth and compassion that made him forget everything else. David could hardly believe that the corners of her eyes, now slightly puckered with concern, should be feeling sympathy for him. She smiled at him – a smile, he thought that could hold back waves. David held his breath – what was happening? With a dry mouth he picked up his drink, and waited for his heart to settle back in his chest.

For the next hour or so, it seemed to David, there were only the two of them in the room. He established that Alicia had been born in Totnes, Devon – as David had suspected, but now lived in Clapham. There was a moment that hung heavily in the air when she asked David where he lived.

It seemed to David that they were edging ever closer to his home situation; he couldn't lie – wouldn't lie about being married – but he also knew that it would probably mean the end of this wonderful unforeseen interlude - a welcome diversion from all his personal confusion.

'In Sandwich…' he hesitated, knowing what was coming next.

'Sandwich?' Alicia repeated, surprised. 'That's a long commute.'

David could almost see the beads on the accountant's abacus fly, as Alicia tried to find the answer to the problem he had just posed her. A single man would not be living out in the sticks – he knew for certain that's probably what she'd be thinking.

'With my wife, and three children,' he added, before he was asked.

David watched with resignation, the expression on Alicia's face change from interested and bright, to closed – it happened in a second.

'Of course you're married,' she said, disappointment evident after a long pause, and a slight shrug that made her red hair swing for a second and then came back to rest again on her shoulders. David held his breath. 'Why aren't you at home with your wife?' she asked, 'why are you sitting here talking to me?'

'I don't want to go home,' David paused, what an admission he thought. 'Things… aren't too good there,' he said simply, feeling a flood of disappointment that he might not see her again.

Alicia nodded slowly at him. He wondered how often she'd heard that line before.

'I'm sorry,' and he was. He would have liked to live this moment to the full, to be untrammelled by his responsibilities, but he knew that couldn't be. He waited, his breath once more held. She looked away for a moment, and David knew this was a moment that might change his life.

'Have you ever surfed in Devon?' she asked, turning to him once more.

David nodded, and let out his breath, relief flooding through him that they had moved on to safer territory. He could see she was disappointed, but had accepted that a man of nearly forty would have baggage. *Baggage?*

'What about Bantham Beach,' she asked, 'have you surfed there? It's my favourite.' As she spoke, David couldn't work out whether she was still interested in him, or whether she was just making polite conversation. Alicia had changed imperceptibly, he could see that her eyes weren't quite as bright, and her smile not quite so wide. *Damn, damn.*

'Oh yes - many times,' he answered, keen for them to be talking about anything, other than his marital status, 'I was there last summer – you can't beat Atlantic waves for great surfing can you?'

'I was there last summer too,' she answered, her eyes lightening slightly, he saw with relief, 'that's a coincidence, isn't it?' he could see her hesitating, 'I suppose... it was a family trip?' He nodded after a moment, embarrassed.

'And you? Who were you with?' he asked. It was as though he had turned a light back on, David thought, he watched her expression thoughtful at first and then a look of understanding; no one was without... ties, it said. Everyone had history.

'My boyfriend,' she said, unabashed. But he could see she had taken his point.

They talked for a while on safer ground; they talked of places visited in Devon – about a shared love of surfing. An image was slowly forming, unbidden, in David's head of them surfing together, laughing as they rode the waves.

A game had begun, David quickly realised. For the first time in months, maybe even longer, he could feel his sluggish blood picking up some pace.

'I'm off now, David,' Joe said, standing at their shoulders, surprising them both, 'see you Monday.'

'What time is it, Joe? It's early yet isn't it?' David asked.

David wanted the evening to go on and on - it was far too soon for it to end. But when he checked his watch it was much later than he thought - already after eight, and he still had a two-hour commute home. But before he could make a move, he saw Alicia gather up her bag and jacket.

'David, I must go too,' Alicia told him, her face a picture of disappointment, 'I don't want to be home late; I've got an early start tomorrow. It's been lovely… meeting you; maybe see you at the coffee machine… sometime soon?'

He nodded and smiled, 'sure, but perhaps not the coffee machine – if it's coffee you want, there's a good coffee shop on the corner of Tooley Street. He watched her deliberate his more obvious invitation, and then to his great pleasure, she nodded.

'That's an idea – at least we'd live a little longer,' she said, smiling.

'I must get going as well; can I walk you to the tube?' he asked, wanting any excuse to prolong the evening, 'which way are you going - London Bridge?'

She nodded in agreement, 'yes, Northern Line to Clapham.'

David braced himself for the fresh air that would greet them at the door - air that he knew had blown across the Thames bringing with it the smell of reality. The night was inky; lights from Tower Bridge just upstream, were as he guessed the Architect had intended, reflected on the glass walls of City Hall - home to the Mayor of London. They walked along the Embankment towards the tube; a slight awkwardness constraining them when they stepped out of the cocooned world of the bar. The night was so pretty - the stars bright pinpoints in the saffron-yellow moon-filled sky - that it dispelled any awkwardness between them. The reflections of masts and hulls sharp edged on the river, David knew, disguised the sludge and slime hidden beneath.

They parted in the anonymous busyness of the vast vaulted London Bridge station. Should he kiss her goodbye? What did people do these days? As he was trying to decide, Alicia leant over and laid her cool pink lips on his cheek.

She whispered, 'I hope we'll meet again soon.'

David gulped. 'I hope so too,' he replied, and realised in that moment just how much he meant it.

'Let's,' she said simply, before walking towards the ticket barrier. Her meaning, David thought, couldn't be clearer. He stood and watched her until she was out of sight, and then turned to walk towards the Northern Line, to begin his own journey home.

37

Late that Friday night, Ginny woke to the sound of scrunching gravel. She had drifted off to sleep listening out for the sound of David's car, trying to dispel frightening images of what may have happened to him. It was, after all, only Friday, not even a week since the accident. Not even a week since he'd suffered hypothermia, trying to rescue Grace. To her, the time since the accident felt like a lifetime.

Ginny had spent the evening wondering why David hadn't phoned her to say he'd be late. *Where was he? Why didn't he pick up his phone? Was he all right? Should she call the police, tell them he wasn't himself after the accident to Grace?* Ginny knew she was being ridiculous. Finally going to bed around ten, she fell into a restless sleep, dreaming of rushing water trying to choke her.

Even in her sleep, she recognised the sound of David's car as it swept up the drive. Flinging on her dressing gown, she stood at the top of the stairs waiting for him.

'Where on earth have you been?' Ginny asked, relief that he was safe, morphing quickly into anger. 'Why didn't you tell me you'd be this late?' Looking at her watch, ' what have you been doing all this time? Where have you been?'

Ginny couldn't be bothered to hide her resentment, tired and irritable, she didn't wait for a reply. 'Is staying out late and not letting me know where you are, your answer to what's bothering you?'

'I don't know what you mean,' David said, 'nothing's bothering me. My phone's dead that's all, and I didn't realise I'd be quite so late. I was out with work-friends celebrating the end of a big deal.'

She was itching to yell her frustration at him. 'You know what I mean,' she said quietly, 'you just don't want to talk about it,' she stood blocking the stairs, her arms held tightly round her, as though trying to hold her emotions in.

'Where's my loving husband gone?' she challenged him. 'There's got to be something wrong the way you've been treating me, it's…unbearable. I don't know how long… ' And with these words, and the anger with which she said them, she could see by the discomfort on David's face she had, at last, got through to him. She had punctured his distant composure. He stood still at the bottom of the stairs looking up at her, astonished at her words. Without saying anything further, she watched him turn his back on her and walk away into the kitchen.

Her out-pouring of emotion had surprised Ginny too. Where had it all come from? Ginny wondered. The look of astonishment on David's face said it all. Neither of them recognised the other.

'David, I asked you a question. Why don't you answer me? What is the matter with you?' She shouted at his retreating figure. She felt so exasperated she didn't bother to wait for an answer; turning on her heels she flounced back into the bedroom.

'Erm…there's nothing wrong,' she heard him call up to her, as she slammed the bedroom door shut behind her. It was her turn to choose tonight. She chose to sleep alone. It wasn't long, lying in the now cold bed, before she began to feel oppressed by the gloom and emptiness of the bedroom. It took all her strength of will to stop from running to him.

38

The next morning, Saturday, after an almost sleepless night, Ginny woke to the pre-dawn light. The stillness of the outside world would last for only a few moments longer before the birds began their morning call. She knew she would never get back to sleep now. Her eyes felt gritty and a headache, arriving overnight, was quietly throbbing. As she lay in bed thinking, she began to regret her outburst of the night before – she knew it would have done nothing to help matters between them. It would probably have made everything worse – much worse.

An hour later, Ginny was surprised to find David already in the kitchen and dressed for running. It was the only time she ever saw him look anything but smart. He looked much younger, she thought, in his grey hoodie and tracksuit bottoms. But she could see lines of worry on his face. He was looking at her, waiting expectantly.

The atmosphere in the house thrummed with their disagreement. Ginny advanced as far as the table and stood with her hands on the back of the chair, more for moral support than anything else, and looked at him silently. The words of regret, of love, of needing forgiveness that fought to be said, stuck in her throat.

They had so much together, she thought sadly, glancing around her at the glossy kitchen, her Orchid House beyond, her precious garden, their sons - it would be such a waste to just let it all turn into ashes. *Would it?* David had caught her look - had he read her thoughts?

With sinking heart she heard David murmur, 'see you later,' as he left for his run. The click of the door behind him reverberated in the empty house; there was to be no resolution that morning.

She pottered about for a while, trying to forget her troubles, taking comfort in the mundanities of life: filling the dishwasher, putting on the washing machine, emptying vases of wilted daffodils but soon ran out of jobs to occupy her. Needing to escape the feeling of suffocation that was pervading the house, and not wanting to be there when David got back, she decided to visit her mother.

Bertie's excitement was uncontainable when she picked up his lead. 'Sit, or I'll leave you behind,' she said, and at the sound of his mistress's stern voice, and the sight of her admonishing finger, Bertie, sat, and for a fleeting moment became the perfect dog. 'You haven't fooled me for a second, Bertie,' she muttered, slamming the door behind them, eager to escape.

The air was fresh, as Ginny walked along Sandown Road, passing fields as she went, with the first lambs of spring gambolling joyously. The sound of lost lambs bleating for their mothers heralded spring, and with it, Ginny thought, a sense of renewal seemed to pervade the air; she could feel her spirits lift with each step. As she walked she imagined her problems floating out to the estuary, taken there by the silt-grey waters of the river Stour.

Twenty minutes later, walking briskly past burgeoning hedgerows and fields dotted with sheep and cows, brought

Ginny to her mother's small flint walled cottage. Climbing roses framed the doorway, getting ready to bloom in a few weeks time.

The familiar sight of her mother, Ellen, in her kitchen, hands deep in bread dough, rosy cheeked with exertion, chased away any of Ginny's remaining gloom. At the sound of Ginny closing the front door, her mother stopped what she was doing and beamed. She looked as she always did, Ginny thought with a smile: grey curls, pulled into what had been a severe bun that morning, had escaped and now framed her heart-shaped face.

'Ginny, darling, how lovely to see you,' her mother said. Ginny felt reassured that there were still some things in her life that remained constant.

She sank gratefully into her favourite, worn but comfy leather armchair, and watched idly as her mother, with an expertise she could only dream of, knead life into the dough.

'I'll just finish this, and then I'll make you a cup of tea,' Ellen said. 'You look peaky, are you OK?'

Ginny saw the look of concern on her mother's face but didn't feel ready yet to talk.

'How are the boys? Are they doing all right at school?' Ellen asked.

Ginny nodded, the tears that had been threatening all morning, began to slide down her face.

'I'm sorry, Ginny,' her mother said, coming over to her, wiping her hands free of flour first, she put her arms around her. 'You must miss those boys, and that accident can't have helped either,' she said, 'it's no wonder you and David are… '

'That's exactly it though, Mum,' Ginny said, 'what *are* David and I? Because I'm sure I don't know anymore.'

'Come on then, Ginny, let's talk this through,' her mother said, going over to the sink to fill the kettle.

Returning home a couple of hours later refreshed, she wondered if David was home so they could sit down and have a talk together. Calling his name, she went to find him, but there was no sign of him downstairs and just as she was about to go upstairs she saw that unusually the door to his study was closed.

Standing outside the door, she felt tempted to knock first - there was something about that closed door – it felt impenetrable somehow. She reminded herself what her mother had advised only that morning, and Ginny knew she was right. Every marriage, had its ups and downs - and from the sad look on her mother's face - it seemed to her, that her mother was speaking from remembered experience.

With trepidation, she opened the door to find David sitting with his back to her, staring out of the porthole window onto the garden. That window was one of the reasons she had fallen in love with the house. She had imagined herself looking through that circular window, no bigger than a dustbin lid, thinking big thoughts - but David, to her chagrin, had seen its potential too, and had soon made it his office.

'David?' she said, and waited while he slowly turned to face her. He looked white, and the look in his eyes made Ginny panic.

'David, what on earth is it? What's happened?' she said, rushing to him, all thoughts of their argument gone. She knelt beside him putting her arms around him. She hoped he wouldn't push her away, and felt relief when he didn't.

'David, what's wrong?' she asked, her voice high with anxiety, 'you look terrible.'

She just about heard him murmur, 'Grace'.

'What's happened to her?' Ginny asked, startled by David's reaction. 'Has Charles phoned? Tell me – please,' for a second she felt like shaking him - she needed to know what happened to Grace too. 'Come on - you have to tell me what's happened?'

She didn't have the courage to ask if Grace were dead – the words wouldn't come. But she'd been fine, Ginny thought, what could have gone wrong? She stroked his soft curls so thick, so short, so… familiar, so… David. She could feel his shoulder blades through his t-shirt, he felt too thin, she could smell the earthiness left over from his run. She breathed in the smell, and felt a stirring of something… memories of intimacy floated unexpectedly into her head - shaking herself she brought her thoughts back to today's reality.

'David, whatever's happened, come on we can sort it out together. Can't we?' she implored, 'that's all I want for us - to be together, to be a team again. We always used to be,' her voice trailed off, as he had once more turned away from her.

It was all so bewildering this rush of love, of yearning. She wasn't sure if he was listening to her, so she said again, 'you and me… how it used to be? Remember? I want that – do you?' Ginny held her breath, this was as close as she had come to declaring herself, laying herself bare, open, vulnerable. Waiting.

'Charles has just phoned,' David explained, his voice strained and quiet, ignoring her pleading.

These weren't the words of love that Ginny hoped for.

'He told me that Grace is out of her induced coma,' David said, 'and that she lost a lot of blood when they… '

David stopped, and Ginny held her breath, as she waited, anxiety making her feel dizzy. She looked out of the porthole as David tried to find the words to tell her - her imagination in overdrive.

'What's happened to Grace?' she asked, still crouching, still his wife, still caring. 'Grace – come on, David, tell me about her. Please.'

'She's had to have her foot… ' David spluttered over his words, '… amputated. They couldn't save it. They tried to reconnect it, but the operation failed. It's all my fault, if only I could have rescued her sooner they may have been able to save her foot.' He turned away from her.

'Oh, David,' she managed to say at the horror of it, 'poor, poor Grace,' she stood up and walked to the window. Amputation - it didn't get much bigger than that, Ginny thought, for a young girl whose life hadn't really started yet. It was too much to take in. 'She's alive though because of you,' she said with relief almost to herself, 'she's still alive – you mustn't forget that.'

When he didn't reply she knelt down again, 'David?' she asked, gently smoothing his back, 'is there anything I can do? We can do?'

'Nothing,' David said, still staring out of the window. 'I asked Charles if there was. But it's a family thing, she only needs her family now.'

Ginny sat next to him for a long time. Laying aside her own feelings, she waited with him. Eventually, she heard him take a deep breath, and watched as he slowly got up from his chair and left the room, without a backward glance for her.

A little while later, sitting in the kitchen, wondering how they could move on from this, Ginny heard the slam of the front door, and then the roar of an engine scattering the gravel. She stayed where she was, watching the sun fade through the porthole, and thought about Grace, wondering what her childhood would be like now.

39

B ella twitched the curtains back for the hundredth time that morning, while she waited for Ginny to arrive. It was only a week since she had first spoken to Debbie in Ginny's Orchid House. She daren't think too much about what lay ahead. The day had started the same as any other Monday: the children had gone to school - complaining quietly, Steve had gone to work, angry – his tongue flaying her. But there the similarity ended. Today she and Ginny were going to visit the women's refuge in Dover. She would at last meet Debbie Harris, the calm reassuring voice on the other end of the phone.

The thought of the meeting with Debbie was making her feel sick with anxiety but at the same time she could feel a bubble of excitement growing. She could barely see out of her living room window, as raindrops falling so fast were blown by a determined wind into a slanted sheet of water. Clouds - grey and with dark intent - rushed past overhead - out of control; much like her own life felt, Bella thought.

Come on, Ginny.

The few people Bella could see from her living room window scurried past as best they could. Their heads were bowed against the wind and rain struggling with umbrellas that had suddenly become combatants in the strong squalls. She shivered at the sight.

Dreading the thought of the day ahead - Bella had to fight

the instinct to run. And then, before the thought could bloom into action, she saw Ginny's calypso-blue mini pulling up outside the house.

Bella let out a breath she hadn't realised she'd been holding, and grabbing her old brown raincoat and woolly hat, still damp from her walk to school that morning, she stepped out into the rain and wind. Looking back at the house, she had the feeling that when she returned everything would be different.

'I was so worried you weren't coming,' Bella said, her words torn from her lips in the wind as she clambered in the car.

'Why on earth wouldn't I come?' Ginny asked, 'I said I'd be here didn't I?' and with a reassuring smile she reversed out of Bella's narrow lane. 'I got stuck behind a dustcart, that's all,' Ginny said, as she squeezed the car through some narrow bollards, placed to protect the ancient timbers of Brant House. 'There's plenty of time - don't worry. Did everything go all right this morning?'

'There weren't any problems, not really,' Bella replied

Seeing the sceptical look on Ginny's face, the muscles of her mouth twitched as she tried to forget the awful names Steve had called her before he left for work.

'And Steve… ?' Ginny asked.

'Well… apart from Steve being in a horrible temper,' Bella hesitated, 'but that's normal for Steve. He told me this morning that it was going to be different from now on.' Bella shook, remembering his barely veiled threat. 'I asked him what he meant. He didn't say exactly - just made a threatening grunt.'

'Well he's right, isn't he?' Ginny said. 'Things *are* going to be different, now he's been made redundant.'

'Probably very different, Bella - but in a good way,' Ginny said, returning to the subject, 'because soon you'll have somewhere to go. Somewhere to escape to - somewhere where they'll know how to... handle these difficult situations.'

'I couldn't do this without you, you know,' Bella said, turning to look at Ginny. 'I'm still really scared. I keep wondering if I'm doing the right thing.'

'Of course you're scared, it would be impossible not to be, and of course you're doing the right thing,' Ginny answered, still concentrating on her driving, 'but in some ways, Bella, you don't have a choice - do you? One day Steve's anger might turn on the children. That was what you were most worried about. Remember?'

Bella did remember; how could she forget? It was the children that were driving her to be brave. She dreaded Steve turning his anger on Izzy and Ben. She couldn't bear to think about it.

It was the baldest of truths and Ginny was right, what other choice did she have? But what a choice, she thought - a women's refuge - running away – leaving her home – an unmapped future.

'How could I forget?' Bella said almost to herself.

'We're in plenty of time to get to Dover and park,' Ginny interrupted her bleak thoughts as they bowled along the empty dual carriageway, free at last of the confines of Sandwich.

'I'll drive into the centre of Dover, while you're with Debbie,' Ginny told her, filling the pensive silence that was permeating the car, 'although, I'm not sure there's much to look at, I doubt I've time to visit the castle.'

Bella nodded, trying to look more positive for Ginny's sake, knowing Ginny was more worried about her than she was letting on.

'I won't be far though, so just call me. OK?' Ginny said, and for a second, took her eyes off the road to give her a reassuring smile.

They swooped down the steep hill that took them from the top of the cliffs to sea level, and the ferry port hove into sight. Before them lay a huge expanse of sea glistening in the sun; the wind had done its job - chasing away the clouds to reveal the brightest of blue skies. The white cliffs of Dover, tall and straight welcomed them.

'Just phone me when you're ready to come home,' Ginny said, as though they were doing nothing more than a girls' day out, 'it'll be all right, Bella, you'll see.'

40

There seemed to Bella, something reassuring about the four-storey Edwardian building that Ginny dropped her off outside. Neat rows of timber sash windows that faced the castle on the upper floors. On the lower ones, they would have a view of people walking past on the pavement, hurrying to their appointments. The building stood in good company, Bella noticed, standing as it was amongst a number of solicitors' offices, and doctors' and dentists' surgeries. It wasn't how she had imagined a women's refuge to be. She had expected a run-down building in a back street, hidden away – much like abuse itself, she thought. This fine-looking building felt welcoming.

Bella found the front door, freshly painted in navy-blue, already open. All she had to do now was find the courage to step through it. 'Go on, Bella,' she heard Ginny call from the car. 'You can do it.' And she could. A few moments later she walked into a cheery reception area: bright-white with eye catching yellow blinds, and chairs. Her gaze was drawn to the woman sitting behind the reception desk, smiling at her warmly.

'You must be Bella?' the dark-haired woman said. 'You're here to see Debbie, aren't you?'

The woman spoke quietly, confidentially, making it unnecessary for Bella to do anything else, except nod. Filled with trepidation Bella didn't trust herself to speak.

'I'm, Aisha, and here is a card with my number on, if you ever need to call here urgently.'

There was no need for her to explain why Bella might need to call the refuge urgently.

'Take a seat,' Aisha said, smiling encouragingly at Bella, 'and I'll tell Debbie you're here. She won't be long.'

'OK,' Bella said quietly, taking the card from the woman's hand. 'Thank you.'

'There's some water over there, if you'd like a drink,' the young woman said, pointing towards the water dispenser. Bella nodded her thanks. But before she had time to sit down, she saw a middle-aged woman with mid-length brown hair tied back in a black velvet ribbon, and an open friendly face, appear from around the corner.

'Hi, you must be Bella? I'm Debbie Smith,' the woman said warmly, as she walked towards her with a hand outstretched in greeting.

Bella shook the woman's hand, and very quietly said, 'Hello.'

'Come with me to my office, it's just around the corner,' Debbie said, in a reassuring voice. 'Did you get here all right?'

Bella nodded, all power of speech deserting her. They reached the open office door, where Debbie ushered her in, saying gently that she was going to make them both a cup of tea.

'I don't know about you, but I'm gasping.'

Debbie pointed to a scruffy, muddy-blue sofa, 'sit down, Bella; it's not the most comfortable of sofas I'm afraid, but if you tuck your feet up under you, it seems to work.'

Bella sat gingerly on the edge of the sofa, suddenly noticing that all her joints were aching, and her head felt it might be about to burst. She hoped she wasn't coming down with flu; she needed to be feeling strong to cope with what lay ahead of her.

'The springs have gone, I'm afraid, but nothing to worry about though,' Debbie explained, busying herself with kettle and cups. 'We buy nothing new here, it's all donations and sometimes we wished it hadn't been.'

Bella knew that Debbie was trying to put her at her ease, with her simple words and tried to smile back. Her fingers worried at her hair while she tried to make sense of her surroundings. There was not much to see, the room was functional: magnolia walls – plain white blinds, slightly obscuring the view, a chaotic array of papers on the large pine utilitarian desk, filing cabinets - drawers open showing a large number of manila files - stood along the walls, and the brown shrivelled remains of a potted plant, adorned the windowsill. Just an ordinary messy office – nothing scary about it at all, Bella thought with relief. *Maybe I can do this after all.*

Bella lifted her eyes from the floor, and for the first time really looked at Debbie. She saw a woman with a generous figure, wearing a flowing kaftanesque top in multi-shades of blue over wide dark blue trousers, neat shoes on small feet peeped out from the bottom of the trousers. She had a relaxed aura of strength, and experience, comforting somehow - Bella felt instinctively she could like her. She took a deep breath to try and steady her nerves, and almost missed hearing Debbie ask how she had got there.

'My friend Ginny, drove me,' she answered. The everyday question, and the knowledge that Ginny was somewhere nearby, calmed her. She took another deep breath and felt some strength begin to seep back into her body.

Debbie meanwhile, was arranging the mugs and plate of biscuits on the table between them.

'You're safe here, you know, Bella,' Debbie assured her before sitting down on a chair opposite her, and handing her a cup of tea. 'Everything is said in confidence – nobody will know you've been here, unless you want them to.'

'Thank you,' Bella said quietly, unsure of what else to say.

'Nobody deserves to be abused,' Debbie said. 'Nobody.'

Bella repeated the words in her head; these were the first words of understanding and recognition from someone who knew what her world was really like. Her hidden world. Her secret world. Bella felt tears begin to well, at the acknowledgement of all that she had gone through.

'Nobody deserves to be abused,' Debbie repeated, slowly, her voice calm, hypnotic. She was right, Bella realised - all she had tried to be was a good wife.

Debbie passed her a box of tissues.

'It's OK, Bella – there's no rush, so take your time,' Debbie said.

Bella tried her best to smile at Debbie's kind face, with the warm brown eyes that held unmistakeable compassion.

'When you're ready,' Debbie added gently, watching her intently. 'You might like to tell me something about yourself.'

Bella was surprised at the question, and wondered what she could tell this woman that was of any interest? Where could she begin? Her life before Steve, that didn't exist anymore - her family life had all but disappeared with Steve's controlling ways.

'For example you might like to start with your family,' Debbie suggested. 'Do you have any brothers or sisters?'

'Two brothers,' she said, her tongue sticking to the roof of her mouth, it was so dry. She picked up her mug and took a sip of the scalding tea.

After a few moments of silence, while Bella arranged her thoughts, she began to tell Debbie about her home life. She spoke slowly at first, her voice sounding strange to her, almost as though it was another person speaking, somebody that had a voice. She told Debbie first about her father, who hadn't worked since she was a child, about her hen-pecked mother, who was now in a nursing home with dementia, and finally she told Debbie about her brothers, who had followed in her father's footsteps, and only one step away from being in prison. 'They don't feel like my family anymore,' she said, saddened at the idea.

'And your husband, what's he like?' Debbie asked, breaking into her thoughts.

Bella was surprised by her instinct to defend Steve – particularly her decision to marry him. She wanted to explain what he had been like at his best before… everything else happened. She began to tell Debbie, hesitantly, still afraid that Steve would know what she had gone and done. It felt like a betrayal of him..

'He was the loveliest person, you know,' Bella began, almost to herself, remembering the first time they met, '… to begin with.' She stopped talking, as the image of the first time Steve hit her exploded across her vision.

'Steve could be charming one minute, 'Bella continued, 'and then… he would… Not much at first, but slowly, gradually… he started wanting to change everything I did. He began ruling my life in small ways, like what clothes I wore, how I wore my hair. At first I thought it was because he loved me and was interested, but now...' She had to stop again. The words coming out of her mouth didn't seem to belong to her.

'I'm not allowed to make any decisions of my own now, not without deferring to him first. *Any* decision,' she said again, emphatically, and wondered if Debbie understood what she was saying. 'It's terrible not even being able to buy my own clothes and underwear, my own food, or my own books.' She stopped, not knowing if she had the courage to say what needed to be said, 'and what happened in the bedroom. I had no choice about that ever.'

'Do you want to tell me about that?' Debbie asked.

'I might,' Bella whispered, shaking her head, 'but not now.'

Debbie nodded.

'And now...' Bella went on, 'I've nothing of my own. I've lost touch with all my friends, and as for family... ' Bella shrugged, 'I'm allowed to see my mother - occasionally,' and with a sob, and a twist of the tissue in her hand, 'she doesn't recognise me anymore.'

'There's plenty of time, Bella,' Debbie said, 'you don't need to say anything more than you want, today.'

They sat quietly for a moment – the silence comforting, unthreatening. After a while, warmed by the tea, by Debbie's presence, by this safe space that she could run to if she wanted – or needed - she felt ready to continue.

'When did you begin to realise that Steve's behaviour was not that of a loving husband?' Debbie asked. 'That not all husband's behaved in the way Steve does?'

Bella thought about this for what seemed a long time. It was such a difficult question to answer. 'Only recently really; I hid everything from everyone, including myself and the children - kept myself apart from other people – it was what Steve wanted, you see.' Bella heard the sadness heavy in her own voice. How must she sound to Debbie, she wondered? 'I was in denial. I know that now. I was surviving.'

'So what made you want to come here?' Debbie asked. 'What changed the way you felt about your married life?'

Bella paused, and remembered Ginny's concern - that concern had broken down barriers.

'It was Ginny,' Bella explained, 'it was meeting her that changed how I thought about… things.'

'Would you like to talk about her?' Debbie asked.

Bella sighed with the relief of being able to talk about something more cheerful. She noticed Debbie had kept completely still, while she talked, only looking at her with a keen intentness, and in response to that Bella could feel the knots in her muscles begin to untie. It was a wonderful feeling, she thought.

'I don't know why - but Ginny took a liking to me,' Bella explained. 'She wasn't put off by my… anxiety. I know I look a fright too – I didn't always look so… dowdy, so horribly unattractive. That was Steve's doing. He said he liked me in brown.'

'Ginny is a good friend then?' Debbie asked, but it sounded more like a statement to Bella. She was the very best of friends.

Bella nodded, dabbing at the tears gathering at the corners of her eyes.

'Ginny was the first person I told about Steve's behaviour - she noticed the bruises, you see,' Bella shrugged with remembered embarrassment, 'and eventually, she wouldn't believe my stories anymore about doors and tripping up.'

Bella fell silent for a moment, while she thought about that serendipitous meeting on the rec – the start of their friendship.

'Ginny made me see I couldn't hide my bruises any longer - that I couldn't hide my secret life any longer,' Bella explained. She didn't persuade me, or anything like that, Ginny just… sort of made it possible for me to have the courage to face up to things. It's really difficult to explain.'

Bella could see Debbie nodding encouragingly, accompanied by a small smile of understanding at her words. She'd no doubt heard them all before.

'Ginny made me see,' Bella continued, amazed at herself for being so honest, 'that I couldn't carry on hiding away from my bruises – or from Steve's behaviour.'

Bella turned towards the window silent now, while she thought of all the people she had hidden her real life from. In the distance, all of a sudden she noticed a church spire pointing towards the heavens, above the jumble of rooftops. Even at a distance there was something familiar about it, Bella thought, and then suddenly she knew what it was - it reminded her of the church where she and Steve got married.

She was instantly transported back to the moment in the small church porch ready to walk down the aisle on her father's arm - he had been sober for once. She remembered walking the few short steps into the high, luminous-cream vaulted church. The space had been drenched with colour, as the sun streamed through the stained-glass windows. The years collapsed. She felt again the smooth feel of Steve's cashmere jacket under her fingers, and the smell of his after-shave - remembered as though only yesterday.

The rest was a blur of wedding nerves. But Bella, even now,

ten years later, could remember leaving the church a married woman so proud of her husband; her heart beating fast with excitement at the future ahead, and then suddenly they were showered with real pink cherry blossom floating on the breeze. It was a sign, she remembered thinking – nature had spoken its approval.

Bella's fingers worried at her hair, twisting and pulling it, as she went back in her mind to revisit the memories of the first few happy months of their marriage, before everything started to go wrong.

Forgotten by Bella, Debbie sat waiting, quietly, patiently.

41

Bella was remembering the day, eight years ago when Steve first hit her; it was etched on her mind - forever.

She and Izzie had been in the nursery, the first time Steve hit her. The baby had been only a few weeks old, she told Debbie, just as she had told Ginny. She felt tears at the back of her eyes at the thought of her darling, sweet smelling, innocent Izzie. Recounting the story again, she found was not nearly as difficult as telling Ginny the week before. She seemed to have found her voice. She began to tell Debbie what she had already told Ginny by the pond, about his temper. It was easier somehow telling Debbie, Bella thought, she felt more composed, less embarrassed - none of the hysteria she had experienced with Ginny. *Poor Ginny.*

'There was no warning,' she told Debbie, 'I was sitting in the nursery, feeding Izzie. It was a beautiful sunny day, and I remember feeling so happy with my little family.' Bella had to drag herself back to what happened next.

'He never did explain what it was that made him want to slap me hard on my face, that first time,' Bella said. 'And I'll probably never know.'

'What did Steve do after he slapped you?' Debbie asked.

'That was the odd thing,' Bella recalled, 'he just walked out of the room, and when I saw him a few hours later it was as though I had imagined it.'

'And there was a next time?' Debbie asked.

'Yes,' Bella nodded, miserably, 'it was nearly two years later. The second time, was a day no different to any other, either. Ben, our son, was only a few weeks old, just like Izzie had been.'

These were the days Bella treasured, so short, so precious – happily immersed in nappies, feeding, washing, and not sleeping.

'Izzy was still not yet two,' Bella carried on, 'so life had become more fraught - more chaotic, more sleepless nights, nothing as it used to be - everything constantly upside down. I loved it. But Steve was getting more and more irritable – I could sense his temper beginning to wear thin,' she told Debbie. 'And as with the first time, he slapped me across the face and then turned and walked out of the room.'

Bella still remembered the noise of that slap, like a crack of a whip.

'That second time,' Bella said, 'I realised with chilling clarity, that it may not be the last.'

Bella looked away from the church and its spire, back to Debbie, 'I'm not sure I can escape him – I'm too weak. That slap was by no means the last… '

'You're not on your own any more,' Debbie said into the silence, 'we'll be here helping you make whatever decision you want to take. And it will be *your* decision, Bella – nobody else's,' Debbie emphasised.

The room was silent again for a moment, while Debbie let Bella process what they had discussed. Bella, sitting quietly, felt the deepest relief, that the worst of her story was out. She felt exhausted; she just wanted to curl up on the mangy sofa and go to sleep for a long, long time.

Over the next hour or so, Debbie led her through a myriad of corridors where memories of the worst of Steve's excesses, had been locked away. Debbie hadn't been shocked. She just murmured her understanding, and when Bella needed reassurance to continue Debbie soothed and asked how she was feeling – always ensuring that she was feeling all right. Bella knew she didn't feel all right at all – but she also knew it had to be done – she had to get it over with, if she was going to change her life. She wanted it done.

'Shall we have a break now?' Debbie asked, Bella nodded, feeling that all the stuffing had been taken out of her, she felt limp and hollow. Debbie had pulled her story out of her, like yarn from a bobbin, layer upon layer, unravelling slowly.

Bella straightened herself up, and in the background heard for the first time, laughter and the voices of children. How long had she been there? Bella wondered.

'So, Bella, *what next,* you must be thinking?' Debbie asked, 'Today you've taken a huge step,' and to Bella's amazement, Debbie added, 'you're very strong, stronger than you think. But what you need now is time to get your breath back. If you like, I'll take you to meet some of the women who are staying here at the moment. Maybe, if you feel strong enough, you can have a chat with some of them. You may find their stories chime with your own. And after that, I will - with your permission - set up meetings – one of which will be with a solicitor.'

Bella felt her breath suddenly pulled out of her.

'Are you all right? Bella,' Debbie said, urgently. 'What is it? Sit down, you've gone terribly pale.'

The concern in Debbie's voice brought Bella back from the brink of fainting.

'Are you OK, Bella?' Debbie repeated, you gave me a fright.

Felling the blood slowly returning, Bella opened her eyes, and found Debbie's concerned face looking at her, 'I'm sorry – it was just the idea of seeing a solicitor - made it all seem… I don't know… a bit overwhelming.'

'Don't apologise,' Debbie comforted, 'you've been through so much just to get here. Our legal team is very dedicated - they really are the best.' Debbie said, gently putting her arm round Bella's shoulder. 'And don't forget, it's all totally confidential. Steve won't know you've been here. But it's your decision to make, of course it is – so take your time and think about it. Nothing's going to be done, without your consent. There's been enough of that in your life already.'

'Will I have to pay?' Bella asked, worried that she would have to use her small escape fund she had managed to hide from Steve. Her mother had given it to her, in one of her more lucid moments.

'You won't have to pay for anything, Bella,' Debbie reassured her. 'I'll explain all that later.'

'I'm all right now, really,' Bella said, standing up, her legs still trembling, as she followed Debbie towards the door, 'can we still meet some of the others?'

Bella followed Debbie down the pale blue corridor. There were doors on both sides of the corridor. Some were ajar, allowing Bella her first sight of where she might one day stay. As they walked, Bella could see some of the women standing in their doorways chatting. They all had a quick smile for her - and Bella thought she could see understanding in their faces, and felt an immediate connection with them - they of all people would know how she felt. Debbie had a quiet word for each of them as they went past.

Through the open doors she glimpsed more of the donations that Debbie had wryly talked about - blowsy curtains and mismatched furnishings. But what struck her, and what she would take away with her to be remembered in the dark moments that she had no doubt were ahead of her, was the sound of the women's laughter. She envied them that. She held on to that.

42

Bella couldn't remember what she and Ginny spoke about on the drive back to Sandwich. It had begun raining again, while Bella had been talking to Debbie. As they drove past the cliff-tops, Bella could see seagulls escaping the churning white-tipped waves - their flight chaotic, their screams raucous.

Her mind was so full of all that had happened that morning – Bella almost couldn't believe what she had just done.

'Did I just dream all this, Ginny?' Bella asked.

'I expect it was more like a nightmare?' Ginny observed wryly, as she peered through the windscreen into the lashing rain.

'This bloody weather,' Ginny observed, 'I suppose this is what you'd call an April shower? More like a deluge.'

The road to Sandwich was empty, not yet school-time; they made their way slowly through the narrow streets of the town to the car park at Gazen Salts on the riverbank. It was tucked away out of sight. They hadn't discussed the need for caution - it seemed instinctive somehow. They sat for a few minutes watching the boats bobbing about on the ebbing tide of the Stour. Life here seemed so peaceful, so uncomplicated, Bella thought.

She tried to thank Ginny for all that she had done, and to ask what she could do in return, but Ginny stopped her.

'There's no need for thanks, Bella, not now anyway,' Ginny said, smiling at her. 'I'm sure I can dream up something in the fullness of time – but not now.'

She caught a flicker of something behind Ginny's words that she didn't quite understand, but she was too exhausted to work it out.

'I'm such a nuisance though,' Bella lamented, shaking her head sorrowfully.

'Not to me, you're not,' Ginny reassured, 'it's not your fault – any of this – don't forget that. OK? You must be exhausted – so you can tell me what happened when I see you next – but just tell me this, so I can stop worrying about you – did everything go all right?'

'Better than all right,' she answered. And it had been, Bella thought, much, much better. Ginny reached over and gave her an awkward hug, 'I'm so… pleased.'

'I know,' Bella said, smiling, 'I couldn't have imagined anything like this happening to me. It's just wonderful.'

' And don't forget you've got supper on Saturday to look forward to as well,' Ginny said.

'I haven't forgotten, but are you sure you want to meet Steve after all I've told you?'

'Of course I do,' Ginny said, 'I want to keep you in my sights – make sure you're OK. And in a funny sort of way, I want to meet Steve. Is that a bit weird?"

'No, I don't think so,' Bella said, 'I'm just a bit worried how he'll behave, that's all.

'I hope the evening goes well,' Ginny said

'Why wouldn't it?' Bella asked, puzzled.

'Oh, nothing,' Ginny said with a shrug, 'nothing.'

The two women parted reluctantly, each to face their own particular dilemmas. Each concerned about the other.

43

Excitement about the Friday evening ahead, was making David unusually quiet, as he and Joe walked over to Hays Galleria after work. The week since he had last been here - since he had first met Alicia - had seemed endless. He had thought about nothing else all week. Thoughts of Alicia were the balm that had begun to heal his sadness about Grace.

'Are you OK, David?' Joe asked, turning to look at him, 'you seem...'

'Sorry,' David said, embarrassed, 'I've just been asked to attend the directors' meeting on Monday morning. So I'm... a bit preoccupied. It was a bit of a surprise you see.'

He couldn't tell Joe, that his preoccupation had little to do with promotion, it was more the thought of red curly hair, and a smattering of freckles..

'The directors' meeting?' Joe asked, dragging David back from thoughts of Alicia's long shapely legs. *What was happening to him?*

'You've kept that quiet,' Joe added, 'I'm not at all surprised though.' David could hear the admiration in Joe's voice. 'A possible directorship for you – do you think?'

'I don't know,' David said shrugging, 'there have been rumours but... I'll have to wait and see.'

At that precise moment though, it almost seemed unimportant, he thought with surprise. The promotion he'd been waiting years for, suddenly really did seem so inconsequential – he couldn't believe it. Alicia had done that. *Am I being a fool?*

Arriving at the grand glass doors of the Galleria, the two men parted company after a moment's surprise when he told Joe he was meeting up with a colleague. He didn't tell Joe who the colleague was, of course.

He waited until Joe was out of sight, and then turned his attention to finding Alicia. He searched the crowded room for that distinctive head of red hair. Catching sight of her eventually, chatting happily with friends, he breathed a sigh of relief. She was there – for one awful moment he had begun to fear she wouldn't be.

He stood for a moment just to enjoy the sight of her – but some instinct must have told her she was being watched. She turned and he saw with pleasure her face light up when she saw him. It wasn't his imagination after all, he thought, she really did liked him. She'd been waiting for him too. He raised his glass to her with a question – did she want a drink? He saw her nod, and while she said goodbye to her friends, he ordered her a cold glass of Sauvignon Blanc.

'Hello, Alicia,' David said, when she had scrambled through the scrum to him. Deciding against a greeting kiss, he was unable to resist putting his hand lightly on her arm for the merest of seconds. Alicia quickly looked down at his hand, and then back up to his face - the gleam of pleasure in her eyes was unmistakeable – he thought he might not be able to breathe again.

'I've got you a glass of wine,' he said, passing the glass to her, and as he did so, he noticed his hand trembling slightly. 'I hope that's what you want. I'm sorry we couldn't meet in the week,' he explained, 'this new project… ' He shrugged, and felt he didn't need to say anything more. He was sure she would understand.

'It doesn't matter,' Alicia said, 'I've been out of the office too this week. Do you remember the project in Exeter I mentioned last week? Well I'm officially on the team now.'

'That's terrific,' David said, and meant it. Bright and ambitious – she would do well, he thought. He didn't let on he'd had a word with her boss – but he was beginning to realise she wouldn't need his help to get on. She already had all the skills that were needed – enthusiasm, intelligence and a love for numbers.

They chatted for a few minutes about their week, struggling against the noise and the crush of people.

'Why's it so busy tonight?' Alicia asked, 'it's difficult to hear and I'm getting squashed. Should we go somewhere quieter?'

'OK,' he said, unprepared for the thrill racing through his body, at her suggestion.

'There's a good Italian place further along the street. What d'you think?' she asked, leaving the suggestion hanging in the air. 'I passed it the other day - it looked nice. David saw a rose-blush of embarrassment bloom on her cheeks.

He nodded, 'great idea,' he said quickly, before Alicia changed her mind. Possibilities for the evening ahead, made him feel dizzy with anticipation.

They walked through the Galleria; the shops now closed, and like any other couple out for a stroll, they looked at the over-priced goods in the windows as they went, wondering who would be mad enough to buy anything in them.

'More money than sense, Alicia said, 'that's who.

That was something else he liked about her – she was level-headed. It was all he could do to stop himself reaching for her hand – it seemed the most natural thing to want to do.

Alicia turned to say something, but his face must have shown what his thoughts were. It was his turn to feel the heat of embarrassment. He watched Alicia raise an eyebrow in question, and smiled when he gave a small shrug. She had known what he was thinking.

'Here it is,' Alicia said, indicating the restaurant ahead. 'It looks busy too - I hope they've a table for us.' He shivered at the thought of her word - *us*.

'I'm sure they'll be able to find a corner somewhere for us.' David reassured her - and that's exactly what the Italian waiter with jet-black hair and a white-toothed smile, was able to do.

The table, the waiter found for them, was in the bay window, set apart from the other diners. It couldn't be more perfect, he thought. They sat opposite each other, accidentally knocking knees, in the small space, treading on each other's feet as they squeezed into their cramped seats. The half-darkness leant a feeling of intimacy - cocooning them in their own world. He desperately wanted to reach out over the table and hold her hand.

He had to stop himself from telling Alicia he had never done anything like this before. It would just sound crass, he thought, and anyway what was *this*? After all, they were only having a meal alone to escape the crush at the bar. That was all wasn't it?

He desperately wanted to let Alicia know how exhilarated he felt – and how these feelings had been missing from his life for so long. He knew this feeling of thrill and pleasure, was what he had been searching for without even realising it. Excitement.

He wanted to tell her all that - but it wasn't the right time yet. One day soon - maybe. Instead, he smiled at her. His stomach suddenly tightened at the sight of the smooth cream skin she had glimpsed at her neckline, as she leant towards him.

Alicia liked her food, he discovered, as she tucked into her spaghetti alle vongole without embarrassment. His own appetite had suddenly disappeared – it felt so... confusing to be here with her, but at the same time he didn't want to be anywhere else.

'What?' she asked, when she caught him gazing at her.

'Nothing,' he said, smiling. It wasn't long before David worked out, what a minefield conversation was going to be. He couldn't just gaze at her he would have to make conversation. Ginny and his children threaded through every part of his life - except for work and running, he had little else that didn't directly connect back to Ginny. And Alicia was easily ten years younger than him so what did they have in common? *Was this mad?*

Alicia maybe had guessed his dilemma, he thought, and was chatting for both of them – she talked and he listened. She chose safe topics they both had in common; work, projects, colleagues, Joe. It was when Alicia turned the subject to what she was reading and listening to that David realised he hadn't heard, seen or read most of what she was talking about. *Where had he been this last ten years* But then he saw her smile at him, and he knew somehow it would be all right. They would find a way. They would find their way. *What on earth was he thinking about, he'd only just met her, he was married, she was over ten years younger than him – what did he mean 'their' way?*

'OK, David,' Alicia suddenly said, leaning back in her chair observing him, 'you've not heard of most of the music or films I've been talking about, have you? Come on, be honest now.'

Alicia's directness had taken him by surprise - he was found out - his smiling and nodding hadn't fooled her for a minute.

'Well erm… not really,' he finally admitted.

'What have you been doing if you don't read or watch films?' she asked, 'what do you do to relax?'

Relax? What was that he thought, and suddenly realised she may have a point, too much work had caused him to lose touch - he had been on a treadmill - work and then more work. Bringing up a family. Married. That's what he'd been doing.

'Working,' he answered. 'It's all I've done for the last nearly twenty years. You want promotion so you work longer, later and then you commute to get a better job – more promotion and before you know it – you're just going home to sleep. That's where I've been.'

He watched Alicia process this sad state of affairs.

'I listen to Oasis and Nirvana when I run – does that count?' he noticed she didn't look too impressed.

'I'll just have to take you in hand,' she said, in a quiet voice sending excitement coursing through his body.

The waiter arrived back at their table to take away their plates; the sound of the waiter's accent made him think of Florence and how much he would love to take Alicia there. 'Deserts?' the waiter asked. 'Tiramisu?' the waiter prompted.

David laughed at her *absolutely* reply.

'Perfect,' Alicia answered the waiter, with the eagerness of a child.

Knowing what he must have been thinking the look she gave him then, had absolutely nothing of the child in it – Alicia's eyes spoke of possibilities.

'You've not eaten much, David,' she said, 'is there anything wrong?'

If he told her he was feasting his eyes on her, and that was enough for him, she would think he had been reading Mills and Boon. Instead, he smiled and shook his head,' big lunch,' he lied.

'Tell me what *you* do when you're not at work,' David asked. 'What, for example are you doing tomorrow night?

Why did I ask that, for goodness sake? It's was the last thing he wanted to hear about – would he feel jealous?

'Oh, I'm off to a club in Brixton with friends from uni. It's called Electric Brixton - heard of it?' She laughed at David's expression. 'I'll take that as a 'no' then, shall I?' David hadn't reckoned on the stab of jealousy he felt at her words. *Yes, he most certainly did feel jealous. What was happening to him?*

'What about you?' Alicia asked, 'what are you up to this weekend?'

'We're having a dinner party tomorrow night,' he admitted reluctantly, 'Joe and his wife, are coming over and a few other friends.'

A half-drunk glass of red wine in her hand, and her Tiramisu finished - fingertips licked – Alicia looked up and suddenly asked, 'why are you here, David - why are you not at home with your wife?'

It was the second time Alicia had asked that question. David nearly choked at her directness he hadn't been expecting it - not tonight anyway - he'd hoped it would remain something unspoken, for a while longer anyway.

'You asked me to come here… and I wanted to,' he finally decided on saying. It was far too soon to dive into the murky waters of his marriage.

Alicia smiled and nodded. Looking at him pensively for a moment, her features tightened with concentration. It seemed to him that Alicia was trying to make up her mind about something.

She picked up her glass, and raised it towards him, waiting for his response. He picked up his own. He couldn't remember ever feeling so alive as he did in that moment; her eyes in the shadows looked green and smoky, a question was held in them. He moved his glass slowly towards hers - he carefully and slowly touched her glass with his. They didn't speak – just looked. It was such an exquisite moment, he couldn't ever remember experiencing one like it in his whole life before. Not even with Ginny.

The door to the restaurant opened, and David watched with horror as John Samuels, one of his directors, walked in. David scooted his chair over quickly so that he wasn't so visible. *Damn. What a fool to come here so near work.* Just what he needed, to be seen out with Alicia by John, one of the biggest gossips in the company, and what was worse he would be at the directors' meeting on Monday. *Hell and damnation.*

'David, what's wrong?' Alicia asked, turning her head to follow his gaze. 'Who is it? Is it someone from work?'

'It's nothing… no one,' he lied, shaking his head. They had to get out of here, before he was spotted. Reality had very much made its presence felt and so quickly. He swore long and hard under his breath.

'David,' Alicia said, quietly reminding him that she was still there.

'I'm sorry,' he said, 'it's one of the directors. We'd better make a move; it's getting late anyway.'

He saw her look of disappointment, and felt the beginnings of regret. Life wasn't going to be as simple as he'd hoped. It still mattered after all, how he behaved - what others thought of his actions. He was still a married man. A married man with a girl friend.

He paid the bill and left the restaurant feeling ridiculous, and embarrassed – he let out a slow breath of relief as the door closed behind them, pretty sure they hadn't been seen. What a stupid thing to have done, he thought, to have gone somewhere were they would both be known. He was new to this world of subterfuge. He'd have to be more careful in future. *Was there going to be a future for them, though?* The idea was exhilarating.

Deciding to walk along the Embankment, putting off the moment when they'd have to go their separate ways, they reached the Thames. David could smell the river, could see the lights on the buildings, and the boats bobbing on their moorings, and the slapping sounds as the ripples of water hit the banks of the river. But tonight, for once, he was more aware of Alicia than these sights and sounds he had grown to love. Her perfume drifted on the air. He noticed the delicate way she had of tucking a stray curl behind her ear – he wanted to be able to do that for her. To touch her. In that moment, it was all he could think about.

A sudden squall of rain had them leaping into the nearest doorway to shelter, legs and bodies inadvertently touching in the confined space. David turned to Alicia to apologise for rushing out of the restaurant, but the look in her eyes stopped his words from ever reaching his lips.

He didn't have to think about what he did next – it was pure instinct. He reached over and gently pulled her into his arms. She didn't resist. Their faces only inches apart now – it would take so little – so very little, to make that last step. But he hesitated, and in that moment Alicia, sensing his indecision leaned her face towards his and gently touched his lips with hers. She then retreated and waited. Did he, or did he not want her? She seemed to be asking him. It was time to make up his mind – she couldn't have been plainer. He wanted her. She wanted him. He couldn't believe it.

David became vaguely aware that somebody else was in the doorway. But in that moment of abandon with Alicia, all David's conscious thoughts were elsewhere. There was nothing and no one that could distract him now, except the feel of Alicia's body leaning into his - her perfume, subtle – desirous, her lips, soft – seductive. He laid his first kiss on her mouth. It was thrilling and terrifying in equal measure. He was disturbingly aware of having stepped over the line into the heady and uncertain world of secrecy.

Someone shouting at them brought them back down to earth. A young emaciated looking man suddenly sat up from under a pile of cardboard and old duvets.

'Go away. This is my bloody doorway,' he roared, shaking his fist, the other hand holding a whisky bottle, 'go away.'

'Sorry,' David said, 'I didn't…' he had been about to say 'see you there,' but somehow the man's plight deserved better than that. Rifling in his pocket for some change, he apologised again. They left the safety of the doorway, giggling with embarrassment.

'Thanks, Guv,' the homeless man slurred, 'I can see why

you didn't notice me, she's a looker that one.' She certainly was, David thought, smiling, desire still fizzing through his veins. He caught the wink the man directed at her as they walked away.

As they headed towards London Bridge, David felt a small, warm hand placed in his own. He gave it a squeeze. It felt so right, her hand in his, and somehow he had known it would. He wished the moment could last forever.

After waving Alicia off on her train, he made his way to St Pancras where he managed to jump on the Ramsgate train, which was waiting at the platform. As it sped towards Sandwich, its wheels racing over the tracks, and the wind streaming over the carriages, David closed his eyes and smiled to himself. His thoughts drifted back to the feel of soft, pink, greedy lips, and to his own longings. He looked out from the window, as the train hurtled out of the velvet darkness, onto the starlit Rochester railway-bridge - a gloriously intricate, Victorian cast iron structure. Moonlight shone on the scruffy-brown river Medway below. Everything, David thought, suddenly felt exquisitely intense.

44

It was nearly eleven when David's train glided into Sandwich Station, empty except for him. The Friday night drunken passengers, had long since found oblivion in their beds. He should have been home hours ago; Ginny would be livid with him. *Why didn't I phone her?* But he knew exactly why – the sound of Ginny's voice would have brought him back to reality. Would have made what happened tonight impossible.

'Sorry, for being so late,' he mumbled, closing the front door behind him, 'got caught up with something at work,' making straight for the kitchen hoping to escape her ire.

'Another bad day at work - was it?' Ginny asked, from the doorway her arms folded, her body rigid. She was angrier than he had ever seen her. He heard her scathing tone, and knew he deserved every word of it.

'I've a meeting with the directors on Monday,' he tried explaining, 'maybe promotion. I've been prepping for it with Joe.'

It sounded feeble even to his own ears. He was beginning to discover he lacked guile. He had never needed its benefits before. It was only then, he asked himself if he were to be promoted, would Ginny be part of that future?

'Really. Again?' she asked.

He could see disbelief written all over her face. He couldn't blame her. None of it sounded at all plausible.

He felt Ginny's eyes scorching his back, as he quickly left the kitchen to go up to his bedroom. He felt exhausted. Emotional exhaustion. Exhilarated.

He wondered, as he got ready for bed in the spare room, if Ginny might guess about him and Alicia. Had it shown on his face, maybe? Did he smell of her delicious perfume? Was there lipstick on his shirt collar? Quickly taking off his shirt, he rolled it into a ball, and disposed of it in the laundry basket.

Sliding into bed, his mobile buzzed - his breath caught in his chest as he saw who it was - Alicia had sent him a red heart, pulsing. David's thoughts turned to their dark luscious kiss as he drifted into sleep.

45

All day Saturday, Ginny had tried to shake off a feeling of foreboding; it had woken her about six that morning, with the dawn chorus. She slipped out of bed and went to the window. She was in time to watch the sunrise creep, inch by inch over her garden: trees shrouded in grey, slowly emerging - greys turning to pink, and then to the pale green of newly formed leaf buds. A mist lingered at their base, creating an eeriness that appeared otherworldly.

The day slipped by slowly, painfully, the atmosphere so tense between her and David, she could almost taste it. Metallic – acid - burning.

Preparations for the dinner party that evening kept her busy; it stopped her from thinking about where David had been the night before, and the previous Friday night. Ginny knew - she didn't know how - but something was definitely different about David. He seemed glowing almost, but Ginny also knew, it had absolutely nothing to do with her. *Then who?*

At nearly seven, desperate for the day to be over, Ginny sat down at her dressing table to apply a mask of thick make-up to hide behind. She had less than half an hour before their dinner guests arrived. Despite the make-up, Ginny could see the mirror was still reflecting the truth; one that she was trying to avoid – she looked wounded, desolate.

The hurt of the last few weeks of David's unexplained, out of the ordinary absences, was clear to see in the mirror. She saw only too acutely that her unhappiness had dimmed her innate attractiveness. She had tried to paint it back on, with eye-liner, lipstick, blusher – the works. The faint purple shadows beneath her eyes, the lines on her face now etched slightly deeper – they all still spoke of her pain. She turned away. She didn't need her reflection to tell her how shockingly awful she was feeling. Feeling barely able to cope, it was only the thought of Bella and Leila coming that had made her carry on.

A knock on the bedroom door startled her, turning towards the door, she saw David come almost stealthily into their bedroom.

'Sorry,' David said, 'I need some clothes for tonight.' He looked embarrassed, she thought. He was wearing his dressing gown; she could see he had just showered, his silver blonde hair, tousled and damp, his cheeks pink from heat. Her stomach clenched with a sense of loss so strong it took her breath away. She still loved this man; his body even now, had the power to cause her body respond with longing. But now, they were teetering on the edge of the abyss, and she felt powerless to save them both from falling.

'Of course,' she said, looking at him forcing a bright smile, 'it's your bedroom too after all.' He flushed at her words and moved quickly to his cupboard.

'Ginny…' David started to say, he was facing her, clothes bundled in his arms, looking like a fresh schoolboy. Her heart yearned to reach out and touch him. She watched him stand there, uncertain, strained.

'Yes?' she said, her heart beating rapidly with hope. She could see he was trying to decide on something.

'Nothing, it's all right' he said to her abject disappointment. What had he been about to say? The moment had passed - the balance, she knew, had swung. He had just made a decision. She gulped back her tears, and turned away.

The doorbell rang a few moments later.

'David, will you get that?' Ginny called. She didn't feel ready to face anyone just yet. She needed just one more minute to catch her breath.

Ginny stood up, and a last fleeting look in the mirror confirmed that she had at least done her best: Armani dress red, and sassy - determined not to let David see what he had done to her. She walked out of the bedroom with resolve - her head held high - determined to deceive.

46

The days had seemed endless to Bella since Tuesday, and her visit to the refuge, but Saturday, the day of Ginny's dinner party, finally arrived. Days of trying to avoid Steve, days of keeping out of trouble with him, days of nail-biting anxiety, days of having to hide a bubbling up of hopeful thoughts had taken their toll. She felt exhausted. And now here they were, at last, she thought, just like any other couple on a Saturday night - getting ready to go out to dinner.

She tried not to think about how close she had come, to being found out about her visit to the refuge. To her horror, Steve had been waiting for her when she got home from the refuge - he had been sent home from work. Redundancy in Steve's case had really meant – dismissal. He was on gardening leave. It had taken all of Bella's wits to think up a plausible excuse for her absence.

'Where've you been?' Steve said, glowering at her. He was still in his work suit sitting at the kitchen table, a beer in front of him. Petulance showing on his face - Bella's spirits sank - he couldn't be drunk already surely?' she thought, it wasn't even two o'clock yet.

'I went for a walk,' she explained, 'I had a headache,' she quickly backed out of the kitchen, out of his way – unwilling to give him a chance to probe further.

Stupid woman, she heard him mutter as he stomped into

the living room. Minutes later at the sound of the television blaring, Bella let out an enormous sigh of relief; she had got away with it.

Bella slipped into her forget-me-not blue dress; an old friend from happier days, rescued from one of Steve's angry purges. Bella stood in front of the mirror: the young woman who had worn the forget-me-not blue dress, the one who had returned home, radiant from her date with Steve, an engaged woman - was gone – long gone – ten years gone. Silky blondish hair – had been replaced with mouse-brown, all shine lost; eyes a sparkling pale blue – now tired, pale, washed out with tears. But tonight, Bella thought, she'd been given another chance to wear the dress; another chance of happiness.

Lipstick poised, the palest of pale pinks so Steve wouldn't notice; she imagines herself young, carefree, as the pale slick glides on her lips. She smiled. Anything was possible.

'What are you smiling about? Hey?' Steve said, suddenly coming into the room, startling her. 'Where did that rag come from? I thought I'd thrown it out.'

'I found it in the back of the wardrobe,' she answered, breathing slowly not to give her lie away. He threw her a look of disbelief, but must have decided there wasn't enough time to pursue it.

'Hurry up for God's sake, will you,' Steve said, leaving the room – tension vibrating in the air.

Bella didn't think the moment would ever come, but it did; the slam of the front door behind them told her it had. They walked, not hand in hand like two people that loved each other, but side by side as far apart as the narrow, cobbled pavements would allow.

To calm her nerves, Bella thought of the reassuring telephone conversation she'd had with Ginny the evening before whilst she hid in the courtyard shadows, her teeth chattering.

'Debbie sounds really supportive,' Ginny had said, after Bella told her what had been said.

'I've got to speak to a solicitor next though,' Bella said, 'it sounds really scary.'

'I'm sure it will be OK,' Ginny said, and Bella was calmed, but only slightly, 'they'd only use solicitors who had chosen… this sort of work.'

'Didn't you mention,' Bella said, 'that one of your friends did this sort of legal work?'

'Yes, Leila Mistry,' Ginny answered. Bella heard the pause and wondered what it was about, 'you'll be meeting her tomorrow night at dinner - don't panic though.' Bella knew that Ginny had heard her quick intake of breath, 'you won't be talking about anything like that tomorrow – it wouldn't be… professional. And she doesn't know it's you. I promise you it will be all right.'

At Ginny's words, Bella breathed a sigh of relief.

'Are you sure you don't need any help tomorrow?' Bella asked, wondering how she could with Steve at home.

'No thanks, just make sure you enjoy yourself,' Ginny replied, 'that'll be the biggest help.'

There was something in Ginny's voice that Bella didn't quite understand. She remembered now that she'd heard it the other day too. Could Ginny have problems of her own? Bella wondered. She'd ask tomorrow at supper.

47

Ginny plastered a smile on her face, and went down the stairs and crossed the blonde wood hall. She could hear a murmur of voices coming from the living room and wondered who it was that had arrived.

Taking a deep steadying breath, Ginny walked into the living room, and saw with pleasure Leila, and what she assumed was Matt, standing next to the French windows.

David, she could see, was taking people's coats and in exchange, handing them a pink bubbling cocktail. He was doing a good job as usual, of making people feel welcome in his home - at least he hadn't forgotten how to do that, she thought bitterly. She walked over to greet them, comforted at the sight of Leila.

She thought of the long chat she and Leila had earlier that morning, when she phoned to cancel their horse ride together.

'Oh no, Ginny, why not?' Leila asked, her disappointment making her feel even worse. 'I was so looking forward to it.' Leila added, 'has something happened?'

Ginny gulped, thrown by Leila's disappointment and her question. There was an easy way to answer it, and a hard way. There was a lie and then there was the truth.

'I'm sorry, I was looking forward to it as well it's just that,' Ginny paused, and then the dam burst and all the fears she had managed to bottle up for months, came tumbling out.

'It's David, he came home really late last night,' she found herself telling Leila, 'and there was something about him – it's difficult to explain. When you've lived with someone for nearly twenty years - you just know when something is… it's a feeling… you know?'

Ginny struggled to put into words an instinct, something without any actual foundation. Knowledge without knowing, 'and,' Ginny continued, 'there was the Friday before that too.'

'Go on,' Leila said, her voice sounding alarmed.

'I don't know why it should be bothering me so much - but it is. He came home looking so… shining, and if he sees me watching him, he turns away as though he's embarrassed. It's as if he's got something to hide. And something else,' Ginny continued, 'he seems all of a sudden to have forgotten about Grace. He was so distraught when he found out Grace had to have her foot amputated, but only a week later he's stopped mentioning Grace at all.'

Ginny could feel her voice catch. 'Or maybe it's *because of* Grace?'

'What do you mean, because of Grace?' Leila asked, 'in what way?'

Ginny didn't exactly know herself what she meant – it was based on gut feeling. Her mind looped, and paused. 'To forget her… maybe? Do you think it's another woman? It can't be – can it?' *Was he being unfaithful? No. He couldn't. Could he?* Ginny's head started to swirl. She was surprised to hear Leila speak, she had forgotten for a moment she was on her mobile.

'Ginny, hang on,' Leila said, 'you don't know that for certain, do you?'

'I don't know for certain,' Ginny admitted, 'I feel it though.

I know that sounds lame. It would explain a lot… if he was.'

'I'm sure he isn't,' Leila said, trying to be reassuring, 'I wouldn't think he's like that. He seems so… calm, and from what you've told me you've always worked as a team.'

'You're probably right,' Ginny agreed, reassured to hear Leila's sensible words, and let out her breath in a long sigh. 'I'm probably… overreacting. I know you'll want to get to the stables now – I just wanted to catch you before you went. Can we talk again soon – not at the dinner party though.'

To Leila's offer of help for the evening, she replied, 'no thank you - not with the food – at least I've got that under control,' Ginny answered. 'I just follow my mother's advice: keep it simple, and use fresh ingredients.'

Pushing the grim thoughts of the morning's phone call away, and replacing them with a welcoming smile, she kissed Leila on both cheeks.

'Leila, you look so pretty - turquoise really suits you. And you, of course must be, Matt?' Ginny said, stretching out a hand in greeting.

Leila had somehow forgotten to tell her how handsome Matt was, Ginny thought. Leila had mentioned he was Argentinian, but she found she was not prepared for the sight of this tall, lean, man. A lecturer at University College London, Ginny remembered - it explained his casualness: the not quite shaved look, the slightly over-long, crow-black hair, curling over the back of his collar – a modern-day conquistador, she thought.

'Yes. I'm Matt,' he answered with a bright smile, teeth white against olive skin. 'I've heard about the fun you have horse riding with Leila,' he said, directing a cheerful smile at Ginny, and then back to Leila.

She smiled back – his smile was infectious.

'You're a lecturer, I remember Leila saying?' she asked, 'I can't remember what your subject is though.'

'Mathematics,' he replied.

Ginny shuddered as memories of incomprehensible equations flashed through her head.

'I saw that shudder,' Matt said, with a large grin, 'wrong teacher that's all - it's easy really.'

'Hmm,' Ginny said, looking at Leila for agreement. But she could see Leila didn't agree. 'I suppose you liked Maths, Leila?'

'I did,' she answered, almost apologetically. 'We happened to have a really inspiring teacher,' Leila paused, and Ginny wondered why she should suddenly look sad, 'I wanted to do a Maths degree, but… it wasn't to be.'

'Oh, why was that?' Ginny asked, surprised as Leila always spoke of her work so passionately.

Leila shrugged, 'my father… ' Her words trailed to a halt.

'What about all these women, you're helping to put back on their feet?' Matt asked, putting his arm round her shoulder. 'You'd have been an accountant instead, working for capitalists. You'd have hated it, Querida.' They all laughed. *Querida.* Ginny thought, how romantic, and envied her this man.

'What about you, Ginny,' Matt asked, 'what do you do besides creating a fantastic home?'

She wanted to hug him, 'thank you – it's been quite a project.'

'It's so tranquil here,' he said, looking around the room with admiration. And the garden from what I can see of it, looks amazing.' They could just see in the floodlights, the garden stretching out into darkness.

She heard the doorbell ring again, more insistent this time. Where was David for goodness sake?

'You'll have to excuse me,' she said, interrupting Matt, 'I think there's someone at the door. We can chat later, though.'

She turned 'I'll look forward to that,' as she went to look for David.

48

B ella stood with Steve waiting on the doorstep to Port Lodge, nervously wondering why no one was answering the door.

She and Steve had walked silently, side by side, through the streets of Sandwich, their footsteps echoing in the darkening light. Old-fashioned black iron lampposts were creating pools of yellow light on the ground by their feet. Bella shivered, her cotton dress though pretty, did nothing to protect her from the chill breeze off the sea. Even this late in the evening, Bella could hear lambs, in the distance, bleating soulfully for their mothers. I know how you feel, she thought.

'You've got the wrong night, haven't you? It's not this Saturday at all, is it?' Steve accused her - mirroring her own fears. *Stupid cow,* she could hear him mutter. 'I reckon they've got more money than sense these people,' he commented sourly, look-ing around him, and peering into a downstairs window. 'Oh, and before I forget, I hope you're not going to embarrass me tonight, with your nonsensical opinions? Just don't embarrass me – hey.' Bella felt a shove in her back.

'Of course not, Steve,' she murmured, more meekly than she felt. She worried that it was going to be him that was going to be the embarrassment.

Bella had surprised herself since visiting Debbie, to find some courage returning to her. She still felt much too much like a frightened mouse - but she felt the mouse was growing ever so slightly bigger and stronger.

'And don't think, we're going to make a habit of visiting Mr and Mrs Port Lodge,' Steve continued, jerking Bella from her thoughts, as he seemed to do so often these days. 'I only agreed to come tonight,' he went on in a harsh voice, 'because it might be useful to get to know David – you told me he plays golf at St George's – I hope you're right. Come to think of it, after tonight I don't want you seeing this friend of yours again – understood?'

So that's why he agreed to come, Bella realised, he wants David to sponsor his membership for St George's.

'And don't you dare tell them,' Steve added, trying to grab at her arm, as he spoke, but she was too quick for him, she managed to dart out of his way causing him to stumble. When she saw a puzzled, suspicious look on his face, she wished she'd let him grab her. And then remembering what he'd been in the middle of saying, Steve continued, 'don't you dare tell them I've been suspended from work.'

Dismissed, more like, she thought rebelliously.

49

Ginny opened the door to find Bella standing at the side of a tall, broad-shouldered man. She was taken aback at how imposing Steve was. A big hawk like nose stood under thick black eyebrows, his eyes, dark and piercing were scrutinising her intensely. She shuddered. How on earth did Bella cope with this man? Ginny didn't like the look of him one little bit. *So that's Steve.* Ginny felt furious, at the thought of what this man had put Bella through.

She drew them into the hall, and wondered again where on earth David was? She needed him to take their coats, and give them a drink.

'Hi, Bella,' Ginny greeted them with the biggest smile she could muster, 'and you must be Steve?' She kissed Bella briefly on the cheek, and held out her hand for Steve to shake; he nearly crushed her fingers in his. She kept smiling, determined not to show how much he was hurting her. In that moment, Ginny began to have an inkling of what Bella's life was like.

She led the way into the living room, and was relieved to see that David had reappeared again. *Where has he been all this time?* He was holding a silver tray of glass flutes with delicate pink bubbles, bouncing on the surface. 'Prosecco and rose hip,' he explained to Bella and Steve, smiling urbanely. 'I'm David - Ginny's husband. You must be Bella and Steve?'

'Yes, Steve Boswell, and Bella. Not for me, thanks,' Steve

said, making a dismissive movement with his hand over the cocktails. 'I wouldn't mind a beer, though,' he added, looking around him.

'Of course, if you can wait a minute,' David answered. 'I'll just take these round first.'

'I'll have one of those please, before you go, David,' Ginny said, pointing to the glass flutes.

She was beginning to feel a strong need for alcohol, and had a feeling the evening was going to be more difficult than she had even imagined.

'So you found the house all right?' Ginny asked, looking at Steve, and avoiding Bella's eyes. She didn't trust herself not to give away Bella's visit to the house, a few days before.

'Well, it wasn't that difficult,' Steve answered, with an undertone of sarcasm.

'No, I suppose not,' Ginny replied, at a loss as to how to continue a conversation with this brusque man. He wasn't even trying to be polite, she thought.

'It's a beautiful home, Ginny,' Bella said quietly, trying to cover up for her husband's rudeness.

'Thank you,' Ginny replied.

'Must have cost a packet,' Steve said, rudely.

'We've done a lot of work to it,' Ginny replied, furious that he had put her on the defensive. Why should she need to justify anything to him?

What to say next, Ginny panicked? Every potential conversation it seemed could lead Bella into trouble: work – redundancy, that was out, anything to do with the house and garden, was out too, meeting Bella anywhere was out – what could she say?

Ginny was desperate to get away from this man, and she'd only met him a few moments ago. But for Bella's sake, she had to make an effort. How did Bella cope? She wondered.

'I'll introduce you to Leila, and her boyfriend, Matt,' Ginny said, pointing them out to Bella and Steve.

Ginny could see Bella was trying to manage her fears, about meeting Leila. *Damn, should I have warned Leila about her?* Too late now, Ginny thought. She noticed Steve didn't look at all impressed. He seemed to be sneering at everything.

'This is a lovely room, Ginny,' Bella said, as they stood in the doorway, 'all those neutrals, makes it look so peaceful. I love the splash of colour as well, that fuchsia-pink is gorgeous.'

Ginny smiled at the compliment – relieved Bella was going to be all right after all. 'I'm going to chase David about that beer, Steve. I'm sure he'll bring it to you in a minute.'

She didn't like the expression on Steve's face; he seemed to be looking around the room glowering - but why? Ginny wondered, what was wrong with the man? She was beginning to wish she hadn't invited him. Not a good start, Ginny thought. She could tell he had once been handsome; the beginnings of flabbiness, was now against him. Taller and more impos-ing than she'd expected - he towered over Bella, who seemed diminutive next to him.

'Leila's a solicitor, and we ride our horses together,' Ginny explained, as they walked across the room to meet them. 'Matt, is a mathematic's lecturer at University College, London.'

After the introductions, Ginny was pleased to see Leila and Bella immediately strike up a conversation - they both enjoyed living in Sandwich.

'If you'll excuse me, I have some things to finish off in the kitchen,' Ginny explained starting to walk away, 'it shouldn't be too much longer now.'

David seemed to have disappeared again. He wasn't in the kitchen – and his study was empty. Where was he? Ginny wondered? Knowing she didn't have any more time to search for him, she decided she would just have to get on without him – she was beginning to get used to that, she realised. And then she thought – *I could phone him.* Phone your own husband, at a dinner party? That's really weird but… well he's behaving weirdly too, she thought. She picked up her mobile and pressed his number – engaged. *Who the hell was he speaking to?*

Sure she would feel better if she just got on with things, and forgot about David for the moment, she started on the final flourishes to the shrimp and tarragon crostini – an easy last-minute job – and the fillet of beef, that had been marinating in balsamic vinegar, soy sauce, garlic and honey since the night before, smelled delicious and just needed flash grilling. Fresh green vegetables from her greenhouse, stored lovingly over winter, completed the dinner. For dessert, forced pink rhubarb from her cold frame; rhubarb, she had been excited to find, had in a very timely manner poked their noses through the dark April earth and grown enough to be served that evening with homemade shortbread, and the local farm's cream.

Everything, she thought, was nicely organised - as it should be. Except for the fact that her husband was missing, and was probably having an affair. Except for the fact that David was chatting on his mobile to someone in the middle of a dinner party. She tried phoning his mobile again, and found he was still chatting. So *who* was he talking to on his mobile, on a Saturday evening in the middle of supper?

Feeling frazzled and alone, she stood for a moment looking out of the kitchen window at her beloved garden, and let a wave of prescience roll over her. Ginny's gloom laden thoughts were disturbed, when the back door opened to reveal David. At exactly the same moment, the front door bell rang. He obviously hadn't been expecting to see her in the kitchen, judging by the flush of embarrassment on his face.

'David, where the hell have you been? We've got guests,' she said, trying to keep her anger from showing too much. After all, they had to get through this evening, 'I need you here? There's someone at the front door, there's people without drinks, and I've had to leave guests on their own, so I can sort things out here in the kitchen.' She could hear her voice rising in anger. And…' She paused should she tell him she had just tried to phone him. Deciding not, '… nothing. Just get Steve a beer will you, I can tell he's going to be difficult.'

'Well, you invited him, not me,' David replied, ' so calm down,' he said, dismissively, 'I just had to take a call, that's all – nothing to get in a flap about. I'll get the front door, and a beer for Steve,' he said, grabbing one from the fridge, as he went. Ginny stood open-mouthed at his rudeness, as the door closed behind him.

She could hear David greeting the last guests to come. He sounded affable, friendly. Her anger soared at his off-hand treatment of her. She suddenly wondered, if he could have been chatting to another woman? That would explain his embarrassment, she shied away from the idea - it was just too horrible to contemplate, not when there were all these people in the house. She would leave that thought to later.

Leila's boyfriend, Matt, could see Bella was in pain. Her mouth had suddenly shut tight, as if to stop a sound emerging – had she just been stung? Could Steve have hurt her somehow? From where he was standing, he could see Steve's hand lying loosely on her arm, and just below his hand Matt could see a red mark beginning to flower. Had her husband squeezed her arm too hard? How could you do that by accident? Matt wondered.

Matt knew nothing about Steve or Bella, and nor did Leila. They didn't seem to fit though, with what Leila had told him about Ginny, or at least Steve didn't. Bella, he thought, was rather sweet, but exhausted looking. He sensed immediately when he'd been introduced to them, that there was something definitely not right between her, and her husband, Steve. He had no idea what – it was some sort of tension. Had they had an argument before coming out?

Bella seemed so fragile, Matt thought - her gentle face, somehow reminding Matt of a horse about to take flight - eyes wide, anticipating danger. Her husband, he thought, couldn't have been more different: physically imposing, taller than himself, broad shouldered, but beginning to run to fat. Bella on the other hand, he thought, looked petite against Steve's bulk. But what Matt found unpleasant, was the sour expression on Steve's face

'Are you all right, Bella?' Matt asked, but when he saw the look on Steve's face, Matt gave Leila a sideways glance as much as to say - *what the hell is going on here?* She didn't respond. When he looked back he saw why - Steve was staring at Leila, with a dark look on his face waiting for her to respond.

Matt swallowed hard, and took Leila's queue, 'so, Steve, what do you do?'

It seemed to Matt that the two women relaxed, as the attention was deflected away from them.

'I'm a chemist,' Steve said, 'at Pharbos. What about yourself? A lecturer, did Ginny say?'

Matt heard the disdain in Steve's voice. It really annoyed him that he had to be in this horrible man's company for the evening, especially when Leila looked so incredibly beautiful tonight: her hair, raven-black glossy and sleek, her dress, resembling a sari, turquoise-blue, the hem edged in gold. He would infinitely prefer to enjoy the evening with her on their own, instead of having to talk to this objectionable man.

'Yes, I'm a maths lecturer,' Matt replied flatly, 'in London. I expect you went to university, Steve, as you're a chemist?'

'No,' Steve said, abruptly, 'I learnt everything I needed to know on the job, or in the lab, not the ivory groves of academe.'

Matt heard the unpleasantness in Steve's tone, and sighed. He wished he'd never begun this conversation - it wasn't going the way he'd hoped. He thought Steve an arrogant idiot, but the last thing he wanted to do, was embarrass Bella who had the misfortune to be Steve's wife. He decided to be as conciliatory as possible.

'Well, yes,' Matt replied, determined to try to be polite 'I do teach in the academic world, and what I teach is fairly abstract, but there are many new applications coming up, almost every day, for applying maths in the real world.'

Steve gave a brief nod and a curt disbelieving grunt. Matt wished, not for the first time, that he and Leila hadn't come. Much as he'd wanted to meet Ginny, this was turning out to be an unexpectedly awful evening. He was relieved when Leila smiled, and changed the subject, asking Steve whether he used a golf course in Sandwich.

'Which one?' Steve asked, 'there are two.'

'Oh, really, I'm afraid I'm not sure; I don't know that much about golf,' Leila replied, 'sorry.'

Matt could tell she absolutely wasn't sorry. Matt found himself wanting to laugh. Her voice sounded even more resolute than usual.

'Haven't you heard of the Open Golf Championships?' Steve asked, disbelief evident in his voice. 'It was held here only a few years ago. If you live in Sandwich, you've got to have noticed the traffic jams in town, surely?'

'I've lived here less than a year, so I must have missed it,' Leila replied, with what Matt heard as careful tact. 'I'd like to hear about it though, Steve. Did you go?'

It was obvious to Matt, that Leila was leading this man away from anything contentious. She was using her court skills, as Matt knew Leila hadn't the least idea, or any interest in golf, but she had recognised that Steve did. Well done, Leila.

Steve began explaining to them why Sandwich was such a great golfing location: not only was the place blessed with two golf courses, but according to Steve the courses were among the hardest in Britain, being links courses. Leila asked what a links course was, and Steve patronisingly explained, at great length, that it meant there were sand dunes under the grass.

Finally, after what in fact was a speech of only a few minutes, but which to Matt seemed interminable, and just about the most boring he'd ever heard, and not excluding those of various chairpersons at the administrative meetings he was forced to attend, Steve finally shut up. Possibly, Matt decided, because he'd run out of breath.

To forestall Steve from teeing off about golf again, Matt quickly filled the ensuing silence by asking Bella how she and Ginny had met. But was surprised to see Bella's face flush pink. What had he said? Matt wondered, to cause her embarrassment.

Bella then said quietly, without looking at Steve, 'we met out, walking our dogs and at church. She and I, have been doing some campaigning together, too.'

Well done, lovely Bella, Matt thought, don't let that creep undermine you. But why had Bella begun to stutter?

'Campaigning? That sounds interesting,' Matt said, not waiting for any remark from Steve.

'Does, it? Anyway I'm off, ' Steve cut in, taking out a cigarette packet from his pocket and waggling it about in front of Matt, 'I don't suppose I can smoke in here, what do you think?'

'I think you're probably right,' Matt said, 'you'd be better off going outside, there's plenty of lights on out there.'

'I don't know about anybody else, but I could do with something to eat,' Steve said, before he left them.

Matt saw a look of relief matching his own, settle on Leila's and Bella's faces as they all watched Steve step out of the French windows onto the terrace. *Take as long as you like,* Matt thought grimly.

'What the hell's up with him for goodness sake?' Matt said shaking his head in disbelief. 'He's got all the charm of a snake.'

He saw the shocked look in Leila's eyes and realised what an idiot he'd been; in fact he'd been just as rude as Steve had.

'Bella, I'm so sorry,' Matt said, turning to her, feeling a complete fool. 'You're so sweet that... I'd forgotten he was your husband. Will you forgive me?'

He could see Bella blushing and biting her lip, 'I'm sorry too for how badly he's behaving; I just hope he's not spoiling the evening.'

'No, of course not, Bella. Matt, why don't you... '

'Take a running jump?' He interjected, and was so thankful when he saw Bella and Leila look at each other, and giggle.

'No Matt, not a jump, but a drink for Bella. Please.' Leila asked him, together with a look of admonishment. He felt the schoolboy, she had intended him to feel. 'To make amends.'

'Ginny's great, isn't she?' Leila said, turning to Bella, 'we have fantastic fun riding together, but we don't get the opportunity, nearly as much as we'd like to: she's so busy, and with my work... '

Matt coming back with pink Prosecco, saw Leila shrug, and then hesitate, before falling silent. It was as though for some reason, he couldn't fathom, she didn't want to talk about her work. Now why was that? Matt wondered. He knew she loved her work, and setting up the legal side of the women's refuge was a challenge that she was embracing with relish. He missed seeing her as much as they used to, but he hoped it would only be for a short while. After Leila had explained to him what her new job entailed, Matt realised he couldn't begrudge Leila's time spent trying to help these unfortunate abused women.

Matt watched, as Ginny came back into the room – and wondered, why she looked so unhappy? He noticed, she kept glancing over at her husband in a rather odd way – was she annoyed with him about something? He did seem to be disappearing rather a lot. Had they had a row?

David at that particular moment, he saw, was deep in conversation - reluctantly, he guessed - with Steve. What were they finding to chat about, he mused? Golf, perhaps? He wondered if it was the same boring spiel they'd had to listen to earlier.

Not for the first time that evening, Matt tried to work out why Ginny seemed so… overwhelmed. He would have thought a dinner party for eight guests, from what Leila had told him about all the charity events she organised, was well within her capabilities. But tonight, only knowing what Leila had told him, he sensed that Ginny was floundering. Had Leila noticed too?

Matt watched Ginny going round the room, turning on all the table lamps; she was right, he thought, the room, had suddenly become gloomy with the darkening of the April sky, the lamps, large, with cream satin lampshades on heavy brass candlestick bases, created an immediate softer, more mellow atmosphere. Just right for an intimate evening with friends, Matt thought, keenly aware of the irony. *Were these all really Ginny's friends?*

As Ginny passed him to reach the floor lamp in the corner next to him, he turned to her, 'Ginny, the garden is wonderful; those flood-lights make it look so incredibly dramatic.'

'Oh, thank you, Matt,' Ginny replied, a smile lifting her worried frown for a moment, 'how nice of you to say so. Do you know much about gardening?'

'Not a thing, I'm afraid,' Matt answered, smiling at her, 'but I know a beautiful one when I see it. And to give me a bit of a helping hand, I have to confess, Leila has mentioned your wonderful garden to me more than once.'

Ginny laughed, and Matt realised what an attractive woman she was when free of her worries. *What was going on in this house tonight?*

'I just wish you could see more of the garden from here. Over there, where the floodlights don't quite reach,' Ginny explained, pointing to the far corner of the garden which was now in complete darkness, 'is a small woodland we planted years ago, and at the moment it's full of the most wonderful bluebells. You must bring Leila back, before they've all gone - it would be such a shame to miss them.'

Ginny had class, Matt decided, but somehow he felt he wasn't seeing her at her best tonight; her red dress and heels told him she had an innate sense of style - they suited her perfectly, he thought admiringly. She was statuesque, her height adding drama, and Matt had the feeling she would usually exude confidence, but for some reason not tonight: tonight he thought, she looked pale, her face taut - was it with worry? He wondered again if it had anything to do with David's repeated disappearances.

'How are you all getting on?' Ginny asked Leila and Bella, as she closed the French windows behind them. 'You didn't get too chilly, I hope?'

'We're fine,' Bella answered, and Matt saw a relieved smile cross Ginny's face. Why would Ginny be so relieved? It was all a puzzle.

'Dinner's nearly ready by the way,' Ginny said, turning to leave them, 'I'll get back to the kitchen for a few more minutes, and then we can all sit down.'

'Are you sure you don't need any help, Ginny?' Leila asked, Matt could see she was willing Ginny to say yes, he knew Leila would love nothing better than to help her.

'No, I'm fine thanks, really - you stay and chat.'

Matt watched her turn to walk away, her body language spoke of burdens. It was then he remembered Leila telling him that David and Ginny had three children; where were they? He wondered. The only sign he could see of their presence in the home, were three photographs, one of each son, he assumed, in gold frames on one of the side tables. He was surprised, it wasn't one bit like his own mother's home - where every moment of his and his four siblings' childhood was chronicled for all to see – however embarrassing it might be. Maybe it was his mother's Argentinian blood; children and family were the focus of their lives. Would his and Leila's children be at the heart of their lives? *Oh my God, where did that thought come from?*

Matt looked at Leila, talking quietly with Bella, and he knew with a certainty he had never experienced before, that Leila was the one he wanted to be with forever. Such was its power this feeling of overwhelming love, that Matt felt he had been punched in the solar plexus. He had to ask Leila to marry him - and soon. They'd only known each other not even six months, he thought. *Was it too soon?* When it happened, it happened, he reasoned - you couldn't control that - he just knew he loved Leila and would love her forever. Leila had turned away from Bella to say something to him, but she must have seen something in the expression on his face, because she stopped what she was about to say and gave him an enquiring look instead. He returned her look with a raised eyebrow, and basked in the warm smile she returned. Had she guessed what he was thinking? Matt wondered. Did she feel the same? She'd obviously forgiven him for his earlier *faux pas*.

With a second glass of pink Prosecco in his hand, and Leila and Bella's enjoyable company – Steve thankfully had gone into the garden for another cigarette break - Matt decided he could relax and enjoy the evening. After all, he thought, it was none of his business if his host and hostess were having a row – it would have blown over by tomorrow anyway, he guessed. Leila was here, and she seemed to be enjoying herself chatting to Bella about living in Sandwich, politics and books - that was all that really mattered to him. He stood quietly for a moment enjoying his thoughts.

Matt's mood plummeted when he saw Steve come back in and was now standing next to Bella, with his arm slung loosely over her shoulder. Suddenly, to Matt's horror, Bella's face turned red, and she began coughing as though she were about to choke.

'Bella, are you all right?' Matt asked, instinctively going to her side.

'She'll be all right,' Steve said with a small smirk. 'There's no need to make a fuss. Is there, Bella?'

'A glass of water, maybe?' Matt suggested, as Bella carried on spluttering, and at the same time he saw her inching away from Steve, 'what do you think, Steve?'

Matt watched him shrug. It was only when Bella half turned towards him, that he saw two half-moon shaped nail marks high on Bella's arm. They were just below the red patch he had watched bloom earlier. *Had Steve just hurt Bella in front of them?* But what surprised Matt, was that Bella didn't seem more shocked by what Steve had just done; it was almost as though there was nothing unusual about it. The absolute bloody brute - poor, lovely Bella. He had to do something to stop this awful man. But what? Hit him? Matt nearly laughed out loud at the very idea. He could feel his fists clenching.

'It was so interesting what Bella was saying about St Clement's Church - wasn't it, Matt?' Leila asked. Her meaning clear - Matt got her message - *don't cause trouble.* Leila must have spotted his clenched fists. 'I've always wondered how old that church was,' Leila continued blithely, as though nothing had happened. He could see her staring at Steve, a hard challenging stare.

'Do you enjoy living in Sandwich, Steve?' Matt asked, hoping to give Bella the chance to recover. He knew he had interpreted Leila's message correctly, when he saw understanding and gratitude in her eyes. It was worth anything, Matt thought, to make Leila happy - even if it was not being able to tell this brute of a man what he thought of him.

'The bells get on my nerves,' Steve replied, 'especially on a Sunday morning when I want to lie in. Still I suppose the bells if nothing else, help get me on the golf course early. Which reminds me,' Steve added, 'I must have a chat with David, about membership at St George's Golf Club. If I can find him, he's rather like the Scarlett Pimpernel this evening, isn't he?'

So Steve was right about something at least, Matt thought, as he looked around himself for David's whereabouts.

'Isn't Ginny's garden beautiful, even in the dark?' Leila carried on nonchalantly into the silence - Bella and Matt turned to look out the window. Murmurs of agreement followed, relief could be felt, as comparative normality was restored once more. Except that Bella was still rubbing her arm.

As if to make up for his earlier absences, David appeared at their sides, and remained standing with them, making what seemed to Matt extremely awkward conversation.

'Do you follow, any sport, David? Cricket, football perhaps?' Matt asked.

'Neither – actually,' David replied. Sounding apologetic, Matt thought.

'I quite like running – I run most weekends,' David added, 'and when I get the chance, I enjoy surfing. Not much good at it though – usually fall off, most of the time. But it's fantastic fun trying. Do either of you surf at all?'

Matt and Leila both shook their heads; they didn't run either and the awkward conversation began to falter. Matt wondered why David should seem so ill at ease in his own home.

'If you'll excuse me, 'Leila said, 'I'm just going to see if Ginny needs some help in the kitchen.'

'I'll come with you,' Bella said, following her out of the room. 'Do you know where the bathroom is?'

Matt wished he could go with them, instead of being left to talk to Steve and David - he hoped Leila would return soon and rescue him.

S tanding on his own by the French windows, contemplating
the eerie shapes the floodlights were creating in the garden,
Matt reflected that the evening was throwing up many unanswered questions.

'What exactly is the deal with David, do you think?' Matt
asked Leila, when she arrived back at his side. 'And as for Steve
– I can't even begin to start to fathom him out. 'Poor Bella.'

'Actually, darling,' Leila murmured, 'I'm more concerned
about Ginny. She and David are so obviously not getting
on right now, and I think Ginny is desperately trying to get
through this dinner party. But listen,' Leila said, and Matt felt
Leila pull him closer to her, so that no one else could hear,
'she's asked me to keep an eye on Bella. Also she could really
do with some help in the kitchen.'

'Would Ginny let me help her, do you think?' Matt asked.'
Anything's better than having to listen to another of Steve's
monologues. And of course I'm really happy to help Ginny,'
Matt quickly said when he saw Leila's raised eyebrow. 'I'll just
go and wash my hands, and then I'll try and give Ginny some
help,' he said, cheerfully, as though it was an everyday occurrence at dinner parties for guests to turn cooks.

Ginny not only felt terrible, but the reflection in the glass door of the kitchen cupboard, told her she looked terrible too. Her make-up was no longer doing its job, she'd asked too much of it, and it hadn't fooled Leila for a second. Leila had seen in an instant, that she was falling apart. She scrubbed at her cheeks trying to bring some colour back into them.

'Right,' Leila had said to her, in a voice stern enough to quell any abusive husband, 'you're going to have some help, whether you want it or not. Now who do you want to help you?'

'Not Steve,' Ginny said, reducing both unexpectedly to giggles.

Ginny, could feel the giggles quickly turning into tears, so she splashed some cold water on her face at the kitchen sink.

'Can I help?' Leila asked.

'I want you to look after Bella, keep her company,' Ginny said.

'So that leaves Matt,' Leila said, 'I'm not sure how skilled he is in the kitchen, but I do know he'll be very willing.'

Ginny nodded, reluctantly – she couldn't understand why the meal wasn't on the table already - nothing seemed to be going right. *What is the matter with me?*

Regretting as soon as Leila had left the room, having agreed to Matt's help. She tried practising a bright smile. She didn't want Matt to find her looking miserable – however much she felt it. What needed doing next? She wondered, bemused by her own confusion. *This is so not like me.*

Damn, she thought, realising she'd forgotten to pick up the menus for the table, from David's office printer. It was a touch she knew guests appreciated, and she loved seeing the curlicue font lavishly adorning the edges of the menu. She hurried across the hall to David's office; her stiletto-heeled footsteps echoing on the wooden floor as she went.

Reaching over David's desk for the menus, which were lying in the printer tray, she saw his mobile lighting up under a couple of his papers. She was taken aback about finding his mobile lying there - David never left it lying around in case of urgent calls from his clients.

She tried ignoring the beeping mobile, but in the end she found she couldn't resist looking. Who, she wondered, would be calling David at this time on a Saturday evening?

She could see the message came from a caller named simply, 'A'. Heart banging in her chest – Ginny wondered if she dared read on. Was this mysterious, 'A' the reason David kept disappearing? Was 'A' a he or a she? *Or am I just being over dramatic?* Jumping to conclusions, perhaps? But the hairs on the back of Ginny's neck, were telling her all she needed to know; 'A' was definitely a woman. Why else would David hide the caller's identity? Ginny found her breathing had become so fast she was beginning to feel dizzy. *Calm down, Ginny – it's probably nothing. Take a deep breath.*

She knew she had to find out who it was phoning David, so persistently. She suspected, based on nothing but intuition and almost twenty years of marriage, that David was trying to hide something. Hiding 'A's identity, Ginny felt certain, wasn't laziness – it was deceit.

The reason why David looked so... furtive had become

all too clear now to her. She sat down heavily on the black leather swivel chair next to his desk, and wished with every fibre of her being she hadn't picked up his mobile. She began to read the list of missed calls, unable now to resist the temptation to find out more. At first the letters swam in front of her eyes, so overpowering was her dread of what she might learn. When her vision steadied she saw 'A' had called at least four times that evening, and left two voicemails. No wonder David had been absent, all these calls to answer. Feeling panic welling - she listened with a dry mouth, and heart racing, to the last voicemail. She so wanted it all to go away, and to be proved wrong.

'*Hi, David, it's Alicia, again,*' the voicemail said, '*I keep on losing signal - I hope I'm not disturbing you? Ring me again later,*' Ginny heard a pause, and then, '*… if you want, we could meet up again on Friday?*'

The loud music in the background nearly drowned out the woman's soft laugh; but Ginny had heard enough. More than enough. *Again. Meet somewhere on Friday.* The words clanged in her head; she knew now with a vicious clarity, that left her clutching the sides of the chair to stop herself from falling, that her life had been heading towards this moment for months.

Not wanting David or anybody, to find her in his office, she slipped back to the kitchen. David's mobile firmly hidden in her pocket, and the menus gripped tightly in her hand, she reached the kitchen without anybody seeing her. Slumping into one of the chairs at the table her legs crumpling; she gave way to the wracking sobs she had been holding back for what seemed like a lifetime. She had known this would happen; it had almost become inevitable, it seemed to her.

Who was Alicia?

The question whirled around her head, like dough in a processer; colliding and bouncing its way in interminable circles - with no escape – all to the backdrop of a fearful din.

Why had she been so stupid? What had prompted her to pick up David's phone? Why hadn't she just ignored it? But she knew why - she had needed to know.

Ginny wished more than she had ever wished for anything before, that she didn't know of her husband's betrayal. The terrible thud of understanding that life wouldn't ever be the same again, had winded her. The pretence, the collusion in each other's denial of there being nothing wrong, was now absolutely over.

Right now though, she knew she needed to deal with the pain – a visceral pain – deep rooted and bloody. She suddenly became aware of how dizzy she was feeling, and it was all she could do to calm the waves of nausea gripping her. It was as if, she thought, all her blood was draining away from her body, leaving her cold and clammy. She lay her head on the kitchen table, and wept hot, desolate tears.

Betrayal - was cold - they were right, she realised - as cold and lonely as a corpse on a steel gurney. A being without life - that was what she felt like now. Something had been ripped out of her.

But a moment later, outrage at David's betrayal rose up, threatening to overwhelm her. It was then she remembered David's mobile still in her pocket. She flung it - chronicling as it did, David's link with 'A' - with all the anger their betrayal had created. The mobile phone smashed against the kitchen wall and slid to the floor in pieces. Fragments of shattered glass sprayed everywhere – she didn't care. He deserved it.

Somehow she had to get through dinner; her pride, she realised demanded it. *And David? What then? Do I have to share this house with him tonight?* Repugnance at the idea rose, threatening to suffocate her. How was she going to face him? When what she really felt, was a deep dark, destructive hatred for him. Air left her lungs in a hiss at the thought, and she had to fight to draw another breath. What would David want? Ginny wondered. *Do I even care?* He couldn't stay here now - could he? Would David want to anyway? Ginny wondered. Wouldn't he want to go to Alicia? She clamped her hand to her mouth to stop the shriek of pain she could feel forming deep within her.

Through the haze of her overwrought mind, Ginny wondered what David's reaction would be when she told him, she now knew everything about his Friday evenings. Was there more to know? Would he bluff it out, would David deny it, would he? What were the questions? What were the answers? Ginny couldn't figure out what the rules were about infidelity. What wife did?

Overwhelmed by her sense of betrayal and the thought of the loneliness ahead, Ginny didn't hear the kitchen door open; she sensed a presence though. Feeling now that nothing mattered anymore - not even if it were David - she didn't bother to hide her distress. She knew she was laid bare for all to see. Her grief exposed to the world – a living desperate thing - she couldn't pretend otherwise. She was an empty, wrung-out woman, with a faithless husband. Ginny realised she had no strength left to fight him.

In amongst this morass of emotion she suddenly became

aware of a warm, comforting arm placed gently round her shoulders. Relief flowed through her body when she realised from the distinctive scent of his aftershave, that it was Matt. Someone to help her – someone to share her burden. She knew instinctively, she could trust this man. Leila wouldn't have sent him otherwise.

53

The kitchen was awash with light when Matt walked through the door. Expecting to see Ginny bustling about in her kitchen getting the meal ready, he was unprepared to find her sitting down at the kitchen table with her head in her hands. It took him a few seconds to work out with rising alarm that she was sobbing, and then he noticed with dismay that her whole body was shaking. What the hell had happened? Matt wondered in panic. *Was this a mad house he had walked into by mistake?* Whatever it was could only have happened in the last few minutes, between her leaving the living room, and now. *So what on earth had happened?*

Matt had never in all his life experienced anyone looking so distraught, as Ginny did now. She was muttering something; he couldn't make it out at first. But eventually he heard David's name, and something about a mobile phone.

Matt squatted down awkwardly in front of her, and as he did so he heard a scrunching sound from under his shoe. When he looked down there were tiny shards of crystals, shining like diamonds scattered all over the floor.

'Ginny,' Matt spoke her name quietly, 'are you OK?' *Of course she isn't. Don't be an idiot, Matt.*

Putting one of his hands gently on her left shoulder, he asked quietly so as not to frighten her, 'what's happened, Ginny? Are you hurt?' And then he caught sight of her face.

'Ginny,' he tried again, more urgently this time, 'what's happened? Should I get somebody to help you – David perhaps?' He had caught her attention at last; Ginny looked up at him in dismay, and shook her head violently.

'It's all right, Ginny,' Matt said softly, 'I won't do anything you don't want me to.' It was at this point that Matt realised, it was up to him to help her.

OK, Matt thought, standing up, and brushing off the glass from his knees. *What the hell was all this glass?* Feeling completely out of his depth, and realising that Leila would know instinctively what needed to be done - didn't help him one little bit. In fact it made him feel even more inadequate - if that was at all possible, he thought.

'Ginny, look, I've found some tissues for you,' he said, kneeling down in front of her.

'Do you want to talk about it?' Matt asked, quietly, 'it might help. Can I get you anything? Some water? Brandy?'

He waited, as he watched her scrub her face with the tissues, leaving black trails of make-up, snaking their way down both her cheeks. She looked so vulnerable, Matt's heart squeezed with hurt for her.

Once more he hunkered down in front of her, his knees telling him there was still something sharp on the floor. He'd ask about that later, he thought. He put both his arms gently round her bare shoulders. She shuddered at his touch, but he noticed she didn't try to pull away. Matt could feel her skin, clammy under his fingers. Something traumatic had happened - that much was clear, but what? Matt wondered, looking around the kitchen for clues. The kitchen wasn't giving him any answers. It all looked as it should do: clean, bright, tidy, and expensive.

A testament to how Ginny spent her life. *Except for the glass…*

'Is it something to do with David?' Matt tried again in desperation, feeling that he maybe stepping over the line into what were more personal matters. He didn't really know Ginny at all, but he knew he had to help her. She was so white, Matt was worried she was about to faint.

After a short while of silence, Matt wasn't sure Ginny had heard the question, Ginny nodded, and began to cry again, shielding her face from view in her hands, a damp, torn tissue clutched in them.

Outside, Matt could see a moon filled sky – so lovely. Matt caught himself wishing the evening had turned out differently. He could imagine, quite easily, walking in those gardens with Leila – hand in hand stopping every few steps to kiss her and maybe even… no it was too soon to propose, he didn't want to frighten her away. What was he thinking about? Matt wondered guiltily, when Ginny needed help.

He suddenly became aware of a small blip from a smoke alarm, and glad of the excuse to ease the pressure off his knees, he went in search of its source.

'Ginny, I think maybe something might be burning,' he said hesitantly, returning to her side. 'I'd better deal with it, and try to turn off the smoke alarm. You don't want everyone in the house trooping in here in a panic, do you?' At the idea of others seeing her, she suddenly looked about her with dismay and fear. It was almost as though, she didn't know where she was, Matt thought.

'I'll be back in just a second,' Matt reassured her, assailed once more by a fierce worry for her. Her face now white, had livid red blotches splattered all over; he had never seen such manifest pain before. Did she need a doctor? He wondered. *What the hell had David gone and done? And then all of a sudden he knew what it was that David had gone and done. Bastard.*

'I'll just turn the pan off, Ginny,' Matt called to her from the stove, and then I'll have to do something about all this glass and mess on the floor. We might cut our feet. Do you know how the glass got here?'

Ginny looked down at the smashed innards of David's phone and wore a look of puzzlement when Matt mentioned the glass. How could she not have noticed all the mess before? She glanced at Matt again, and lifted her shoulders as much as to say - *I don't know where all that came from?*

She must be suffering from shock, Matt suddenly realised. He tried wracking his brains to remember what he should do for shock; the first aid class he attended when he had first started lecturing at the university seemed far too long ago. *Come on, Matt, what did they say to do?* And then he remembered - a cup of tea with lots of sugar and a good slug of brandy – that's what she needed. But first he had to find everything.

He hoped opening the windows and the door into the garden had done enough to stop the smoke alarm going off again. The charred remains from the frying pan were now smouldering in the sink. Goodness only knows what it had been, he thought. *What was everybody going to eat now?*

'Ginny,' Matt kept talking quietly, to reassure her, 'the kettle's on, and while we're waiting for the kettle to boil perhaps you can face telling me what's happened. So I can be of more help to you.'

He saw the look of panic in her eyes, 'it will help, you know, to talk about it – Leila always says that, and you know she's always right,' he added, with a smile.

Ginny looked up at these words, and Matt saw with relief the start of a tremulous smile on her face. And although the sobbing had stopped for a moment, she still looked a broken woman.

It was while Matt was looking in the kitchen cupboards for tea and mugs, that he suddenly realised the broken and smashed mess of glass plastic and innards was actually a mobile phone. Was this the one David had been looking for? Matt wondered. Was this the one Ginny had been muttering about when he came into the kitchen? Had Ginny broken it? Was this the key to the mystery of David's absences? Questions flew through Matt's head - the pieces of the jigsaw were slowly locking into place. But what part had the broken mobile played in tonight's drama?

There was nothing for it, he realised, he was just going to have to try and get her to tell him, 'Ginny, is this David's mobile?' As Matt saw her nod, he watched fresh tears well up, and roll down her face. This time they were silent, which Matt found even more unnerving. Where was Leila, with her gift for intuitive understanding of human nature, when he needed her?

'Ginny,' he said, 'did you… break David's phone?' he waited, she raised her face after a few seconds and nodded.

'Why?' he asked and held his breath, waiting for what he hoped might unlock all the events of that evening.

Matt saw Ginny consider his question for a moment, and then he saw her close her eyes and take a deep breath.

'David's having an affair,' Ginny said simply, and hung her head in what looked to him, a deep anguished shame.

Matt felt as though the wind had drained from his lungs, he gulped for air. 'I'm so sorry,' he said, feeling completely shocked. What it must have cost her to tell him, Matt could only guess at. He gathered her up in his arms, and held onto her for a long silent moment.

'I don't know for how long,' he heard her say indistinctly, her voice muffled against his jumper.

'You poor, poor, love,' Matt whispered, stroking her hair.

'He's doesn't love me anymore,' she said assailed by a fresh bout of weeping. Her head was still resting on his shoulder, as she spoke, 'and hasn't for a while now.'

'I'm so sorry,' Matt said again softly, feeling there was nothing more he could say. He really didn't want to get it wrong - Leila would find the right words for her, but that would come later. All Matt felt he could do right now, was murmur soothing words and hold her steady. He didn't ask again about the mobile – he could make a good guess at what part it had played in tonight's events. He'd have thrown it too. He'd have stamped on it and hoped that Ginny had too.

This is going to be a long night, Matt thought still holding onto her, as they sat in a tableau of grief. In that time Matt tried to decide what he ought to do next.

There was now, in the cast, of this particular drama, Matt counted mentally on his fingers: David, an unfaithful host who seemed to have forgotten he'd got guests; Ginny, a hostess who was now in deep shock; Steve a sexist bully; and Bella a possible victim of abuse; a couple of guests he hadn't even met yet; and of course Leila, his darling happy Leila trying to keep everything together in the living room. Last, but no less important, all the food was burnt. He could have laughed if it weren't so terribly sad.

Matt was glad to see the cup of tea he'd made for Ginny had begun to revive her slightly; she no longer looked quite so white, and her tears had begun to subside, and she was beginning to look calmer. After a few more minutes, she moved away from him slightly, as though only just becoming aware of their closeness.

'Ginny,' Matt said, 'why don't we send everyone home? You're in no fit state to entertain guests. I can always say you've suddenly come down with flu, or something – malaria perhaps?'

Ginny gave him a telling look, and he agreed with her, it was definitely not the time for jokes.

'He's not going to see me broken,' Ginny whispered, so quietly that Matt nearly missed it, 'I've got my pride – you see. I know that might seem ridiculous to you. But I've got to show David I'm not broken. That he's not broken me.'

'OK,' Matt said, understanding exactly what she meant.

How on earth was she going to be able to provide food, and sit down and chat to guests after receiving such devastating news? Matt wondered. She wasn't in any position to prepare any more food. Matt suddenly realising - in a cold panic - that it only left him to pick up the pieces. Both literally and metaphorically as he heard the scrunch of glass under his foot. He looked anxiously around Ginny's kitchen; at all her shiny sophisticated steel appliances, and realised he didn't know how to work any of them. *Where on earth should I begin?*

'I'm going up to my bedroom for a minute, Ginny suddenly surprised him by announcing in a quiet strained voice, 'I can't let anyone see me looking like this - could you tell Leila to come up, please.'

'Ginny, Matt suggested again, 'please send everyone home, they'll all understand – you look... so... ill.'

'What will they understand, Matt?' Ginny asked in a quiet voice.

'That you aren't well?' Matt said, realising it was useless - she wasn't going to listen to him.

When Ginny left, he quickly raced into the living room, and took Leila aside to whisper briefly about what had happened. He noticed luckily that everyone else in the living room, including the couple he hadn't yet met, appeared to be chatting quite happily. How on earth had that happened? Matt wondered. He realised all of a sudden, that David was looking over at him and Leila, with a questioning look on his face. *Bastard.*

Leila only needed to be told the barest of details, before leaving the room to find Ginny. Matt breathed a deep sigh of relief to know that Ginny was in much better hands now. All he had to do was find some food for everyone. All? Matt thought in panic.

Returning once more to the kitchen, Matt set himself the task of throwing together some sort of a meal. Anything to eat would do now. Quickly raiding the freezer, he shoved four bags marked, 'curry', into the large microwave to defrost. He knew how to work one of those at least, he thought thankfully. Meanwhile, feeling very pleased with himself at his resourcefulness, he found some bread and salad to accompany the curry. Not haute cuisine that was for sure but a meal of sorts.

It seemed only a short while later, that the microwave pinged; the meal was ready, the curry was steaming hot, he hadn't dared taste it, everyone was going to have to eat it no matter what. He piled the bowls of curry, salad and bread onto to a couple of red plastic trays he'd managed to find in a cupboard. And as a final touch he even threw a few bits of parsley, he had spotted growing on the windowsill, onto the bowl of curry. He doubted though, if anyone would notice.

As Matt crossed the hall into the dining room with the impromptu supper - he was surprised to see Ginny coming down the stairs with Leila at her side. He was greatly relieved to see how much more in control Ginny looked – her face a mask once more – the pain now only showing in her eyes, and in the tightness of her mouth. What a transformation they'd managed, he thought. *Brave, wonderful girl.* He was beginning to recognise the strength that lay at the heart of Ginny. His admiration for her soared, in those moments, while he watched them both descend the stairs.

Maybe this could just about work, Matt realised with relief, seeing the resolve on Ginny's face, and the set of her back – ramrod straight. She managed a weak smile for him, followed by the slight raising of an eyebrow when she saw the tray of food. He replied with a shrug, and an embarrassed smile. With a determined expression, Ginny led the way into the dining room.

54

A clear night sky, sparkling with stars, greeted Matt and Leila as the door to Port Lodge closed behind them.

'Please let us stay,' Matt had asked Ginny one last time, as they stood in the porch saying their goodbyes. Leila added her pleas to his, 'at least until….'

'I'll be fine,' Ginny answered, interrupting them both, and ushering them out. 'I'm going to bed - I'll lock all the doors. He's got his keys – I'd rather not see him tonight anyway. I need time on my own to think. But thank you both, I couldn't have done it without you.'

They could see she was absolutely exhausted from holding herself together; dark circles under her eyes emphasised her pallor and lines that had suddenly appeared, were etched deeply into the corners of her eyes. Ginny's heart was breaking, and Matt felt powerless to do anything.

'I do wish Ginny had let us stay,' Matt said to Leila as they walked up the driveway. 'Where on earth did David go? He just seemed to disappear after we'd eaten.'

They'd waited, until all the dinner party guests had left, but there was still absolutely no sign of him.

The streets of Sandwich were eerily empty, and although it was only just after midnight the town was already in bed, as Leila and Matt made their way home. A wedding party at the Bell Hotel, which graced the quayside, could be heard across the silent streets sounds of gaiety suddenly filling the air.

'I wish we'd gone there instead, it looks much more fun,' Matt said, as satin waist- coated wedding guests spilled out onto the pavement - a drink in one hand and a cigarette in the other. Realising how insensitive that must have sounded to Leila, Matt immediately regretted his words remembering Ginny's tearful gratitude as they left her house.

'I'm sorry,' Leila said, her face downcast. 'I did so want you to meet Ginny; she's such a good friend of mine, and now… '

'Don't be silly,' Matt said, firmly anchoring his arm around her shoulders, 'life's all about timing – right? Next time will be different.'

They each wondered what the next time would bring for them all.

'I'll phone her in the morning,' Leila said, brightly. A plan of action making her feel happier, 'that's what I'll do.'

'Great idea,' Matt answered, 'and if she wants us to, we could go round in the morning and help her out.' Matt was pleased to see a smile at last on Leila's face.

'I'll never forget that meal though,' Leila said, her eyes twinkling once more. 'Who'd have thought lamb curry and salad, would have made such a delicious combination? And why would you ever need rice?'

'Leila, that's really mean,' Matt said laughing, 'I did my best.'

'God help us all then,' Leila teased.

Matt saw a shadow appear on Leila's face, becoming serious once more,

'Don't worry,' Matt said, trying to dispel the gloom, 'Ginny's stronger than she looks. I saw that tonight. I've never seen anyone pick themselves up from such utter disintegration – you didn't see what I did, Leila. And the way she managed to carry off the rest of the evening with such dignity, really impressed me.' Matt turned to Leila, and added, 'I couldn't believe it, Leila, when I saw her walking down those stairs with you – her head held high – back, ramrod straight - so very regal, so very determined. She was definitely going to show David what she was made of - and show him she did.'

'I know, Matt, but…'

Matt interrupted her, 'no buts,' he said, 'she's a street fighter that one. I wouldn't have missed the expression of utter manifest horror on David's face when Ginny handed him his mobile at the dinner table. *'Is this what you've been looking for, David? I think it may have been dropped.'* She said it so innocently too. No, I wouldn't have missed it, Leila. I'm just sorry it had to have happened like this for her.'

'I know,' said Leila, 'the look of shock on David's face, and the realisation dawning right there in front of everybody, that Ginny knew what he'd done. And then, I couldn't believe it, Matt - she actually asked him if he wanted any more salad. I wanted to laugh so much, until I saw the devastation in her eyes. And then all I wanted to do was hug her. I just don't know how she managed it. Do you?'

Matt tightened his arm around her shoulders, 'she's a tough one – I'm not saying it won't be hard for her, but I know it'll all work out in the end. She'll make a much more satisfying life for herself when she's not anchored to David's career.' *Bastard.*

They walked passed the twin round towers of the Barbican – the medieval entrance to Sandwich - still guarding the bridge centuries later. Matt and Leila's thoughts were more occupied with the present and the future, to notice. More battles to be fought, but probably this time in the courts, Matt thought.

'Do you think Bella might be one of those abused women? Like the ones you help,' Matt asked, not really wanting to discuss the dreadful subject.

After twenty seconds or so, while Matt guessed Leila was trying to decide what was confidential and what was not, Leila nodded.

'I don't know, maybe,' Leila answered, 'Steve was certainly acting in a particularly strange way, and Bella did look frail. There was something about Bella that I really liked though. Did you?'

'Yes, she was very sweet,' Matt answered, adding darkly, 'but that husband of hers, I did not like one bit.'

'Unfortunately, we can't help anyone until they seek us out,' Leila said

Matt decided not to pursue the subject, it was far too serious, and they'd had more than enough drama for one night.

'What an evening, I hope I never have to experience something like that again,' Leila sighed. Matt felt her shiver in the cold misty air, and pulled her closer to him for warmth.

'Me neither,' Matt said with feeling, 'poor Ginny, poor Bella, what a dreadful muddle. Not to mention David… ' Matt added, '… how could he do something as awful as that to Ginny?'

Leila shook her head; her incomprehension similar to his own. 'You were brilliant, you know, Matt,' Leila said.

Brilliant! Now that was a rare compliment, Matt thought enjoying the idea - he was more than a little curious to know why.

'You saved the day, you know, I was so proud of you. Ginny was falling apart, and you managed to get her back on her feet.

And to make a meal for us all – I just don't know how you managed that. I was so completely surprised.'

'I didn't do anything, Darling,' Matt said, shrugging, 'that anybody else wouldn't have done in my place. Come here,' he said, stopping to encircling her with his arms. 'Let's forget about this evening - just for a while,' he added quickly, as Matt knew none of it would be forgotten - not for a long time to come, 'we have each other, and that, my darling girl, is important too.'

Matt pulled her closer to him to ward off the chilly night air, the soft drizzle, and the unexpectedly worrisome memories of the evening. He loved this woman — he couldn't ever remember feeling so joyous, despite everything that had happened. Matt could hear their footsteps ringing dully on the cobbled pavements, as they hurried home to Paradise Street. It was comforting, he thought, to think of others treading the same cobbles throughout the centuries. It was strange that Sandwich seemed to always make him aware, as no other place did, of past centuries: from Dutch Gables - to the timber cowl of the Oast House. It all spoke of the working lives of centuries before.

An urgent desire to get them both home quickly, gripped Matt, all of a sudden. It had nothing to do with the dampness of the night, nor the dark mean sky above. Under a cast iron lamp, standing inside its pool of yellow light, Matt stopped to pull Leila into his arms and kissed her; he saw the surprise in her eyes quickly replaced by desire.

'I'm sorry, but I've been dying to do that all evening,' he explained. 'No, actually I'm not sorry at all. The look in his own eyes he knew communicated ancient desires, as ancient as this town and ages beyond. 'You looked so beautiful tonight, so radiant, so like… everything I've ever wanted my future to hold.' Matt stopped, fearing he may have already said too much.

'Matt...' Matt could see Leila struggling to find the words; her face told him of her surprise, her mouth parted ready for words to flow. None came.

Matt realised too late, how clumsy he had been - laying himself at Leila's feet. No romance, no fine architecture, no fine dining, no fine words, just a kiss under a lamp in the dreariness of the damp, empty wet air. He had robbed her of speech. *You idiot.* She wasn't ready yet – it was too soon – he had been a fool. All these thoughts raced through Matt's head – *too soon* echoed in his head, the dank night mocked him.

Matt didn't know what to do for the best; should he just walk on and pretend it wasn't the declaration of love that it sounded like? He stood still, silently praying in the yellow lamplight, and waited. There was no going back now; Matt knew his words had shouted as loudly as any megaphone could, his desire for a deeper more intimate relationship.

Leila looked at him: pensive, thoughtful, questioning, and much more, her face so open, so emotional - showed all these things. Matt read every one of them.

In the silence, Leila's eyes roamed his face, as if seeing it for the first time. Her hand came up, and he felt her touch his cheek, a touch that was so light he barely felt it. *What did she see? What did she feel?* He waited, his heart pounding a beat that stopped and started, as though to music that hadn't yet been written.

'I...' Leila started and then stuttered to a halt.

His heart beat another tune, new, dissonant, fast, too fast, too slow. Matt could no longer breath. *What had he done?*

'I... want that future too,' Leila said, quietly, her cheeks blush-pink, her breathing he noticed with joyous pleasure, matched that of his own. Fast, erratic.

Matt held his breath as he looked into Leila's eyes, and saw all that he himself felt mirrored there.

'Come on,' he said, taking her hand, 'let's get home.' The sound of that word, *home*, he felt suddenly had taken on a different resonance - it meant two - not one, it meant the future. Their future. He shivered with excitement.

'Leila, I've been thinking,' Matt said, as he pulled the front door of Leila's cottage, closed behind him, 'we can't solve anyone's problems tonight. But we can prove, just to ourselves, that there was at least one happy couple at that dinner party tonight.' Matt took Leila's hand, and pulled her gently towards the stairs.

Matt saw with a thrill, a small smile begin to hover at the corners of her mouth, leaving a glorious sexy dimple behind. After only a small moment of resistance, Leila allowed him to lead her up the stairs to the bedroom. As they went, he whispered in her ear that he had something to ask her.

He smiled as he saw a questioning look appear on her face, to be quickly chased away by sudden understanding.

'Matt…?' she said, but before she had time to say anything more, he swept her up into his arms. Now was not the time for words – words were for later. Much later.

'We'll talk later,' Matt said, stopping any more words with kisses.

55

David heard the house phone ring just as he was saying his goodbyes to Joe and Elsa. He could feel a new constraint between himself and Joe - he wasn't at all surprised. By the end of the evening all the dinner party guests must have guessed something shattering had happened between him and Ginny.

David wanted so badly to be able to speak to Alicia, wishing at the same time, this terribly awkward, and embarrassing evening was over. He looked around the table, and saw what appeared to be a group of people trying to enjoy themselves, he felt unconnected from the proceedings - isolated. He had seen as soon as they had all sat down that Ginny had found out about Alicia, when she handed him his completely smashed phone. It was a message from her to him – no words were needed. Her wrecked face told the rest of the story; her make-up, her bravado at dinner, hadn't fooled him for a moment. Ginny knew, and loathed him for it – the phone signalled the smashing of their marriage. Was this really what he wanted? David wondered, panic beginning to set in.

David found himself having to pretend not to notice that Matt, Leila and Bella were supporting Ginny. He had to also pretend that he hadn't noticed that Joe now seemed colder towards him. It was just Steve, then, who carried on unaffected by the undercurrents - too consumed with his own destructive intent. He hadn't missed seeing him pinching Bella at the table, and her heroic attempts to hide her pain; it was the stupid smirk that had gone with it that revolted him to his stomach.

David hoped he would never have to see Steve again - he certainly didn't want him as his only ally. He'd rather stand on his own. And the realisation, all of a sudden, hit David, that his life here with Ginny had been decimated by his actions. Life was never going to be the same again, in so many ways, he thought – and all because of those sweet tracing of freckles. How he yearned for Alicia, even in the midst of all this chaos. Would Ginny forgive him and so they could carry on as before? Did he want to be forgiven? Did he want to carry on as before? *Come on Alicia ring on the house-phone.*

David realised with shame, he didn't have the courage to face Ginny and the inevitable recriminations.

Thankful the house was empty at last, and realizing Ginny must have gone straight to bed, David decided to head out into the garden. He couldn't go far, the range of the house-phone wouldn't allow him any further than the rose-entwined pergola, but at least he could shelter there from the drizzle.

'Alicia,' David said, with relief to be finally speaking to her, 'where are you? It's very noisy.'

'I'm at the club, at Brixton,' Alicia answered, her voice blurred. 'The one I told you about, you remember? Why don't you come over; we can have a boogie?'

A boogie? 'I can't, Alicia,' David said, determined his old-fashioned dancing wouldn't be put to the test – not just yet anyway. 'What are you doing tomorrow? Perhaps we could do something together?'

David heard the hesitation humming down the phone.

'Erm, maybe,' Alicia said, 'it's just that... '

'Just that what?' David asked, 'I'd really love to see you.'

He heard the hunger in his voice.

'Can I...' Alicia said and then the phone went dead.

'Alicia,' he called more loudly. Cursing, David stood up and ran through the rain back to the terrace where there was some shelter. *Bloody, bloody phones.* He tried phoning her again but there was no answer. Dreading facing the atmosphere that would greet him in the house, David decided he would just get in the car and drive to Alicia's. He realised he had nothing to lose, and he didn't want to stay at Port Lodge a minute longer.

It was then David noticed the outside lights were not on; the motion sensors should, by now, be searching for an intruder. He had to fumble for the back door latch in the blackness – and discovered to his dismay it seemed to be locked from the inside. How had that happened? David wondered. He began checking all the other doors to the house and discovered they were also locked and bolted. *Ginny has locked me out. Hell and damnation.*

David looked around him for inspiration; his mind, still blurred from the effects of the wine he'd drunk that evening, wasn't functioning well. Darkness surrounded him, wrapping him in the unwelcome and devastating realization, that Ginny didn't want him in the house - just as much as he didn't want to be in it. *Shit, shit, shit.* This was Ginny's answer to Alicia. The conversation between them had been said. She wasn't going to forgive him, and their lives were not going to go on as before. Ginny had told him all that - without saying a word. Ginny, in locking all the doors had stated her intent.

He stood in the front porch shivering, feeling at once both foolish and angry. Luckily his car keys were in his pocket; he would have to go and see Alicia just as he was. He could pick up some essentials in the morning. Not ideal, but it would have to do - a part of him had begun to feel excited at the turn of events, even though he would have preferred it to have been a bit more… planned.

The Clapham policeman, on his second circuit that night, knocked on the car window, shattering David's sleep. He rolled the window down and was taken aback at the looming figure peering in at him; it took him a while to register that it was in fact a policeman.

'Is this your car, sir?' the policeman asked, suspiciously.

'Yes, Officer,' David said; the first sense of his foolishness making its presence felt. 'I'm waiting for a friend to come home.'

'OK, Sir,' the policeman said, 'I hope for your sake they return soon, it doesn't look at all comfortable in there.'

'So do I, officer, and it isn't,' David replied, beginning to realise with a thud that he would definitely fail a breathalyser test. *Oh my god please don't even think of it Mr Policeman.*

David sat up straight, and brushed his hair into some semblance of order with his fingers trying to look more respectable.

He watched with relief as the policeman walked away. *What an idiot I've been driving here.* He settled back into the driver's seat feeling cramped and cold, and realised he didn't have any other option now but to wait for Alicia to get home. *Where the hell was she?* David hoped the policeman's patch was a large one, and that he wouldn't be coming this way again for a while.

A second knock on his car window woke him up with a start.

Where the hell was he and why was he aching everywhere and freezing cold? Then he remembered. This time it wasn't the policeman it was Alicia, looking confused.

Stiffly getting out of the car, he stood on the pavement stretching and yawning.

'I thought it was you, what the hell are you doing here?' Alicia asked, looking bemused at him; the red tail lights of her taxi, fading in the distance.

'I wanted see you,' he said, smiling awkwardly at her. He'd already decided it would be better not to tell Alicia just yet, that he'd effectively been thrown out of home. A lie of omission, he thought, was not a good start. But they'd be plenty of time to discuss all that another time – at the moment all he was interested in, was those freckles. 'I just wanted to see you again, and we kept on getting cut off before I could tell you, so… here I am.'

As he watched her swaying slightly sobering up in the cold fresh air, he felt his first misgivings. Had he behaved ridiculously foolishly? *Yes he had - but so what?* He realised with a sinking feeling that Alicia wouldn't have ever considered the possibility he might one day just turn up on her doorstep. He realised the way he looked right this moment: rumpled shirt, tousled hair, bleary eyes, not to mention the beginnings of stubble – was a million miles from the suave city man she was attracted to.

'You'd better come in then,' she said, 'the place is in a mess, and it's tiny – definitely no cats can be swung.'

David laughed with her, a warm feeling beginning to replace the indecision and unhappiness of the last few months. This was what he wanted – and it looked as though Alicia did too, judging by the way she was dragging him back to her flat. *Who cared about cats anyway?*

He followed her down stone steps, leading into the basement flat of a four-storey converted Edwardian terrace. Fumbling with her keys, Alicia managed at last to open her front door and switch on the lights. His first sight of her flat confirmed that she hadn't been exaggerating – you couldn't swing a cat. It was as tiny as she'd promised, and untidy to the point where every surface was covered with the detritus of single living: clothes, plates, mugs, wine bottles, glasses, make-up, clothes – it was all there, scattered absolutely everywhere.

'I did warn you,' she said, embarrassed.

'You did warn me, but even so… Come here,' David said smiling at her, his arms outstretched, 'it's you I've come to see, not your terrible untidiness, although mind you, I don't think even as a student, I can recall anyone being quite this untidy.'

'Oh shut up,' Alicia said laughing, as they both fell on the bed.

'Ouch,' David cried holding his head, 'what the hell was that?'

'Sorry, it's just some shoes,' Alicia said, 'are you all right?'

'I will be in a minute,' David replied, throwing everything off the bed, shoes, clothes, damp towels, onto the floor. 'That's better,' he said.

He began a trail of kisses that traced a line from the tip of her ear to where the swell of her breasts began. He heard Alicia's soft moan.

56

David woke on Sunday morning in a dark, unfamiliar bedroom to a feeling of heady contentment. He lay drifting in the thrilling sensation of Alicia's body next to his – he leant over and placed a kiss on her bare shoulder, careful not to wake her. He wanted just a few moments on his own, to think about the staggering changes that had occurred in his life over the last few weeks: first Grace, then meeting Alicia, and the ending of his marriage, and then this… in bed with the most delicious woman he had ever met.

He watched her sleep; one arm flung over him, pinning him down, and let his thoughts of her roam unchecked. The exquisite feel of her skin – downy, like ripe peaches, her sweet perfume - reminding him of roses, her chestnut hair - riotous now, after their night of passion. This was what he imagined heaven to be like. A feeling of sheer pleasure washed over him, as he lay listening to her quiet breathing. Life was perfect.

After a few moments David's eyes adjusted to the gloom of her bedroom; he hadn't noticed much about it the night before, but now he could see how incredibly small the room was; in daylight the untidiness looked even worse, if that was possible, David laughed to himself. Still perfect.

This was it then, he decided - this was what he had been searching for, without knowing. This was the adventure he craved, the adventure he had denied himself all his life. He had always trodden the path expected of him: he was a bright boy - his parents had pushed him to achieve excellent grades at school, at university, he had done everything they had wanted - for them but not for himself. By then his course was set - hard work – work hard. Taking a risk had not been part of his upbringing – it was all about responsibility, conformity, there was no room for anything else. Ginny and her pregnancy, he thought was the one and only event that hadn't been mapped out beforehand. He wasn't going to think of Ginny now, David decided, he was going to put all thoughts of her aside for the moment. Because how he felt now, his soul was soaring, was a new experience. He liked it; he never wanted it to end.

'What are you smiling about?' Alicia asked in a sleepy voice, slightly croaky, but very sexy.

'Morning, Sleepyhead,' David replied, 'I was just thinking about you, believe it or not.'

'That's nice,' she said, still sounding half awake. 'About anything in particular?'

'Well,' David said, with a shiver of pleasure, as his hand trailed lightly down her back, 'I was thinking… '

'Mmm, go on,' Alicia said, nudging him in the ribs.

'I was thinking… ' David said, trying to sound reluctant, 'how extremely tidy you are.'

'Ouch,' David said, laughing as she nipped him with her fingers.

'I'm going to have to make you pay for that,' she said, sitting up next to him, and pulling the duvet up to her chin.

David thought how adorable she looked, with her long chestnut curls fanned out on the duvet.

'I can't wait,' David said, pulling her to him, and kissing her on the tip of her gorgeously freckled nose. 'What shall we do today?' he asked, his chin resting on the top of her head – her hair still smelled of the expensive orange blossom shampoo, he knew she loved – delicious. It was then he had an awful thought that she might be busy. Or even worse, she might not be interested in spending more time with him. Last night may have been a 'no-commitment' affair. Would she be expecting him to go now? He felt a lurch of apprehension – this was new territory, and he no longer knew the rules.

'Don't you have to go home now?' she asked, as if reading his mind. David could feel her eyes, bright, and sharp, searching his face.

'No,' he said, 'no, I don't. I really don't. But would you like me to go?' David held his breath.

She shook her head, and rested it on his shoulder, 'no, I want you to stay,' Alicia replied simply, her voice muffled against his skin. 'Can you?'

David groaned with disbelief. Was this really happening, he wondered, could it possibly be real - this beautiful woman wanted him to stay?

'Yes, I can, and I do really want to stay,' David said. A wave of embarrassment suddenly hit him, when he realised how ardent he sounded.

'Good,' Alicia said,' that's that then. What shall we do? There's Clapham Common just up the road - there's always something going on there. Do you fancy that?'

David, realising he had no idea what time it was, noticed a clock on the bedside table.

'Important things first,' he said, nuzzling her neck, 'I'm starving, and it's past lunchtime, already.'

But then he felt a butterfly touch on his neck, and then another, and all thought of food vanished from his mind as Alicia's kisses reached his mouth.

As dusk began to make its presence felt, David realised they still hadn't eaten properly – you certainly couldn't consider the meagre contents of her cupboards as nourishment. To his amusement, he found himself sitting in Alicia's bed eating packets of crisps, and some less than recently bought cheese and biscuits - the total result of her foraging. But David found he couldn't have wished for anything more delicious, or to be anywhere else.

David stroked the silky skin on the base of Alicia's neck, as she lay with her head on his shoulder. His fingers idly tracing a path down her arm, through her golden freckles.

'I think I've just found Orion,' he said.

'Orion? That's a star isn't it? But it's not dark enough yet is it?' Alicia said, tilting her head so she could see out of the window.

'Your freckles,' David explained, leaning down to kiss the tip of her nose, 'that's where I've found Orion.'

He watched as Alicia slipped out of bed, laughing, 'I'm going for a shower, maybe you could make us a cup of tea?'

'Another one?' David said, 'why don't we make it a glass of wine instead, and a meal to go with it?'

'Sounds good to me,' Alicia answered, her eyes dancing, 'I promise I won't be long.'

'You'd better not be,' he called after her.

David could hardly believe how beautiful Alicia was, as she walked about the room, totally at ease with her nakedness; just as she reached the door, she turned and gave him a smile, which seemed to him, to hold the promise of an infinity of happiness - she blew him a kiss. He felt his stomach flip over with desire.

Searching for his clothes, he eventually found them scattered around the room where they'd fallen, in their haste to undress. Realising how dishevelled he must look - he raked his hands through his hair, and tried to smooth out the creases in his shirt. He felt his chin and found stubble. Could he go out with Alicia looking like this? He would have to, he thought.

He needed to ask Alicia where he could get some urgent provisions; at the very least a change of clothes, razor, and toothbrush. And then suddenly, questions arrived intruding into the paradise island they had created for themselves. Where was he going to stay tonight? How was he going to get to work? He couldn't go to work looking like this. How was he going to get his clothes, all his belongings from Port Lodge, where was he going to put them? What? Where? When? Questions whirled around his head. *Why couldn't we just both stay here in this lovely cocoon?*

He decided very quickly that he couldn't move into this flat of Alicia's. Even if he was invited it was far too soon. And even if her flat weren't the size of a cupboard, that is, - he chuckled to himself at the idea. But he definitely didn't want their burgeoning relationship to falter through lack of space.

David dressed, and tidied himself as best he could, using her small make-up mirror to tell him what he already knew - he needed a shave and a wash —despite that he could see how relaxed he looked. It all felt good – in fact, he thought, it felt absolutely wonderful.

Sitting on the edge of her bed while he put his shoes and socks on, he could see the busy street below from the bedroom window. The sight of other people getting on with their every-day lives, made David suddenly feel an unexpected surge of total happiness.

Arm in arm, with Alicia snuggled up close to him against the cool night air, they left the warmth of the Italian restaurant, and were now heading to the cinema.

'Please, can we go?' Alicia had begged. He didn't have the heart to say no. He couldn't tell her he hadn't been to the cinema for years.

'I've been dying to see, Love from Melissa, but none of my friends wanted to. It's got Justin Goodman in,' she said.

Not wanting to betray the fact he'd never heard of Justin Goodman, or Love from Melissa, David found himself agree-ing to go, but only on the understanding that they sat on the back row, and bought some popcorn. Before very long he found himself with a tub of popcorn in one hand, and a drink of something fizzy in the other. Settling themselves down on a luxury sofa at the cinema with the lights dimming, David heard Alicia's delightful giggle as he pulled her to him and began to kiss her.

57

Monday started beautifully – David woke to gentle kisses on his face.

'Mmm, I wish I could wake up to your kisses every day,' David said, still drowsy, the words having left his mouth before their significance hit him.

'You can if you want,' Alicia said hesitantly, kissing him again, 'but it's definitely time to get up though, if we want to get to work on time.'

'I don't want to get to work at all,' David said, burrowing back down in the bed and covering his head with the duvet. He realised with a thud he meant it – he couldn't believe it, and him a career driven man all his life would prefer, to hunker down with this wonderful woman. In just a few days after meeting her - work had, all of a sudden, lost its place as his reason for existing; he wanted to stay in this cocoon forever.

'Nor do I, but…' Alicia said, giving him a push.

'I know, I know, it was just a wonderful, beautiful thought,' he said, getting out of bed and making his way to the bathroom for a shower and shave. 'Won't be long,' he said, as he left the room.

He tried to shave looking in an old mirror that was nearly opaque with brown age speckles. *God knows what I really look like.*

They walked hand-in-hand, as they made their way to

Clapham Common tube station. When David had finally seen the area where Alicia lived in daylight he immediately saw why she had been prepared to live in that - barely more than a cupboard – flat. To have lush parkland with ponds and woods on your doorstep must be such a treat in London.

They turned into the park to walk along a wide sandy path, that as well as pedestrians was being used by runners, and cyclists; even at seven in the morning, the park was alive with activity. The trees, David noticed, edging the path were alive with newly migrated birds; the birds rejoicing to have returned to their summer roost. He knew exactly how the birds felt, and gave Alicia's hand a gentle squeeze to convey his appreciation of all that was around them. She returned the squeeze. He couldn't remember ever feeling this happy.

The streets, still wet after the rain of the night before, glistened with puddles, and for once the London air, felt clean and fresh - there was a sense, David thought, of winter being over, and spring having at last arrived. He noticed everything around him with a sharper clarity than ever before - Alicia had done that for him. She had woken him up to the world around him - the drive to achieve, suddenly and unexpectedly mellowed by a world that was shining and bright – full of possibilities.

A feeling of pride shot through him, as he saw admiring glances cast in Alicia's direction. They were right to be interested, he thought - she was stunningly beautiful; a thrilled sense of proud possession, gripped him as they walked along, making the world their own and nobody else's.

'Will you be coming back tonight – after work?' Alicia asked him suddenly, in a voice whose loveliness and hesitancy made him tingle.

He stopped in the middle of the pavement, not caring who saw, and pulled her into his arms.

'God yes,' David said, whispering in her hair.

They parted company reluctantly, in Tooley Street, a few streets away from work; it was instinctive, but it made David feel the first hint of guilt. It had indeed been a cocoon they had been living in since Saturday – and now - he was going to have to face, not only the reality of work but also the reality of Ginny; his marriage, and the rest of his life.

58

Around seven on that same Monday morning, Ginny was woken to a loud and insistent banging on her front door. Still groggy from taking a sleeping pill the night before, she went to open the front door, irritated with whoever it was that had woken her.

As she traipsed down the stairs, she suddenly realised she hadn't been in touch with Bella, since the dinner party on Saturday night. *How could I have been so selfish? What sort of friend am I?* It didn't seem to matter now to Ginny, that she herself, had spent the whole of Sunday facing her own demons, feeling alone and dejected. Why on earth hadn't she phoned Bella yesterday? Ginny felt flooded with guilt and selfishness.

Catching sight of herself in the hall mirror, as she headed for the front door, Ginny was taken aback by how terrible she looked: she was still wearing the red dress from Saturday night - badly crumpled now - her hair, completely awry, was standing up on end, and her make-up - wasn't where it should have been. She couldn't possibly answer the door looking like this. They would just have to come back another day. Turning to go back upstairs to shower and dress and restore herself to some sort of normality – she heard more banging - but this time it was accompanied by shouting. Suddenly fearful it might be Bella needing her help, Ginny retraced her steps and raced to the door and flung it open.

To Ginny's utter astonishment, it wasn't Bella standing on the other side of the door, but Steve. His fist was raised ready to give the door another pounding. Shock quickly turned to apprehension when Ginny saw how angry he looked: his dark features were twisted into a black, menacing ugliness. Ginny gulped with a deep and frightening foreboding.

'Where is she?' Steve asked, in a voice that held a steely chill.

Taken aback by his words, it took Ginny several seconds to understand what he was asking. Steve, with barely contained impatience, was expecting to find Bella in her house. It didn't make any immediate sense to her groggy brain. *Why did I take that damned sleeping pill? Was Bella all right? Why was Steve looking for her here?*

Purely working on instinct, Ginny tried to shut the door to prevent Steve from coming in, but she was a second too late. His foot shot out and was now, to her horror, firmly wedging the door open.

'Oh no you don't,' he said, pushing past her, 'I want to know where my wife is - and I think you know.'

'Why would Bella be here?' Ginny asked, genuinely surprised. 'Why would I know where she is?'

Starting to feel threatened, alone in the house with Steve, she decided she had to get rid of him somehow. And quickly. But she found to her dismay that her brain, was still refusing to function properly. *Think, Ginny, think for god's sake.*

'Of course you know where she is,' Steve accused, 'you're her friend, aren't you?

'Yes, I'm her friend, but I still don't know where she is,' Ginny said. 'I haven't seen or heard from her, since the dinner party.'

'And you expect me to believe that?' Steve snarled. 'Well I

don't - not for one minute.'

'When did you last see her?' Ginny asked, beginning to feel really worried for Bella – where on earth was she?

'Since Saturday night,' Steve snarled back, 'as if you didn't know.'

It hadn't taken Ginny long to realise she was no match physically for Steve; even though she was much taller than Bella – Steve was taller still, and much broader. But it was his anger, rather than his size, that made him seem so threatening. No wonder Bella felt intimidated, Ginny thought.

'Steve, I really think you should go,' Ginny said, mustering up some sternness in her voice. 'I haven't invited you into my house, and I don't want you here. I want you to leave.'

'Where is she?' Steve repeated, raising his voice. 'I know she's here - where else would she go? She has to be here.'

'I don't know why you would think that,' Ginny said, concern for Bella making her braver than she was feeling in the face of this angry, red-faced man. 'I told you I haven't seen her since Saturday evening. Now, please would you go.'

'No I won't, and further more, I think you're lying to me,' Steve said, jabbing his finger in her direction. He swivelled his head around, 'what's in there?' he asked, pushing open the door into the Orchid House.

'Oh, very nice,' Steve said, standing stock still, as he took in the beauty of the conservatory full of orchids with their exotic perfume filling the air. 'Wow,' Steve added, sounding impressed.

She thought for a second that he was genuinely charmed. But then to her surprise, he turned to her, 'your husband doesn't know when he's well off, does he? All this,' he added, his arms

337

outstretched to capture the whole of the beautiful Orchid House, 'and he wanted more.'

Steve's words mirrored her own nocturnal thoughts with horrible accuracy, making Ginny feel as though she had been physically punched. She gasped for air and choked back her tears.

'So where is Bella?' Steve demanded. 'I know you and that bitch are hiding something.'

Ginny saw in an instant, that Steve's calm was beginning to deteriorate.

'I want you to phone her,' Steve instructed, 'right here, where I can see you.'

Ginny reluctantly took her phone out of her pocket and called Bella; she listened to the phone ringing unanswered. Ginny was desperately trying to think of a way to get rid of him. *Should I call the police? Where the hell was Bella?* When Bella's phone went on to voicemail Ginny started to really worry about her. Had Steve done something to her after the dinner party? Ginny wondered.

'Have you got through to her yet?' Steve demanded, looming over her so close she could smell his rancid breath.

Ginny shook her head, not trusting herself to speak; she didn't want him to know how frightened she was becoming for Bella and for herself.

Ginny looked at Steve, 'the phone's gone to voicemail,' she said, her hopes fading at the sound of the recorded message.

'OK, well at least she'll see that you've tried to call her,' Steve said, settling himself in one of the wicker chairs in the Orchid House. 'We'll wait here until she decides to ring you back. A cup of tea would be nice while we wait,' Steve said, as though it was a friendly visit, 'and maybe a biscuit. I didn't have breakfast. I've not been able to sleep all night worrying about where my wife is – and where she's taken the children. I think she's left me.'

Ginny couldn't believe what she was hearing. 'But didn't you see her leave? How could you not have done?'

And to her absolute astonishment, he began to cry. This frightening, angry man was sitting among her orchids, crying over the woman he regularly abused. It seemed surreal.

'I've a meeting with my solicitor in half an hour, and I must go and get ready,' she said, ignoring Steve's emotional outburst – he didn't deserve one jot of her sympathy. 'And as for the tea and biscuits... ' *You can go hang.*

She didn't want him to see that the news that Bella may have left him, made Ginny's hopes soar – was she already at the refuge in Dover with the children, safe and sound? Ginny fervently hoped so.

Steve looked incongruous sitting there, sunlight was pouring through the glass roof onto his face. His solidity was incongruous, against the fragility of the flowers and his tear-stained face.

'I'll give Bella another call, and leave a message for her this time,' Ginny told him. 'But first I'm going to change. I can't stay like this.'

'Nope,' Steve told her, shaking his head emphatically. 'You stay right here where I can see you, until we hear from Bella and then you can do whatever the hell you like.'

Ginny knew she had no choice; he had an ugly look on his face that was beginning to terrify her. She pulled her dressing gown tightly around her, thankful that she still had her dress on underneath. But when she phoned Bella again, her fingers were trembling so much she couldn't get the number right at first. There was still no answer.

'Bella, it's Ginny - can you ring me - urgently?' Ginny said leaving her a message, 'Steve's here with me at Port Lodge, and I'm worried about you.'

And myself, Ginny thought.

'Why did you say that?' Steve said jumping up from his chair and walking towards her menacingly. 'Why did you tell her I was here?'

'Was Bella all right when you last saw her - or had you… ?'

Ginny wished immediately she'd not asked the question, when she saw Steve's furious face.

'It's none of your bloody business,' Steve thundered. 'This is all because of you, you know – putting ideas into her head. It's all your fault.' He said pushing her.

Ginny could smell alcohol on his breath, and from his nearness, she could see broken veins on his nose. He was by now so close to her; he looked quite mad, with his chin thrust out and a white blob of spittle on his lip. Ginny took a step backwards to get away from his terrifying aggression – she didn't think she'd ever been so frightened for her own safety in her life. *What must have Bella endured?* She was suddenly assailed by a - never before experienced - need for her own self-preservation. *I've got to get out of here somehow – he's going to attack me* – was Ginny's last thought before she turned and ran. She could hear Steve's laboured breath as he gave chase knocking over plants and furniture as he went.

'Oh no you don't, 'Steve screeched, grabbing at her with his thick hands, 'come back here, you bitch.'

Ginny could feel herself losing her balance, and tried to grab at anything to stop herself falling. She knocked over some plants, as her legs and arms flailed about her, and suddenly she felt her balance go - soil, and delicate pink petals fluttered to the floor with her.

As she fell, Ginny saw in vivid slow motion, the edge of the cast iron table coming inexorably towards her – and in a moment of other-worldliness - amidst the sound of a blood-curdling shriek, Ginny heard a sickening crack.

She didn't hear Steve yelling out to her – nor feel him grabbing at her to try and save her. It was all too late. He watched in horror, as in slow motion Ginny hit her head. The first knock was the cast-iron table: the second, the concrete floor of the Orchid House. Everything went black, and she felt herself sliding into a different world. A pitch-black empty world.

Ginny lay completely still in front of him, soil, leaves and petals scattered all over her. He bent over her and to his horror saw blood pouring from her head. *Oh god, I've killed you,* he whimpered to Ginny's prone body. His whimper, the only sound in the otherwise completely silent house.

He knelt down, brushing off some of the soil from her face.

'Ginny, Ginny, are you all right?' Steve beseeched, shaking her. 'Wake up, come on. I didn't mean to… '

Panic engulfed him, as Steve thought Ginny might not be breathing.

'Police, ambulance or fire brigade?' The voice on the other end of the phone asked.

'I don't know,' Steve sobbed down the phone. 'I think I've killed her.

59

Closing his office door behind him, David sat down at his desk to prepare some notes for the Directors' meeting at ten o'clock. Instead, turning his leather swivel chair to see what was happening on the River Thames fifteen storeys below, his thoughts turned to Alicia and their plan to meet at lunchtime.

He looked out of the large picture window; there was always something of interest going on. Today it was a police boat skimming along the sludge-grey water at speed. Where was it going and why? He wondered. And that was the beauty of it - the not knowing. Every minute different.

Watching the river had become his favourite place for thinking; solutions would sometimes appear when he let his thoughts drift along with the flow of the river. David sat hoping an answer to the conundrum of his marriage and Alicia, would reveal itself. It had all seemed so... simple in Alicia's tiny flat, where no intrusions from the outside world could make their presence felt.

He sat there cogitating the balance of freedom and responsibility he knew he had to face somehow - and then laughed at himself, ever the accountant, he thought, trying to balance the books.

He had to get this right, David thought; it felt a daunting prospect. Alicia and Ginny. Ginny and Alicia. Did he really have to choose this soon? David wondered. Could he not just enjoy, for a short time, this wonderful experience that had suddenly appeared in his life? And then all of a sudden, he realised Ginny might be the one making those decisions for him. Locking him out on Saturday night was definitely telling him something. It was a forthright message from Ginny – there could be no misunderstanding, David thought. He wouldn't be going back to his old life. The message clearly stated.

The phone on his desk rang, jolting David out of his unresolved problems. He hid his irritation at being disturbed by his secretary.

'David, it's a call from the police,' his secretary announced. He was surprised to hear the concern in her usually unruffled voice.

'Put me through then straightaway, Wendy, please,' David asked. 'Did they tell you what they wanted?'

'No, they didn't want to tell me,' she answered, apologetically.

David's stomach contracted suddenly, with unaccountable worry.

'Mr Jackson? David Jackson?' The policeman asked over the phone.

'Yes,' David replied, warily.

'It's Detective Inspector Clark, here, Kent Police,' the policeman informed him, in tones of such seriousness that David found he couldn't breath.

'Your wife has been injured,' the police officer told him, 'she's in Kent and Canterbury Hospital.'

David willed him to stop. Not wanting to hear anymore.

'What do you mean? Has there been a car accident or…?' David instantly felt breathless with worry.

'No, sir, not a car accident,' DI Clarke explained. 'Your wife has been assaulted, Mr. Jackson.'

David barely allowed him to finish. 'Assaulted? How? Who by? When?' the questions coming thick and fast, incomprehension fogging his mind, panic making his blood race. He wiped his forehead, finding it already sticky with sweat and sat back down in his chair – the river flowed by - unnoticed now.

The DI's voice, deeply calming said, 'your wife's going to be all right, Mr. Jackson. She's not on the critical list; but she is in Intensive Care – only as a precaution though, you understand? The doctor looking after Mrs. Jackson, told me to make sure that I said as much to you.'

'But what happened,' David stumbled over his words, 'why is she in intensive care?'

'She was attacked at your home,' the policeman said, 'we have a man in custody, but at this point we are unsure of the events leading up to the assault. Your wife's going to be all right, Mr. Jackson,' the inspector repeated.

'I still don't quite understand,' David said, feeling bewildered. 'I'm sorry, I'm having trouble taking all this in.'

David was trying to get a grip on his panic: Ginny injured - his thoughts, usually so orderly, were rushing chaotically round his head.

'It's shock, Mr. Jackson,' the policeman explained calmly, 'quite natural I assure you. Mrs. Jackson, as far as I know, is suffering from concussion, but you'll be able to find out more when you get to the hospital. Her friend is with her at the moment.'

And with those words, David suddenly realised what the policeman was trying to tell him. He was needed at the hospital - of course he would have to go - Ginny was, after all, still his wife. He was still her next of kin, whether they liked it or not.

After putting the phone down, David quickly made his way over to his secretary's desk, and briefly explained what he needed her to do. Five minutes later, coat and briefcase in hand, he was hurrying to London Bridge tube station, along the same route he had taken earlier that morning holding Alicia's hand. If only she could be with him now.

The high-speed train ride home, seemed endless. David wilted in his impatience to be at the hospital – nearly twenty years of marriage – couldn't be abandoned overnight. The scurry of the train wheels as they raced past stations, leaving all in their wake silent, until the boom of the train wheels as they went over Rochester Bridge, eclipsed all thoughts of Alicia. The speed and the roar were taking him nearer and nearer to Ginny. *Damn, damn, damn.*

A curl of resentment, from deep inside, grew - why did the accident have to happen right now? Why today of all days? David wondered. Why now? Why right this very moment? When he had just found the beginnings of happiness? He couldn't even begin to imagine what Alicia might think, if she knew he was going to Ginny? Would she mind?

David dreaded the idea he might lose Alicia.

60

Arriving at Kent and Canterbury Hospital on Monday after-noon, after a journey of two hours, that had felt more like twenty to David. Each rumble of the train wheels, separating him from Alicia and taking him nearer Ginny, did nothing to lower his feelings of stress.

Jumping out of a taxi, David hurried through the entrance of the hospital. His last visit to this hospital had been with his youngest son in the summer. Although Tim had been warned not to climb the old oak tree as it was unsafe – he had. Consequently he had fallen and broken his arm. *Little fool.*

'Cheerful Sparrows, Love. It's the general women's ward, up the stairs and on the left,' the kindly pensioner told him with an encouraging smile, 'that's where you'll find your wife.'

Pushing open one of the double doors to the ward, David saw a row of curtained beds. He made his way slowly down the ward and eventually found her alone in a side room. He stood for a moment looking through the viewing panel in the door, shocked to his core at how fragile she looked - so unexpectedly vulnerable - he found it difficult to catch his breath.

David hadn't thought Ginny would look… so wounded; he had been selfishly bound up in his own feelings he stupidly hadn't really considered how she would be. She was lying in the bed, ramrod straight, with a crisp sheet up to her chin - her skin, so translucent, he could see her veins pumping the blood back to her heart. The same heart he had so thoughtlessly, so unforgivably, broken. He suddenly felt terribly afraid for her - the hospital didn't know her as he did; she couldn't sit still – always, always – doing something. Doing something for others. Not still, like this. Not so alarmingly frighteningly still, like this. Had they got it right? Was she really going to be all right?

Dragging a chair over to her bedside, he became suddenly and piercingly aware, that what he felt for Ginny now, was pity - not love. He foolishly thought after their long marriage, he would still feel some vestige of love - he felt certain he would. He felt certain that under the circumstances, something would rekindle.

He needed her to be well, David thought, he wanted her to be well, so he wouldn't feel so guilty about returning to Alicia. He knew how terribly, terribly selfish he was being. Turning his face towards the window - away from Ginny – he could see small patches of cotton-wool clouds scurrying along, unhampered; he was envious. His own life at the moment felt ravelled, beyond anything he had ever experienced before. The coils of responsibility had tightened around him once more, because of Ginny's accident - he wanted to be free. *Bastard.*

David thought all this, while Ginny lay oblivious, asleep - healing. He turned back to face her, and a flood of resentment rose, shattering his new found peace of mind. What if Alicia left him, because she suspected he was still in love with Ginny? *If I lose Alicia because of this…*

Desperately trying to calm his fears, David watched Ginny sleep; but memories of happier times came unbidden, unwanted. He remembered how the future had seemed so full of hope, when they first visited Paris together. But more vivid, more recent memories intruded – Alicia sitting on his knees facing him, wearing only the flimsiest of dove-grey satin and lace. Her long bare legs wrapped around him, kissing him with a passion that drove them far away from the everyday, and into a world of exquisite sensations.

Trying, but not succeeding, to banish these wonderfully disturbing thoughts from his mind - he noticed for the first time, the beginnings of a bruise, purpling on Ginny's jaw, and the edge of a livid gash under her ear. Sitting quietly on the uncomfortable plastic bedside chair, David suddenly felt over-whelmingly sorry for her. He had left her with nothing, and he by contrast, had everything he could ever dream of - Alicia.

With his eyes half closed, sleep nudging his exhausted mind and body, the evocative antiseptic smell, and the hum of machinery in Ginny's room, took his thoughts back to his own stay in hospital in Devon. Memories of that time, swirled unbidden. Feelings of embarrassing shame suddenly rolled through him, like waves battering the shore. He had treated her despicably in Devon. She had sat by his own bedside, he remembered, trying to care for him; his words to her then had been cruel and callous. And now, here was Ginny in hospital herself, and he suddenly understood how worried she must have been for him after Grace's accident. He thought of how Ginny had tried to help and comfort him through his own anguish of failure about Grace.

If only he couldn't remember how heartlessly he had pushed her away. But it was what he had not said to her that would have wounded her the most. Ginny, he knew, was worried about their marriage and needed to hear words of reassurance, of love even, from him - was in fact desperate to hear them from him. He had said nothing. Deliberately. *Bastard.*

David knew all this in Devon, but he hadn't let on; he had feigned ignorance. He knew all the time what Ginny was trying to do. She was trying to save their marriage, and he hadn't lifted a finger to help. He had allowed their marriage to fall apart – without a care. Without any intervention.

The sight of her now, lying silent and hopeless made him feel cold and ugly - he had cast her adrift on a sea of indifference. So after the long journey of his and Ginny's life together, David recognized bleakly, that the happenings of recent months, weeks, days had inexorably led to this terrible incident. He had left her on her own, in the midst of the chaos of their marriage, to face that bastard Steve. *Oh God, how scared she must have been.*

His eyes were drawn compellingly, time and time again to the sight of those flickerings of life in Ginny's veins, and to the pulse in her neck - she was alive. David felt saved from the abyss of remorse. The possibility that Steve might have done much, much worse made him sick to his stomach. He was tempted to stroke the vein, but no longer knew whether he had any right to touch her. He doubted she would want him anywhere near her now. Instead, he sat and watched and waited; loneliness crept into the edges of his thoughts.

With only the sound of the deep melancholy hiss of the hospital machines for company, David could feel his heart tear into fragments; grief had begun for his lost love. He had hoped to feel so much more for Ginny, no longer love perhaps, but something decent, sentimental even - but he now understood he didn't. He no longer deserved her. It was the shining memories of his time with Alicia that were overshadowing all his past.

All was the future now, he thought. None of it was Ginny's fault - but it was Ginny who lay in the hospital bed, seriously injured, and alone. All she had done was to be generous with her love – and he? He knew he had been as selfish as it was possible to be. But his life had changed irrevocably; it was now on a different trajectory. All of a sudden it came to him, that despite his guilt and shame - there was no going back. *Had those heady hours with Alicia really existed? Really happened in reality or had they been some extraordinary dream?*

He needed to get back to Alicia - he felt, surrounded by the living, breathing hospital equipment keeping Ginny safe, such a Catholic guilt about how much he needed to touch her again, and breathe in her delicious perfume. The thought of never making love with Alicia again, made his chest constrict with fear. Was it possible to feel so overwhelmingly in love with another human being? *Yes. Most definitely, yes.*

David could feel tears of sadness welling, as he began to see Ginny as he had once seen her, and had forgotten – beautiful, caring, and endlessly generous with her time and love - he had thrown it all away, out of boredom for what their marriage had now become.

Restless now, his thoughts making uncomfortable companions, David slowly and quietly moved about Ginny's room, not wanting to disturb her. He didn't feel ready to see the expression of hurt, or even anger on her face, when she woke and saw him for the first time since she found out about Alicia. He didn't want her first conscious thought, to be one of anger at him.

A plump, and kindly looking nurse popped her head round the door, saving him from any more drear thoughts.

'Mr. Jackson?' the nurse asked.

'Yes… ' he answered, gesturing with his hand towards Ginny, 'I've been told my wife's going to be all right - but she still looks so pale, and the stitches on her face?'

'She's going to be fine,' the nurse replied, giving him a reassuring smile as she set about her duties: adjusting Ginny's drip, the smoothing of already crisp un-creased sheets, the temperature taking, the blood pressure monitoring. To David it seemed endless.

'Don't worry about the drip,' the nurse explained, 'it's just for hydration, your wife's had a nasty shock, and of course painkillers; we're just monitoring your wife's blood pressure, and temperature as a precaution. We're not worried about her now, she just needs some rest after the concussion. She was lucky your wife's friend acted so promptly - calling the ambulance straight away,' the nurse said, leaving the possibility of disaster hanging in the air.

David nodded, not even wanting to contemplate what may have happened – what had already happened was bad enough. *Who was this friend?* He suddenly wondered.

'My wife looks so… ' David interrupted the nurse's stream of chat, 'ill.'

'She's going to be fine,' the nurse repeated, putting a hand on his shoulder for reassurance. 'Oh, I nearly forgot, the ward sister wants to know if there'll be anybody at home to look after Mrs. Jackson?' The nurse asked while she wrote something in Ginny's notes. 'It would only be for a week or so when she can't be left on her own. Will you be able to take time off, do you think?'

'Yes of course,' David answered, not wanting to talk of their marital confusion – he doubted somehow, even if he was able to, that Ginny would want him anywhere near her. He would have to think of some other way - he was desperate to get back to Alicia. *The nurse didn't need to know that.*

'You need to get some lunch,' the nurse suggested, 'you look exhausted.'

He picked up his phone, no longer able to avoid writing the text.

My darling Alicia, (you don't know how much I enjoyed writing that!) I'm not going to be able to make lunch today. I've been suddenly called back… for an emergency at home.

David paused for a moment; how was he going to tell Alicia that he was now unexpectedly at the hospital with Ginny? *Can I tell her the truth?* No, he couldn't, David quickly decided - they hadn't really had any meaningful discussion about Ginny yet. It was far too soon to embroil Alicia in his marital mess. David sighed, at the thought of how complicated his life had suddenly become.

I hope to get back to you tonight, darling one, but will let you know as soon as. Dxxxxxxxxx

61

David wandered out into the hospital corridor, avoiding trolleys, porters, and beds as he went in search of coffee and a sandwich.

Following signs for the Terrace Café, he found himself in a large poorly lit canteen. He could see that the white melamine tables and steel frame chairs were largely unoccupied. He made his lunch choice from an unappetising assortment of sandwiches, and pastries, wishing instead for a Mexican wrap from the local deli near work.

Deciding to sit at a table overlooking a courtyard to eat his lunch, David watched a couple of robins fighting over a food scrap. He turned away from the window and was tidying up the mess of his half-eaten sandwich and it's packaging, when he spotted a woman sitting at a table on the other side of the canteen. He couldn't be certain but there was something familiar about her. Could that possibly be Bella? Yes, he was sure it was.

'It is you, Bella? I thought I recognized you,' David said, as he walked over to her table. 'What are you doing here?'

And then catching sight of her plaster cast, and the purple bruising on her face, David fell silent, wondering if he should leave her in peace. 'Sorry, I didn't see you were hurt... I didn't mean to disturb you.'

David suddenly saw how ill Bella looked. He remembered at the dinner party thinking her quite pretty, if a little exhausted and pale. Now though, her eyes were bloodshot, and she looked as though she'd been crying.

'Have you been in an accident, Bella? Ginny's here in hospital too – I don't suppose you knew…'

David's voice trailed off… it was too much of a coincidence, he thought, that both Ginny and Bella should be at the hospital, at the same time.

'Bella, do you know Ginny's been hurt?' David asked, eager to find some answers.

Bella nodded but said nothing further

'How do you know? Were you with her?' David asked.

Without asking permission, he sat down heavily; weary beyond words, and held his breath while he waited. He saw with a terrible unease, how much her hands were shaking.

'I don't know what's happened,' he tried to explain. 'All I know is that Ginny was attacked at home the police said, and there was a friend that helped her. Was that you that helped her? How did you help her?'

Why wouldn't Bella look at him, David wondered, and then it dawned on him, Bella knew he had been… unfaithful to Ginny. Bella looked at him for a second, her eyes spoke of her dislike for him.

'I'm still her husband,' David said defensively, and watched Bella blush – he'd been too harsh, he realized.

A sudden horrified idea dropped into his head. *No it couldn't be surely?* 'If you were the friend that helped Ginny, does this… *incident* have anything to do with Steve?' David asked, with an explosive dawning of understanding. Bella didn't need to

354

answer. He could see from her stricken expression that he had guessed correctly.

Bella's eyes met his. They seemed to him, to be full of hopelessness and profound sadness – she gave a slight but definite nod.

'Tell me please, Bella,' David begged, running his hands through his hair in incomprehension, 'how on earth could Steve have been involved? It really doesn't make any sense to me. Surely you can see I need to understand what happened? If Steve was involved, why was he at Port Lodge in the first place?'

David watched Bella bite her lip anxiously, 'David, I'm so sorry… Steve was there looking for me.'

'At Port Lodge looking for you… ?' David murmured, completely bewildered. 'But why would you be there?'

David realized how rude he must have sounded, 'I'm so sorry, Bella, I didn't mean to be rude it's just that I'm so worried about Ginny.'

'It's OK,' Bella said, 'Steve knew we were friends.'

A moment later, Bella's face crumpled. 'I'm so sorry, David, this is all my fault.'

David understood then, the situation was much worse than he had first thought. He had been imagining that Ginny had interrupted a burglar, and got knocked out as a result – but this was all now starting to feel much more horribly personal.

'Bella,' David said as gently as he could, and at the same time laying one of his hands on her shoulder. 'It's going to be all right, you'll see. I can see how worried you are – what's important is that Ginny's going to be all right. I'm going to get you some tea, and then you can tell me what's happened to you, and what's happened to Ginny. I have a horrible feeling they are both linked.

'Thank you,' Bella said when he returned with the tray of tea and biscuits.

Letting her sip her tea for a moment, David hoped the question he was about to ask, wouldn't upset her too much. She was silent as she stirred her tea with the hand that wasn't plastered to the wrist - David could see her thoughts were anywhere but this hospital canteen.

'What did any of this have to do with Ginny? The police called me about ten, at work this morning, you know,' David explained. 'I don't know how they knew where to find me. Do you? All the detective told me, was that someone had been at Port Lodge, and hurt Ginny. He didn't elaborate about what had gone on: perhaps he couldn't.'

Bella shrugged, but still didn't say anything further. Her attention seemed to be caught by the same robin he'd seen earlier. 'David, it was me who told the police where to find you,' Bella answered at last.

David breathed in relief; for a moment he was worried that Bella wouldn't be able to tell him anything. 'Your mobile wasn't working, and that was the only number in Ginny's medical records. You're her next of kin - so I told the detective where you worked.'

David saw a look flash swiftly across Bella's face. And then David, all of a sudden, knew what that look meant – she knew exactly what had happened to his mobile. *She did know about Alicia.*

'So it *was* you who helped Ginny?' he asked, still unsure if he had any more understanding of the events of that morning. It didn't seem to David that Bella could look after herself, never mind help anyone else, and as for facing up to her domineeringly obnoxious husband, David didn't think that would be at all possible. He could only wonder why Bella had chosen to marry Steve in the first place.

Bella gave an emphatic nod. David felt astonished. 'Yes, it was me that helped Ginny.'

'Ginny's going to be all right, you know,' he repeated, 'and without a doubt you certainly helped her. Or at least that's what I've been told.'

Bella gave him a dismissive smile. It was clear to David, Bella didn't believe him.

'I'm really grateful to you,' David said. 'The nurse told me, your quick action helped save Ginny. But I still don't understand why Steve was looking for you at our house?' David asked again, trying to keep any sign of impatience out of his voice this time.

'I... I've... left home. I left Steve on Sunday morning while he was playing golf.' Bella explained, at last, looking at him, her eyes full of despair. 'Steve was looking for me at your house.'

'Go on,' David encouraged, gently.

'I've had a really rough time with him,' Bella started to explain, 'he's... not been a good husband. He's been... abusive for most of our married life.'

What an evil, evil man. It seemed to David that Bella just needed to make a start; her words were now tripping over themselves to be heard.

'Ginny has been helping me with all of it. I didn't tell Steve what I was going to do – he would have stopped me. We are now, me and the children, at the women's refuge in Dover.'

'And Ginny helped you with all this?' David asked, incredulous.

Bella nodded, 'yes, she's been so wonderful. But never mind about me - it's Ginny you will want to hear about. Don't forget, I wasn't actually there when she was hurt - I came into the Orchid House just after, but I think it was only a few moments later.'

'Go on, Bella,' David encouraged quietly, 'why don't you start from the beginning – I know there is one. Please don't be afraid I'll tell anyone else about what's happened between you and Steve.'

Bella smiled, a faint but grateful smile, 'it all started on Saturday night… ' Bella said,

'… things didn't go too well at home, after Steve and I got back from your dinner party. Steve was dreadfully angry with me… he said I'd been flirting with Matt.' He saw Bella lift her arm - he needed no further explanation. Steve had broken her arm that night.

Bella gave a short scornful laugh.

'It's hard to believe, isn't it?'

'What is… ' David asked.

'That anyone could think of me as a flirt, but I didn't always look like this, you know. I was quite pretty once… '

'You're pretty now,' David said.

Bella managed a smile, 'thank you,' she lifted her shoulders in a small shrug, as if to say, *you're kidding me.*

'Ginny's the only one who knew about Steve, and what he did to me, apart from the manager at the refuge. I've kept it all… hidden,' Bella explained, her face pink with embarrassment.

'I see,' David said, involuntarily bowing his head so as not to meet Bella's gaze. He was beginning to feel totally at a loss hearing about this awful world that Bella inhabited. He wanted to tell her that not all men were like Steve, but realized that in his own, but very different way, he had been cruel to his wife too. He could see Bella was looking grimly at him, as if she knew what he was thinking.

They were both startled when David's mobile suddenly started ringing from the pocket of his trousers. Dragging it out, he was just in time to see Alicia's name flash up on the screen before it went onto his answerphone.

'Answer it, David,' Bella said, 'it could be important.'

David wondered if Bella had some inkling of who it might be phoning him. The phone rang again, but this time he put it on silent, and sent a wordless apology to Alicia.

'It's nothing important,' he lied, hoping Alicia would forgive him for his dreadful words, 'just someone from work.' David glanced at Bella, at least the bit about Alicia being a colleague was true - Alicia *was* his colleague. 'I'll quickly text them back – if you don't mind?'

'That's fine,' Bella said, once more rummaging in her bag, this time bringing out a crumpled tissue.

My dear Alicia sorry can't take your call right now – I'm tied up in a meeting until a bit later. Will call you back then Dxxx

'Please go on… ' David said, putting his mobile back in his trouser pocket.

'On Sunday morning, after the dinner party,' Bella began again, her eyes focusing far into the distance, 'Steve went off as usual to play golf.'

'What – you mean he left you hurt?' David interrupted, his voice full of utter contempt, 'and went off to play golf after he had broken your arm?'

Bella's eyes told him everything he needed to know – they were bleak with pain – physical and emotional pain. David was at last beginning to understand, what the friendship between Ginny and Bella was about - no wonder Ginny was anxious for her. David had a sudden memory of Ginny mentioning something about Bella, but to his mortification, he hadn't taken any notice at the time.

'Ginny helped you on Sunday?' David asked.

'No,' Bella said, 'I didn't call her… because she had… problems of her own.'

David knew he was the *problem*. He saw Bella's face begin to crumple, as she closed her eyes and lips tight, as though trying to hold back a dam of emotions.

'I didn't want to bother her – she had already done enough for me. This is all my fault,' Bella said, quietly crying, 'I should never have involved Ginny. She didn't deserve to be hurt.'

What a terrible life this poor woman must have suffered, because of her vile husband, David thought.

'You didn't deserve to be hurt either,' David said, reaching over and gently putting his hand on her good arm. 'If it's anybody's fault, it's Steve's. Anyway go on – tell me what happened next.'

'After… he'd been angry, Steve always behaved… as though he hadn't done anything cruel. He just carried on the next day as normal, as though nothing had happened. But this time, there was one difference.'

'What was that?' David asked, looking at her intently, he didn't know what to expect – he was learning fast - it was unlikely to be anything good.

'This time - Steve started to whistle... cheerily. Blocking out all his guilt, I expect. I know he felt it... ' Bella trailed off, and for a few seconds David had to wait for her to regain her composure – he was so tempted to put his arms around her – but he knew she wouldn't want that.

'But the whistling,' Bella said, rubbing her hands together nervously, 'was almost worse that anything else – I can't explain why. I think it was because afterwards... I felt so terrible – in pain, and so upset, and so worried for the children, and he just sounded so cheerful, as though he didn't have a care in the world.'

'Bastard,' David muttered, inaudibly. What a complete and utter bastard, David thought, to hurt a woman as gentle, and defenceless, as Bella.

'I made my mind up, in that moment, to leave him,' Bella said. 'There he was, with his golf clubs slung over his back, whistling and smiling his goodbyes as he left the house, as though his world was just perfect - I knew then I couldn't put up with one moment more of Steve's abuse,' Bella explained, 'I knew if I stayed with him for too much longer... '

It was a moment of the darkest comprehension – Bella didn't need to explain to him, David knew with a clarity of the most frightening kind, what it was Bella was trying to tell him. He had read in the paper only recently about a woman who had been killed at the hands of a violent husband. He shuddered at the thought.

'So, while Steve was out playing golf,' Bella resumed her story, 'I hurriedly phoned Debbie at the women's refuge, and told her what had happened.'

'The refuge? Debbie?' David asked, feeling a tsunami of

incomprehension sweep over him.

'We went to the refuge, last week, Ginny and I,' Bella explained, 'to meet Debbie – she's the manager of a refuge in Dover, for abused women. Leila's there too.'

'Ginny went with you?' David asked, surprised, 'I'm sorry, Bella, I don't know anything about this.' David put his head in his hands. *What more is there, I don't know about Ginny? What more have I missed while I've been falling in love with Alicia?*

'I didn't want Ginny to tell anyone,' Bella continued, 'I wish now, I hadn't even told her. I should never have involved her. If I hadn't… she wouldn't be lying in a hospital bed with concussion.'

David leant over, and placed one of his hands on top of hers; it seemed to him she'd definitely been hurt more than enough already.

'Ginny's alive, and will recover. This is all Steve's doing – just try and remember that,' David said, more emphatically than he'd intended. Suddenly he noticed the people on the next table were looking at them with interest. 'It really isn't your fault,' he said more quietly, 'and in fact – the nurse said that a friend - and that was you, had helped Ginny.'

David felt so sorry for her, and he recognised despite the tears and Bella's nervousness, that this woman wasn't as weak as he'd first thought. It had to be an extremely brave woman he reckoned, who made plans to leave a determinedly abusive husband.

'I couldn't call Ginny on Sunday, until the evening,' Bella said, looking to see if the people on the next table were still trying to listen. 'I spent most of the day waiting at A&E in Ashford, getting my arm X-rayed and put in a cast – it takes forever. Then I had to settle the children at the refuge; they were so upset about leaving their home I nearly... couldn't do it. I so very nearly went back home. But I had to try and make the best decision for the children's future too.'

David nodded, he felt exhausted for her.

'Is it OK at the refuge?' David asked, hopelessly at a loss for what it might be like

'It's not too bad,' Bella answered, 'everyone's trying really hard to be friendly and helpful. I suppose they must know how I'm feeling – they've all been through something similar themselves.'

'I think we could do with some more tea,' David said, feeling suddenly as rung out as Bella looked. Looking at his watch, he was surprised to see he had been away from Ginny for nearly an hour. He had to let Bella finish – he was desperate to know what had happened to Ginny.

'I tried several times to call Ginny on Sunday evening,' Bella said, as soon as he returned with the tea, 'but her mobile must have been switched off. So this morning, early, I phoned her again. I wanted to make sure she was all right after... '

David watched Bella blush again with embarrassment – he knew she meant after Ginny had found out about Alicia. And he knew why Ginny's phone had been switched off. She hadn't wanted to speak to him.

'It's OK, Bella, I know Ginny and I have a lot to work out between us.'

What opinion must Bella have of men? David wondered – with an abusive husband, and her friend's husband having an affair.

'Ginny didn't answer my call,' Bella added, 'and she hadn't called me either; I think she would have done - she hadn't wanted me to go home after the dinner party because Steve was behaving so spitefully - so I started to worry. I took the children to school, as usual - they're still at school in Sandwich, you see. And then went over to... your house.'

'Bella? What's wrong?' David asked, suddenly panicked by her ghostly-grey colour. She looked to him as though she might be about to faint. 'Are you all right, Bella?'

To David's relief, he could see she was quickly starting to regain some of her normal colour. 'Bella, please don't do that again - you really gave me a fright. You and Ginny are safe from Steve now - I presume? You did say he was in custody didn't you?'

'Are we? I don't really know where he is now,' she asked, turning around and checking who was in the canteen.

'I'm sure the policeman who phoned me this morning, said he was in custody,' David said, 'but it was such a shock, I didn't really take in everything he was saying.'

'The police took Steve away with them, from your house,' Bella said, 'but I don't know anything after that.'

'Although it looks bad at the moment, Ginny has only got concussion and a gash on her cheek which required some stitches. That's all – I promise you. It could have been so much worse. Unlike you, Ginny has no broken bones, only bruises,' David said, trying to reassure her. 'Whilst bad, it's definitely not life threatening. And as for Steve – you've done the hardest part by leaving him. And at the moment he's with the police – he won't be able to fool them easily. They'll know what sort of despicable man he really is.'

'But it was Steve, who hurt Ginny,' Bella began, again, 'and he's my husband – I feel so responsible.'

David heard the anguish in her voice.

'I know what Steve looks like when he's angry,' Bella explained, 'it's absolutely terrifying. Ginny would have seen him angry - she must have been so scared. If it weren't for me, she wouldn't be hurt. If I hadn't left Steve, he wouldn't have come looking for me – would he?'

'You're not the guilty one,' David replied, looking intently at Bella, '*you've* done nothing wrong, except try to love and be the best wife possible, to a man who doesn't even know the meaning of love, and certainly by what I've only now heard, doesn't deserve your love,' David added, quietly.

Bella's voice sounded stronger when she began to speak again. Perhaps she was beginning to believe him at last, David thought.

'When I arrived at your house, just after nine, this morning,' Bella said, shaking her head, 'it feels a lifetime ago, but really it's only a matter of hours isn't it?'

David nodded, he understood exactly what she meant.

'I knocked on the front door, but no one answered,' Bella continued with her story, 'I was just turning to get back into my car, when I heard a man's voice shouting. And because it sounded urgent, and maybe a little bit like Steve's voice, I ran round to the back of your house to see if the Orchid House door was open. I don't know what it was, but some sixth sense was telling me Ginny was at home and needed me.'

David sat silent, fascinated, but at the same time terrified for what may have been happening to Ginny.

'I don't think,' Bella said, trembling, 'I will ever forget the sight that greeted me when I opened the door into the conservatory. I saw Steve kneeling on the floor surrounded by soil, empty flowerpots, broken orchids and petals everywhere. My mind couldn't take it all in – what was he doing there, in the Orchid House? And where was Ginny? He seemed to be in there on his own. None of it made any sense, at all.'

'Have some of your tea, Bella,' David said pushing her mug towards her. 'Take a breath.'

'I was also worried what he might do to me when he realised I was there,' Bella said. 'Such a selfish thought, I know.'

'Bella you can't blame yourself for being worried,' David said, 'look what he's done to you.'

'I couldn't understand why there was such a mess everywhere,' Bella said, 'I called his name quietly, but he didn't seem to hear me - he was just staring at the floor motionless, almost as though he was in some sort of trance – I think it must have been shock. Eventually, I crept over to him – I didn't want to get too near in case he was just... playing some sort of game with me. As I got nearer he must have heard me and turned round towards me, and as he did, I saw to my complete and utter horror Ginny was lying on her back on the floor next to him - in the middle of all the mess, and next to her head,' Bella choked on the words, 'there was all this blood. I could see she wasn't moving - she was quite, quite still.'

David looked away for a moment, trying to take in what Bella was telling him. He could imagine the scene - so vivid had been Bella's description. He could envisage Ginny lying unmoving on the floor, covered in debris from her beloved orchids – it made him feel sick to his heart. If he could get hold of Steve that minute he would... what? Even under this extreme provocation, he still didn't think he could hit anyone.

The canteen was now bleached of colour: dull grey clouds had descended blocking out all sunlight, David shivered. The canteen had suddenly become a horribly gloomy room, or maybe it was Bella's frighteningly real story.

'For a moment, I was frozen with shock,' Bella said, shaking - she tugged her brown oversized cardigan tight around her. 'I just couldn't believe what I was seeing, I couldn't move – it was Steve's urgent cries that finally brought me round. '*Is she dead? Is she dead? Is she dead?*' Steve kept asking me, over and over again.'

"What have you done," I shouted at him, "what are you doing here?" but he just went on muttering, 'is she dead? I couldn't get any sense out of him at all.'

David was finding it difficult to breathe - he hadn't been expecting anything so spectacularly dramatic as this.

'I rushed over to Ginny,' Bella said, looking up at David, ' I had to get Steve out of the way somehow first - he was still bending over her, you see. I was so afraid of what he might do next, either to me or Ginny – but uppermost was my desperation to find out what Steve had already done to Ginny – I was so worried for her.'

'Bella, you were so incredibly brave,' David cut in. 'I can't imagine how afraid you must have been.'

'I didn't feel brave at the time, I can tell you,' Bella continued, 'I managed to persuade Steve, I needed to tidy up the mess before anyone saw it.' Bella continued, 'Steve was absolutely obsessed with tidiness, and I just hoped he would forget about Ginny for a second or at least enough time for me to persuade him to sit on one of the chairs out of the way of Ginny. It worked thank god. Steve stood up and went and sat on one of the chairs at the table. He was sort of keening – a low pitched moaning, and he looked devastated.'

'Do you know what Steve had done to her,' David asked.

'Not until he had moved out of the way - I knelt down beside her. I could see blood, but not much, oozing out from under Ginny's head, and there was a gash on her face. But Ginny wasn't moving at all, and her eyes were closed - it was this more than anything that terrified me. I tried listening to her chest, and then to my utter relief I saw she was breathing - slowly and faintly, but still she was breathing. I thanked all the gods,' Bella added. 'You just can't imagine, David, the relief I felt when I knew she was still alive.'

'I think I can,' David said, quietly, 'and then what happened.'

'I turned round to check on Steve,' Bella continued, 'he was standing right next to me, saying very quietly, over and over again, '*I didn't do it. I didn't do it. I didn't push her. It's not my fault*'. I coaxed him back to the table again, and he calmed down a bit when I told him Ginny was still breathing, she wasn't dead, and that she was going to be all right. I didn't have any time to ask Steve what had happened - I knew I had to look after Ginny.'

'You did well, Bella,' David said, 'you were so very brave to deal with Steve, and at the same time, look after Ginny.'

'I ran into the living room as quickly as I could – I didn't want to leave Ginny alone for too long with Steve,' Bella continued, ignoring David's words completely, 'to get a blanket from the living room sofa to put over Ginny, and a couple of cushions for under her head – I was worried she might be cold, and the floor in there is very hard - while I was in the living room I called an ambulance, and the police – I didn't want Steve to hear me - I wasn't sure what he'd done or why. I thought the police were the right people to sort all that out.'

'Bella, you were so… incredibly brave.'

'There was nothing else for me to do after that,' Bella said, 'except hold Ginny's hand, and wait for the ambulance. I kept Steve calm by talking to him, I had to keep reassuring him Ginny was going to be all right – I didn't want him to start getting agitated again – and I kept checking Ginny was still breathing. That was all I did – so you see I didn't really do much.'

Bella laid her head on her hands, and David put his arm round her shoulders, and let her rest for a moment. She must be unimaginably weary, David thought, with everything she'd gone through that morning - and before.

'I think I can guess the rest, Bella,' David said, 'the ambulance came, the paramedics took over, and I suppose you must have come to the hospital in the ambulance with Ginny?'

David only just heard her agreement, muffled by her hands, 'and did it take long for the police to come?'

Bella lifted her head, he could see how drawn her face looked – she desperately needed to go home, he thought.

'It seemed like hours,' Bella said with a faraway look, reliving this nightmare, 'but in reality it was probably only five or ten minutes. And while we waited, Steve didn't move or say another word. I tried asking him what had happened, but he wouldn't tell me. The police took him away, you know – it was the most dreadful sight – and the look he gave me as he got into the police car – I'll never forget it. Steve's eyes were accusing me of betrayal.'

'Steve abused you,' David said, trying not to sound too angry about it, 'don't ever forget that, Bella. You look absolutely exhausted – you've been through more than enough these last few days. Why don't you go home now and get some rest? I'll stay with Ginny until this evening, and then I have to get back to London. I'll be back tomorrow though,' he added quickly, when he saw Bella's scathing look. 'You could come back, later on today, or tomorrow.'

'I just wanted to make sure… ' Bella said, hesitantly.

'That Ginny's OK?' David finished for her. 'She is OK and is going to be sleeping most of today – so why don't you go and see her now for a minute, and then go home? She'll be pleased to see you in the morning, and I'll be here until nearly six – I have to get back to London, tonight, you see.'

Bella gave him a fierce look – *she did see*, as her expression accused him of disloyalty, and much else besides.

'What about Ginny?' Bella demanded. She looked directly at David. *What about Ginny*? Her eyes repeated the question. 'You deserve to feel shame. And I hope you do.'

David watched Bella stalk away, out of the canteen to Ginny, leaving him feeling as though the breath had been knocked out of him. He hadn't expected her outright condemnation – but he knew it was deserved.

62

Ginny slowly became aware of a sensation of floating; her body felt like cotton-wool – light, adrift - at peace, so wonderful. Ginny wanted it to go on forever. But all of a sudden, voices fractured this peace – voices sounding persistent and demanding – she didn't want to listen. She wanted to stay cocooned in this warm comforting world. She realised she had no idea what time or what day it was. Or in fact where she was. She also realised she didn't care that much.

'Ginny,' a man's voice - insistent, and familiar, pushed through the soft white mist surrounding her. 'It's all right, Ginny - you're in hospital - everything's going to be all right, now.'

Hospital? Ginny wanted to flee back to the peaceful place of a moment ago. She reluctantly opened her eyes a little - she wasn't ready yet to leave her safe world behind; she could sense an unpalatable truth awaiting her.

Trying to focus, Ginny felt the back of her eyes sear in the brightness of the overhead lights - she quickly closed them, retreating once more into the woolly mists.

'Hello, Mrs Jackson,' a bright business-like voice said, 'how are you feeling?'

She tried to speak but found she couldn't; a pain, sharp and hot tore through her face. 'Aaargh,' was all Ginny found she could say.

'Don't try to speak, Dear,' the kindly voice said, 'It's going to hurt for a few days – I'll give you something for the pain in a minute.'

'Ginny, it's all right,' a familiar voice said, 'you're safe now. Try and relax.'

She began to breathe more easily; the red-hot pain in her face was becoming unbearable. *Why?* Then the unmistakeable smell of antiseptic unexpectedly caught in her nostrils; she was in hospital - that's what they'd been trying to tell her, she realised.

'Ginny,' the familiar voice spoke again, but the pounding in her head were making his words muffled and indistinct. 'How do you feel? Don't move your head, you've had a bad knock, but it'll be perfectly all right in a few days. So don't worry.'

Ginny tried opening her eyes again, this time the blinding light seemed to have dimmed – she was surprised to find a doctor standing beside her bed.

'Mrs Jackson,' the doctor said, 'you've received a knock to your head and jaw; it will be difficult for you to speak for a few days, because of the bruising. Do you remember what happened, Mrs Jackson?

Ginny tried to shake her head, regretting it immediately.

'Do you remember,' the doctor asked, gently, 'being at home, and somebody... attacking you?'

Ginny lay for a moment, searching her memory – she couldn't remember anything – she felt the beginnings of panic fluttering in her stomach.

'Don't worry, Mrs Jackson,' the doctor reassured her, putting her warm hand on hers, 'you'll remember shortly.'

Ginny watched the doctor leave the room, her file tucked

under her arm – she hoped the doctor was right. She closed her eyes, she felt so terribly tired – she just wanted to sleep.

'You gave us such a fright, Ginny,' the familiar voice said.

She opened her eyes once more to find it was David, sitting in a chair next to her bed. *David?* She saw to her surprise, David wipe a tear away, she wondered why. Ginny saw compassion in his deep blue eyes - compassion for her; for a moment she saw love, and tried to smile.

She put her hand up to her jaw, and for the first time felt the heat of the swelling, and it's tenderness to the touch. No wonder it hurt, she thought, and then suddenly, out of nowhere, she was swamped by memories. And then she remembered what David had done, and why she had wanted to stay in that warm cosy world of a moment ago. Her smile faded into a tight-lipped frown.

'What day is it?' Ginny asked, slowly trying to find a way of talking that didn't hurt so much. She knew she had to speak to David. But definitely not now – and she didn't want him at her bedside. *Go away*, she wanted to shout.

'It's Tuesday afternoon,' David answered, 'you slept the whole of Monday, and this morning – they gave you painkillers.'

'… here all the time?' Ginny asked. From the puzzled expression on David's face it was clear he was having difficulty understanding her.

'I went back to London,' David explained, finally understanding her, embarrassed.

There was a conversation that was starting to go round and round in Ginny's head. She had to get it out. She had to say the words, she had to face him with her hurt and betrayal; he had to know what pain he had caused her, and how her life was now in total turmoil. There was so much she had to say to him; to hurl at him; to rant at him - so much that she could barely breathe.

'Did you go home?' Ginny queried.

'Yes,' David answered, 'I needed to collect some clothes and… stuff.'

Ginny hadn't imagined David would ever step foot in Port Lodge again. She felt a flush of anger - he had taken advantage of her being in hospital to sneak back in.

'… not yours,' Ginny said, wishing they didn't need to have this conversation when the pain in her head was so excruciatingly terrible. But the last thing she wanted, even now, was misunderstanding about the future. *They had no future. Their future was over – forever – gone.*

'… your… stuff?' Ginny asked, closing her eyes against the pain in her head, and the feeling of nausea that had suddenly arrived.

She watched him nod; 'I'm sorry,' David said, 'I thought you wouldn't mind…'

'I mind,' Ginny managed to say. She made absolutely sure her meaning was clear.

'… boys?' Ginny asked, suddenly realising they would be worried about her. '… OK?'

'Yes, I rang the school last night,' David told her, 'they wanted to come and visit you in hospital. Could they come tomorrow perhaps? Do you think you would feel up to it?'

'… collect them?' she asked, and then realised suddenly David should be working. '… work?'

'I've taken a few days off,' David explained, 'The nurse said you'd need some help for a week or so – she wondered if I would be able to... look after you.'

'No need,' Ginny said. 'I don't want you to look after me – please go.'

There, I've said it. It felt wonderful to have said those two simple words – *please go.* Ginny felt as though she had taken the first step in regaining some control of her life. Feeling too weak to be able to deal with the aftermath of their marriage, when all she really wanted to do was to escape into sleep, she closed her eyes, hoping when she opened them again, David would be gone out of her life. She could feel her eyes welling up with tears. *I must not cry.*

'Shall I come back later?' David asked. 'Bella said she would be here this morning. Did you know she was here? We had a long talk about what happened. She told me about Steve – how he... mistreats her. She's left him – you know? That's why she was at Port Lodge – Bella wanted to tell you, but your phone was off.'

'Bella was at Port Lodge?' Ginny exclaimed in surprise moving too quickly, and let out a loud cry of pain. She had forgotten for a moment about her injuries. 'Left, Steve?' *Damn, Damn,* Ginny thought. She remembered now turning her phone off, in case David called – she must have missed Bella's call. *Damn.*

'Yes. That's why she came to see you,' David explained.

'... she's all right though?' Ginny asked.

Bella had left Steve, how did that come about? Ginny wondered. *What could have happened for Bella to make that incredibly difficult decision?* I wasn't there when Bella needed me, and felt a sad regret for her friend having to make such a huge decision on her own.

She turned her thoughts away from Bella, and lay studying David for a moment. This was the man she had married and loved for nearly twenty years – over half her lifetime. He looked the same on the outside: short cropped curly hair – silver at the edges, distinguished, as slim and athletic looking as ever, still wearing cashmere jumpers, smart shirts and well pressed trousers – conservative as ever, but still achingly attractive, she thought – but that was only the outside of David; inside he was no longer the man she knew - now so unutterably different. Those feelings of love and warmth, she had once had for him, had completely died – to be replaced with a cold implacable heart. Alicia had done that, and so too in an unintentional way – Grace. *Poor Grace an unwitting catalyst.*

Ginny found, to her surprise, even in her injured state, she could talk to him politely, but she felt nothing for him – her heart was now and forever closed to him. She suddenly had a feeling of lightness, of a burden at last lifted; a step had been taken – and she had taken it. Maybe she didn't need to have that conversation after all. *It was over.*

'… not stay at Port Lodge,' Ginny said, feeling a calmness, that had been absent from her life for so long now, and it was oh so welcome. She made a decision. 'Collect your stuff… friends will look after me.'

'But…' David stammered. She turned her back on him, as he had once done to her. It felt as though her future had started at last.

63

Late afternoon the next day, April sunshine shone as Bella hastened up the stone steps of the hospital, eager to see if Ginny would be awake today.

Making her way along the endless gloomy hospital corridors with a posy of garden flowers, and a horse magazine for Ginny, she couldn't resist reliving her encounter that morning with Will Green. She had driven carefully, her arm unstrapped and pulsing with pain, to his house before coming to visit Ginny. She wanted to put his voting papers through his front door - she didn't admit, even to herself, that she wanted to see him again. So when he pushed the front door open and found her on the step, she was unprepared to find her heart fluttering with pleasure.

'I'm so… sorry to bother you,' Bella stammered, 'but I've brought this for you,' handing him his voting registration.

'Bella, isn't it?' he said, as surprised as she was. 'Come in, I'm just having some coffee.'

She stood dithering; her face hot with acute embarrassment. This wasn't what she had expected to happen – not at all.

'I didn't think you'd be in,' she eventually managed to say.

'We could sit outside in the garden,' he said, 'if you'd prefer?'

She knew immediately he'd guessed at her discomfort. She nodded, her agreement.

'For a minute,' she said, unable to resist his smile, which was just as she remembered: two dimples, and a gleam of laughter in his eyes. She followed him into his kitchen and saw it was filled with clutter and life.

'It's a mess I'm afraid,' he said, with no embarrassment. 'It's what happens when you live on your own. You become lazy.'

'It's lovely,' she said, and meant it. *I could live here in this mess with this man.* She shook her head to banish her unruly thoughts. 'I must go. I can't stay, after all. I'm sorry,' and with that she turned and almost ran to the door.

'It's OK, Bella, really,' he said, kindly. 'Another time, come and visit and I'll show you around the garden.'

He must have seen her delight at the idea.

'You like gardening then?' he asked.

'Oh, yes, I love it,' she breathed, unable to disguise her pleasure.

'Come after school one morning next week,' he said, 'that's if you want.' He obviously could see she did. 'And I have an idea. But I'll tell you about it next week. Wednesday?'

She nodded in bemusement, 'Wednesday.' She agreed.

What was happening? Steve would kill her.

Bella's thoughts were interrupted at the sight of David ahead of her in the hospital corridor. She slowed her pace; she didn't want to speak to him again today. She'd said all she wanted to say yesterday. But from the droop of his shoulders, and the slowness of his walk, she began to wonder, with rising alarm if something had happened to Ginny. *Is he going home? Already?*

Bella hurried into the brightly-lit women's ward with trepidation, but the sight of Ginny sitting up in bed felt like an unexpected gift – one, all the more welcome for its surprise. Ginny's face looked worse if anything today, Bella thought:

bruises, now royal-purple and blue were spreading fast across her cheeks and down her neck. With her swollen nose, and half closed eye, she looked more like a boxer after losing a big fight.

'Do I look that bad, Bella?' Ginny asked, her words still coming out mangled from her half-closed mouth.

'No you look… you're sitting up - that must mean you're feeling a bit better? I hope,' Bella asked, as she leant over to kiss the bit of Ginny's face that wasn't bandaged, or sore looking.

'For a moment I was really worried,' Bella explained, 'I've just seen David, and he didn't look happy. I thought something had happened to you.'

'No,' Ginny said, 'and you're right he wasn't happy. He wasn't happy at all. I'd just told him our marriage was over.'

'… I'm so sorry,' Bella said, tears forming in her eyes. 'I feel so responsible – if it hadn't been for me… for Steve… '

Ginny lifted her hand to stop Bella saying anything more.

'Difficult to speak… hurts when I open my mouth,' Ginny explained.

'Don't worry,' Bella said, 'I can understand you fine. Has David gone now?'

Ginny nodded, and then gave a little wince of pain, 'he's gone. I'm so glad you're here - I want to thank you.'

'Thank me?' Bella asked, astonished.

Bella sat down; the discomfort of the chair no longer a surprise.

'For looking after me,' Ginny continued.

'I didn't do anything,' Bella said, 'and I should never ever have involved you in my… in mine and Steve's difficulties.'

'I'm glad you did. It was an accident you know,' Ginny said. 'I tripped, and fell onto the table. Steve didn't push me - he was very angry though, but he didn't touch me apart from jabbing me with his finger. I'm going to explain everything to the police when they come back. I don't know what Steve would have done, if I hadn't tripped and knocked myself out... But anyway what did happen - was an accident.'

Bella wiped away a tear, and took one of Ginny's hands in her own, 'I'm so relieved Steve didn't actually hurt you. I know he's ultimately to blame, but the thought of him... hitting you – I'd never have been able to forgive myself.'

They sat together silently for a moment.

'Tell me more about David,' Bella asked, breaking the silence, 'why has he gone? He looked so defeated somehow, when I saw him out in the corridor.'

'Yes,' Ginny said, with asperity, '... I sent him away.' Bella had to strain to hear, as Ginny's voice had suddenly become much quieter. 'I told him our marriage is finished – I think he was eventually going to tell me the same anyway. He's seeing another woman. And I don't mean *seeing* - he's made love to her – I can't stay married to him after that.'

'I understand - of course I understand. Are you all right?' Bella asked, concerned at the sadness on Ginny's face.

'We couldn't go on as we were,' Ginny answered, 'something had to change – I just wasn't expecting it to be another woman, that's all – it's taken me a bit by surprise.'

'Of course it would,' Bella said, taking her hand. 'And you never told me all this was going on – I've been so selfish, monopolising you when you had your own problems.'

'I wanted to help you,' Ginny said, 'and I would have told you - but your problems were so much more immediate than mine.'

'But you know about time and healing don't you?' Bella asked. 'Well it is true, even after only a few horrible days I feel different. I feel as though my future is no longer bleak. All of a sudden it feels lighter somehow. Give yourself time, and these dark days will fade.' Bella was rewarded with the beginnings of a smile.

'You still look... fragile,' Bella said, 'how will you manage at home without David? You'll need some help won't you?'

Bella sensed that Ginny wasn't ready to answer her question yet.

'It'll be OK,' Ginny went on quickly, 'but much more important is what's happened to you since the dinner party. David told me you've left Steve, but I wouldn't let him tell me anymore. You don't know how difficult that was, I was so worried about you – I've been sitting here waiting for you to visit.'

'Yes, I've left Steve,' Bella said, unable to hide her sadness, 'I only told David enough to explain what Steve was doing at your house – I don't think David had ever encountered domestic abuse before; he seemed really shocked when I told him about Steve.'

'That's because, it is shocking,' Ginny said.

'Steve was looking for me, because we weren't in the house when he came back from golf on Sunday afternoon, and we didn't go home that night either. We went to the refuge on Sunday morning.'

'Oh, Bella,' Ginny said, reaching across for her hand. 'Tell me what happened on Saturday night. I assume that something must have happened after the dinner party.'

Bella nodded, and pointed at her broken arm and the bruises on her face.

'These are what happened on Saturday night?'

'I'm so sorry I didn't phone on Sunday, but after all the... trouble with David, I took a sleeping pill and didn't wake up until the middle of Sunday, and then felt so peculiar - I'm not used to sleeping pills - I went back to bed and by then it was Monday morning. I was about to phone you just as Steve started banging on the front door looking for you.'

'So much has happened,' Bella said, 'I can't grasp it all - can you?'

'No, I can't,' Ginny answered, gingerly feeling her jaw, and touching the lump on her head, 'but I feel so awful right now, I can't really concentrate properly at the moment. I'm just so pleased you're safe from Steve. I suppose he's with the police – do you know anything else yet?'

Bella looked at her watch, surprised to see she would have to go so soon, 'I'm not sure where Steve is at the moment. All I hope is that he is having a truly uncomfortable time. I've a meeting with Leila later this afternoon at the refuge, that's where the children are right now, Leila's finding out what's happening with Steve. She may have to get an injunction out for me, she told me – can you believe it? Steve still doesn't know where I am.'

'Before you go, though, I've got something to ask you... ' Ginny said, and paused.

Bella was intrigued to know what was causing Ginny to look so embarrassed.

'You were right about me needing help,' Ginny finally admitted.

Bella knew how much it would cost Ginny to say that.

'The nurse told me it would be just for a week or so, and

unfortunately I think she might be right - I feel as weak as a kitten, and my head feels as though it's being ground up in some sort of mixer.'

'Go on,' Bella said, giving her a nudge of encouragement when the silence had become too long, 'have you thought of a plan then?'

'Mmm. I thought that maybe... if you and the children came to stay for a couple of weeks or so, and... only if you wouldn't mind. You can say no, of course. You might be too busy sorting everything out with Steve, and all that you have to do, and don't want to take on nursing duties. And you might not want to move the children again.'

'Stop, Ginny,' Bella said, laughing. 'Of course I'll come and look after you. I can make some sort of amends that way. But I'll need to speak to Debbie, first though – I don't know how any of this works, but I'm hoping it won't be a problem. I'll come back tomorrow – you'll be feeling a bit better by then, and we can talk some more. Meanwhile, I'll speak with Debbie and Leila. We've got to make sure we'll all be safe from Steve. Oh and by the way, your Mum is coming tonight, she told me to tell you – I hope you don't mind but I remembered you telling me where your Mum lived, and I went to see her to tell her what had happened. She's been here a few times already, but you've been asleep.'

'It would be so good to see, Mum,' Ginny said, a tear rolling down her face. 'I've a lot to tell her – she must be worried about me?'

Bella leant over and gave Ginny a kiss, 'she was worried about you, but not anymore – and don't worry about David – he'll survive, and so will you; you did everything you could to make your marriage work - David didn't. You've got nothing to feel any guilt about.'

Bella turned to wave to her at the door, and caught the melancholy expression on Ginny's face. Bella knew it would take time for them both to heal after the awful events of the last few days. But heal they would, Bella thought with firm resolution.

64

Easter Saturday morning, Sandwich sunny and warm, was bustling with visitors for the annual *Le Weekend*. Along the quayside, burnished classic cars with their proud owners alongside, were being examined by enthusiasts; picnickers sat in the shade of the weeping willows along the river edge; aromas of all things French, were wafting through the town enticing visitors to the green and white striped food tents for their annual serving of tartiflette, and les moules; pungent cheese stalls were tempting gourmands and repelling everyone else; visitors, wanting nothing better to do than to sit in the sun and drink warm beer, occupied cafe tables on the pavements. A festival feeling filled the air.

Today was exactly a month since the accident, and a month since Bella and the children had come to Port Lodge to stay with her. But to Ginny, time still felt horribly distorted, one minute it all seemed in the past, and the next it was as clear and terrifying as though it had just happened. Flashbacks apparently, the doctor had said. And David's treachery with Alicia, remained as fresh in her mind as the day she'd found out about them. At least, she thought, he had the grace to let her live at Port Lodge until she wanted to move out. Only that morning he'd written to tell her he was renting a flat in London, until everything was more settled. She had no intention of replying to him, except through his solicitor. She no longer cared where he lived.

Reluctantly eschewing the festivities because of her toppling vertigo, a result of banging her head, instead, her and Bella were sitting chatting in the Orchid House. Ginny had taken up what had become her favourite convalescing position: feet up on an elegant antique chaise longue - pink tweed with scrolled cherry woodwork. Bella had managed to drag the chaise longue in from the living room to replace the wrought-iron table and chairs that had been at the heart of the scene of the *accident*. Neither could bear to look at them. A grateful charity had been delighted to take them away. And they had been equally delighted to see them go.

'Despite what's happened here,' Ginny said, thinking aloud, 'I still feel more relaxed amongst my plants, than anywhere else in the house. Too many memories of David everywhere else, he never really came in here.'

Bella looked at her, and felt a deep concern for her friend. 'It will get better I promise you. But for the here and now, I'll be glad when you're well enough, to take over the job of looking after your orchids,' Bella added, to try and cheer her up. 'I'm horribly afraid I'll have killed them all by the time you're able to do it yourself.'

'Don't you dare,' Ginny said. 'It would mean my lifetime's work is ruined. 'I'm joking, Bella, don't look so worried. They'll live, like me they're tougher than they look, and anyway I'm beginning to wonder if I shouldn't grow something else in here now. I still can't get those last few moments out of my head when I was showered with all that soil and pots, and orchid petals as I fell.'

Bella nodded in complete understanding, turning back to carry on with her watering. 'Those memories *will* pass, Ginny, I promise you. I'll help if you want to plant something else, and I can see, that however beautiful these orchids are, why you might want to start again.'

'That would be great, Ginny said mustering a smile, 'but first I have to decide some other stuff. Like, how long I'll be living here at Port Lodge.'

The sound of knocking interrupted them, making them both jump.

'Don't forget to put the chain on the door before you open it, Bella,' Ginny called out, still worrying that it might be Steve at the door.

'It's all right; I can see it's Leila,' Bella shouted back from the hall.

'Leila, how lovely, come and join us,' Ginny said when she walked into the room.

'You're both looking so much better,' Leila said, smiling at them both. 'Ginny, your bruising's nearly gone, and you now look a much better colour without all those horrid blues and purples. And you Bella, I can't believe how much prettiness was hidden under all those brown clothes.'

'I just wish this dizziness would hurry up and go,' Ginny said to Leila, 'it's holding me back, and I have so much to sort out.'

'You have to be patient,' Leila said, putting her arm around Ginny, 'it's not been that long, you know. It'll take time.'

'I know but...' Ginny answered and then gave up the fight - Leila was right, she would get better in time. 'I didn't expect to see you today. I thought you'd be out with Matt, enjoying the sunshine.'

'I'm meeting Matt in a minute, but first I have something important to tell you.' Leila said, looking pleased with herself.

'Leila, what is it?' Ginny asked, her stomach flipping over in alarm. 'What's happened?'

'It's Steve,' Leila said, taking out some legal looking documents from her capacious handbag.

Ginny immediately looked at Bella who she could see was gripping the arms of the chair in sheer panic.

'I'm sure it's good news, Bella,' Ginny said quietly to her. 'Leila wouldn't be looking quite so pleased about it I'm sure, if it were bad news.'

'Yes, it definitely is good news,' Leila said, quickly. Ginny could hear Bella breathe a sigh of relief. 'I had an email last night,' Leila explained. 'Steve's injunction has been extended for another six months.'

'That's wonderful news,' Ginny exclaimed, with deep relief. 'Just think, Bella, you won't have to worry for another whole six months.'

'He has to appear in court at the end of the summer,' Leila added, 'and the court has asked for a psychological assessment.'

Ginny looked over at Bella, and wondered why she didn't seem pleased. 'That's really good news - isn't it Bella?'

Bella nodded, 'it's just that I can't quite believe it yet. I still feel he's going to walk through that door any minute, demanding I go home with him.' She shivered as she spoke.

'I know it's going to be hard to believe for a while yet,' Leila said, standing up to put her hand on Bella's shoulder. 'But one day you'll suddenly realise it's true. He'll end up in prison if he comes anywhere near you again. You're all quite safe now.'

'Thank you so much for coming to tell us,' Bella said, beginning to smile again. 'I'll just have to keep reminding myself that it's true and that he can't hurt me...' and seeing Ginny's pale face as she lay on the chaise longue still recovering from what Steve had done to her, '... he can't hurt *us* anymore.'

'Don't forget Bella, you're not in his power anymore,' Ginny said. 'You're much stronger now, and if he did turn up you'd be able to tell him to go. You're definitely not the same person you were.'

'Leila, you're looking really beautiful today,' Ginny said, admiring her sunshine yellow dress, and the simplest of leather sandals. The effect was stunning. 'You look, I don't know... glowing somehow.'

'Well, there is something else I have to tell you,' Leila said, her eyes bright and her face full of happiness. 'I've something to celebrate.'

'Come on, Leila, don't keep us in suspense,' Ginny and Bella said in unison.

'Matt and I, we're... getting married,' Leila revealed, unable to hide her good news any longer. 'He proposed on the night of the dinner party. And what with all that's gone on it just didn't feel the right time to tell you. But now you're both looking so much better, I couldn't wait any longer.'

Ginny manoeuvred herself slowly to standing, to give Leila a congratulatory hug. 'I couldn't be happier for you. I'll never, ever forget how much Matt helped me that night.'

Ginny found she couldn't go on. Every time she thought of the night she found out David was having an affair, an implacable anger robbed her of breath. But this wasn't about her, she chided herself; this was about Leila.

'That's wonderful, I'm so pleased for you too,' Bella said, coming over to join them.

Ginny could see Bella's hands hovering, unsure whether she should hug Leila or not. 'He's so lovely, I know you'll be… '

'What a pair we are,' Ginny said, to cover Bella's confusion. 'But I know that despite what's happened to us, you'll be really happy with Matt.'

'Thank you' Leila said, her acorn-brown eyes gleaming. 'One day it'll come right for you, too. You're such wonderful people that there is definitely someone out there for you both. It has come right for me, and look how many prospective husbands I've had to turn down to find Matt.'

'What about your Mum, though, Leila?' Ginny asked, remembering how upset Leila had been several months ago when she'd confessed that her traditionally Asian parents were threatening to disown her, if she didn't agree to an arranged marriage.

'I'll have to wait and see what happens,' Leila said, sadly. 'I just hope they won't refuse to speak to me. But I've decided, despite what my family threatens to do, I'm still going to marry Matt.'

'Your parents love you,' Ginny said, 'I'm sure they'll come round in time to you marrying Matt. After all, they couldn't be getting a better son-in-law.'

'We should celebrate,' Ginny suggested quickly to dispel the gloom she could feel descending in the Orchid House, 'you and Matt are happy together, and that is definitely the most important thing of all. Your parents have had their own chance of happiness – now it's your turn.' Turning to Bella, she asked if she would make a drink for everyone, so we can celebrate.

'A pity it can't be champagne,' Ginny said, 'but as soon as I'm better we'll definitely open a bottle. Until then, I'm afraid it's going to have to be a cup of tea.'

'That sounds great. I'll help you, Bella,' Leila said, jumping up.

Out in the kitchen, Leila asked quietly, 'how is Ginny really? She looks so sad to me. I know she's trying hard not to show it.'

'She is sad,' Bella agreed. 'But you know what Ginny's like? She doesn't like to talk about herself. She's such a selfless person. But what David did to her has really shaken her to the core. She's making plans though for her future, which is a good sign, isn't it?'

'Bella, you're doing an amazing job looking after her,' Leila said, hugging her. 'She'll get better so much more quickly with you here with her.'

'Her neighbour Carl, has been really attentive,' Bella said, 'he's called in every day with fresh fruit and vegetables from his garden and stays to chat for quite a while. He's asked her to help him restore the Salutation Gardens. But I'd better let her tell you about the rest.'

'Well don't tell me anything more then,' Leila said, 'I'll ask her myself, and don't worry she won't know it came from you.'

Leila walked through into the Orchid House carrying the tea tray, 'and how would Madam like her tea?' She asked, Ginny.

'Hmm, funny,' Ginny said laughing at Leila. 'Did Bella tell you her job interview next week is at the Manor House, no less?'

'It's just that I met Will Green, the head gardener, while I was canvassing there,' Bella explained quickly, blushing, 'and I had to go back again with some voting forms for him, and we sort of got talking about gardening, and he offered me a job...' 'Bella trailed off. 'It sounds, I don't know, unbelievable. But I do have to have this interview with the owner first, and I'm so nervous, I'm sure I'll make a mess of it,' Bella confessed, frowning.

'You'll be great,' Leila told her, 'Ginny said you've done wonders with your own garden. You're a natural apparently; I've never heard her so complimentary. She just sniffs when she sees mine.' They watched Bella's face suffuse with pride, at the compliment.

Ginny turned to Leila. 'What Bella's managed to achieve in her tiny garden is truly amazing. Will Green will be lucky to have her. While *you*, Leila, are... better at other things.'

'Thank you, Ginny,' Leila replied grinning, 'OK, so I won't take up gardening.'

'Is that a promise?' Ginny asked, laughing.

'What about bringing some photographs with you,' Leila said, 'if the garden's as good as Ginny says it is, they'll be sure to be impressed.'

Bella nodded, 'photographs are a really good idea, and Will said he'd like to see some too. Thanks, Leila.' Ginny and Leila looked at each other with raised eyebrows. 'Stop it you two,' Bella said giggling. 'I don't really know Will at all.' But in Bella's mind the word "yet" lurked.

'Now, Ginny, who's Carl?' Leila asked, with a grin on her face.

Ginny smiled at her two friends, and in that moment, she suddenly realised with a clarity that lifted her spirits, and dispelled her headache for the first time in weeks, that with the help of these two wonderful friends at her side, her life was going to be all right after all.

She knew it was going to take time, maybe even a long time: she still had a divorce to get through; a home to sell;

the children to help get through their parents separation; and lastly, a new career to forge. But despite all the obstacles she knew lay ahead, Ginny had an unexpectedly strong sense of conviction that her life was going to change so much for the better. It would be her very own life for the first time since leaving home for university as a naïve and immature young girl.

Ginny reflected that, in the aftermath of that horrific day in the Orchid House, she had made a promise to herself as she lay in her hospital bed, that she was not going to let either David or Steve defeat her. And she had also promised to herself, that she was going to do her damndest not to let Steve hurt Bella ever again. And now weeks later, the resolve to change her life that had started in hospital was gathering momentum.

Ginny realised that no one could have foreseen what Steve would do to her that day, or what he had done to Bella for many years. Neither could she have foreseen, or even imagined for a heartbeat that David would fall out of love with her, and in love with someone else. But she knew the friendship between the three of them, herself, Bella and Leila, each helping the other, would all, in time, conquer the many obstacles that stood between them and their future happiness.

She raised her mug, a tear glistening on her cheek, 'to the future.'

'To the future,' they all chorused.

THE END

Acknowledgements

To my children Britta, Joe and Frances for being in my life. My thanks for your support each in your own way.

To my editor James Essinger, for his faith in me to write the book it became under his guidance.

To Leslie Goldsmith, for always thinking the best of me.

To Rachael Quin for being there right at the very beginning.

And of course there are others… Thank you.